PENGUIN BOOKS

NUNQUAM

Lawrence Durrell, a British citizen of Irish parentage, was born in the Himalaya region of India in 1912. His first ten years were spent in India. After schooling in England he decided to become a writer. Throughout the 1930s Durrell devoted most of his talents to poetry, which has won much acclaim. His first novel, *The Black Book,* was published in Paris in 1938 and was cited by T. S. Eliot as "the first piece of work by a new English writer to give me any hope for the future of prose fiction." World War II temporarily interrupted Durrell's literary career. During the war years and for some time thereafter, he served Great Britain in various official and diplomatic capacities in Athens, Alexandria, Cairo, Rhodes, and Belgrade. His published works now encompass poetry, essays, and novels, including the famous Alexandria Quartet—*Justine, Balthazar, Mountolive,* and *Clea* (1957–1960)—devoted to an examination of the various aspects of love. Recognized as one of the greatest and most important writers of our time, Lawrence Durrell currently lives in the south of France. His most recent books are the nonfiction *The Greek Islands* and the novel *Livia, or Buried Alive.* Penguin Books also publishes his *Prospero's Cell, Reflections on a Marine Venus, Sicilian Carousel* (travel books about the island of Corfu, the island of Rhodes, and Sicily), the novels *The Dark Labyrinth* and *Tunc,* and his translation and adaptation of Emmanuel Royidis's *Pope Joan.*

By Lawrence Durrell

NOVELS

The Alexandria Quartet:
Justine, Balthazar,
Mountolive, Clea

The Black Book

The Dark Labyrinth

Livia, or
Buried Alive

Monsieur, or
The Prince of Darkness

The Revolt of Aphrodite:
Tunc, Nunquam

Pope Joan *(translator)*

POETRY

The Ikons

The Red Limbo Lingo

Selected Poems

The Tree of Idleness

Vega

HUMOR

The Best of Antrobus

Esprit de Corps

Sauve Qui Peut

Stiff Upper Lip

TRAVEL

Bitter Lemons

The Greek Islands

Prospero's Cell

Reflections on a
Marine Venus

Sicilian Carousel

DRAMA

Acte

An Irish Faustus

Sappho

LETTERS AND ESSAYS

Lawrence Durrell and
Henry Miller:
A Private Correspondence,
edited by George Wickes

Spirit of Place,
edited by Alan G. Thomas

FOR YOUNG PEOPLE

White Eagles over Serbia

Lawrence Durrell

NUNQUAM

A NOVEL

PENGUIN BOOKS

Penguin Books Ltd, Harmondsworth,
Middlesex, England
Penguin Books, 625 Madison Avenue,
New York, New York 10022, U.S.A.
Penguin Books Australia Ltd, Ringwood,
Victoria, Australia
Penguin Books Canada Limited, 2801 John Street,
Markham, Ontario, Canada L3R 1B4
Penguin Books (N.Z.) Ltd, 182–190 Wairau Road,
Auckland 10, New Zealand

First published in the United States of America by
E. P. Dutton & Co., Inc., 1970
Published in Penguin Books 1979

LIBRARY OF CONGRESS CATALOGING IN PUBLICATION DATA
Durrell, Lawrence.
Nunquam.
Reprint of the 1970 ed. published by Dutton, New York.
I. Title.
[PZ3.D9377Nu 1979] [PR6007.U76] 823'.9'12 79-15616
ISBN 0 14 00.5189 9

Printed in the United States of America by
Offset Paperback Mfrs., Inc., Dallas, Pennsylvania
Set in Baskerville

à Claude Vincendon

Aut tunc, aut nunquam,

"It was then or never. . . ."

Petronius, *The Satyricon*

MERLIN: The international corporation that seeks to control the destinies of us all.

FELIX CHARLOCK: Scientist whose brilliant machine, *Abel,* makes him indispensable to *Julian,* Merlin's elusive chief.

BENEDICTA: Felix's wife; Julian's sister.

IOLANTHE: Formerly a film star and courtesan whose pagan innocence attracted both Felix and Julian.

CARODOC: An elegant architect and talker.

DR. NASH: Merlin's house psychiatrist.

MARCHANT: Felix's co-worker.

ONE

Asleep or awake—what difference? Or rather, if there were a difference how would you recognize it? And if it were a recognizable difference would there be anything or anyone to care if you did or not—some angel with a lily-gilding whisper to say: "Well done"? Ay, there's the rub.

My head aches, it isn't only the wound—that is on the mend.

"Guilty in what you didn't know, what you hoped to escape merely by averting your face." Ah!

He wakes, then, this manifestation of myself so vaguely realized that it is hard to believe in him: he wakes in a room whose spare anonymity suggests one of the better-class hotels; no feudal furniture, no curtains smelling of tobacco or cats. Yet the towels in the bathroom are only stenciled over with a capital "P." The Bible beside the bed is chained to the wall with a slender brass chain; owing to some typographical mishap it is quite illegible; the ink has run. Only the title page can be made out. Well, where am I, then? In what city, what country? It will come back, it always does; but in waking up thus he navigates a long moment of confusion during which he tries to establish himself in the so-called reality which depends, like a poor relation, on memory. The radio is of unknown provenance; it plays light music so characterless that it might be coming from anywhere at all. But where? He cannot tell for the life of him—note the expression: for the life of him! His few clothes have no tabs of identity, and indeed some have no buttons. Ah, that strikes a vague chord! There is a small green diary by the bed; perhaps that might afford a clue? It has the other one's name in it. Felix Ch. But the book seems very much out of date—surely the Coronation was years ago? It seems, too, full of improbable Latin-American itineraries; moreover in the middle a whole span of months is missing, has been torn out. Gone! Vanished months, vanished days—perhaps these are the very days he is living through now? A man with no shadow, a clock with no face. Something about Greece and Turkey? Had he ever been to Turkey? Perhaps it was the other one. That blow on the head had occluded his vision: the darkness turned violet sometimes and was apt to dance about in his skull. (How she trembled in bed, this astonishing revivalist of a dead love.) But of course he had!

April to October, but where were those vanished weeks, and where was he? I would give anything to know. It doesn't look like spring at all events; from the window the snow meadows tilt away toward tall white-capped mountains; a foreground of pearling sleet upon windowsills of warped and painted wood. Some sort of institution, then? (Dactyl, you are rusty and need taking down.) Nothing of all this did you notice until the image in the mirror one day burst into tears. Well, keep on trying. No luck with the soft descriptive music. I must have had a meal, for the remains lie there, but they are quite unidentifiable. Last night's dinner? I turn over the remains with my fork. Brains of a hall porter cooked in Javel, one hundred francs? I press the bell for the maid but nobody comes. Then at last I cry out as I catch sight of the little Judas in the door. The pain of regained identity. Ahhhh! It opens for a second and then slowly closes. This is no hotel. Doctor! Mother! Nurse! Urine!

Someone starts banging, fitfully, on a wall nearby and screaming in a frothy way; thud upon the padded wall, and again thud: and the peculiar reverberation of a rubber chamber pot upon the floor. I know it now, and the other knows it too—we slide into one identity once more, as slick as smoke. But he feels desperately feverish and he takes my pulse, and his sweat smells of almonds. O all this is quite perfect! Hamlet is himself again. Fragments of forgotten conversations, the whole damned stockpot of my life memories has come back to me; and with it the new, the surprising turn of events which has given me the illusion of recovering Benedicta (Hippolyta saying: "How sick one is of *les petites savoirs sexuelles*").

I can see no reason why all this should have happened to me, but it has; they go on, these harpies both male and female, tearing their black hearts out. "I received nothing but kindness from him (her) and repaid it with double-dealing though meanwhile unwaveringly loving (her-him). Staunch inside, infirm without, lonely, inconstant, and mad about one woman (man)." These raids on each other's narcissism. And yet, if what she tells me is true? It would be going back to the beginning, to pick up that lost stitch again; going back to the point where the paths diverged. Hark, someone is calling my name—yes, it is my name. Lying beside her I used to reproach myself by saying: "You were supposed to know everything; you arrived equipped to know all, like every human being. But a progressive distortion set in, your visions withered slowly like aging flowers." Why did they, why have they?

She says that now she is allowed to visit me because neither is observably mad; we are simply mentally mauled by sedatives. "And you, as usual, are pretending." But then if I like to be mad it is my own affair—doctors are scared of schizophrenes because they can read minds, they can plot and plan. They pretend to pretend. Ah, but I care for nothing anymore. Quick, let us make love before another human being is born. More and more people, Benedicta, the world is overflowing; but the quality is going down correspondingly. There is no point in just people—nothing multiplied by nothing is still nothing. Kiss. Eyes of Mark, beautiful gray eyes of your dead son; I hardly dare call him mine as yet. (And what if you are lying to me, that is the question?)

> *Matthew, Mark, Luke and John,*
> *Bless the bed that I lie on,*
> *Ano-Sado-Polymorph*
> *Bless the pillow I slide off,*
> *Giving Sascher-Masch the slip*
> *With his twice-confounded whip.*
> *Let them take me from behind,*
> *But not too very sudden, mind.*
> *Polymorphouse and perverse,*
> *Reveling in the primal curse.*

Serenity, senility. Serendipity . . . ah, my friend, what are you saying?

Of course I am on my guard, watching her like a hawk. A hawk, forsooth? She will feed me on the fragments of field mice still warm, broken up tenderly bit by bit in those slender fingers. She will teach me to stoop. Of course a lot of this material is dactylized, belonging to lost epochs; they have recovered my little machines for me and returned them to me (give the baby his rattle now!) . I recover bits here and there which in the past Abel might well have appreciated. Turn them this way and that, they smell of truth —however provisional it is; as when raising those deep blue, very slightly unfocused eyes she said: "But the sexual act is by its very nature private, even if it takes place on the pavement during the rush hour." When I ask why I have been brought here, she adds, on an imperious note: "To begin again, to recover the lost ground. There is much that will be explained to you—a lot by me. For God's sake trust me this time." It is as enigmatic as her way of saying "Help me" in the past. Must I resume the long paper chase once more, Benedicta?

I suppose that I owe my survival to the last-minute breakdown of Abel, or something of that order. I can't believe that any other consideration would have motivated my capture. Of course nobody knows how to put it right except me and I won't show them under duress. All this is surmise, of course; nobody has said anything. And I am shown every mark of sympathy and consideration: many of my toys have been returned to me, and a place set aside for me to work if the mood is on me. I resist these soft blandishments, of course, though it is hard in a way: time hangs heavy. I admit that I took up an offer to work on the Caradoc transcriptions, largely out of curiosity. The executors want some "order brought into them," whatever that means. Indeed the notion itself is unwise, since this type of material, by its very haphazardness, creates its own kind of order. "Attempt to capture the idea quite naked before it strays into the conceptual field like some heavy-footed cow." Thus do I kill time till time kill me.

And now, as I have explained, she has come back, for how long I don't know, or for what reason; but changed, irremediably changed. Yet still the beauty of the domed egg-of-the-high-masted-schooner visage which smiles turn into a stag: still the slant calamitous eyes. Illness, imprisonment, privation—might not all this have brought us close together? I wonder. Why, she even helps me with my papers now. The boy's death hangs over us, between us, the something unspoken that neither knows how to broach. Resilient as I am, that was a thrust right through the heart of my narcissism; and the bare fact does not yet seem to correspond to any known set of words. So I shuffle paper a bit, reflect and allow my moods to carry me where they will. As for the executors, they do not care what I do with the material, provided it goes into covers and provides money for the estate. But . . . there are no inheritors to claim it, so some committee of cranks will divert it to crank projects: old men smelling of soap and singed hair. Pelmanism for rodents, birth control for fairies . . . that sort of thing: everything for which Caradoc, if indeed he is dead, did not stand. (I hear those growls, I have them recorded.)

And then, from time to time among my own ruminations float fragments which might almost seem part of another book—my own book; the idea occurs fitfully to me, has done on and off for years. But so much other stuff has to be cleared first: the shadows of so many other minds which darken these muddled texts with their medieval reflections. Abel would have been able to give them shape and position and relevance; human memory is not yet whole enough to do so. Was it, for example, of Benedicta that I once said this—or was it Iolanthe? "Perhaps it is not fair to speak abusively of her, to note that she never thought anything which she did not *happen* to think. No effort was involved. Shallow, unimpeded by reflection, her chatter tinkled over the shallow beds of commonplace and platitude, pouring from that trash box of a head. But what beauty! Once in her arms I felt safe forever, nothing could happen to me." Prig!

Today is cold again, a Swiss cold. It has all started to become very clear. The leaves are falling softly and being snatched away across the meadows like smoke. My God, how long must I stay here, when will I get out? And to what end if I do? My life is covered in the heavy ground mist of an impossible past which I shall never understand. I sleepwalk from day to day now with a hangover fit for a ghost.

As for these scribblings which emerge from my copying machines, the dactyls, these are not part of the book I was talking about, no. Would you like to know my method? It is simple. While I am writing one book (the first part might be called *Pulse Rate 103*), I write another about it, then a third about *it*, and so on. A new logic might emerge from it, who knows? Like those monkeys in the Indian frescoes (so human, so engaging, like some English critics) who can dance only with their index fingers up each other's behinds. This would be *my* way of doing things. Smell of camphor: I must not get too vivacious when Nash, the doctor, calls. I must remain as he sees me—an eternal reproach to the deathbed, the dirty linen, the urinals clearing their throats. Yet vivacity of mind is no sin, saith the Lord God.

As far as Caradoc is concerned, what ails me in gathering up this inconsequential chatter is that there are several different books which one could assemble, including some which couldn't have been foreseen by those who knew him; is everyone built on this pattern?—like a club sandwich, I suppose. But here for example is a vein which would be more suitable to Koepgen—perhaps it is the part of Caradoc which *is* Koepgen, or vice versa. I mean *alchemy*, the great night express which jumps the points and hurtles out of the causal field, carrying everything with it. Alchemy with all its paradoxes—I would have logged that as Koepgen's private territory. But no. The vein is there in Caradoc, under the fooling.

I mean, for example: *"Pour bien commencer ces études il faut d'abord supprimer toute curiosité"*; the sort of paradox which is incomprehensible to those afflicted by the powers of ratiocination. Moreover, this, if you please, from a man who claimed that the last words of Socrates were: "Please the gods, may the laughter keep breaking through." Contrast it with the fine white ribbon which runs through the lucubrations of Aristotle—the multiplication tables of thought to set against this type of pregenital jargon. (In between times I have not been idle: on the little hand lathe I have turned a fine set of skeleton keys in order to be able to explore my surroundings a bit.) Is it imperative that the tragic sense should reside after all somewhere in laughter?

Yet now that I am officially mad and locked away here in the Paulhaus, it would be hard to imagine anywhere more salubrious (guidebook prose!) to spend a long quiet convalescence—here by this melancholy lake which mirrors mostly nothingness because the sky is so low and as toneless as tired fur. The rich meadows hereabouts are full of languid vipers. At eventide the hills resound to the full-breasted thwanking of cowbells. One can visualize the udders swinging in time along the line of march to the milking sheds where the rubber nipples with electricity degorge and ease the booming creatures. The steam rises in clouds.

Billiard rooms, a library, chapels for five denominations, a cinema, a small theater, golf course—Nash is not wrong in describing it as a sort of country club. The surgical wing, like the infirmaries, is separate, built at an angle of inclination, giving its back to us, looking out eastward. Operations one side, convalescence the other. Our illnesses are graded. A subterranean trolley system plus a dozen or so lifts of various sizes ensure swift and easy communication between the two domains. I am not really under restraint. I am joking; but I am under surveillance, or at least I feel I am. So far I have only been advised not to go to the cinema—doubtless there are good clinical reasons. Apart from the fact that I might see a film of Iolanthe's again, I do not care: the cinema is the No play of the Yes-Man, as far as I am concerned. I am for sound against vision—it runs counter to the contemporary trend: I know that, but what can I do? *Konx Ompax* and *Om Mane Padme Hum* are the two switches which operate my brain box: between the voting sherd and the fetal pose of the sage.

There are many individual chalets, too, dotted about on the steep hillsides, buried out of sight for the most part in dense groves of pine and fir. They are pretty enough when the snow falls and lies; but when not, the eternal condensation of moisture forms a light rain or Scottish mist. The farther snows loom indifferently from minatory cloudscapes. One sleeps well. No, I won't pretend that it is anything in particular, either comminatory or depressing or enervating: except for *me*, the eye of the beholder. For I am here against my will, badly shaken, and moreover frightened by this display of disinterested kindness. Yet it is simply what it is—the Paulhaus. Subsoil limestone and conglomerate. Up there, on the farther edge of the hill among the pines, are the chalets allocated to the staff. Our keepers live up there, and the lights blaze all night where the psychoanalysts chain each other to the walls and thrash each other with their braces in a vain attempt to discover the pain threshold of affect-stress. Their screams are terrible to hear. In other cells the theologians and mystagogues are bent over their dream anthologies, puzzled by the new type of psychic immaturity which our age has produced—one that is literally impermeable to experience. When he is here Nash lodges with Professor Pfeiffer whose dentures are loose and who has a huge dried black penis on his desk—a veritable Prester John of an organ. Swiss taxidermy at its best. But nobody knows whose it is, or rather was. At any rate it isn't mine.

Here they must discuss poor Charlock in low tones, speaking of his lusterless eye, the *avain* quality of his gaze. "Such a lack of *theme*," Pfeiffer must say. It is his favorite expression. And there opposite him sits Nash in his bow tie, author of *The Aetiology of Onanism*, in three volumes (Random House). Little pissypuss Nash. You wait a bit, my lads. My goodness, though, it was worth the journey, it was worth the fare. Mind you, it is easier to get in than to get out—but that is true of other establishments I have known. . . .

It was not entirely my fault that I awoke with a head like a giant onion—swathed as it was in layer upon layer of surgical dressing. Like the Cosmic Egg itself, and I damned well felt like it. Chips of skull (they said) had to be removed—like a hard-boiled egg at a picnic. No damage to the Pia Mater. Clunk with a couple of pick helves as I reached for my knife. Then a kind of bloody abstract but rather lovely abdication of everything, with darkness hanging like a Japanese print of an extinct volcano. *Angor Animi*—fear of approaching death. It haunted me for a while. But now I have gained a bit of courage, as a mouse does when the cat does not move for a long time. I am just beginning to scuttle about once more . . . the cat must have forgotten me. Actually they must see that I am on the mend; by special dispensation I have been allowed some of my tools back, as I say; along with them some private toys. One, for example, has enabled me to discover the position of the two microphones in my room. Instead of plugging them as a clumsy agent might have done, I fill them with the noise of cisterns flushing, taps running, dustbin lids banging—not to mention the wild howls and squeaks of the tapes played backward; and music too, prodigious wails and farts in the manner of Alban Berg. Poor Pfeiffer, he must shake his shaggy head and imagine he is listening to the Dalai Lama holding a service.

Lately Nash has taken to visiting me regularly about thrice a week—hurried and apologetic harbinger of Freud. Pale with professional concern. "Come, Nash, let us be frank for a change. Julian had me captured and brought here so that you can try to break my will with your drugs." He laughs and pouts, shaking his head. "Felix, you only do it to annoy, because you know it teases. Actually he saved you just in time, for all our sakes. Seriously, my dear fellow."

Nature becomes almost transparent to the visionary eye after even a moderate period of sedation. I could see so to speak right into his rib cage, see his heart warbling out blood, see his timid and orderly soul neatly laid up in dusted ranks like a travel library. A telephone rings somewhere. "Felix," he says tenderly, reproachfully. "I suppose," I said, "you must have dreamed of escaping once, when you were very young. Where has it gone, Nash, the impetus? Will you always be the firm's satrap, its druggist?" His eyes fill briefly with tears, for he is a very emotional man and suffers when criticized. "For goodness' sake don't give way to delusional ideas of persecution, I implore you. Everything has turned out right after a very nasty and dangerous passage. When you are rested and well and have seen Julian, there is no need why you shouldn't send in your resignation if you wish. There is no obstacle—all that is a comic delusion of yours. We want you with us, of course, but not against your will. . . ." I can't resist acting him a little of a private charade based upon Hamlet's father's ghost—nearly managing to secure the heavy paper knife which I make to drive into his carotid. I bulge my eyes and wave my ears up and down. But he is fleet enough when danger threatens, is Nash; once round the table and to the door, ready to bolt, panting: "Cut it out, for God's sake, Felix. You can't scare me with these antics." But I have, that is what is mildly engiggling. I throw the paper knife in the air and catch it; then place it betwixt my teeth in pirate fashion. He comes back cautiously into the room.

"You want me mad," I say, "And you shall have me so." I comb out my overgrown eyebrows in the mirror and try a stern look or two. He chuckles and continues to talk. "It's lucky you have caught me during my safe period," I say. "If it had been any other woman . . ."

"D'you know," he says effervescently, "I have a patient who makes up natural mnemons just as Caradoc used to; he was a famous philosopher, and he illustrates the ruins of his dialectical system with them. Free association is the Draconic law, no? *La volupté est la confiture des ours*—how is that?"

"Woof! Woof!"

"Felix, listen to me."

"*Ja, Herr Doktor.*"

"These dreams you are turning in to Pfeiffer—anyone can see they are faked. I ask you, psychoanalysts riding on broomsticks and sliding down moonbeams with fairies . . . a joke is a joke, but this is going too far. Poor Pfeiffer says . . ."

I play a little game with him for a while, chasing him round and round the table, but he is nimble and I tire rapidly; I suppose that I am rather ill still, weak in the knees, and of a tearful disposition: and he knows it.

"And Benedicta?" says he.

"Was sent to help me compromise my reason and my feelings."

"Good heavens, Felix: how can you?"

"How did it all happen to me, Nash—to Felix Ch., eh? Perhaps a desire to poke some frivolous and egotistical strumpet, to plow up some sexual ignoramus? Ah, listen to the alpha rhythms of the gray matter." I hold up a finger to bid him listen. He shakes his head and sighs. "Poor darling," he says. "You wrong her and soon you'll know it. Anyway she will be back on Tuesday and you'll see for yourself. In the meantime you see how free you are to walk about, even without her. Even walk into town if you want one afternoon. Treat this like your own country club,

Felix. It won't be long before we have you back in our midst—I've never been more confident of a prognosis. Meanwhile I'll send you plenty of visitors to cheer you up."

I must have given him a woolly look, for he coughed and adjusted his bow tie neatly. "Visitors," he added in a lower key, filling out a longish prescription form with deft little Jap-type strokes, and adding the magic word in block capitals at the foot of the page. "This for the nurse," he added sportively, waving it as he stood up. "Until next week then, my dear Felix. Julian sends his warmest regards. . . ." He just got through the door in time before the heavy chair burst upon it; a leg fell off, a panel was cracked right across. The German nurse came in clicking like a turkey, a strapping girl with the square walk of the sexually unrealized woman. She had a big bust and an urchin cut. I liked her white smooth apron and her manicured capable hands. Nash had fled down the corridor. I helped her gather up the pieces and redispose the furniture. I asked her if it was time for my enema, but she registered shock and disapproval at this sally. "If not, then will I to the library go," I said and she stood aside to let me pass. As I walked, still puzzled by everything, I told myself: "Benedicta and I come from a long line of muddled sexers, specters of discontent. What dare I believe about her, or about anyone?"

Over the weekend I tested my freedom in tentative fashion by disappearing for the afternoon: no, not into town where I am always followed at a discreet distance by a white ambulance; but into the dangerous ward. Who would ever have thought of looking for one there? I reappeared in my own quarters as mysteriously as a conjurer's rabbit and simply would not tell them where I had been. Would they have believed me? I doubt it. The thing is that I found I was actually picking up the thought waves of a schizo on one of my little recording devices. He was knocking on the wall at the end of the corridor and singing a bit. I sneaked to the locked door and passed him a wire with a tiny mike on it. (Of course I myself have lots of tinnitus, which is only static in loony terms.) But we hit it off wonderfully well. He didn't really want to get out, he said; he was only troubled by speculations as to the nature of freedom—where did it begin and where end? A man after my own heart, as you see. He turned out to be a wife murderer; higher spiritual type than the rest of us. Our electronic friendship flowered so quickly that I felt it about time to test my set of keys. The second worked like a charm and I was inside the ward with the red light, shaking hands with my friend. He was a huge fellow but kindly, indeed almost diffident about his powers. The padded ward was just like anywhere else; spotless and obviously well conducted—and with a much more refined class of person than one finds in the rest of the place. Yes, I liked it very much, even the corridor with its sickly saintlike smell: smell of sweaty feet in some Byzantine cloister? And then all the pleasant diversified humors of Borborymi. Woof! Woof! There would be no visitors between teatime and supper, so we were free to play at nursery games—on all fours, for example, barking in concert at a full moon, trying to turn ourselves into wolf men.

You see, anxiety is only a state of deadly *heed*, just as melancholia is only a pathological sadness. I might have foundered here, I suppose, had she not appeared; foundered out of sheer exhaustion, out of defiance to Julian's obscure laws. I could have retreated by sheer imitation into a genuine hebephrenia, to follow out the dull spiral of some loony's talk; under the full sail of madness steered this cargo of white-faced gnomes toward the darkness of catatonia. A Ship of Fools, like the very world itself. My friend speaks of freedom without quite being able to visualize its fartherest reaches; yet he is *almost there. Ah! Folie des Gouffre!* But cerebral dysrhythmia will respond to a cortical sedative, even in some cases of cryptogenic epilepsy. . . . You ask, Nash! *Om.*

The thing is this: coming round in the operating theater, under the arcs, surrounded by a ballet of white masks (white niggers, appropriates of a blood sacrifice) : bending down to plunge needles into me: I heard, or thought I heard, the quite unmistakable tones of Julian. They spoke, all of them, in quiet relaxed voices, like clubmen over their cigars while I lay there, a roped steer, with wildly rolling eye and flapping ear. I knew that the operation was over by now; I was just waiting to be wheeled away. The figure I mean stood just back from the circle and was obviously neither surgeon nor dresser, though he was masked and gowned like the rest of them. It was this one who said, in the tones of Julian: "I think the X-ray findings followed up by a pneumogram should tell you. . . ." Talk filled the interstices of his phrases like clods raining down upon a coffin lid. Explanations proliferated into jargon. I felt perfectly well by now, the pain had gone with the tachycardia, leaving only the spear-pointed attentive fury of the impotent man. Someone spoke of brainstem sedatives, and then another voice: "Of course, for a while he will undergo what will seem like electric charges in the skull—weird haptic sensations." Hence, I suppose, the longish period of surveillance among the odors of guilty perspiration; life among bedridden schizos under insulin torpor therapy, beings whose "Rostral Hegemony" is faulty—to quote the brave words of Nash. Much of this is a blank, of course, punctured by dim visions. I daresay I ran the gamut of D Ward. Petit mal to grand malheur. Bed-wetting is common. By day their speech exhibits uninhibited lalling. Welcome, electrically speaking, my newfound friends, possessors of the spike-and-dome discharge! I see the anxiety rising in the centrocephalon, the rapid 25-per-second high-amplitude rhythms of the grand mal, the focal seizures rising in the cortex. Last week the Countess Maltessa had an unrehearsed, unsupervised epileptic fit; she died from the inhalation of her own vomit. "It so often happens," Pfeiffer will be saying, shaking his head. "You can't watch everyone all the time."

I do my best to try and remember this war, but in vain; nor indeed do I remember its inhabitants with their diversified idiosyncrasies, though of course some of them I have known about, have heard about. But if I met them during my last sojourn here I have retained no memory of the fact. They are all freshly minted—like for example the famous Rackstraw, who was Io's screenwriter, responsible for some of her most famous work. I would have been glad to remember him; and yet it is strange, for I recognized him instantly from her descriptions of him. She used to visit him very often I recall. He himself had once been a minor actor—and, some say, her lover. In its way it was quite thrilling to see this legendary figure face to face, weighed down by the Laocoön toils of his melancholia. "Rackstraw, I presume?" The hand he tenders is soft and moist; it drops away before shaking to hang listlessly at his side. He looks at one and his lips move, moistening one another. He gives a small cluck on a note of interrogation and puts his head on one side. Watching him, it all comes back to me; how well she described his imaginary life here in this snowbound parish of the insane.

How he would sit down with such care, such circumspection, at an imaginary table to play a game of imaginary cards. ("Is it less real for him than a so-called real game would be for us? That is what is frightening.") I hear the clear dead husky voice asking the question. Or else when walking slowly up and down as if on casters, he smokes an imaginary cigar with real enjoyment; smiles and shakes his head at imaginary conversations. What a great artist Rackstraw has become!

His hair is very fine; he wears it parted in the middle

and pasted down at the sides. It is someone else who looks back approvingly at him from the mirror. His ears are paper-thin so that the sunlight passes through them and they turn pink as shells, with all the veins illustrated. He will appear to hear what you say and indeed will often reply with great courtesy, though his answers bear little relation to the subjects which you broach. His pale blue eye gazes out upon this strange world with a shy fishlike fascination. What a feast of the imagination, too, are the interminable meals he eats—course after course—cooked for him by the finest chefs, and served wherever he might happen to be. Who could persuade him that in reality he is nourished by a stomach pump? No, Rackstraw is a sobering figure only when I think that these long nerveless fingers might once have caressed the warm smooth flesh of Iolanthe. (The final problem of intellection is this: you cannot rape yourself mentally, for thought creates its own shadow, blocks its own light, inhibits direct vision. The act of intuition or self-illumination can come only through a partner-object—like a host in parasitology.) If one is tempted to kiss, to embrace Rackstraw, it is to see if there is any of Io's pollen still upon him. Can one leave nothing behind, then, that is proof against forgetfulness?

But Ward D is only another laboratory where people are encouraged to live as vastly etiolated versions of themselves—and Rackstraw has taken full advantage of the fact. At certain periods of the moon his old profession seizes him and he fills the ward with his impersonations of forgotten kings and queens, both historical and contemporary; or will play for hours with a doll—a representation of Iolanthe in the role of Cleopatra. At others he may recite in a monotonous singsong voice:

Mr. Vincent	five years
Mr. Wilkie	five years
Emmermet	ten years
Porely	ten years
Imhof	ten years
Dobie	five years

and so forth. At other times he becomes so finely aristocratic that one knows him to be the King of Sweden. He mutters, looking down sideways with a peculiar pitying grimace, lips pursed, long nose quivering with refined passion. He draws hissing breaths and curls back his lips with disgust. He sniffs, raises his eyebrows, bows; walking about with a funny tiptoe walk, lisping to himself. When the evening bell goes and he is told to go to bed, he bridles haughtily, but he may mount the bed and stay for a long time on all fours, thinking, "Rackstraw's the name. At your service." His every sense has become an epicure. On the wall of the lavatory near his bed someone has written: *Mourir c'est fleurir un peu.* Then also for brief spells, with the air of someone looking down a well into his past, he will produce the ghastly jauntiness of the remittance man —he is living in the best hotel. "I say some ghastly rotter has pipped me . . . top-whole Sunday . . . the boots doesn't clean suede properly. . . ." He has become the professional sponge of the twenties, cadging a living from the ladies.

But the difference between Rackstraw's reality and mine is separated by a hair—at least as things are now. For me, too, reality comes in layers suffused by involuntary dreaming. Some mornings I wake to find Baynes standing by my bed with his silver salver in hand, though there is never any letter on it. He says: "Which way up will you have your reality, sir, today?" Yawning, I reply in the very accents of Rackstraw. "O, as it comes, Baynes. But please order me a nice L-shaped loveproof girl of marriageable age, equipped with learner plates. I have in mind some heart-requiting woman to lather my chin; someone with sardonic eyes and dark plumage of Irish hair. Someone with a beautiful steady walk and a thick cluster of damp curls round a clitoris fresh as cress." He salutes and says, "Very good, sir. Right away, sir." But at other times I think I must be dying really, because I am beginning to believe in the idea of Benedicta.

I had been about and around for several days when I caught sight of her, sighted along the length of the long corridor with its bow window at the end, standing in the snow in a characteristic distressful way. She had rubbed a small periscope in the frosty glass in order to peer in upon me, her head upon one side. A new unfamiliar look which somehow mixed diffidence and commiseration in one; I gave her the sort of look I felt she merited—O, it was all I could afford: a tired frog's smile: it was a package, a propitiatory bundle of nails, hair, menstrual rags, old dressings—everything that our joint life had brought us. But it contained little enough venom—I felt too bad about it all, too emotionally weak to expend more upon the encounter. And yet there was something in her face at once touching and despairing; her inner life, like mine, was in ruins. It was the fault of neither. So when she tapped with her nail upon the glass, I said not a word but unfastened the glass door into the garden and let her in. Of course it was suspicious. We stood, featureless as totems, gazing at each other, but unable to thread any words on the spool. Then with a soft groan she put her arms out—we did not embrace, simply leaned upon one another with an absolute emptiness and exhaustion. Yet the personage in my arms in some subtle way no longer corresponded to any of the old images of Benedicta—images she had printed on my mind. A qualitative difference here—you know how sometimes people return from a long journey, or from a war, completely altered: they do not have to speak, it is written all over them. What was written here? There was no discharge of electrical tension from those slender shoulders— the vibrations of an anxiety overflowing its bounds in the psyche. Her red lips trembled, that was all. "For God's sake be kind to me," was all I said, was all I could think of. She started to cry a little inwardly, then began to *cry*. She cried buckets, but without moving, standing quite still; so did I, too, from sympathy, just watching her—but inside like usual: tears pouring down the inside of my body. "I am coming to you tonight—I have permission. Somehow we must try and alter things between us—even if it seems too late." Only that, and I let her go, a snow demon in her black ski clothes against the deep whiteness of the ground and the clouds. She walked carefully in her own imprints toward the trees and disappeared, never once looking round, and for a moment this whole episode seemed to me a dream. But no, her prints were there in the snow. I swore, I raged inwardly; and when night fell I lay there in the darkness of my room with my eyes open staring right through the ceiling into the snow-sparkling night sky. I have never understood the romantic cult of the night; day, yes—people, noise, motors, lavatories flushing. At night one recites old phone numbers (Gobelins 3310. Is that you, Iolanthe? No, she has gone away, the number has been changed). Recite the names of people one has never met, or would have liked to sleep with if things had been different. Mr. Vincent five years. Mr. Wilkie five years. Yes, the night's for masturbation and death; one's nose comes off in one's handkerchief, an arm drops off like Nelson's. . . . .

The minutes move like snails; the faintest shadow of a new hope is trying to get born. It will only lead to greater disappointments, more refined despairs, of that I am sure. Yet thinking back—years back, to the beginning—I can still remember something which seemed then to exist in her— *in potentia*, of course. I wrestle to formulate what it was, the thing lying behind the eyes like a wish unburied, like a transparency, a germ. Something like this: what she herself had not recognized as true about herself and which she was all but destroying by running counterclockwise to the part of herself which was my love. (Go on, make it clearer.)

Every fool is somebody's genius, I suppose. Just to have touched again those long, scrupulous yet sinister fingers gave me the sense of having reoriented myself with reference to the real Benedicta; it was because I myself had also changed a skin. Past suicide, past love, past everything—

and in the obscurest part of my nature happy in a sad sort of way; climbing down, you might say, rung by rung, heartbeat by heartbeat, into the grave with absolutely nothing to show for my long insistent life of selfish creativeness. Put it another way: what I have left is some strong emotions, but no *feelings*. Shock has deprived me of them, though whether temporarily or so I cannot say. Ah, Felix! The more we know about knowing the less we feel about feeling. That whole night we were to lie like Crusader effigies, just touching but silently awake, hearing each other's thoughts passing. I thought to myself, "Faith is only one form of intuition." We must give her time. . . . Are you stuck, then, dactyl? Come let me clear you. . . .

Later she might have been more disposed to try and put it into words: "I've destroyed you and myself. I must tell you how, I must tell you why if I can find out."

To find out, that was the dream—or the nightmare—we would have to face together; following the traces of her history and mine back into the labyrinth of the past. No, not simply looking for excuses, but hunting for the original dilemma—the Minotaur, which itself seemed to connect back always to Merlin's great firm which had swallowed my talents as Benedicta had swallowed my manhood. It is this fascinating piece of research which occupies me to the exclusion of almost everything else now—perhaps you can guess how? With the help of my keys I have vastly extended the boundaries of my freedom; for example, I can now traverse Ward D, and make my way into the central block without being specially remarked by anyone; but more important still I have found the consulting rooms of the psychiatrist and the library of tapes and dossiers which form a part of Nash's patrimony. Up the stairs, then, past the ward with the huge Jewesses (big bottoms and nervous complaints: fruits of inbreeding). Down one floor and along to the right, pausing to say a timely word to Callahan (pushed through a shop window, cut his wrist: interesting crater of a dried-up carbuncle on his jaw), and so along to the duty consulting rooms where the treasure trove lies. The tapes, the typed dossiers, are all grouped in a steel cabinet, according to year—the whole record of Benedicta's illnesses and treatment. . . .

I thought at first that she might find this prying into her past objectionable, but to my surprise she only said: "Thank goodness—now you will trust me because you can double-check me. After so much lying to you . . . I mean involuntary lying because things were the way they were, because Julian came first, his will came first; then the firm. You have already guessed that Julian is far more than just the head of Western Merlin's for me, haven't you?"

"Your brother."

"Yes."

"So much became clear when I discovered that simple fact—why did you never tell me?"

"He forbade me."

"Even when we were married?"

She takes my hand in hers and squeezes it while tears come into her eyes. "There is so much that I must face, must tell you; now that I'm free from Julian I can."

"Free from Julian!" I gasped with utter astonishment at so preposterous a thought. "Is one ever free from Julian?" She sat up and grasped her ankles, bowing her blonde head upon her knees, lost in thought. Then she went on, speaking slowly, with evident stress behind the words: "There was a precise moment for me, as well as one for him. Mine came when the child was shot—like waking from a long nightmare."

"I fired that shot."

"No, Felix, we all did in one way and another."

She pressed my hand once more, shaking her head; continued with a kind of scrupulous gravity. "The image of Julian flew into a hundred pieces never to be reassembled again; he had no further power over me."

"And from his side?"

"The death of that girl, Iolanthe."

"How?"

"He described it to me in much the same words, a suddenly waking up with a hole in the center of his mind."

Yet in Julian's case the emptiness must always have been there; one could imagine him saying something like: "A faulty pituitary foiled my puberty, and even later when the needle restored the balance, something had been lost; I had lived a complete sexual life in my mind so the real thing seemed woefully hollow when at last I caught up with it." Hence the excesses, the perversions which are only the mold that grows upon impotence and its fearful rages against the self.

So lying beside her thus in the darkness, I found myself looking back down the long inclines of the past which curved away toward the Golden Horn and the breezes of Marmora; toward the lowering image of the Turkey I had hardly known, yet where my future had been decided for me by a series of events which some might regard as fortuitous. What a long road stretched between these two points in time and space.

Real birds sang all day in the gardens, while indoors the mechanical nightingales from Vienna had to be wound up; at certain times one became aware of the beetles ticking away like little clocks behind the damascened hangings, full of dust. The corridors were full of beautifully carved chests made from strange woods—delicately scented sissu, calamander, satinwood, ebony, billian, teak or camphor.

Somewhere among the wandering paths of these old gardens overgrown with weeds and brush-marked by cypresses, I saw the pale figure of Benedicta wandering, stiff and upright in her brocade frock, holding the hand of a nurse. How would it be possible to bring her back here again, to my side in this cream-painted sterile room among the snows? It was a puzzle made not the less complicated by the new tenderness and shy dignity which now invested her, and which aroused my worst suspicions; I could not see how a new array of facts alone could clear the air, could exculpate her—or for that matter myself. Ironic for a scientist who cares for facts, no? We sat here side by side on the white bed, eating mountain strawberries and staring at each other, trying to decipher the pages of the palimpsest. "You see," she said slowly, staring deeply into my eyes, "we have lived through these fearful experiences together, killed our own child, separated, and all without ascribing any particular value to it. It has brought us very close together so that now we can't escape from each other anymore. The numbness is wearing off—you are beginning to see that I was in love with you from the very beginning. My appeals for help were genuine; but I was in the power of Julian—a power that dates back to my early childhood. I loved him because I was afraid of him, because of all he had done to me. I was trapped between two loves, one perverse and sterile, the other which promised to open up a real world for me, if only you could see in time how truthful I was—and act on it." Then she bowed her head like a weary doe and whispered: "It's easy to say, I know. Nor is it fair perhaps. You were as much in Julian's power as I was, after all, and he could have had you killed at any moment, I suppose, had he not been in doubt about losing me forever. He took refuge from me in this strange love for that girl you call Io—and that perhaps saved us from his wrath, his fearful impotent fury which he hides so well under that calm and beautiful voice of his." I said nothing for a long time. In my mind's eye I saw once more those steamy gardens abandoned to desuetude, those chipped and dusty kiosks standing about waiting for guests who never came: the stern sweep of the tombs decorating the beautiful slopes of Eyub. "In the cemetery there—it was your mother's tomb?" Benedicta nodded sadly. "She hardly enters our story. She was ill, you know. In those days syphilis, you couldn't cure it."

It dated back, dated right back. "Nothing could have exceeded the passionate rage and tenderness of Julian for

Mother." Here as she lay, after so very long, anchored in the crook of my arm: and talking now softly, rapidly, unemphatically: I saw come up in my mind's eye (beyond the golden head) the sunburned mountains and peninsulas of Turkey rising in layers toward the High Taurus. "Jocas was the illegitimate one, the changeling; he was never allowed to forget it. He was ugly and hairy. Whenever he spoke, my father would get up without a word and open the door into the garden to let him out. And Julian smiled, simply smiled." Though I had never seen Julian I seemed to see very clearly that aquiline smile, the sallow satin skin, the eyes with the thick hoods of a bird of prey. I saw too the landscape of their minds, locked up together in those tumbledown seraglios; a Turkey that had been so much more than Polis with its archaic refinements. Plainland and lake and mountain, blue days closed by the conch. "There was only hate or fear for us to work on after my mother died." Yes, it was not simply themselves she evoked, the tangled pattern of questions and answers their lives evoked; but more, much more, which could only find a frame of reference within the context of this brutal humble land, kneeling down like a camel in the shadow of Ararat snow-crowned. Her inner life lay with Julian, her outer with Jocas; one represented the city, the drawn bowstring of Moslem politenesses, the other the open air, the riding to falcons, the chase. Remote encampments on the rim of deserts mirrored in the clear optic of the sky: to sleep at night under the stars, balanced between the two open eternities of birth and death.

It was much more than the facts which mattered, which had shaped their peculiar destinies; it was also place. I mean I saw very clearly now the tiny cocksure figure of Merlin, senior, walking the bazaars, dressed in his old blazer and yachting cap; high white kid boots and high collars fastened with a jeweled tiepin: flyswish held negligently in small ringed fingers. Behind him strolled the resplendent kavass—the Negro dressed in scarlet and brocade, carrying the drawn scimitar of his office, with the blade laid back along his forearm. This was how it all began, with Merlin shopping for the firm, which at that time must have consisted only of a raggle-taggle of sheds and godowns full of skins or poppy or shrouds. Yes, shrouds! The Moslem custom of burying the dead without coffins but wrapped in shrouds had not passed unnoticed by that blue jay's eye. (Was it the little clerk Sacrapant who mentioned this?) Seven shrouds to a corpse, and in the case of the richer and more distinguished families, no expense was spared to secure the most gorgeous embroidered fabrics the bazaars could offer. Old Abdul Hamid used to order hundreds of pieces of the choicest weave—China and Damascus silk. These were sent to Mecca to be sprinkled with holy water from the sacred well of Zem Zem. Thus the dead person was secured a certain translation of Jennet, the Moslem Paradise. It was not long before the caravans of Merlin carried these soft bales. But all this was at the very beginning, before Julian could say of the firm: "It has great abstract beauty, the firm, Charlock. We never touch or possess any of the products we manipulate—only the people to a certain extent. The products are merely telegrams, quotations, symbolic matter, that is all. If you cared for chess you could not help caring for Merlin's." He himself loved the game in all its variety. It is easy to see him aboard the white-winged yacht which the firm had given him, anchored upon the mirror of some Greek sound, sitting before the three transparent Perspex boards in stony silence; playing three-dimensionally, so to speak. How beautifully those little Turkish warehouses had metastasized, so to speak, forming secondary cancers in the lungs, livers, hearts of the great capitals. In the long silences of Julian one saw the slow curling smoke of his cigar rise upon the moonlit sky.

"But, Benedicta, all that rigmarole about them being orphans and all that. . . ."

"My father invented that to get round some complicated Turkish legislation about inheritances, death duties."

"But he said it with such feeling."

"Feeling! Jocas had murder in his heart for many years against Julian. But by repressing his hatred he turned himself into a fine human being; he really did come to love Julian at last. But Julian never loved him, never could, never will. Julian only loved me. Only me."

"And your father?"

"And my father!" .

She said it with such a withering emphasis that I instantly divined the hatred between Merlin and Julian. "Julian would not let me love him, forced me to hate him: at the end drove him out. He too had reasons, Julian."

"Drove Merlin out?"

"Yes. As he had driven out my mother."

In the long silence which followed I could hear her shallow breathing; but it was calm now, confident and regular. "Nash always said that real maturity should automatically mean a realized compassion for the world, for people. This Julian never had, only sadness, an enormous sadness. Nor for that matter did my father. He was a bird of prey. What was I to do between them all—with no real human contact to work upon? I dared not show my sympathies for Jocas even, hardly dared to speak to him. You know, Felix, they were all killers by temperament. I never knew who might kill who—even though Julian was away so much, being educated. If they met, they met on neutral ground, so to speak, usually some dead spa like Smyrna or Lutraki. All staying at different hotels with their retainers. A sort of armed truce somehow enabled them to survive—it is very Turkish, you see. Formal exchanges of meaningless presents. Then discussions, perhaps in a special train on the Turkish frontier. That was all. Later of course the telephone helped; they did not need to meet, they could be cordial to each other in this way."

"But you were lovers."

"Always. Even afterward. We found ways."

But I was mentally adding in the data derived from the steel cabinets—or as much of it as I had had time to read. It was not hard to picture them there, the two children, in some deserted corner of the dusty palace among the tarnished mirrors with their chipped gilt frames. The swarthy intent face of Julian, his eyes blazing with almost manic concentration, his lips drawn back from white teeth. Each held a heavy silver candlestick with a full branch of rosy lighted candles. They confronted each other thus, naked, like contestants in some hieratic combat, or like Oriental dancers. Perhaps too among the wheeling shadows of the high rooms and curling staircases they must have seemed to anyone who saw them (Merlin himself did once) like gorgeous plumed birds treading out an elaborate mating dance with all its intricate figures. So they shook the burning wax over one another, thrust and riposte, hissing at its hot tang; they were drenched as if with molten spray. What else was there left to do? They had learned and unlearned everything before puberty—disordering their psyches, forcing them on before they were ripe. Will those who do this not prejudice their sexual and affective adult life: live forever in fantasy acts of sexual excess? Never get free?

Well, who am I to say that? But I could see deeper now into the pattern of their lives which had become so very much a reflection of Turkey—the miasma of old Turkey with its frigid cruelties, its priapic conspiracies. This fitted in well with the small ferocious Calvinist soul of Merlin, bursting at its seams with guilty sadistic impulses. (And him with all the quiet diligence and the family grace of feature!) Here at least he was at home. One saw him during those long winter evenings, sitting over his books with some green-turbaned teacher, drinking in the charm of the language with all its gobbling sententiousness, its lack of relative pronouns and subordinate clauses. Sitting with the amber mouthpiece of a nargileh in his hand, allowing one-half of his mind to play with the idea of its cost—silver-hilted amber (worth perhaps two hundred English pounds?).

Or else up on the bronze foothills (they all shot like angels), following the cautious dogs—himself not the less cautious between the accompanying guns. They walked in an arrowhead formation so that Jocas and Julian and the girl were a trifle ahead of him. Up here, though, in the exultation of the open life of the steppe, they were almost united in spirit, almost at one with each other. Disarmed around a campfire at evening, they would listen smiling to the ululations of tribal singers, stirred into an exultant tenderness by the magnificence of the night sky and the hills. From this part of their lives single incidents stood out forever in her memory, clear and burnished. Like when the little man was walking alone along an escarpment and was pounced upon by a pair of golden eagles. He must have been near their nest, for they fell whistling out of the sky upon him, wingspan and claws powerful enough to have carried off a full-grown sheep. He heard the whistle and the swish of the huge wings just in time; he had glimpsed their shadows as he ducked. The others rushed to help him—he was defending himself with the unloaded gun, beating the eagles off; but by the time they arrived, one of the birds lay breathless on the rock at his feet and the other had gone. He was panting, his rifle was twisted, the stock was cracked. He took a cudgel from a Turk and beat the quivering eagle to death with white face, his teeth showing in a grin. He had deep wounds in his back, his shirt was torn to rags. Then he sat down on a rock and buried his white face in trembling hands. Watching him she understood why she could never bring herself to call him "Father"; he was quite simply terrifying. Julian says laconically: "I can see their nest," and taking a shotgun blazes away at it until it disintegrates. If she closed her eyes and held her breath, she could feel the weight of Julian's mind resting upon hers. It was something more than the drugs; he held her by the scruff of the mind, so you might say. "He performed an elaborate series of psychic and physical experiments on me—of course in the Levant there is nothing very uncommon or shocking about it." When the telephone came into fashion, she learned to ring him up and recite a string of soft cajoling obscenities until . . . "Of course you can love somebody like that," says Benedicta with her eyes closed, resting her forehead on the cold rail of the bedpost. "Nobody has got more than one way, his own, of showing his love. Too bad if it's uncommon or perverted or whatnot. Or perhaps Julian would say 'too good.' I can't say I didn't enjoy being owned by him, engulfed by him—utterly swallowed. In another perverse way, it is such a relief to surrender the will utterly. Julian turned me into a sleepwalker for his experiments. He led me up to the point of being able to kill." The white face with the closed eyes looked like some remote statue forgotten in a museum. A long time like that in a fierce muse of concentration, still as a burning glass.

Was this before or after? Ah, dactyl answer me. No, I do not care. It suffices that it should form part of the central pattern. While Merlin prospered and bought ruined palaces and cypress groves, the children loved and despaired away their youth in sunken gardens guarded by a retinue of impersonal servants, governesses, retainers. Jocas was born to the chase and was always glad to escape to the Asiatic side with his hunting birds and his kites. Julian the tranquil, thoughtful, the vicious, was never without a book, and was already the master of several languages. Yet withal he had in him some of the heavy-souled impersonality of the sleepy Ottoman world where the humid heat lay upon the nerves with the weight of lead. Julian and his sister! Later they were to be separated and his personal hold over her suffered a metamorphosis—he held her through the firm and the needs of the firm, no longer through the body and the personal will. That was how she became the near-witch Benedicta. But during this early time he taught her to fence; naked again, they faced each other on the stone flags and the room rang to the dry clicking of buttoned foils. Then lying in the great bedroom with its mirror ceiling, in each other's arms, as if at the bottom of the ocean they made love, watching each other watch each other. He was soon to meet his peculiar medieval fate—the fate of Abelard; for Merlin knew all. Somewhere inside himself Julian was not really surprised when they all walked in holding candles—Merlin himself dressed in an old-fashioned nightgown and soft Turkish slippers with pointed toes. Julian closed his eyes, pretending to sleep, until they touched his shoulder and led him away. Benedicta slept on, slept on. The tall bald eunuch held the long-shanked dressmaker's scissors reverently, like an instrument of sacrifice, which indeed they were. Also the sterilized needle and the thread to baste the wound and stitch the empty pouch up like a gigot. It was not pain that turned Julian into a raging maniac; it was quite simply the indignity. When she told me this, I could see suddenly the whole pattern of things lit up by the phosphorescent white light of his anger, translated out of impotence. No, the cruelest thing about impotence is that it is fundamentally a comic predicament. His father had not only punished him but had mocked him as well. A phrase creeps back to mind from some other forgotten context. "They were bound by a complicity of desire and purpose far stronger even than love, perhaps even independent of death." I hardly dare to touch her, to put my hand upon her shoulder when she looks like this. The closed eyes stare on and on into the center of memory. "All this I will have to be punished for someday I suppose," she said between her teeth. "I was afraid you would find it endearing—another delightful feminine weakness to add to your collection." I had already begun to undress. I said, "I am not going to indulge your sense of guilt anymore." I told her to take off her ski pants and sweater and climb in beside me. The sense of familiarity combined with the sense of novelty—new lives for old: a new version of an old model: new wine in old brothels: it held me spellbound. Nor were her kisses any longer contaminated by nervous preoccupations—the stream was flowing clear, undammed at last. "Tell me how you killed him, the husband." Between quickly drawn breaths she said: "Now?" "Yes, Benedicta, now." While she spoke I was making love to her, I was happy.

They had been mounted, had ridden far across the fields and valleys to a marsh where he had been promised game to hunt. By the side of a long narrow causeway ran a group of abandoned clay cuttings with a rivulet flowing. Beneath the causeway was quicksand, or rather a quagmire. Urging her horse with her spurs, she found it no hard matter to press his mount toward the end and softly push it over. He landed in a huge sucking surprised calm, almost disposed to laugh, looking up at her from under the brim of his soft straw hat. The sandy moustache. Two realizations gradually welled up simultaneously in his fuddled mind: namely, he was slowly settling in the black viscous mud, and that she had become suddenly motionless, her eyes staring down at him with an almost expressionless curiosity. But the horse knew and sent forth an almost human wail as it flailed with its legs to free them from the soft imprisonment, the anaconda coils of the mud. Appalling sounds of the sucking farting mud. As for the man, he watched himself, so to speak, reflected in the pupil of that blue scientific eye, watched himself sinking down and away, out of time and mind: out of her life and out of his. Surprise held him silent. Only his youthful handsome face, now pale with sweat, held an expression of pained pleading. The treachery was so unexpected: it seemed that he had to revise the whole of their past life, their past relationship in the light of it. It was not only his past which swam before his astonished eyes but his future. He whispered "help" from a parched throat, but his lips barely framed the word. The moustache! But she only sat down upon the parapet, turning her mount loose, and watched the experiment with a holy concentration, forcing herself to memorize the whole thing unflinchingly so that she might recount it to Julian when the time came, when she would have to.

So he settled slowly as the westering sun itself was settling beyond the hills. They stared at each other in bitter silence, almost oblivious of the death struggles of the horse which blew its muddy bubbles and groaned and rolled its eyes as it slowly heaved its way downward, suffocating. The mud sounded jocose. Soon he was there, buried to the breastbone like some unfinished statue of an equestrian knight. "So that's it," he said, with a wondering croak. "So that's it, Benedicta."

"That's it, my darling."

She lit a cigarette with steady fingers and smoked it fast with shallow inspirations, never taking her eyes off his. But now it was horrible, he had begun to sob; the harsh sniffs broke down the features of his face into all the planes of childhood. He was getting younger as he died, was becoming a child again. And this was hard. A hopeless sympathy welled up in her, battling against the deadly concentration. It was becoming harder to watch with all the promised detachment. He was panting, head on one side, his mouth open. His hands were still free, but his elbows were becoming slowly imprisoned. There might still have been time to throw him a rope and pass it round a tree? She fought the thought, holding it at bay as she watched. It wasn't the fear of death so much, she thought, as the ignominy of her betrayal—that was what lay behind the tears of this adolescent, this infant in the straw hat. But in a little while he decided to spare her feelings, his tears ceased to flow; a lamblike resignation came over his face, for now he knew he was beyond hope. Quickly she cut a slip of reed, cleft it and passed down the lighted cigarette so that he might take a puff. But he brushed it away and with a small sigh turned his face inward upon himself and floated thickly down in slow motion, with little shudders and no more sound—not even a reproach, a curse, a cry for help. Not a bubble. It was so quickly over. She watched and went on watching until only the hat still floated on the quag. She could hardly tear herself away from the spot now. Muttering to herself, she felt all at once as if she were in a high fever; a fiery exultation possessed her. She had shown herself worthy of Julian. She managed to secure the straw hat—she would carry it back to him like someone carrying the severed head of a criminal. The valley was silent, oppressively silent. She tried to sing as she went, but it only made the silent dusk more eerie. Once or twice she thought she heard the sound of horses' hooves behind her; and she wheeled about to see if there was anyone following—but there was nobody to be seen.

There! Easy to recount, to bring to memory, hard to assimilate. It still stuck in her throat like a bundle of bloody rags she could not swallow.

"And it's no good saying I am sorry; yes, I am, of course. But what really ails me is the wound to my self-esteem, to find myself, my wonderful unique beautiful self guilty of so petty a betrayal. You see what a trap the ego sets you?" She raised a white fist and drummed softly on my breastbone, and then sinking down she fell, mouth to mouth in a suffocating parody of sadness which swallowed itself in the new unhindered sexual paroxysms. "But by far the most absurd and humiliating thing that happened to me was to fall in love with you at first sight. It was unbearable, such a blow to my self-esteem, such a danger to my freedom. And also to you—you were in such danger for such a long time. Poor fool, you wouldn't have believed it; how could I tell you? I did not believe it myself. All that comedy of errors with the little clerk, remember? He was supposed to kill you in the cisterns. Poor man! First your hesitation about signing, then this poor foolish clerk being told to do away with you—he was unfitted for such a task, even though his own life depended on it. All that excursion you found so funny was a sort of dress rehearsal for the job Sacrapant had been set. Mercifully you hesitated about signing, and this gave me a chance to reach Julian. I persuaded him to countermand the order. 'Leave him to me,' I said. 'I will suck him dry. He has lots to offer us as yet. If necessary I will marry him, Julian, until we can dispose of him.' But in all the delay of sign and countersign, the suspense became too much for poor Sacrapant, he knew he could never do it, that his time was up."

"So he fell out of the sky?"

"So he fell out of the sky. Kiss me."

"He sacrificed himself for me in a way."

"Not really, there's no such thing. I did."

I began to see a little deeper into the meaning of those first encounters, those first brushes with the firm. They had already had a chance to see my notebooks which were from their point of view crammed with promises.

"Benedicta, darling, tell me one thing."

But she was asleep now with her blonde head against my breast, rocked by our mutual breathing as a sea gull is rocked by a calm summer sea. "I see," I whispered to myself, but in fact I saw only relatively. I recalled Jocas talking about the impossibility of ever tracing the real causal relationship between an act and its reason. And in the context of beloved Sacrapant, too, I saw the little man's pale water-rat face in the wallowing water light of the great cisterns.

It was here in Turkey that Julian first contracted that thirst for the black sciences which has always colored the cast of his mind; for here every form of enquiry could be pursued in absolute safety. "The idolaters of Syria and Judaea drew oracles from the heads of children which they had torn from their bodies. They dried the heads and, having placed beneath the tongue a golden lamen bearing unknown ciphers, they fixed them in the hollows of walls, built up a kind of false body beneath them composed of magical plants fastened together: they lighted a lamp under these fearful idols and proceeded with their consultation. They believed that the heads spoke . . . moreover it is true that blood attracts larvae. The ancients, when sacrificing, dug a pit which they filled with warm and smoking blood; then from the recesses of the dark night they saw the feeble and pale shadows rising up, creeping, chirping, swarming about the pit. . . . They kindled great fires of laurel, alder and cypress upon altars crowned with asphodel and vervain. The night seemed to grow colder . . ." (Julian silent in a high-backed chair with a book open on his knees.) Moreover, "if integrally and radically the woman leaves the passive role and enters the active, she abdicates her sex and becomes man, or rather, such a transformation being physically impossible, she attains affirmation by a double negation, placing herself outside both sexes like some sterile and monstrous androgyne."

I was beginning to see him much more clearly, and in ideas like these I thought I caught a glimpse of the *altera* Benedicta, that lovely petrifact which destiny had transformed back into the loved original, the beloved outlaw I had almost forgotten in all this exhausting struggle. As for her mysterious and elusive lover, why should he not aspire to the mastery over age and time that Simon Magus first achieved? "Sometimes appearing pale, withered, broken, like an old man at the point of death: at others the luminous fluid revitalized him, his eyes glittered, his skin became smooth and soft, his body upright. He could be actually seen passing from youth to decrepitude, childhood to age." Nor did there seem to be any perversity in these speculations which swarmed in the young Julian's mind; everything was tinged with the vast Oriental passivity of the place. Down below the jetty at Avalon you could still see, if you dived, the weighed sacks with the heads of the women—some forty—done to death like cats by Abdul Hamid in a sudden rage of revulsion against sex. Those that did not sink at once were beaten to death with oars in the green evening; their wails were piteous to hear, the boatmen had tears running down their faces as they worked. And Hamid? Do you remember the description of Sardanapalus, the great king? "He entered and saw with surprise the king with his face covered in white lead, and all bejeweled like a woman, combing out purple wool in the company of his concubines and sitting among them with blackened eyes, wearing a woman's dress and having his beard shaved close and his skin rubbed with pumice. His eyelids too were painted. . . ." Then the great pyre he built to end his days; several stories high it stood: and the conflagration lasted for weeks. Everything, to the smallest of his belongings, went up.

Mind you, only once did she dare to say that she loved him to his face, only once. His look of horror and fury was quite indescribable. He struck her across the face with a book, without contempt yet deliberately. "Hush," he said on a deep resonant note. "Hush, my darling." He was trying to say that it was not love, it was possession, and that her use of the word diminished the truth of the sentiment. Sentiment? No, that is not the word. She endured every kind of physical and sexual humiliation at his hands with the deepest joy, the profoundest pleasure. Julian was born never to weep. It was Jocas who took the scissors and embedded them in the wall of the cellars with their handles protruding. It had been decided that Julian was to go away, to be educated separately; partly it was the strain of the internal hatred between them all that decided the matter. But it was also dictated by the future needs of the firm, the firm that was going to be; for Merlin's quiet calculations were all bearing fruit slowly. His subtleties put many a fruitful project in his way: as when Abdul Hamid had given a concession for the purchase and sale of tobacco *en régie* to a company unwise enough to order Austrian cigarette paper stamped with the Sultan's *tougra* or monogram. Nobody would have noticed this except a man like Merlin. Was the sultan, he asked, content to have his effigy spat upon daily by tens of thousands of cigarette smokers in the kingdom? It was the same with the postage stamps which bore the monster's head. Were these also to be spittled over by scribes? Within a short space of time he secured both concessions for himself, for the firm.

A kiss is always the same kiss, though the recipient may change from time to time; her kisses were the only thing which had remained young still about her, fresh as spring violets. So many of our gestures are not prompted by psychological impulse but are purely hieratic—a whole wardrobe of prehistoric responses to forgotten situations. (The sex of the embryo is decided at coition; but five whole weeks evolve before the little bud declares itself as vagina or penis.) Io had suffered from a small and useful abnormality in being temporarily sterile: the closure of the lumen of the Fallopian tubes by scar tissue resulting from an early gonorrheal infection. . . .

Much of this I could not stand, could not bear hearing, bear knowing. I took refuge in the frivolity of my illness—purely in order to alarm her, to see if she cared. Master Charlock has been naughty this week; he has thrown his porringer on the floor, beat upon the table with his spoon, spilled his soup, roared like a bull, wet his trousers. . . . *Inventeur, Inventaire, Eventreur.* . . . I lie just looking at her, so far from the invincible happiness of possession; all this dirt, all these contaminated circumstances turned my love to vomit for a while. But this will not last; something which will prove to be stronger than the sum of these experiences will forge itself—is already rearing its flat head like a king cobra. If the sex thing remains the way it is, I will not falter again.

But even as I lie thinking this, looking into her eyes, the other half of my mind is following her out across the Cilician plains where once she used to be sent to hunt the harmless quail with the women of the little court. They alight in great flocks during the spring when the sesame crop is ripening—from far off they seem to be one huge moving carpet of birds, running along the ground like mice, with a subdued chirping. The women hunt the little creatures with a light net and an *aba,* a strange prehistoric contrivance shaped like a shield, or one side of a huge box kite, a skeleton of sticks covered in black cotton, but pierced with eyelets. Wearing this over their heads they advance in open order, staring through these huge eyes at the quail, which begin by running away: but soon appear to become mesmerized. They sit down and stare at the advancing shapes, allow themselves passively to be scooped up in the nets and transferred to the wicker hampers. Turning her mouth inward upon mine, I think of Dr. Lebedeff and his *délires archaïques.* Turkish delight, onanism in mirrors.

"It was not only Julian's life which was aberrant," she says clearly, trying to get it all off her chest, "it was the place, too. My father had me sexually broken, as we say in Turkish, by his slaves." Inexpressibly painful to her to retrace her steps over this poisoned ground, yet necessary. There in the night of Turkey I saw Julian as more of a goblin than a youth. The dust devils racing across the plains, some spinning clockwise some counterclockwise. "You can see from the way they fold their cloaks which are female and which male," say the peasants. In those days to bring rain two men used to flog each other until the blood poured down their backs and the heavens melted. (They pissed on Merlin's eagle wounds to disinfect them properly before dressing them.)

"Not all our eunuchs were artificially formed. There were some villages on the high plateau which specialized in producing strange but natural androgynes with an empty scrotum like a tobacco pouch; they were bald usually and had high scolding voices." Fragments of other lore have got themselves mixed up with the transcription somewhere here. (A skeleton whitewashed and painted the color of blood, to present its reemergence in the world. Or a phrase underlined by Julian in a book, *"Il faut annoncer un autre homme possible"*; you will see from this how deeply he was concerned with his own soul, and for the fate of man. It is not possible to consider him simply as an unprincipled libertine, or an alchemist who went mad under the strain of too much knowledge. No. His concern was with virtue, with truth. Otherwise why should he have said that the most devastating criticism ever made of a human being was in the *Republic* where the phrase occurs: "Now he was one of those who came from heaven and in a former life had dwelt in a well-ordered state, but his virtue was a matter of habit only and he had no philosophy"? I do not really know him as yet; perhaps I will never know him now.)

Autumn is well on the way with its moist coloring, its rotting avenues of leaves; but these wards are quite seasonless. Blood-orange moons over the Alps. But I am miles away still in the heart of Turkey with Benedicta. There is still so much to comprehend. They have changed my nurse for a great big sad dun-colored creature with eyes like conjugal raisins. In the dangerous wards they are playing backgammon with little moans of surprise; men and women like outmoded, damaged pieces of furniture. "Smoking spunk!" cries Rackstraw with peevish vexation. "What has the dooced boots done with my suedes?" There is no answer to the question. Then at times a touching half-comprehension of his situation comes upon him—in the mirror on the white wall he will talk to himself thus: "Ah, my lifelong friend, I have led you up to this point, past so many deceits, so many suicides. And you are still there. Now what? Something the blood deposits as it moves about like an old snake. But the reticence of these ghosts is amazing. Io! Io!" He listens with his head on one side, then turns away, shaking his head and whispering: "I was sent here because I loved too much. It was out of proportion. I had to pay for it with all this boredom." Drawing in breath on the windowpane with a long yellow finger, he will suddenly change mood and subject and exclaim: "Has anyone seen Johnson lately? I wonder where he's gone. I last heard he'd been locked up in Virginia Water for making love to a tree."

Where indeed was Johnson and why did he write so infrequently? "They may have moved him from Leatherhead to Virginia Water. He has had a great crisis of *belief*, Johnson. They are studying his case with care; it is not like me, I am simply here to rest on my laurels." Rackstraw scratches an ear.

"Pthotquyck" he says suddenly, brightly.

"I beg your pardon?"

"Pthotquyck. It's the Finnish for mushroom."

"I see."

"The dooced things get into everything."

From various sources I have managed to piece together the story of his friend Johnson, the great lover. Yes, they are holding him at Virginia Water, in the grip of his fearful but poetical Yggdrasil complex, or so I suppose they must call it. "Things have closed in very much down here," he writes. "The people are kind but not very understanding. Out in the park there are some lovely trees, and next week when I have my first walk I will try and have a couple. Elms!" It was as simple as that—suddenly in the full flower of his sexual maturity Johnson found he loved trees. Other men have had to make do with goats or women or the Dalmation Cavalry, but Johnson found them all pale into insignificance beside these long-legged green things which were everywhere: he saw them as green consenting adults with diminished responsibility, loitering all round him with intent. They beckoned to him, urged him to come on over; they could hardly do otherwise, for a tree has not much conversation. Perhaps it was due to his long and severe training for the Ministry which had all but tamed him. However it may be, long-suffering policemen on the prowl for more unsavory misdemeanors used to chase the skinny figure round and round Hyde Park. Johnson showed a surprising turn of speed, running distractedly here and there like a cabbage white, doing up his trousers fervently as he ran.

For several orgiastic weeks he led them a dance, and perhaps they would never have caught him had not the indignant prostitutes organized an ambush for this harmless satyr. He was distracting trade they said, while some people were even complaining that the trees were getting bent, several of them. This was pure jealousy, of course. So Johnson, priest and dendrophile, was committed to the doctors for attention. And now Rackstraw is here, brooding on the destiny of his friend. He sighs and says: "And Iolanthe—I wonder if you ever heard of her? She was famous in her day; I made her famous. I wrote them all except one—the one about the lovers in Athens. Films. The whole thing came from her diaries; she wouldn't let me change a word of the dialogue. The young man had died or gone away, I don't know. But she could never see it without weeping. It used to upset me. O I wonder what's happened to Johnson. Pthotquyck!"

The woods are full of them, the wards are full of them! Yet they contrive in their disjointed fashion to present a composite picture of a way of life, a homogeneous society almost—even the most alienated. They smell each other's aberrations as dogs smell each other's tail odors. Even the hauntingly beautiful Venetia, the little girl with two cunts, who has specialized in a crooning echolalia which Rackstraw listens to with delectation—as if to the song of some rare bird.

"Who are you?"
"Who."
"Who are you?"
"Are you."
"Are you Venetia Mann?"
"Mann."
"Are you?"
"Are you."

Rackstraw shakes his head and gives a mirthless laugh. "Priceless," he says. "Priceless."

Ah, but one day we will be restored to the body of the real world—O world of Anabaptists, tax dodgers and hierophants, O world of mentholized concubines! Yes, my darling wife, with your bright eyes and snow-burned face, we shall leave this place one day, arm in arm. A new life will begin, dining off smoked foreskin in Claridge's, on partridges in Putney. We will leave Rackstraw to play chess with the deaf mute. And Felix will go back to the firm with the same engaging adolescent manner which seems to say: please be nice to me, I have only been educated up to the anal stage. Back to London, back to the *vox pop.* of the banjo group, back to the young with their unpsychoanalyzed hair. Kiss me, Benedicta.

But pouring out a drink with shaking hand she says:

"Julian has said that he wants to see us together."

"Well?"

"I'm beginning to feel afraid again."

"The very word is like a knell."

"He says everything is different now."

"It had better be."

Not tonight, though; tonight we are alone, just the two of us, compounding fortune with all her little treacheries. You will tell me once more, lying half asleep, about the locusts—of how the early winds brought them sailing over Anatolia, darkening the light of the sun. How the hunters would see them first, being the longest-sighted: and give tongue. Whistles and gunshots and the winking of heliographs from the ruined watchtowers of the coast. Away across the bronzy stubble and the mauve limestone ranges, the marauders came in innocent-looking puffs, coming nearer and nearer until the cauldron overflowered and they were on you. Clouds at first soft, evanescent, tempted to disperse: but no, instead they gathered weight and density, formed into the wings of giant bats, spread out to swallow the pure sky.

The camp went grimly frantic with preparations: as if for an Arctic blizzard, for the horny coarse-bodied little insects penetrate everywhere, everything, ubiquitous as smoke or dust itself. Heads wrapped in cloth or duffel, wrists fastened, legs sheathed in puttees or leggings. Then the long wait to determine if the cloud was preceded by an advance guard of wingless green young ones, pouring along the ground with incredible speed, turning the fields to a rippling torrent of scaly green.

Pits were dug, long barriers of tin or wood scooped the advance guard (as far as was possible) into them where kerosene fires smoked and flapped. On they came, pouring themselves unhesitatingly into the pits, piling upon the bodies of their burning fellows, until there were tons of them ablaze. The stench deafened creation. But the fliers approached with that ominous deep crackle—first from far away like thorns under a pot: then nearer, more deafening, like a forest fire, the noise of their shearing jaws. The illusion of fire was also given by the speed with which they stripped the forest of every green leaf, hanging in long strings like bees swarming. Shrubs keeled over with the weight of their bodies. The horses kicked and shied at their horny touch; and however many precautions one took, one always felt the creatures crawling up one's legs or arms, scratching the bare skin, tickling. In a twinkling the whole visible world was stripped of life, bald as a skull. A winter forest as nude as Xmas under the burning sun. A very particular and utterly silent silence followed such attacks for weeks on end: that and the stench of charred bodies burning like straw.

Then camps were broken up, ranks redressed; but exhaustedly, listlessly. Yet there had been no danger. Only it was as if they themselves had been stripped of everything except their eyeballs. In one of the khans a circling vulture dropped a woman's hand into the camp. Well and so back like ants to the skylines, to where the blue gulf carved and recarved itself, smoothing away toward the fitful city.

Deep sleep was good again, though the research ferrets of the unconscious still sniffed around the motives and actions of my silent companion. The past isn't retrievable is it?—too many burned-out bulbs. Try, Felix, only try!

Now this morning an unexpected envelope with a London postmark—this from Vibart; not a real letter, he explains, but a few pages torn from his desk pad. "I should really have come to see you, Felix, but I'm superstitious about bins. Always have been. Suppose you were glassy, eh? Ugh! Even a real letter might be wasted, then. But a few pages from my desk pad will give you news of me, broadening the old mind as we used to say.

> *"Tell me*
> *What strange irrelevance*
> *Dogs the lives of elephants*
> *With trunk before*
> *And tail behind,*
> *With ears of such vast elegance*
> *How they control the state*
> *Of such a massive gait*
> *And still be reasonable and kind*
> *Though almost all behind?*
> *"item*

"It's awkward, isn't it, when the flippant, the effortlessly inconsequent, becomes a tic. We have come a long way together, haven't we, old man? Without being very much together either; from time to time, like model railways our paths cross at a critical junction. Ting-a-ling!

"item

"Cogent Memo in Julian's own hand. (He has begun to write very big and sprawly now.) 'From a publishing point of view the only irresistible themes are Quests, Confessions, and Puzzles in that order. Let Vibart govern his judgment by this unshakable truth.' An odd tone to take with me, isn't it? What about all those poems which give us prestige—poems written with a stomach pump? Koepgen's new volume for example. It's all very well for him, Julian, just off to New York again with his star-spangled manner.

"item

"Felix, I am making a very great deal of money. Yesterday my ideal novel came in. It begins, 'Smith was a nice big man in good health; but because he had been told as a child that his balls would fly off if he laughed too heartily his face always wore a strange twisted expression. He lived in dreadful anticipation until one day the worst happened . . . (now read on).' I have had to refuse it for other reasons.

"item

"One lives and learns. F.V., the novelist, tells me that 'one should know as little as possible about one's characters. The more detail you give the more they sink back into the undifferentiated mass. All you need is one cardinal aspect for each one—a ruling bent, in fact the person's "signature" in the heraldic sense: hunchback moneylender, myopic scholar, deist king. The rest is padding.' And I suppose that the proof of the padding is in the publishing?

"item

"Felix, I'm miserable, how are you? How would F.V. novelize us? I wonder if we might presume ourselves to live in one of his fictions? If only you knew, if only he knew. Pia! The last letters! It is unfair. I can't bring myself to throw them away: yet what purpose would they serve if I kept them? They are fading anyway. Time is very generous in some ways. 'Death comes always by a sort of secret intention, a compact. Like a love affair, one *disposes* toward it, one *inclines*, one intimates the secret need.' I sometimes wish myself in the Paulhaus with you—at times I almost merit it. My dreams, you should see them! What an extraordinary fauna and flora sprouts from the infernal regions.

"item

"And all the time she was staring at me with those candid and unflinching eyes, she knew that she was quietly and confidently betraying me all down the line. She had decided I wasn't a man, I suppose. And with whom? Guess! Yes, with Jocas. I really can't believe it myself as yet. The caption doesn't fit the picture. And yet it's all there, written out in her own fair hand. The riding lessons! Then when we had to go away they both got ill from the separation. How sordid. All those doctor's bills. Damn.

"item

"The fear of solitude is at bottom the fear of the double, the figure which appears one day and always heralds death. The triumph of death over the hero is ineluctable—*le triomphe ignoble du mal remplit le monde d'une immense tristesse*. Would you buy a manuscript with such things in it?

"item

"'Pia says: 'What matter? One day my teeth will fall out like rocks out of a hillside. Only the dignity of the mouth—its outline—which once haunted men might linger a little in certain postures. Musculature giving in like an old banjo. Then I shall die—but I *have;* while you are reading this I *am*. The process has started. Let's imagine Pia in a state of infinite dispersion, infinite extension, inhabiting every nook in imaginable space. It will be hard to part with all my jewelery and clothes—even the *toc*. And what of that family of little homeless shoes? How could I do it to them? But I must, I *have*. Yet I cannot bring myself to leave them to anyone, for death is only apparent and mostly by scheming. I would have liked to embrace you once, good and warm—but you would decipher my intention from my kiss. I dare not risk it. Only Jocas knows the date, the time, the minute; I am taking him with me in a funny sort of way, as a fellow passenger. He will still be on earth of course, and quite unchanged in the physical sense; but in a special sense not. The not-part will have been expropriated. I am trying not to punish him too much. He did me one inestimable service in love—taught me to "listen with the clitoris" as he called it.'

"Well, and then it gets mixed up with my obligatory reading. Listen, 'Love, then, as both teleological and biological trigger.' The weight of these massive ponderations illustrated by Pia's dead gnome's face. Damn them all, the philosophic cutthroats. Mumbo jumbo, cant and twaddle. In a book on esoteric something or other, she has underlined a passage which goes: 'Nothing is hidden, there are no secrets. But you can tell people only what they already know. That is the infuriating thing. And while they may know it, they may not be conscious that they know. Hence the jolt provided by the dry-cell batteries of art. In such a thing all that has been done is to create an area of self-recognition. The reflected light plays upon the observer, he sees, becomes a see-er, a self-seer.' The wisdom of other lands and other time, my lad. What avails it all?

"Alcibiades,
Alcibiades!
Feeling it rise and recede
Feeling the Pleiades, bids us
Take heed.
'One gets tired of elderly parties
Even when they are as wise as Socrátes.'

"item

"So here I am, your old pal Vibart, still walking these rain-benisoned streets, rising morning after morning at cock

[58]

sparrow lantern to face the terrible effrontery of a bowl of porridge. I listen to the news before checking latchkey and leaving house. In the tube inhale the twirpy twang of urban English. Life has no sharp edges.

"item

"Lately I have all but managed to see Julian face to face—I've been playing your sly game with him, just to tease him, I mean. I even waited in his flat for a while as you did —of course with no result. I found it much as you told me I would. But those great blowups of Iolanthe, they were all slashed as if with a pair of scissors. Someone too had written across one in Greek, 'Αρχείτω βίος! Ιώ! Ιώ!* For the only time in my life my classical education proved of some use—for I recognized the quotation. I don't know why it gave me such a pang. Is it possible that such a man feels?

"item

"I see a lot of Pulley, but in the question of Caradoc-Crusoe some new and ambiguous developments have thrown us into a state of indecision. At any rate Robinson has been expropriated by the Australians and has disappeared. They want his island as a proving ground for one of your toys, ironically enough: something Marchant has modified and perfected. May one perhaps see the hand of Julian in all this—or perhaps we exaggerate? I'm sick of looking over my shoulder. At any rate that is all we know about Robinson. Meanwhile I enclose two little items from the usually so sedate *Informateur* of Zürich which you may find highly suggestive. Could they be . . . ? *Aimable jogl cherche nonne enculable que mariage.* Box 346 X. Also this: *Young flesh fervently sought by aged but eclectic crosspatch.* Box 450 X.

"item"

I stifled a cry of amused amaze, but my involuntary start must have jolted her out of sleep. She lay with eyes closed,

* Enough of life! Io! Io!

[59]

but awake and drowsy. "My goodness," she said at last in a luxurious whisper, settling that slender body warmly against mine, revising its posture so that it fitted as nearly as possible into the hollows of my own. "You have begun to believe in me as a possibility at last." It was only our sleepy minds making love, or recovering the part of it which had been so long left unmade. Kiss.

"Caradoc may be alive, do you hear?"

"Of course."

"Did you know it?"

"Not for certain; I sort of felt it in my bones."

"We must try and find out." In my enthusiasm I all but forgot the equivocal nature of the "freedom" Nash had so heartily conferred on this patient. Free, yes. To walk along the lakeside at twilight, hand in hand with B. if need be; but always following on behind us after a discreet interval came the small white ambulance, keeping its exact distance. This was just in case I should become overtired. Once I amused myself by entering a cinema and leaving at once by another entrance, but it was not long before they caught up with me. The town is small, the streets short. Besides I was, I am, tired; moreover I have no projects, nothing to look forward to, nowhere I would rather be than in this clinical paradise. A philosopher out of work. Benedicta must have been following my thoughts with great accuracy for she said: "No, you won't be followed anymore. Let's go and try and find him, if you wish. I know because Julian is here. He telephoned about a meeting. He said so, and you know he never lies." So we sat down to eat together and plan. It was unnerving in its unfamiliarity—I mean the simple act of eating off the same tray. (In the age of chivalry, husband and wife, knight and lady, ate off the same trencher, he feeding her.) Well, I want to keep an exact record of all this; I still don't trust anyone, except sporadically Benedicta herself.

TWO

The offices of the *Informateur* were easy to find; in an old building smelling of drains and printer's ink. The editor a tiny mollusk in powerful spectacles. The cuttings rather startled him, and he went to files to assure himself that they had indeed appeared in his august journal. It was unusual, it was bizarre. He was a little troubled on the grounds of good taste.

At any rate the offices which handled the advertising were at Geneva, and he thought that current practice would prevent them giving me the address of an advertiser. It was a private matter, after all. I would have to write. This was disheartening; but since the project itself might well prove hopelessly chimerical, it wasn't worth being too cast down about it. We sent a couple of telegrams to the box numbers, one from some young flesh signed by Benedicta and one from an "enculable nonne" signed by myself, offering every enticement we could. Then we wandered for a while in the streets, chafing ourselves upon the windows with all their finery, admiring everything. "Buy me something," said Benedicta suddenly. "I want to be given something, anything small and cheap. In bad taste if you like." But I had forgotten my wallet and while she had plenty of money on her it "wouldn't do," for some reason or other, it *wouldn't do!* For some esoteric reason this made me suddenly happy. I felt an absurd disposition to tears almost. She stood me coffee and cream buns in a deserted café with plush seats and barely any light; and suddenly I felt a desire to rid myself of my cocoon of bandages, which I did in the lavatory. "Good," she said. "Good. Don't look rueful even if the hair hasn't covered the scars as yet. The move is in the right direction."

"Loving," I said, sinking back into my seat with a sigh, though the word had a strange translated ring to it; it was as if I were trying it out, like a shoe. Benedicta nodded, her blue eyes bright.

"Loving," she said, as if she too were trying it out.

Then she added as we rose to walk back up the hill to the Paulhaus: "No more of it for us. We've done it. We've committed it, and need never think of it again. Unless . . . How sure do you feel of yourself?"

"I don't know. Remember a piece of my brain is missing; suppose it's the piece (like in the old phrenology skulls) which had the fatal word written on it? Then what?"

"Nothing. I've done it, I've had it, I am it."

"My God, is happiness so simple then?"

"When you are committed; when it's a fact."

"Benedicta, what are you planning, what are you dreaming about?"

"For the first time nothing. I'm just content to be, to have escaped Julian, to have persuaded you to try and rediscover me. Let's just let go, shall we, until we see Julian?"

The long walk, the long silence, the plenitude of it, refreshed instead of tiring me.

"This is very absurd."

"I know."

In some vague and unspecified way the wind of destiny

seemed to have shifted. A mild sun fumed upon the fir-clad slopes, filling the valleys with a ghostly mist; but now all benign. Even the winding paths, the firmly shuttered look of the buildings, the cars parked in rows along the concrete drive-ins—they had all participated in this subtle shift of emphasis. It only takes a little thing like an outing when you are a loony . . . No, but there was substance to it. "Come and spend tonight with me up at the chalet. It's all right. Just tell them." Just tell them! I wondered where she discovered this fund of easy insouciant optimism. Nevertheless I returned for a bath and a change of the small dressings and with nervous sangfroid did as I was bid. No objections were raised—though when I think of it what objections could have been raised? It just shows the state of mind I had got myself into.

It was ten minutes' walk over the hill to the chalet with its little chaplet of firs; there were lights on inside, but soft lights suggesting candles. I kicked off my snow and slush and tapped. She was in the little hall, already changed into a long dress cut like an aba and made of some heavy damascened material; she was in the act of combing out the newhead of curly blonde hair. "It all fell out during the course of my troubles and I inherited a new head from who knows where? My mother perhaps. There's a lot of white in it, Felix." It was quite simply beautiful, much silkier and lightly curling. The face I had so often seen lined with suffering, sulky, anemic—it had also renewed itself; the so often lackluster eyes (turning toward gray in candlelight) had a recaptured vivacity. She could tell I liked her this way, better than ever. Someone was moving about the little studio with its warm smells of polished wood, its crude peasant curtains. Baynes was setting a small table for us before the throbbing log fire. It was too much. I reached toward a forbidden whiskey, saying, "My God, Baynes, is it really you? I thought I dreamed you up." Baynes smiled his wooden smile and said: "I came in once or twice to see you were all right, sir." So he was really here. No dream was old sobersides Baynes, but our very own reality. "Here let me touch you to prove it." It was partly that, and partly an excuse to embrace Baynes without causing him an attack of blushes. Baynes submitted to these proofs of his existence like an elder churchman, modestly benign.

I walked around the little place which had been her self-imposed prison for so long with all the curiosity of a visitor suddenly entering the imperial apartments on St. Helena. The disposition of everything suggested some far-reaching shift of values. The old litter of half-empty medicine bottles, uncut French novels, widowed slippers, clothes tossed in corners—there was no trace of all this. Even with a dozen maids to clear up after her, the old Benedicta could leave her thumbprints on her quarters after half an hour in residence. The telephone rang, but it seemed to be a wrong number. "O I forgot all about it," said Baynes penitently, "but a gentleman rang up and left a message for Madam. I wrote it down." Sitting by the fire she took it and read it with a chuckle. "There's your answer," she said. "I told you so."

Baynes had laboriously transcribed it with a few spelling errors, but in sum it said: "Amiable yogi will meet green fruit at Manwick's English Tearoom Geneva Saturday for crumpet and butter. Only place in Europe for crumpet."

I felt the blood rush to my heart. "He's alive." And characteristically the feeling was succeeded by one of vexation for all the amount of missing him I had done. "Damn the old fool," I said. And now a different set of preoccupations raised their heads. Benedicta was putting a disc on the record player. "What is it, Felix?"

"I don't want to prejudice him—to make a *gaffe* and lead Julian to him. That's what I was thinking."

"I think Julian has seen him," she said. "So that isn't a problem. In fact I bet you he has been trying to get Julian to take him back into the firm."

"What?"

"Yes. I bet you. And now probably Julian will refuse to do so!"

"Caradoc!"

It was an unheard-of departure after all this elaborate disappearance and fictitious immortality. "How much do you know about it?" Benedicta lit a cigarette and said softly: "Only what I surmise. Julian said nothing when he spoke to me; but once before he puzzled me because he himself seemed not to be quite sure whether it *was* Caradoc or not. Perhaps Caradoc has changed very much; but I was amazed when Julian said something like 'either our own Caradoc or whoever might be impersonating him so perfectly.' . . . Perhaps it was just one of those things which slip out in conversation and mean nothing. Come, let's meet him."

"He can't live without making a mystery of something," I said angrily. "It's his ruling monomania." Benedicta smiled and took my hand, pressing me down beside her before the burning logs. "I know," she said. "And yet he has nothing really to hide—not more nor less than any man." What made me angry, I think, was this sudden questioning of Caradoc's reality almost before he had been reclaimed from the grave. Yes, that was it.

"And Geneva!"

"It's not far, just a short drive."

"Do you think we can go?"

"Of course."

She seemed so certain of everything, as if something had happened to reassure her; what the basis of this new confidence could be I did not try to imagine. It was good to be here in this way, relaxed within the boundaries of a new understanding that had lost the old fearful vigilance. Outlines of a new maturity of vision? One hardly dared to hope for so much. And yet there we were, effigies of our old selves, sitting in front of the fire and gazing at each other with a curious sense of renewal. "Tonight I want to sleep alone. Can I?" There was no need to ask me, was there? "I want to collect myself a little bit. Count out my loose change, so to speak."

Baynes came and solemnized a little after dinner as was his way before he said good night and set up the little silver Thermos of coffee which was practically the only relic I could recognize from past habits. "Do you still sleepwalk?" Benedicta smiled. "Not for ages now, perhaps never again. Let's hope, shall we?" I stood up to take my leave but she went on with a restraining hand laid upon mine. "Stay just a second. I want to do something with you here; will you?"

She went into the inner room and emerged with an armful of the little leather postiche boxes which had been such a feature of her ancient wardrobe. Opening them she tumbled out upon the floor in precious confusion all her wigs—the fine hair of nuns, of Swedish corpses, of Indonesian and Japanese geisha girls, of silk and thrilling nylon. All tumbled together in a heap. Then one by one, combing each softly with her long fingers, disentangling it, she began to put them on the fire. Black smoke and flame rose from this pyre. I did not question, did not exclaim, did not speak. "From now on nothing that isn't my own," she said. "But I wanted to do it with you, somehow. Just to prove."

It was not a long run, and it was a comfortable one, for Benedicta had unearthed a black sports car with good heating and a turn of rampant speed wherever the surfaces had been cleared. A heavy thaw had set in, the lakeside swam and wallowed in warm mist. The attentive white snarls of white mountain came out and retired again endlessly, like actors taking innumerable curtain calls. She drove with dash, but immaculately. The whole thing was as easy as breathing, or so it seemed to me. Even old Geneva looked its best with its snug Viennese flavored architecture and its melancholy lake views; thawing ice was chinking along the river where the dark arterial thrust of the waters carved their way toward the southern issues— waters which would soon see Arles and Avignon.

We had lunch at the Quatorze, but were both too excited to eat very much. We walked silently by the water until it was time to turn our steps toward Manwick's Tea Rooms—a relic which had been washed up at the end of the Victorian era and had remained as authentic as any Doge's palace, unchanged, unblushing, uncorrupted. . . . It was the headquarters of the nannies of Geneva (like Bonington's in Rome). Very old ladies clad in home-weave smocks wielded cake slices. The tables were as heavy as William Morris, so was the cutlery; the walls were papered in something indeterminate which Ruskin would have admired. There was even a complete set of Sherlock Holmes in a yellowed Tauchnitz edition which lined one window embrasure. O the simplicity of everything was momentous. I mean that we saw him directly we entered, sitting at the far end, with his face buried in a book. It was not very crowded. But we were both suffocated with a sort of weird apprehension—we tiptoed toward him as one might toward some rare butterfly, trying to get a closer view without disturbing the rare specimen.

The fact of the matter is that we sat down at his table like a couple of gundogs in a point. It seemed to last ages, this little tableau, but it could have been only a second or two before he closed his book and said in his familiar deep voice: "So there you are at last." He must already have caught sight of us entering the place. "Caradoc!" He gave a raucous chuckle and threw back his head in a gesture which was familiarity itself. And yet . . . and yet. There was no doubt that he had changed. To begin with his hair, as plentiful as ever, was now no longer tabby, parti-colored; it was white and as fine as the thread of silk. His mouth was mantled by an equally soft and sparse moustache of a mandarin kind. Beard there was none, and his pink rubicund face shone out upon the world like a winter sun. "It's only old age," he said as if to explain, "only old age, look you." Yet in another way he had never looked—I was going to say "younger"—but it might be more accurate to say something like "healthier." His skin was firm and unwrinkled, his eyes glittering with amiable malice and hardly crow's-footed. Yes, one did have a moment of doubt about his real identity, but the voice clinched it. "The death and the resurrection," he boomed, ordering crumpets with a capacious gesture, yet taking a precautionary look into a little leather purse while doing so. An aged lady, all politeness, took his order with an approving smile. She had caught his last phrase and doubtless thought he was some friendly religious maniac—Geneva is full of them. The old darned plaid had been replaced with something of much the same style—a sort of evangelical overcoat with heavy cabman collars. He looked like a rather smart music-hall coachman.

"My God, Caradoc! You owe it to us to tell us all, everything." He nodded briskly, as if he had every intention of so doing. But as a preliminary he took a small silver flask of something which looked suspiciously like whiskey and tipped a modicum into his teacup; then he produced a tiny tortoiseshell snuffbox and tapped it with a fingernail before whiffing up a grain or two from his extended thumb. "Julian, that old body snatcher, wouldn't believe it was me," he said with a certain pride. "That is what it does for you, escaping. I had three lots of twins straight off in Polynesia—bang off like that, without a moment's effort. The little woman was only a child but she had read the studbook, she knew racing form. More's the pity; I've had to leave them all behind because of funds. They would have looked damn rococo in London, I can swear."

"But from the beginning, Caradoc. Why did you cause all this fuss and flurry, cause us such anguish and despair?"

"In one way I had to," he said, "to see how it felt. I had to. And the minute I'd done it I knew that it was the best, the most fruitful thing I had ever done. At the same time I knew just as certainly that it wasn't necessary at all—it could have been done another way. But when someone wants jam on his bread it's no good just describing it. He wants to taste some. So you've got to provide some. But of course the firm was hard to persuade about this—particulary Julian. I bided my time. I thought in fact my chance would never come. Year after year, my boy, all the time getting more and more successful, piling up less and less reasons to leave my beautiful billet. But when the crash came I realized that I had to try. But *aut Tunc aut Nunquam*—it was then or never! And mighty successful it was, what I tasted of it, what I learned from it. All that coconut oil; you should feel my breasts. They are like a woman's only prettier." He poured some more tea, spliced it, and plunged into the crumpets until the butter was running off his chin. "After all," he said indistinctly, "what is it really to buzz off to a remote isle with a tropical Venus? Nothing very much. Time takes on a wonderful never-quite quality. Infinite extension, lad, causality pulling out like a rubber band. At first of course one misses doctors and dentists and Shakespeare and all that. Of course. I don't deny it. One dreams of cod's roe or roasted shad—many the night I've awakened with tears in my voice at a New York restaurant. Waiters always whisked the shad away before I'd eaten it. But it didn't last. Finally a sort of Prosperine feeling came over me. Exhausted by night and droopy by day, living on paw paw and piggy wiggy: I was in the lap of the local lotus-eating gods, I was. Never question it."

"Then why come back?"

"That was another jolt from the blue. The whole group of those islands was scooped up by the Aussies. One morning I woke up and found coast guards all over my place and warships poking about. We were bought out for practically nothing. Expropriated! Then they started nosing into my papers because I cut up so very rough, and I was on rather weak ground there. Apparently Robinson had quite a history behind him about which I knew nothing—he was bigamous to the core, old man, and the continent was studded with women crying out for vengeance and alimony. It was a terrible fix. I had to recover my own identity in order to escape from his wives. Then of course I had the inevitable note from Julian, telling me not to be a fool. While I had no inclination to knuckle under I was in a squeeze and he knew it. I went through a long period of debate and finally I decided I would come back and rejoin the firm on the old terms. It cost me something to come to the decision, but I˙did it. And in a funny sort of way I felt relieved at having done it—as if I learned all I needed to learn from the experience out there with little Inky, the wife, and the funny ten-toed nippers. I bought them a coconut grove with my last cash—in another group—and said a tearful farewell. Landed in England dead broke, dead broke. And now . . ."

"Everything's all right again," I cried.

"Far from it," said Caradoc ruefully. "Very far from it. I am living for the time being on the charity of old Banubula."

"What?" said Benedicta incredulously.

He gave what in stage directions is sometimes called a "dark laugh" and snuffed once, with a pained hauteur. "I rang up Julian when I arrived, but he was awfully evasive though kind: just off on a long trip, you know the sort of thing. I didn't like to talk about reinstatement point-blank and he didn't mention it. And I knew that Delambert had been given all my appointments and charges. Well, the upshot of it was that he told me he would like to see me in Geneva to talk things over; and this he duly did a few days ago, but without any result."

"But it's scandalous," I said hotly. Caradoc shook his head quickly and put out a hand as if to intercept the charge in midair. "O no," he said. "It's not like that. Don't get the impression Julian is out to punish me, to victimize me—nothing like that.' He is far above any such considerations. No, it was as if, in a sense, I had missed a step on the ladder, on the moving staircase, and I would have to wait awhile until the turn came round again. It was all to do with the firm, and the destiny of the firm: of us all, I suppose, in a way. It was a most extraordinary interview.

"It took place in a suitably mysterious setting on the lake some way out beyond the United Nations buildings (by the way, in the course of other matters he said nonchalantly that the firm was hoping to take the building over next year—and I wondered what about the inhabitants, all those people living in the woodwork?) . Anyway I was summoned at dusk to meet a small motorboat. Dead calm oily water, heavy thaw, almost like a late autumn night with a full moon and all those blasted mountains showing their teeth like wolves. It could have been eerie to some, I suppose. Nor was it very far along. Just by a landing stage amid a cluster of tall dark trees there was a rotunda of sorts with a rose arbor, and a table with cold marble chairs surrounding it. He was sitting alone there, waiting for me with a great goblet of wine in front of him; opposite in front of what was obviously to be my chair was another equally heartening-looking one with brandy. It was warm; I feared I might get piles sitting on the marble but the sight of the brandy reassured me. 'Well,' he said. 'At last. I'm so glad it's over.' Quite a promising beginning wouldn't you say? So thought I.

"I advanced to receive his hesitant cool handshake. Of course as always he was sitting with his back to the moon so that he was all outline, if you see what I mean. His face was in half-shadow. Once or twice I saw a moonflake alight on his crown—white hair or very blond, one couldn't say which. And in a funny sort of way the optical illusion created by the watery moonlight gave the impression that he was altering shape all the time; not very conspicuously,

[73]

you understand. But it could be seen; it was like a gentle breathing, systole and diastole. But his voice was just the same as always—the pained-lamb voice Pulley used to call it, remember? He questioned me very calmly and quietly about what I had been doing on my island; showed every mark of considerate attention. Also the brandy was excellent. I roughed in my little crusoe, as you might call it. Then he said: 'And you expected to be taken back just like that? You expected the firm to grant you absolution and a hundred lines and take you back?' I mumbled a bit and scraped the gravel with my toe. Then somewhat to my surprise he went on. 'And of course it will. But you will have to wait until it can find a place for you, having abandoned your own so suddenly. The ranks have closed, you know.' "

Caradoc paused.

"Of course I wouldn't want for a decent living outside the firm; I could get something good tomorrow. But . . . I don't know how it is, yet the idea didn't appeal to me very much. All my adult creative life has been spent with the firm. He said it really wasn't a question of money but of order. If he took me back now, before waiting my turn, he could only offer me relatively menial things to do, things which might waste my gray matter and time and in the long run be bad for my credit and standing. "We have always treated you in the same way, and neither of us can change now,' he added, sadly, I thought. 'We have offered you only things which *nobody else could do, nobody living*. So we will have to wait for our reality jolt as you waited so many years for yours.' I suppose you will think it nonsense, but it carried a queer kind of conviction for me. I drank my flowing bowl and gazed sleepily at him. Really, he is a marvelous character, Julian, a strange one. I'd like to know him better, to know more about it. He seemed sort of hurt, as if he were nursing some sort of internal grievance against the order of things. I don't know. He surprised me by saying: 'Yes, we must wait for it—who knows till when? Perhaps one of these days you will be asked to build a tomb for Jocas out here in Turkey.' "

Jocas! Nobody could have been further from my own thoughts at that moment. "And then what, Caradoc?"

Caradoc performed a rather clumsy mopping-up operation with a spruce handkerchief. "Nothing," he said. "Or practically nothing. He spoke a bit about you, with great affection I must add. He said he still had hopes that you would understand the issues better—whatever that meant. Then he said the time was getting on. Right in the background, outside the large house shrouded in big trees, I had heard the continuous noise of car tires on gravel and seen the sweeping of headlights as limousine after limousine drew up and disgorged its occupants. There was a steady movement into the lighted hallway of the building; it looked like people going to an opera, for I saw women in evening dress. But Julian wasn't dinner-jacketed: striped shirt and speckled bow tie and dark suit, as I could half guess. He caught the direction of my eye and said: 'It's gambling, Caradoc. For the first time I have started to gamble and lose, a thing I have never done. It makes one most uncertain. I had become overconfident and always risked very large sums. I had got used, you see, never to losing heavily. But now, I don't know. I dare not reduce my habits of *play* for fear of altering my *luck,* the basic psychic predisposition to win which I enjoyed over so many years. I hope it doesn't mean something serious. I have always avoided studying the matter of play because I believed in luck, but lately I have been wondering if a computerized study might yield some ideas which would help me. And yet I feel such a thing would be fatal, *fatal.*' He repeated the word with such emphasis that I felt a vague sort of sympathy and alarm for him. 'I'm stuck in a way,' he said, and then abruptly stood up and said good night, keeping himself face forward to me as I went down to the landing stage where the little boat lay. The driver lit the dash and kicked the engine over. I turned and looked back across the inky water, just in time to see the dark indistinct figure of Julian moving away toward the house. He had his hands folded behind his back, his head bowed. I could see the glow of a cigar in his fingers. I don't know what I felt—a sort of confused relief mixed with disappointment and doubt; and also a kind of confidence in him. I felt he'd have told me more if he could—if he had known any more than he did. I must sound preposterous, I suppose, but then the simplest things come to sound preposterous. I don't know. Also, he had not touched his wine. How typical of him to sit there, flower in buttonhole, with a bubble of blood in front of him."

He lowered his massive head on his breast for a moment and seemed to brood, though in fact he was smiling a smile of resignation—or so it seemed, though perhaps I was misled by the new babyish contours of the familiar face. "So there it is, roughly speaking—that is the state of play for the moment. I am not unduly worried even though I realize that it may last forever—I mean I might never get back. At my age, you see." He snuffed slowly once more and sat back in his seat to smile upon us with an unguarded affection as he supplied us with other characteristic details of his earthly life, such as, for example, that owing to his domestic exuberance he had developed a weakness in the belly wall which forced him to wear a suspensory which he called a *soutien-Georges*.

Then abruptly turning back to the original matter of his conversation, he said: "You might say that not having freed myself completely from the firm and yet not having come back either I was in a sort of limbo. Not a ghost and yet still not quite a man." I put out my hand to touch him—I must confess I went through a moment of doubt as to whether my fingers might not meet through his wrist. "Take my pulse," he said. I tried, but could find no trace of one; yet the flesh was solid flesh. "I suppose you don't cast a shadow either like the traditional *Doppelgänger?*" But he was humming a light air and gazing about him with happy abstraction. "The twentieth of every month is the day of Epicurus. I celebrate mildly, ever so mildly. With old *soutien-Georges* here I cannot go the whole hog. *Je n'ai plus des femmes mais j'ai des idées maîtresses.*" But he was not disconsolate or cast down by having to make the confession. He intoned to a fingerbeat.

> *"Surrender and identify and nod.*
> *That's why you came, remember, little God?"*

This was apparently a free translation from some Epicurean proverb. Then next:

> *"Hail!* Ejaculatio praecox,
> *No more love among the haycocks;*
> *Yet psyche chloroformed by science*
> *In poems will breathe her last defiance!"*

He paused, attempted to recover some more verses and failed in somewhat uncharacteristic fashion. Then he gave a simulacrum of his ancient roar and gestured at the door. "There he comes, Horatio the Magnificent"; and we saw with surprise and delight another familiar figure weaving its way toward us. It was Banubula.

Yes, it was Banubula all right, but in a somewhat advanced stage of what might have seemed intoxication. He wove toward us, all elegance, gesturing with the silver knob of his walking stick. He was gloved and circumspectly hatted, not to mention spatted—for he sported his favorite gray spats. Radiant is hardly the word—he smirked his way over to us, smiling with his loose lips and moving his eyebrows about. Our greetings were effusive and somewhat confused. The count turned on Caradoc and said somewhat reproachfully, "I suppose you have told them about me—I suppose they know? How vexatious, I would have liked to boast!" Caradoc shook his burly dogged head. "Not a word," he said gravely. "Not a blasted word. If they do know it's not from me."

"Do you know," said Banubula with breathless coyness, "about me?"

"What?"

"That I'm *in* at last, *in the firm?*" He seemed almost on the point of executing a brief dance.

"The firm?"

He gave a whiff of insipid laughter behind his gloves and sibilated. "Yes, the *firm*. Have been now for several months. It's a post after my own heart and I think I may say that I am giving it everything I've got in me."

"Bravo!" we all exclaimed and I banged his rather portly shoulder blade to register my excitement and approval.

"Coordinator of industrial disputes, no less. I share the job with my old friend, the Duke of Lambitus, who has left the F. O. to come to us. My word, Felix, you have no idea how delicate and yet how all-embracing it is. Everywhere there is a dispute or a falling-off of production or simply tension due to a psychological cause—why, we are there, I with my languages and Lambitus with his courteous diplomatic experience."

"It must be devastating."

"It is," said the count meekly. "It is."

Caradoc grinned at us and dug Banubula boisterously in the ribs. "Tell them about your latest coup," he said, and Banubula was in no way loth to do so. "But I don't want to bore you with shop. Yet this last case does illustrate the enormous tact and psychological insight we have to bring into play. I'd like to tell you about it, if I may?" Inspired by the raptness of our attention he went on. "Well, just as an example: last year we started having trouble with our German branches in the applied industry sector. It was a queer sort of general malaise, nothing one could really analyze, a lack of heart at the center of things. And, of course, disputes of one sort of another, mostly idle and foolish disputes for such an orderly and industrious nation. Julian sent us over as psychological counselors to study the matter and propose means of dealing with it. Now what really was wrong? Nothing we could see really: to account for the falling-off of the statistics, I mean. Simply boredom it seemed to us. At any rate it didn't seem something which salary rises could cure. *And this is where psychology comes in.*" The count pointed a long spatulate finger at his own temple and paused dramatically. His eyes twinkled with keen joy, like summer lightning, like fireflies. "Lambitus finally said: 'The whole thing is this. They are not *enjoying* themselves, they do not know how to. It is our job to find a way, Horatio.' We pondered the matter and at last I hit upon a solution. It may seem simple for such a complex people. Baby Balls, that was it!"

"Baby Balls?" I exclaimed. Banubula nodded and pursued his rigorous exposé with raised finger. "You are perhaps too young to remember how the British sense of humor was saved and revived after the First World War? By the Baby Balls organized by the Bright Young Things."

"But what the devil is it?"

"Simply a ball to which you have to go dressed as a baby, sucking a bottle, and preferably in a pram wheeled by a close friend."

"Well, I'm damned."

"It worked, Felix" he cried. "You would never have believed it. All those huge German businessmen crammed into prams, dressed as babies, sucking on their bottles of milk, and waving clusters of colored balloons. Nothing exceeded in pity and terror the sight of them entering so determinedly into the fun of the thing. We had thought of everything, you see. We had musical chairs, prizes for bobapple, buns and booby traps, cap pistols and those streamers which uncurl when you blow them and go *wheee. . . .*"

He mopped his face and laughed shyly, adding only the vital words: "All Germany laughed and all Germany went back to work and the needle began to mount again on the production board. Do you see the delicacy of the whole operation, I mean?"

To say that our collective breath was taken away would be an understatement. We sat and gaped our humble admiration. The count himself seemed transfigured by this simple but subtle success. "D'you know," he went on, "we had a special interview with Julian in which he congratulated us and said that he would see to it that we got an O.B.E. each in the Prime Minister's next list." The narration of this great *coup de théâtre* had so moved him that there was a long moment of silence while he applied himself to the delicacies of the establishment, giving himself totally, fervently, to the crumpets, and also to the toasted tea cake. Caradoc gazed upon him with what one might call tears of admiration welling up behind his eyeballs. After so many years of waiting, of doing menial little jobs unworthy of his manifest genius . . . and at last to find his real bent in the firm. It was wonderful! Benedicta pressed his hand with sympathy and congratulation. Banubula himself was transported—he was quite beside himself, professionally speaking. I mean that there was not the slightest touch of complacence in his manner when he added, "And this is only one occasion of many, *many* where we have been of vital use to the firm."

"Tell about the Koro epidemic," said Caradoc, who for once seemed generously pleased to let his friend hold the floor.

"Ah, that!" said Banubula rolling his fine eyes. "That really did tax us to the hilt. Lambitus was actually ill afterward and imagined all sorts of things. I wonder if I dare speak of it without indiscretion before . . ."

He nodded toward Benedicta who acknowledged the delicacy with a smile but spread her white hands in supplication. "Yes, please do. It is fascinating."

Banubula mopped his brow, poked his handkerchief into his sleeve and sat back. "This will amaze you I think," he said. "It certainly took us by surprise. We had not heard of Koro before, which is known as Shook Yong to the Chinese of the Archipelago. In fact the first we heard of it was when Nash, who had been sent out with a group of psychiatrists to stem this epidemic if possible, sent a signal back saying that nothing could be done. It was an SOS if ever there was one. Lambitus and I were at the Savoy Grill when we got orders to move in and set our brains to work on this problem which was threatening to disrupt whole sectors of our work both in Singapore and throughout the whole network of islands where we had enormously important sources of raw materials at work for the firm. By morning's early light then, we were in the air, sometimes holding hands a bit as neither of us liked air travel and the journey was bumpy: we were on our way to Singapore. May I have this last one?" He took up the last crumpet on the dish and used it lightly as a baton to punctuate his discourse, pausing from time to time to take a small bite from it.

"Now Shook Yong," he said in a faraway fairy-tale voice, "and its ravages are hardly known to us Occidentals, and when one first hears of it one thinks it rather farfetched. But it is real, and it creates mass panics. What is it? Well, it is a belief that those who contract this disease experience a sudden feeling of retraction of the male organ into the abdomen; this is accompanied by a hysterical fear that should the retraction be allowed to proceed, and if swift medical aid is not available, the whole penis will simply disappear into the belly with fatal results for the owner." He paused for the inevitable smiles. "I know," he went on gravely. "So it struck me at first. But it spreads like wildfire, whole communities get taken with Shook Yong just as our medieval ancestors, I suppose, contracted dancing or twitching manias. It is real, all too real. Now when a community is so afflicted, they experience utter terror and in their anxiety to hold on to their own property they grab and pull it to prevent it vanishing: worse still, they often use instrumental aids such as rubber bands, string, clamps, clothes-pegs and chopsticks, and frequently inflict severe bruising or worse damage on the organ. Now what had caused all this trouble, which spread from Singapore like wildfire and gained the remotest corners of the landmass in next to no time, was a rumor set about (perhaps by the Indians) that Koro was caused by eating the flesh of swine which had recently been vaccinated in an attempt to combat swine fever. At once there was an almost complete standstill in the pork sales in markets, restaurants and so on—but those who thought that they might have been exposed to the disease by accident took fright. So Koro or Shook Yong became an epidemic to be reckoned with.* Everything was done to educate public opinion by press conferences and radio and journalism—but it was all in vain. The Ministry of Health reported that both the public and private hospitals were swamped by mobs of yelling patients holding on to their organs and calling loudly for medical aid. The scenes were indescribable. Oriental mass panic has to be seen to be believed. Poor Nash, who had arrived with some severe-looking but orthodox Freudians, was completely out of his depth, and indeed, when we found him, quite pale with terror at all the commotion. He was holding on to his own organ, not, as he explained, because he felt he had Shook Yong but simply because he feared to lose it in the general melee. I don't mind confessing that for a while the whole problem seemed to me a bit out of our usual range. They hadn't explained in London the meaning of these deplorable crowd scenes taking place all over the city. Freud was no help, however much the disease might have suggested an ordinary anxiety neurosis. You cannot ask a yelling Chinese to lie down on a couch and give you free associations for the word 'penis' when he is holding fast to his own, convinced that it is simply melting away. Worst of all, the telephones were humming from the plantations, telling us

* Koro is a real mass neurosis and not an invention of the author's. For a full account of it see *British Medical Journal*, March 9, 1968.

that the epidemic had already penetrated into the countryside where the people are even more susceptible to mass
suggestion than in the towns. We attended conference
after conference, Lord Lambitus and I, listening to these
grave accounts of a world turned upside down, and both of
us completely perplexed as to what to do to lend nature a
hand. As I gathered that the scourge had already been
signaled among the Buginese and Maassars in Celebes and
West Borneo at other periods, it seemed to me that the
whole thing would sweep over the subcontinent and perhaps die a natural death in Australia where they have
another attitude toward the male organ. But it was very
disturbing all the same. It put us on our mettle. Yet there
we were in the unfamiliar world, with the most arbitrary
sanitation and precious little ice for drinks, beating our
heads, almost our breasts, so worried were we.

"And at every conference the case histories poured in,
collected by devoted and whey-faced doctors. Just to give
you a typical one to illustrate what was happening. A
fifteen-year-old boy was rushed into the emergency ward of
the clinic by his shouting and gesticulating parents calling
for aid. The boy, they said, had contracted Shook Yong.
The youth was pale and scared and was pulling hard on his
penis to prevent it being swallowed up. He had heard
about Shook Yong in school and that morning had eaten a
little pow, which contains some pork, for his breakfast.
When he went to the lavatory he saw that his member had
shrunk very greatly and concluded that he had contracted
the scourge. Yelling, he ran to his parents, who ran yelling
with him to the doctor. Here at least he might receive
sedatives and reassurance provided he and his parents had
reached the stage of evolution when things begin to make
sense; mostly however they hadn't. Well, as I say, Lambitus and I were at our wits' end to devise some equitable
way of ending this intellectual debauch. The Freudians
keeled over one by one and even Nash, who had led the
rescue group, was sent to hospital for a while and put

under heavy sedation. He had, I believe, become prone to the contagious atmosphere which Koro creates, and had almost begun to believe . . . well, I don't know. Anyway, everyone seemed privately highly delighted in rather a cruel way. But still we could make no advance on the problem. The season was breaking up, the monsoons were heralded. And now Lambitus, who is a man of iron nerve, quite unimaginative, as you have to be in the higher diplomacy, began to show signs of strain. He spent an awful long time in the shower room every morning, examining himself for signs of Koro. I began to suspect him of suspecting . . . Well, anyway the situation was desperate. I sat night after night swatting giant moths with a bedroom slipper and brooding on the problem.

"Indeed I had reached the point when I had decided that we should return and confess our mission a failure when—how does it happen: Nash would know?—an old memory of my youth came to my rescue. You may know that when I was first engaged to the countess we went round the world together; she said she wished to see me anew in each continent before deciding whether she would marry me or not—so there was nothing for it. It was a prehoneymoon in a way, and by no means an unfruitful trip. She was an expert botanist, and I was already then working on my comparative folklore of fertility symbols in East and West. We came to Malaya, among other places, and indeed stayed a month on a plantation. From the recesses of these old memories I suddenly resuscitated Tunc or Tunk—the small fertility god which is responsible for so much of the overpopulation in these parts and whose little effigy in clay one sees on cottage lintels. It came to me with the force of a forgotten dream that we might perhaps invoke the little deity's aid once more to counter the nationwide (so it seemed at the time) retraction of the Malayan penis."

"Do you remember," said Caradoc suddenly, "Sipple's account of *his* attack of Koro?—it must have been that. In the Nube, a hundred years ago?"

Of course I did.

"It must have been," said Banubula seriously. "It would have been terrible if such an affliction had spread into England. It could topple a government—I saw it do so. And we couldn't invoke little Tunc there because nobody believes in him or it. Anyway to resume my account of this strange episode: I woke Lambitus and breathlessly outlined my plan. He was ready to grab at any straw and eagerly backed me up. I obtained some *ex votos,* some silk drawings unwittingly issued by the British Council, and set myself to think. In half an hour I had roughed out a more modern effigy which, if fabricated in mauve plastic (the national color, by the way), might have charm and appeal for the afflicted.

"We rang up Julian and flew him home a sample. Of course we had visualized a vast free distribution of this charm, probably sowed broadcast from the air, but as usual Julian's keen mind took hold of the problem and solved it. It would have no value to people unless they had to pay for it, he said, and I quite saw his point. We were to give away only a few thousand through the hospitals but put the rest—some four million at first printing—on the open market in order to forestall some similar kind of effort by the Catholics. Moreover he offered us one percent, which was really very handsome of him, and which has made us both extremely rich men. So was Koro finally brought under control by the kindly intervention of Tunc. I must say I am sentimental about the little god and always carry one on my watch chain for good luck—though God knows at my age . . ."

Musing thus the count produced a new gold watch chain of great luster and showed us a copy of the charm. "A pretty emblem, no?" he said modestly.

"But why in European characters?"

"Foreign magic has great cachet there. This was the foreign issue given away by the hospital administration. There was also a local version for sales distribution. We

were a little worried about religious sensibilities, but
everyone was delighted.

T U N C
U   U
N   N
C U N T

He sighed at the memory of these great adventures and
glanced at the pristine gold watch which depended from
the chain. "I have a conference," he said. "I must run
along. I'll meet you at the plane at six, Caradoc. Without
fail, mind, and don't lose that ticket." And so saying he
waved us an airy good-bye, only pausing to add over his
shoulder, "We'll meet in London, I hope."

Caradoc squeezed the pot dry and took up the final
teacup. "Isn't it marvelous to see what happens when
people really find themselves?" It was, and we said so,
somewhat sententiously I fear. Banubula had emerged
from his cocoon like the giant emperor moth he had always
been and was now in full wingspread. "You know," said
Caradoc polishing up the butter on his plate with a morsel
of tea-cake, "that is all that anybody needs. Nothing more,
yet nothing less."

And so at last the time came to take leave of him, which
we did with reluctance, yet with delight to know that he
was still to be numbered among the living. I spoke to him
a little bit about his papers and his aphorisms and recordings—and indeed all the trouble Vibart and I had been to,
to try and assemble a coherent picture of this venerable
corpse. He laughed very heartily and wiped his eye in his
sleeve. "One should never do that for the so-called dead,"
he said. "But it's largely my fault. One should not leave
such an incoherent mess behind. I didn't know then that
everything must be tidied up before one dies or it just
encumbers one's peace of mind when one *is* dead, like I
have really been, in a manner of speaking. It was too bad

and I am really sorry. We'll order things better next time, for my real death. There won't be a crumb out of place, you'll see. The whole thing will be smooth as an egg, mark me. Not a blow or a harsh word left over—and even tape recordings burn or scrub, don't they?" He walked us with his old truculent splayed walk to the car park and waved us good-bye in the misty evening. I looked back as we turned the corner and gave him a thumbs-up to which he responded. Lighting-up time by now, with mist everywhere and foggy damp, and the wobble of blazing tram cars along the impassive avenues. "I feel sort of light-headed," I said, "from surprise I've no doubt."

Benedicta put her hand briefly on my knee and pressed before turning back to the swerves and swings of the lakeside road. "Perhaps you've contracted Koro," she said.

"Perhaps I have."

"You must ask for an amulet from the firm."

"I think I will. You can never be certain in this world; even the innocents like Sipple can get struck down it seems."

The dark was closing in fast, and soon I was drowsing in the snug bucket seat, waking from time to time to glance at the row of lighted dials on the fascia. "Why so fast?" I said suddenly. "Light me a cigarette," said Benedicta, "and I'll tell you. Tonight we shall hear from Julian. As it may be a phone call, I suddenly had a guilty conscience and thought we should get back." I lit the cigarette and placed it between her lips. "And how did you know?" I said. "I had a postcard ages ago giving me this date, but it slipped my mind and I only remembered it all of a sudden while Caradoc was talking. If it's too fast for you tell me and I'll slow down."

No, it wasn't too fast: but it wasn't a phone message either. It was a telex to the hospital from Berne, saying: "If Felix feels up to it and if you are free, please meet me with a small picnic on the Constaffel, hut five, at around midday on the fifteenth. My holiday is so short that I would like to combine the meeting with a bit of a run on the snow. Will you?"

"The polite request disguises the command," I said. "Shall I decline? And what the devil is the Constaffel?"

"It's where the practice slopes begin up on the mountainside; the Paulhaus always keeps a camper's hut available there for the use of convalescents."

"Look, Benedicta," I said severely, "I am not web-toed, and I am not going to scull about in the mountains on skis in my present state of health."

"It's not that at all," she said. "We can go up with the *téléférique,* and the hut is about five hundred yards along the cliff face with a perfectly good path to it. It won't be snowed up in this sort of weather. We could walk, if you'll go, that is. If not let me send him a cable."

I was tempted to give way to an all too characteristic petulance but I reflected and refrained. "Let us do it, then," I said. "Yes, we'll do it. But I warn you that if he appears disguised as the Abominable Snowman I'll hit him with an ice pick and polish him off for good and all."

"I count on you."

They were easily said, these pleasantries, but in the morning, lying beside her warm dent, her "form," while she herself was making up her face in the little bathroom next door, I found myself wondering what the day would bring, and what new information I would glean from this encounter. I went in to watch her play with this elegant new face, now grown almost childish and somehow serene. She had only half a mouth on, which made me feel hungry. "Benedicta, you don't feel apprehensive about this, do you?"

She looked at me suddenly, keenly. "No. Do you?" she said. "Because there's no need to go. As for me I told you I had come to terms with Julian. I'm not scared of anything any longer." I sat down on the *bidet* to wash and reflect. "I used the wrong word. What I dread really is the eternal wrangle with people who don't understand what one is

[88]

trying to do. I fear he'll just ask for me to come back, everything forgotten, but never to try and run away again. It's what they do to runaway schoolboys at the best schools. Whereas I am not giving any guarantees to anyone. I intend always to leave an open door." Benedicta finished her mouth and eyes without saying anything. Then she went out and I heard her giving Baynes instructions about Thermos flasks and sandwiches. So I shrugged my shoulders and had a shower.

The day was fine and bright and really ideal for non-skiers; this year there had been very little snow and the press had made great moan about the fact that the season would be blighted because of it.

Rackstraw had seen some reference to the matter in a paper and had kept on about it until I could have strangled him. In the old days he had been, it seems, some sort of ski champion. Though no longer allowed out he kept a close eye on weather and form. Anyway, this was none of my affair, and about half-past ten we set off—she in her elegant Sherpa rig of some sort of mustard-colored whipcord—toward the *téléférique* which we found quite empty. Operated by remote control, it was an eerie sort of affair, the doors flying open as one stepped upon the landing ramp and closing behind one with a soft whiff. We had the poor snowfalls and the excited press to thank for the empty car in which we sat, sprawling at ease among our packs and other impedimenta, smoking.

A few moments' waiting and then all of a sudden the cabin gave a soft tremor and began to slide forward and upward into the air, more slowly, more deliciously than any glider; and the whole range of snowy nether peaks sprang to attention and stared gravely at us as we ascended toward them, without noise or fuss. Away below us slid the earth with its villages and tracery of roads and railways—a diminishing perspective of toylike shapes, gradually becoming more and more unreal as they receded from view.

The sense of aloneness was inspiriting. Benedicta was delighted and walked from corner to corner of the cabin to exclaim and point, now at the mountains, now at the snowy villages and the dun lakeside, or at other features she thought she could recognize. The world seemed empty. Up and up we soared until we had the impression of grazing the white faces of the mountains with the steel cable of our floating cabin. "I don't know whether Julian is doing the sensible thing," she said, "in skiing about up here; the surfaces have been flagged here and there for danger and there have been several accidents." The lift came slowly to a halt in all this fervent whiteness, slid up a small ramp and stopped with scarcely perceptible shock. The doors opened and the cold world enveloped us. But the sunlight was brilliant, dazzling, and the snow squeaked under our boots like a comb in freshly washed hair. Nor was it far along the scarp to where the ski huts stood; it was from here that the serious performers started their ascent. Benedicta had the key and we opened up the little hut which was aching with damp and cold, but fairly well equipped for camp life. There was a little stove which she soon had buzzing away—it promised us hot coffee or soup to wash down the fare we had brought. We settled ourselves in methodically enough. Then outside in the brilliant sun we smoked and had a drink together and even embarked on a snowman of ambitious size. There had been several bad avalanches that year and I was not surprised when one took place there and then, as if for our personal delectation. A white swoosh and a whole white face of the mountain opposite cracked like plaster, hesitated, and then broke away to fall hundreds of feet into the valley. The boom, as if from heavy artillery, followed upon the spectacle by half a minute almost.

"That was a good one," said Benedicta.

There were some tree stumps and a wooden table under the fir in front of the hut, and we cleared these of snow and set out plates and cutlery thereon. We had all but finished when by chance I happened to look upward along the crescent-like sweep of the mountain above us. Something seemed to be moving up there—or so it seemed out of the corner of my eye. But no, there was nothing. The unblemished snow lay ungrooved everywhere on the runs. I turned away to the opposite side and saw with a little shock of surprise a lone skier standing among a clump of firs, watching us like a sharpshooter. We stayed for a long moment like this, unmoving, and then the figure, with the sudden movement of a Red Indian sinking his paddle into the river, propelled himself forward and began to ripple down toward us, cutting his grooves of whiteness on the clean snow.

Fast, too, very fast. "Could that be Julian?" I said, and Benedicta, following the direction of my pointing finger with eyes screwed up, said: "Yes. It must be." So we stood hand in hand, watching while the small dark tadpole rushed toward us, growing in size as it came, until we could see that it was a man of about medium height, rather gracefully built in a slender sort of way, and as lissom on his skis as a ballet dancer. When he had reached the little fir about fifty yards off, he swerved and braked, throwing up a white fountain of snow; he took off his skis and made his way toward the hut, beating the snow from his costume with his heavy mittens. "Hullo," he cried with great naturalness, as if this were not a momentous, a historic meeting, but a casual encounter between friends. "I'm Julian at last," he added. "In the flesh!" But of course in his ski getup there was nothing very distinct to be seen as yet. Then I noticed that there was blood running from his nose. It had dried and caked on his upper lip and in the slender perfectly shaped moustache. He dabbed it with a handkerchief as he advanced, explaining as he came. "I tend toward an occasional nosebleed up at this level—but it's well worth it for the fun." His nostrils were crusted with blood, though the flow appeared to have stopped.

We shook hands, gazing at one another, while he made

some perfectly conventional remark to Benedicta, perfectly at ease, perfectly insouciant. "At last," I said, "we meet." It sounded somehow fatuous. "Felix," he said in that warm caressing voice I knew so well (the voice of Cain), "it's been unpardonable to neglect you so but I waited until we could talk, until you felt well and unharassed by things. You are looking fine, my boy." I gave him a clumsy Sherpa-like bow which conveyed, I hoped, a hint of irony. "As well as can be expected," said I. He still kept on his heavy mica goggles, tinted slightly bronze so that I could not really see his eyes properly: also of course the padded suit and the peaked snow cap successfully muffled all clear outlines of his head and body. All I saw was a very delicately cut aristocratic nose (like a bird of prey's beak), an ordinary mouth with blurred outlines because of the bloody upper lip, and the small feminine hand with which he grasped mine. Benedicta offered to swab his lip with cotton wool and warm water but he refused with thanks, saying: "O I'll clean up when I get down to terra a little firma." So we stood, eyeing each other keenly, until Benedicta brought out some drinks and we settled down opposite him at the wooden table to drink gin slings in the sunny whiteness. "Where to begin?" said Julian with a melodious lazy inflexion which was very seducing—the calm voice of the hypnotist. "Where to begin?" It was indeed the question of the moment. "Well, the circle can be broken at any point, I suppose. But where?" He paused and added under his breath, "Running into air pockets, ideas in flight!"

Then he leaned forward and tapped my hand and said: "Our old quarrel is over, finished; with what more you know now of myself, of Benedicta, you must feel a bit reassured about things, less fearful. I've been planning this meeting for a long time, and indeed looking forward to it, because I knew that I should have to throw myself entirely upon your mercy, to try to win your heart, Felix. Wait!" He held up a hand to prevent my interjection. "It is not what you think, it is not how you think. I wanted to talk to you a bit, not only about the firm but about the general questions it always poses for the people involved in it—like this question of freedom." (As I watched him I saw so clearly in my mind's eye the two grave children; he had tied up Benedicta's mind with his excesses, and then tried to liberate her by teaching her to fence! Fool! Dry click-click of their buttoned foils. Now here he was with his nostrils full of dried blood. Another image intervened: Julian tapping away on an Arab finger drum while the monkey on its chain chattered and masturbated furiously. And then Benedicta saying to me . . . O centuries later, something like, "You were such a surprise it was terrifying; I watched you sleep, off your guard, just to try and verify the feeling. Caught between such tyrants as you and Julian, is it a wonder I went mad? With him it was love, but an actor's love—I knew no other.")

But here she was at my side, very composed and smiling, smoking her little cigar and watching us. It was I who was trembling slightly, feeling the palms of my hands grow moist. He was so attractive, this man, that for two pins I could have reached forward and strangled him as he sat there with his poise and his bloody face. "Go on," I said. "Go on."

He made a self-deprecating little gesture with his un-gloved hand and sighed. "I am," he said. "I will. But I was just thinking rather ruefully of how much thought and feeling and will I had put into the matter of the firm over all these years—not only running my side of it as best I could, but trying to penetrate also the meaning of it and the meaning of my own life in relation to it. And of course yours, and everybody's. The firm itself, Merlin's firm," he uttered the proper name with a profound, a sad bitterness, "what is it exactly? It isn't just a loosely linked association of enterprises coordinated under one name; its very size (like a blown-up photograph) enables us to see that it is the reflection of something, the copy of something.

Though on one plane you might consider it a money-making contrivance, the very terms under which it operates reflect the basic predispositions of the culture of which it is only an offshoot. Of course it is both constricting for some and liberating for others, according to their position vis-à-vis the organism; but they can't escape reflecting the firm, just as the firm can't help reflecting the corpus of what, for want of a better word, we must call our civilization. O dear, Felix, reality is kindly—but inflexible.

"It doesn't seem possible to break either the mold of the firm or the mold of ourselves as associates or even hirelings (you might think) of the thing. Yet you seem to think it necessary, I suppose because you are a romantic in some ways. And perhaps it might be possible for some, though not in the violent and ill-considered way you seem to think necessary at your present level of understanding. Ah! You will reply that you have played a part in some of our maneuvers and so you can judge—but I wonder if you can? For example, the whole question of that upset in Athens (such a small, such a trivial part of the whole design) was not simply a question of buying the Parthenon—who would want it? The firm manipulates without owning, that is part of its charm. It is the invisible increment which it tries to conquer. A long lease was all we asked for and a say in its management, if you like. My dear chap, in this, our new Middle Ages, investment has become the motor response of all religion; not in God as he was known (he hasn't changed), not in the psychic Fund of Funds which pretends to chime with the ways of universal nature. (That too is balls by the way.) No, for us *money is sperm,* and the investment of it the ritual of propitiation.

"The pattern is only repeating itself; we have placed an unobtrusive hand on much more than the Stock Exchange. Most of the Indian holy places like the Taj and Buddha's tree and so on are in our hands; the Holy Sepulcher in Jerusalem, Herculaneum, Pompeii, Grant's Tomb. The Parthenon held out for a while purely through the muddle of Graphos, the indecision of Graphos. To wipe out the National Debt and balance the Greek budget for the first time ever . . . and all in exchange for a treaty involving a few dead monuments. For us they still offer a fulcrum of operation and a power yield if looked at from the point of view of our own religion—I use the word in its anthropological sense. We have in fact begun to fit these old things into the corpus of our own contemporary culture where they can be of some use: not just brooding places for sickly poets."

"And the United Nations?" I said.

"That has great value as a relic of the future, like the Rosetta Stone. No less than an Old Master of complete nullity which is overpriced because it happens to be the only one of its period. Do you see? Then let me go a little further. If we are reflections of our culture, and our culture represents something like the total psychic predisposition of man in terms of his destiny, dare we not ask ourselves what makes it come about, what makes it last or decay? At what point does such an animal get born?" He was breathing hard now, as if the effort to enunciate his ideas clearly were a strain. "In a world of brainless drones for the most part this question never gets asked, and it's very few of us who can see that some of the answers anyway lie about in obscure places—like *The Book of Change*, for example. Felix, it's my belief that you can touch the quiddity, the nub of the idea of a culture only if you realize that it comes out of an act of association of which the primal genetic blueprint in the strictest biological sense is the uniting of the couple, man and woman. In the compact and the seed." Here he seemed to be suddenly overwhelmed by sadness. He faltered, hesitated, and then recovered himself to go on.

"Nature, as you know, is very class conscious and builds as carefully as a swallow, always in hierarchies; nothing but the best will do. It's difficult in our age where the tail is trying to wag the dog to descry any shape at all in the overall dog.

"Moreover to attempt to analyze or comprehend such matters through chimerical abstractions like capital or labor—why it's like discussing chess in terms of ludo. The problem is not there at all. I first learned this in watching the pattern of Merlin's investments; among them were several singular departures. Of course in his time specie, bullion bars, tallies, shares and so on still had the relative value they do today. But he went after other things as well; for example, he dreamed of owning (not owning of course, but manipulating) six of the largest diamonds in the world—what they call paragons: that's to say a stone with the minimum weight of 100 carats. I remember him reciting their names and weights which he knew by heart. The old 'Koh-i-noor' of course belonged to the Queen and there was nothing he could do about that—she didn't need money! 106 carats that was. Then the 'Star of the South' 125, the Pitt diamond 137, the Austrian 133, the Orloff 195, and last that monster from Borneo, 367 carats. Some of them he actually did own briefly, though of course not all; but his dream was to hold a sort of mortgage on them. He was looking always for an unchanging value or one which would increase on its own.

"No, looked at in this wider context things become vastly richer and more subtle than our polite social reformers would have us believe. Nature is an organism not a system, and will always punish those who try to strap her into a system. She will overturn the applecart—a horse with its leading rein cut, careering over a cliff: that is what is happening today in a way. On the other hand we ants must use our reason as much as possible in order to try to descry the hazy outlines of human destiny in nature as it evolves around us. We are trapped, do you see?

"Nature improvises out of pure joy, always with a miracle in hand; why can't man—or perhaps he could if he tried. Why do we build these wormcasts around us like

to Julia

civilizations, defensive/walled cities, ghettos, currencies? Then another terrifying thought pops into one's head: the very concept of order may never have entered nature's own head. Man has tried to impose his own from fear of the fathomless darkness which lies beyond every idea, every hope? Is it all self-deceit? No, Felix, it isn't—but how haltingly one begins to see the 'signatures' of things—the sigil left by the master mason, nature. Yes. Yes. Don't shake your head! They are to be seen. The imprint is there in the matter in the form things take, in the way societies cohere about a set of basic propositions, form around mysterious points of mind like God or Love. One little misinterpretation of the data and the thing goes sour. Look at our little love asylum—everyone seeking for somebody with whom he can be thoroughly weak!

"And then all this whine about personal freedom—everyone feels it is his right to worry himself about the matter. They don't see, you don't see, that nothing can be done in this field unless the firm itself becomes free; then and only then could the notion of a personal freedom be assured. And even while the poor fool is waving his arms and talking about free will, he is being subtly grooved by his culture, formed by it—money, fashions, architecture, laws, machines, foods. At what point can he really say that he stands free and clear away from the pattern in which he was cradled and by which he was formed? God! will we never see more than one profile of reality at a time? Yet it has been man's wildest hope one day to turn the statue round and gaze at it face to face. Perhaps this too is a delusion based on faulty conjectures about its sovereign nature."

There was a long pause while he lit a short cigar from the packet which Benedicta had brought with her. "I suppose you might agree that reality is sufficiently implausible to cause people great anxiety?"

"The aphorism refuses to argue, Julian. That is perhaps

its strength—or perhaps its weakness. Look both ways before crossing the road."

"Felix," he said, smiling and patting my knee once more, "I can see that you are following me and it makes me glad. But I have more to say about the firm—this tiny microcosm which has formed itself without consulting us and which is not based simply upon human cupidity so much as on a fear of the outer darkness. It would be like taking a stern moral tone with a pigeon for being forced to eat grain to keep alive. And then think of all the different types of society formed by nature from infusoria and fossils up to helpless dinosaurs with a pea for a head. Don't we belong, culturally speaking, to the same canon—woven out of the invisible by powers we don't clearly understand and can only manipulate in certain tiny areas? Think, Felix."

I was thinking; O yes, I was thinking.

"How do cultures come about, how do they vanish? We would give anything to know. Can the firm and its structure perhaps inform us a little—that's the point? Well, to break a chain you must hit a link, I suppose—the fragile link upon which the whole structure depends. One such link in man's culture is the fragile link of association of one with another, articles of faith, contracts, marriages, vows and so on. Snap the link and the primordial darkness leaks in, the culture disintegrates, and man becomes the coolie he really is when there is no frame of culture to ennoble him, to interpret himself to himself. A crisis comes about. Then the providers, the secret molelike makers of the new, go to work to repair the link, or to put in a new one. How easy to break and how laborious to repair! Only a few men in every age are fitted for the grim task, the exhausting task. For them the job in hand is self-evident, but to everyone else it seems a mystery that has got out of hand.

"Then think how puerile is our conception of such men we label with the word genius—it's on the level of Santa Claus! There isn't such an animal. But when a link is broken these rare men address themselves to the problem. What we call genius occurs when a gifted man sees a relation between two or more fields of thought which had up till then been believed to be irreconcilable. He joins the contradictory fields in an act of intellectual harmony and the chain begins to hold once more. The so-called genius of the matter is merely the intuitive act of joining irreconcilables. There is nothing new added, how could there be? But these men realize that when you wish to do something new you must go tranquilly ahead in the full knowledge that there can only be new relations, new combinations of the age-old material. The kaleidoscope must be given a jolt, that is all.

"I have always wondered whether the firm could not invent something like a death predictor; most of our troubles come from the feeling of human transitoriness, of the precarious nature of our hold upon life. But if you knew, for example, that on the 3rd March next year you were going to die, it would change your whole attitude toward people and things. It would make for resignation, compassion and concentration on the precious instant. It's anxiety over that unknown date which causes so much of the hysteria and consequently panicky judgment and thinking."

"Death," I said. "But the firm itself inflicts death."

Julian nodded quietly. "Merlin deliberately inured us to death—it was part of his code of things. So that from the firm's point of view death itself was only a pastime. One tried to keep one's hand in simply to make sure that one felt nothing about it one way or another. I must confess it meant next to nothing to me: until—well, I should say that I have only once experienced death with its full force and that was not my own but someone else's. I shall tell you more about that anon. But for the moment let me just say that the firm itself, being an organism, feels neither compunction nor conscience nor doubt: it has no guilt—how could it, since nature in making indiscriminate use of her raw material has none either? Felix, a culture is based upon an act of associaton—a kiss or a handshake or a firm or a religion. It communicates itself, flowers, perpetuates itself through a single basic principle, which is sharing. In the genetic twilight of the firm, then, I have had a close look and found it wanting in much. Could we not make a model perhaps, trace out the pathology of memory to follow the broad furrow of the genetic code with its basic structure of the male and female elements? Sex might be the great clue here; certainly the pathology of the imagination was nourished in it, or so I thought. We are still so backward in so many respects—I mean that we so often have to make a model to comprehend a little bit."

In a clean bit of snow at his feet he scratched a few words, but absentmindedly, as if he were doing it for himself rather than for his audience. Like this:

pro CREATION re CREATION.

Then he went on, still half musing. "Such simple acts and such preposterous results! Because every desire wins its response. Hence the danger. Nature is so rich that people only have to wish and they quite literally get what they want. As most of us have unpurged desires the child born of the wish is so often a changeling—in fact the last thing one, in fact, wanted. It is too late by then. This so often happens to the mob wish. Inferior slaves beget inferior masters to parody the awful distortions of the psyches which wish them up. Think of the mob creations like Nero, Napoleon and Lenin—flowering from the bad dreams of masterless men who desired only to be led to their deaths—and had their wishes answered.

"I was thinking of course of the type of human association which gives rise on the one hand to the sexual compact—you'll say that love is more a seizure like epilepsy than a sober and conscious entry into a bond; but it contains in its genes, if you like to put it that way, the basic male-female dichotomy which mirrors itself in every manifestation of language, science or art even. Whether a cave culture, city culture, or a religious culture, or even in inventions like tools or wheeled things, chariots or motor-cars. I was forced to consider all this in order to try to understand a little bit what I was doing, sitting in the cockpit of the firm, trying to direct its motions. I didn't hope for much—but I would have liked very much to become a sort of goldsmith of its ideas. Nor is anything I say the usual criticism which one hears all the time of an age of technology. Technology in every age is simply the passive miracle which flows out of our attitude toward nature, helping the chrysalis to turn itself into the butter-fly. It has nothing to do with the worry about raping nature—you can't: because nature will round on you and punish you for transgressions of this sort. But the idea of push and bite, the hand's scope allied to bronze or steel, gave us a new concept, namely 'spade'. In other words technology comes after the Fall and not before it.

"The first man to put one stone upon another may or may not have been aware that he was building a wall but his delight was great when his sheep could shelter from the snow behind it; but when the stones grew too big or too many to lift, he was joined by his nearest neighbor, and then he by his; and so gradually you got a wall culture based on an act of free association—you got the Great Wall of China, if you wish."

"Yes but *free association*," I said peevishly.

"The minute you join in the act you are no longer free, you are bound by the articles of association not less than by the natural obstacles which are posed the minute you start messing about with the natural order of things. Nature did not invent stones to stand up on one another, and will hasten to overturn them. This problem created a secon-dary one—either stone pruned so accurately that it could stand the ground swell (the Romans, say) or else some new idea—like sheer weight, or another still, mortar. It is when you are in the act of working on your wall that another idea strikes you, namely if ever one did not have a trust in nature and its basic benevolence one would have none in death, and none in man."

He sat there looking at me, a strange blood-caked goblin of a man in his heavy ski clothes and with his mica-tinted glance. He seemed to be waiting for me to say something, but I remained obstinately silent. I still wasn't clear in my mind about where he proposed to lead me. At last he himself sighed and rose to take a turn upon the terrace and gaze out across the dazzle of mountains dancing and shimmering with such purity in the light of the slowly westering sun. He spoke again, but it was almost musing once more, almost as if he were refueling his mind to carry the argument forward upon another plane. "So little time," he said, "in which to realize ourselves, one iota of our selves; and life so precarious in this pathetic overcoat of flesh and muscle; and there he goes, man, babbling about free will with gravity following him about like a salt bitch! The leaden pull of the grave on the one hand and these huge towering structures in stone or paper which he has built to keep out the thought, the unbearable thought of his disappearance. And moreover, each man with different needs, a different rate of acceleration, different physique even. O I forgot, Felix. Koepgen asked for this to be sent to you so I brought it with me." He dug into his breast and produced the slim volume of which Vibart had spoken. I put it carefully away in my pack without stripping it of its cellophane covering. He sat down again, smiling a little, and said: "Koepgen has earned an honorable retirement and he has just realized that many of the infuriating things the firm made him do actually belonged to the plan of self-realization which he had set himself—he's an alchemist by temperament and has spent his adult life trying to smelt himself out."

"You sent him to Russia to buy mercury."

"Yes, Felix. It must have seemed an arbitrary or even harsh decision. But later on he realized that it was a fruitful one on completely nonmaterial grounds. You probably know that what the sea was for Plato, and indeed for Nash's famous Freudian unconscious—namely the symbol of rebirth—mercury is for the alchemist? It is their primal water! I deliberately did not tell Koepgen this; indeed at times I held my breath because he was on the point of disappearing or resigning. Then one day, just in time, he discovered that what he was doing for the firm on the material plane he was also doing unconsciously on the spiritual. He is glad now that he carried out the task."

"Where is he?"

"On an island. He has discovered that prayer, if rightly orientated, can become an exact science. I am quoting, of course, because all that line of enquiry isn't within my own interests. It's the purest rubbish, I believe. But there you are, it makes him happy to think so. Besides, just suppose it were true—prayer wheels for the lazy. We are making some already for the Tibetans. . . ." He smiled a smile of sad malice and shook his head ruefully, as if at the pure extravagance of human beliefs. Then he looked up and said: "I tried to kill you, Felix, and you tried to kill me—in both cases it was a near thing. But you lost a child, and I have been rendered incapable of making one. In a way this makes us quits."

"Yes."

He had become very pale now, and his nostrils were drawn in. He stared at his ungloved hand, as it lay upon his knee, with great intensity, as if he had never seen it before. After a long pause, and without looking up, he said quietly: "Benedicta, will you do us the favor of leaving us alone together for a moment? I want to talk to Felix about Iolanthe." Obediently Benedicta rose, lit a cigar, and, kissing me lightly on the cheek, walked away across the snow toward the tree where Julian had propped his skis. So we sat immobile as the half-finished snowman on the tree stump. I could see that he was wondering where to begin. He wrote in the snow the word "Io" and then raised his head to look me in the eyes. His whole posture reflected a tremendous contained tension—sometimes if a powerful but delicate dynamo isn't properly anchored to its base, its vibrations can make the whole housing ripple and tremble. But his voice was deadly calm, deadly calm. "It's strange the things people have to say about love," he said surprisingly. "About love at first sight, or love at no sight at all, or the love of God or of man. It's a real honeycomb of a sound. But from my point of view, and yours and the firm's, the genetic shadow of the love child is always there, its silhouette hangs over the love match. It is generated by the eyes and the mind perhaps less than by the body. The child is implicit in the transaction. When it goes wrong of course you get monsters; changelings, like the umbratiles of Paracelsus or the angels of Swedenborg, are such productions, formed, so to speak, from sperm which has missed its mark or gone bad.

"I did not," he went on, "choose my own ground for this duel either, the encounter with this weird sort of animal, love. It was chosen for me by Merlin. I saw her, having always believed she did not exist, and the blood rushed to my head—and all the Petrarchian rubbish of our civilization with it! The anaconda coils of an immense lethargic narcissism wrapped themselves round me! But unlike Dante, unlike that fool Petrarch, I could not ingest the love object and transform it into self-love. I suppose because I wasn't that other kind of impotent, an artist. No, I was a whole man in every sense but this vital one—this insult to my honor and my very being."

He had swollen now with suppressed rage, and his face had become flushed, feverish-looking, while the fine controlled voice shook slightly. It was deeply moving to have this tiny glimpse of the driving power of Julian—sexlessness, impotence, fury, rage, sexual ferocity. "I received sex and death in one blood-stained package, thrown in my face like the bundle of discarded bones a butcher wraps up for the dog." He paused to master his breathing and then went on. "One minute you are still there, breathing and planning and hoping: the next you are this appalling beautiful toy which will not respond to the controls. Reality rushes in like some fearful bat and circles round the room, knocking over the candles and banging against the white screens. I learned all this from Iolanthe." He looked quickly around him, as if looking for something against which he could dash a clenched fist, or bang his head; and I was reminded of what Mrs. Henniker had told me of the last night of his vigil, of what she had seen in a brief moment between sleep and waking. It must have been the critical moment.

In his confusion he had been completely disoriented. He was hardly aware that he had a tremendous erection—the death wish of the flesh itself. Little incoherent sounds escaped his lips, little sighs and whimpers. He snatched off the hanging cylinder of transfusion blood which was hanging over the bed, stripped the needle, and drank it thirstily off, putting the rubber capsule in his mouth like a teat. Never had he known such a thirst. Then, with the same little soundless sobs, he went to the mirror of the hanging cupboard and made up his face with her lipstick, staring like a ghoul. He took the candle from in front of the ikon in order to light the spectacle of himself standing here, staring abstractedly at the man called Julian whom he hardly recognized. "Julian," I said, with compassion for his wretchedness. "Steady on." But he was already calm once more, in full control of body and voice. He looked once more at me with a piercing calm and said: "So I come at last to the whole point of the matter. *If the firm could be freed, Felix!* On such a notion we could base a hope however faint of the freedom which you so desperately seek, which I too need. But the only road to freedom of such a kind lies through an aesthetic of some kind. Beauty, from which alone comes congruence and the harmony of dissident parts and which echoes back the great contrivances of nature." He gave a harsh bark of a laugh, as if at the very hopelessness of such an idea. "Beauty, whatever it is, is the only poor yardstick we have; and in my own case Iolanthe's image is the model which suits our book, a universal beauty which has sent her round and round the world in celluloid and which has made her what she is for so many. She has exemplified, projected the wild notion of this inner freedom which we can realize only through the female. She is there like cumulus, she is everywhere like a world dream—O! a twentieth-century shallow trashy dream, if you wish. But not less real than Helen of Troy. Only on her image can be built, only through her can we realize our mad experiment. It is Iolanthe that we must try to realize."

Now something more astonishing happened. He fell on his knees before me and spread his arms in supplication, saying: "Felix, for God's sake help me. *We are building her*."

"*Building her?*"

"I know. It will seem to you like one of those fantasies which go with General Paralysis of the Insane. It is nothing of the kind. We are building her and her consort, just to see. It is terrible to have to make models to comprehend, but it is all we can do. Rubber, leather, nylon, steel—God knows in the matter of technological contrivance we have everything at our disposal. But *memory*, Felix, for the conditioned responses, she will need a vastly extended memory. She must sensitize to sounds, she must be word-perfect in her role— ('Come, darling, open') . She needs you, she must have you, Felix. Nobody else can do it. We have nobody who could do it for us. You know that for a while we all thought Abel was a typical Felix type of hoax. It was only when the machine made *pi* come out that I woke up with a start and realized that in fact you had made something extraordinarily strange and original, a mnemonic monster."

He sat staring at me with a singular expression of exhaustion and triumph—the sort of relief a lecturer might feel at having completed a triumphant exposé of an abstruse theme. "We dismantled it, you know, with the greatest care. Marchant did it. It was perfectly astonishing as an example of technical virtuosity, of technical insolence if you wish. Parts of it you had only sketched out and tied together with string, so to speak. They were only just holding, only just passing a current. But such elegance of thought!"

"I know. I went mad with rage against you and Benedicta and the whole set-up. You see I didn't care if it worked or not; it's when you don't care that sometimes things work out. And really I had need of about fourteen people on the technical side to build such a toy."

"I know you did."

He had by now risen from his knees and dusted himself as meticulously as a cat; he crossed and poured himself a drink with perfectly steady hand. Then he turned to me and said in a low voice, a conspiratorial voice: "I *implore* you, Felix."

But now I was musing, staring at the ground, seeing in my mind's eye the sweating Marchant taking down Abel, probably with earphones like the people who defuse mines (after all the staked shotgun must have worried them); calling back in his firm but squeaky voice the name of every nut and bolt he touched. So they had stolen Abel's memory, a thing still so terribly imperfect of execution. (I have had since a number of new notions about how to extend it.) Here they were clearly thinking about a mnemonic contrivance which acted directly on the musculature—a walking memory; what else is man, pray? It was breathtaking as an idea, and also monstrous. "Yes," said Julian, as if he were thought reading. "It's monstrous all right, but only from one point of view."

"Who would have thought it, Julian?" I said. "Iolanthe as the witch fulfillment, the which fulfillment—how do you prefer it? How did you reduce it all to size to fit it into the confines of the human skull?"

"We can do almost anything with matter, in the field of imitation; all we can't do is *create* it." He said it with such bitterness that I felt at once that he was thinking of his own castration. And then I looked past him up the hill and saw this other blonde monster, Benedicta, leaning against a tree and smoking quietly, with her blue eyes raised toward the sunlight which had begun to weaken now, to send blue shadows racing down to the bluer roots of the snow peaks—and I thought grimly of the long desolating periods of impotent fury I had had to live through because of this man: of the fears and illnesses of Benedicta herself: of a life half lived or at least ill lived (always some cylinders not firing) : and thinking the whole damned cartoon strip through from the beginning I felt a sudden surge of weakness, a lassitude of limb and mind. I took a good swig from the gin bottle and set it carefully back in its place. "So you want me to join forces on the science friction, Julian? I'll have to think it over, you know." But he was already smiling at me in a curiously knowing way, as if he realized how deeply his arguments had pierced my armor, my self-esteem; and also how enticing was the prospect he had sketched in for me. I also had the uncomfortable feeling that he had really gone out of his mind in a queer sort of way. I wanted to say, "You are schizoid, my lad, that's what you are. But with patience and rest and sedation . . ." but I said nothing. On the other hand, in a confused sort of way I began to wish I had never heard of this toy of his. But here he was, still smiling at me with a funny hangdog tenderness, quite impenitent over the past and still hungry about the future.

"I have good hopes of you," he said softly. "I will ring you up in a day or two. I am making arrangements to take Rackstraw back to England. He has moments, you know, when he becomes quite lucid and recalls quite a lot. I have spared no research into Iolanthe, you know—into her character and her habits. Almost everyone who knew her has had something to tell us, and we've built up a huge library on her, crumb by crumb, to feed into the Abel nervous system, if I can put it like that. I think the elegance of Marchant's adaptation of Abel will please you very much— all sorts of new materials are to hand these days for modeling. My dear Felix, I can't believe you'll refuse me. It would be the crown of your life's work, I believe, to help me make her so perfectly that nobody would ever believe it wasn't her."

"Why Rackstraw?"

"He was her lover. I want to suck him dry."

"What can he tell you?"

He gave a small impatient gesture.

"The least thing is important for her. Nothing is too trifling to be overlooked." He said this with such childish impish seriousness that I was tempted to laugh. Quite insane! All this would end in catatonia, some delicious twilight state which would make the doctors croon with joy. O boredom, boredom, Mother of the Arts! But if I didn't do this, what else could I do to escape from it? I was a compulsive inventor, nothing else fulfilled me. I had an irrational rush of hunger and love for this new Benedicta staring into the clouds up there—perhaps she could save me from myself? No. I looked at Julian, and I realized with full force for the first time in my life what the theologians must mean when they speak of being tempted by the devil. The *hubris*, the insolence, to arrogate to oneself the power of the gods! Vaulting ambition, etc. I suddenly wanted to do a pee and be alone with myself for a second. I retired behind the hut for a moment while Julian sat motionless, waiting for me to come back. I did, and sat down. "You are insatiable," I said and he nodded in a thirsty sort of way. The inside of his mouth was very pink, very red, so that in some of his expressions one might descry a touch of vampire. "Iolanthe," he said in a low voice as if she explained everything, the whole earth and the heavens above. "I saw her, you missed her. Now the firm must re-create her. It *must*, do you understand? and you *must help it."*

"And when you have built your Adam and Eve, what then? Will you ask Whipsnade to find a corner for them?"

"I am not going to speak to you as yet about that", he said in a sharp martinet's tone, a soft peremptory flash of fire. "We will face that when and if we succeed in doing what I want done."

"We'll ask Caradoc to build them a pretty little Parthenon to live in, I suppose; dependents of the firm with a firmly guaranteed pension scheme and health insurance. . . ." I badly felt the need to insult him, I loved him so much. Badly. He sat quite still and calm but said nothing. I went on truculently, irrationally, "I shall be forced to regard you as a case of intellectual Koro, artificially induced. A *retractio ad absurdum."* He writhed and gritted his teeth with fury but said nothing, always nothing. It would have been pleasant to hit him with something but there was nothing to hand. Such weakness is despicable.

"I think you will," he said at last. "I don't really see what else you can do, now you know about it." And all of a sudden he expelled his breath with relief and shrunk down to half his size, as if from exhaustion. He became so pale I thought he would probably faint; he seemed suddenly to feel the cold, his teeth chattered. Then after a minute or so his breathing steadied again and he regained his posture, his norm. He became once more the pleasant conversational man. "As for Caradoc," he said, "as you know he is back and *en disponibilité* until the firm finds something worthy of his genius. But even a genius has a few intellectual holes in him and he is no exception; the sense of symbolic logic in architecture escapes him completely. He finds no significance, for example, in the fact that the diameter of the outer stone circle of Stonehenge is some 100 feet which is about the diameter of the dome of St. Paul's."

He stood up again and turned away to stare at the

snow range intently. Then he said, but in a whisper and as if to himself: "One dares not neglect symbolism in either life or art. It is perilous. I threw a lighted torch into Iolanthe's grave!" I was in the presence of someone who had suffered the full onslaught of the European disease, poxier than pox ever was—Love! But of course allied as always to matter, for he added in the same breath, "I own all her films now. I play them over and over to myself, in order to regale myself with all that she wanted to be, all that she could not realize of herself. My God, Felix, you must see them."

"So you bought her out at last!" I simply could not resist the bitter note in my voice. He nodded with set jaw. How I hated this mechanical vulture!

"I finally forced her to abdicate," he said, but sadly now, as if the victory were a hollow one. "She abdicated only after her death; and I could do nothing about her life or about mine. Fixed stars!" In a long sad pause he repeated the phrase like an incantation. "Fixed stars!"

Poor Julian! Rich Julian! Vega and Altair!

"Now I must leave you," he said, "and find my way down to the bottom of this damned mountain." He gloved his precise small hand and stood up. Together we walked across the snow to where Benedicta was. She watched us quietly advancing toward her, unsmiling, calm. *"Eh bien,"* she said at last on a note of interrogation, but there was not much more to be said.

Julian took her hands in his in a somewhat ceremonial fashion. "B., you betrayed us over Count Böcklin, didn't you? Quite deliberately." But there was no rancor in his tone, perhaps just a touch of regret. Benedicta nodded in perfectly composed fashion and kissed him in sisterly wise on the cheek. "I wanted to show myself that I was finally free, Julian." Julian nodded. "That word again," he said reprovingly. "It has a dying fall." B. put her arm through mine. "All too frequently," she agreed. "But not anymore, at least for me. You know, if Felix hadn't disappeared and left me alone, I would have refused the task when you put it to me. But I was scared, I was scared to death of you." Julian started to put on his skis, tenderly latching up the thongs and testing them with precision on one leg and then the other. "And now you can only pity me, I suppose. Don't, Benedicta. That might make me turn dangerous again." Strange, agonizingly shy man!

"No" she said. "You are defused for us, Julian."

He looked from one to the other for a long moment; then he gave a little nod as if of approval of what he saw. "I shall order you some happiness for a change, now that we have crossed the big divide in ourselves. You might even come to love *me* one day, both of you. I doubt, though. Yet the road has opened in front of us. But there is still quite a lot to be done in order to earn it. Felix, I shall ring you up in a couple of days when you have had a chance to reflect."

"No need," I said. "I am your man and you know it."

"What luck," he said in a low voice, "what luck for me to have you at my side once more. And so farewell."

He shuffled his way uphill until he gained the edge of the practice slope and then ebbed forward on his skis, propelling himself with his paddles; gathered momentum, curved up small, and glided away like a swallow into the valley. Suddenly with his going we felt that the world had emptied itself; we felt the evening chill upon us as we returned to the hut to pack up and trudge back to the *téléférique*.

"You are signing on again," she said. "Darling, this time I think you should; now I am at your side and you at mine, armed. I'm holding my breath. Do you think some happi . . .?"

I kissed her breathless. "Not a word, not a single word. Just go on holding your breath and we'll see what happens."

Sinking down the mountain side in the dark purple cusp of evening was more beautiful than the morning ascent; a somewhat inexplicable sensation of delayed shock had seized me. I repeated in my own mind the words, "Well, so Julian actually exists and I have met him in the flesh." The phrase generated a perfectly irrational relief and—indeed why not?—happiness. Also physical relief: I felt done in, exhausted. Why? I don't know. It was as if, during the meeting itself, my mind had been in such a daze that I couldn't fully grasp the fact. I suppose ordinary people might experience this sort of grateful shock anesthesia on meeting an admired film star unexpectedly in a grocer's shop. It was clear for me at any rate. Julian had appeared like some figment of a lost dream flashed, so to speak, on the white screen of the snows. He had disappeared just as dramatically—a dwindling black spot turning back into tadpole and racing away into the huge blue perspectives of the valley. Gone!

Benedicta had burrowed her slender hand into my pocket and was softly pressing mine. "It is fatuous to feel so serene," I said, "and possibly dangerous too. Do you know what he is up to? Building a human being, if you please. Moreover one we know. God, I love you, Benedicta. Wait!"

I had a perfectly brilliant idea for a new sort of jump circuit. It was so rich I feared it might disappear if I didn't make a note of it; yes, but pencil and paper? Fortunately she had a very fine lipstick with her and in her methodical camper's way she had brought a few sheets of toilet paper against emergencies, since she knew there was no lavatory at the huts. Saved! She looked over my shoulder as I blotted and blotched with this clumsy tool. I couldn't stop to explain for fear that the idea might fade. It was my sort of poem to the blue evening, the sliding white mountains, the buzzing prismatic corolla of the sinking sun bouncing off the slopes, the trees, the world, to Benedicta herself. And how patient she was; probably disappointed that it wasn't a love letter but a set of silly pothooks, equations. (If it worked it might spell the death of the ordinary light bulb as we know it.) "I love you," I said. "But don't speak for a moment. O I love you desperately, but shut up, please."

Ouf! But I felt guilt when it was all duly noted down and stuffed into my pocket. So I wrote on the window a rebus based on the word TUNC with a heart in the middle instead of a you-know-what and the words *Felix amat Benedictam*. In fact such was my euphoria that I missed a step on the ramp and fell headlong into a snowdrift.

"That really is a sign of returning health," said Benedicta approvingly after her first concern about broken limbs was allayed. "With the return of absentmindedness on such a scale, we can really prognose a total cure." That is all very well, but in fact I was whacked; I had a bath, got my dressings changed, and was all ready for visiting her at the chalet, but instead I lay down on the bed for a few moments of repose and reflection and fell instantly asleep. It was early morning when I woke to find myself stiff as a lead soldier but wonderfully refreshed. Beside me, scribbled on the temperature chart, was a note from B. which said: "Alarmed, I came to find you. But I like you almost better asleep than awake. You look such a fool, such a contented fool. All the algebra has been drained from your body. You look how one ought to look when one is dead but alas we don't. Anyway I have enjoyed sitting beside you, watching you going up and down in a steady purposeful sort of way. In your Chinese book I read the following passage which pleased me. 'Drunk, in a huge green garden, among flowering cherry trees, under a parasol, among diplomats, what a death, Tu Fu, poor poor dear.' So good night. (P.S. I want to sleep with you.) "

But she had gone into town to do some shopping, so I spent the morning in the so-called danger ward, learning to tie seaman's knots from Professor Plon who was a specialist in the garrote; he had already disposed of a wife and two daughters in exemplary fashion (running bow line?) and was technically not supposed to have any access to rope. But he had found a piece, I don't know how, and was shaping all kinds of elaborate and diverting knots and bows. I finally got it away from him when his attention was diverted, though it was really a pity. He could have emptied that whole ward by lunchtime. But I didn't want poor Rackstraw to go the way of all flesh; though it was almost inconceivable that he should have anything very special to tell us about Iolanthe, it was only fair to let Julian satisfy his curiosity. What else had I been doing but just that? Those elegant debauched hands had roved all over that lovely body, touching it now here, now there, molding the breasts and stroking the marvelous haunches of the paragon girl, the nonpareil. I felt a sort of sick pang of tenderness when I thought of it. Iolanthe the waif, and Iolanthe the breastless goddess of the silver screen; the sick romance of all our Helens, for whom somebody's Troy always goes up in flames.

Rackstraw himself was enjoying a period of rare lucidity. "I have been invited to go away," he said happily, "to a place which is a country house to stay with a man I used to know vaguely I have forgotten his name, but anyway it wouldn't mean anything to you."

"Julian?" I said.

" 'Pon my soul, yes!" said Rackstraw. "You do know him then? He came to see me yesterday and told me about it. It's more like a film studio than a country house: it's full of inventors. They keep popping out of doors and saying things like, 'I've got it, old boy. Look no further. The answer is untreated sewage.' It might prove boring in the long run; but they are going to make a long recording lasting months, perhaps years." Ah, the blessed intervals of insulin coma! But he was radiant in a funny etiolated way. He had cleaned his shoes and was fussing over an egg stain on his waistcoat.

"Rackstraw," I said. "What about Iolanthe?"

"I made the mistake," he said surprisingly, "of treating women as grown-ups without believing in the idea; but later I found to my horror that they *were*. It was I who was the child." He shook his head slowly and looked round him. "If only I could have a word from old Johnson. There's no knowing if he will have a happy Christmas or not, down there in Leatherhead. It is very remiss of him. At our age, you know, there aren't very many more shots on the spool." Then he said "Iolanthe!" in a tone of the greatest contempt, and suddenly shuddered with horror as if he had swallowed a toad. "What does that mean?" I said. He looked at me with blazing futile eyes and hissed: "Have you seen the sharks in the Sydney zoo? Then I shall say no more!" If he went on like this I could see that it was going to be a very long and very costly recording. "To be belonged to!" he went on in the same tone of high contempt. "Pah! She killed someone and I found out because she talked in her sleep." He knelt down and patiently undid my shoelaces, then stood up again apparently completely satisfied with his handiwork. "My success with women," he said modestly, "was all due to my voice. They could not resist it. When I wanted one I used to put on a special husky croony tone which worked like a charm. I used to call this 'putting a lot of cock into it.' It was infallible. Naturally I took great pleasure in their company."

He walked up and down in his strange tottering fashion but with quite a strut of sexual vanity. Then he stopped and raising his hand in a regal gesture said, "Now go! Vanish! Decamp! Vamoose! Buzz off!" So I did, albeit rather reluctantly, for I was intrigued by even this glancing reference to Io. Who knows, perhaps if he sat week after week in the red plush projection room where Julian now spent so much of his time, staring at the films he had helped her to make, something might be evoked in him, some concrete response? And yet to what end? Once dead . . . God, I wondered what sort of toy was in the process of being fabricated; a copy of the human dummy which would pose once more the eternal problem (how real can you get?) without ever being able to answer it. Iolanthe! I had missed her somehow and Julian had never enjoyed the real girl whom Henniker described in the words, "It was her animal fervor, her warmth, her slavishness which won men's hearts, going down to the ugliest client like a humble and devoted dying moon. Later she became tired, and worse still something of a lady: and intelligent, worst of all. She discovered she had a sensibility. This tied men into worse knots, intellectual ones. They were always trying to find metaphors to express things which are best left unexpressed." All right. All right.

I hadn't seen a paper for months, indeed had had no desire to know what was going on in the world. So I was interested to catch myself lifting a copy of *The Times* from a consulting-room desk, to read with my lunch. Nothing very much. I missed Benedicta as I read. Sometimes in some of our expressions, straying into the visual field, so to speak, I saw my son very clearly. Then he dimmed away and she became once more herself. It made me feel shy in a way, and guilty; I had mounted that toy in order to kill Julian and it had recoiled on my head. Bang! I could never have foreseen, even with the help of Abel, that Mark himself might opt out of the whole compact, press the trigger. I had such an ache too when I thought that Benedicta had never mentioned it, never alluded to Mark. I saw now to what extent she had been a prisoner in this fantastic web spun by the firm—a web held firm by the fanatical tenacity of Julian.Well, I read a little bit into the extraordinary fantasy of reality as captured by the so-called press. The world had not changed since my absence, it was the same. Fears of war as usual. They were crying "punish me, punish me." And of course a war was coming. Hurrah! Everybody would be miserable but gay, masochistically gay, and art would flourish on the stinking middens of our history.

I went into the other room to find Benedicta on her knees with half-open trunks all around. "What the hell are you doing?" She said: "Packing." Well, on the one hand it might seem logical enough. "Why?"

Benedicta said: "Nash rang me. You are released, we are both released. Free. Julian is coming to get you tomorrow and drive you back. I'm going by air. Where do you want to live? Mount Street is always there, and also that monster you hate in the country."

"Let me find out a little bit where and how I am working—and at what. Let's go to a hotel first, let's go to Claridge's where the people are so insensitive, shall we?"

"All right, I'll book."

THREE

But you'd have thought that Hitler himself had sent for me if you'd seen the four huge black limousines coming to a halt in the drive of the Paulhaus; Julian traveled like a Black Prince with numerous secretaries, perhaps even gunmen for all I knew. He himself was in the back of the leading car, holding the door open for me. He wore an immaculate dark suit and soft black hat turned well down over his eyes—and, of course, characteristically enough, dark glasses. Chauffeurs bustled about with my luggage. "Come into my floating office and admire it," he said, indicating a shallow panel full of switches. With childish pride he showed me the radio and telex arrangements, a secretary's folding desk; and there was even a telephone which worked externally. A cocktail cabinet. Everything in fact except a lavatory and a chapel to worship Mammon in. "What splendor," I said to humor him. "Could we call London and give them Benedicta's flight number?" He was delighted to show his mysteries off and in next to no time was talking to Baum over the water. Then he sat back in the comfortable seat of the mammoth and lit a cigar. I watched him with curiosity, still consumed by a feeling of unreality; as much as I could see of him, that is, for the glasses shielded his eyes. "Always the passion for disguise, Julian," I said, somewhat rudely, I suppose. "It has always puzzled me." He looked round at me and quickly looked away again. "It shouldn't really," he said. "I have always been terribly . . . shy; but apart from that I have a thing, I suppose Nash would regard it as a complex, about faces. They seem to me quite private things. I do not see why we have to walk about with them sticking out of a hole in the top of our clothes, simply because convention decrees it. I have perhaps overcompensated in one direction; you know that I have had my face made over twice by plastic surgery in order to get it the way I wanted it. It's better than it was but I'm still not completely happy. It is very boring, for example, always to have the same face—and nowadays, thank goodness, it's no longer necessary. Here, I shall be quite honest with you and show you my dossier." He groped in a shallow leather wallet and produced some passport photographs which he handed to me one by one, saying, "That is how nature made me, this is where art stepped in, and this is the way I look now." I gasped and stared incredulously at him. "But it's three quite different men," I said. "Not really. Look more closely. There is much that cannot be changed." Yes, he was there in each if one peered into the eyes, but in each case the change had been accompanied by a different hairstyle. But the differences were more marked than the resemblances. "But, of course," he said coolly, "this may not be the end of the affair if I begin to get bored with the way I look at present. It's a marvelous feeling of liberty to know that you can change when you wish, even though very superficially."

He put the photographs away carefully and pocketed the wallet. "Now you know all," he said, and lapsed into an indifferent silence as he watched the countryside rolling past us. His hands seemed fatter and coarser than I remembered them to be, and he wore a seal ring. But having disposed of the subject of his disguises he seemed to have nothing more to say. In fact he seemed to doze off, to hibernate inside the dark wings of his overcoat.

We lunched in high mountains on smoked salmon and white wine; Julian had a long talk on his pet telephone to a branch in Holland which manufactured paper clips. "We have two lazy men there I shall have to deal with; one sits all day in a bubble bath of self-esteem, and the other is too scared to move: Jaeger, you perhaps know? A Jewish banker like a very very old very sharp scythe."

I had expected him to make some reference to the sort of work he was expecting of me, but he said nothing at all about the Iron Maide, so I contented myself with dipping into unreality again—reading a newspaper, I mean. Dear old London! At it again. A new Labor Party pamphlet which would offer wholesome sex instruction to the under-fours and most probably begin: "Children, did you know that Mummy was full of eggs and that Daddy had to hatch them, and that is how you are here?" Life, as Koepgen never tired of reminding us, is only being let out on parole for a brief while. *Tous les excés sont bons.* Well, let Julian sleep. But I myself was half asleep when late that night we slanted into Paris in a foul gray rain. "I want," said Julian, "to go first to the café where you met her, then to the hotel. I want to see the room you took her to." I protested feebly, but there was nothing for it; a note of such passionate urgency and hunger came into his voice that out of sheer sympathy I felt I had to give in. Sordid rum-whiffing *terrasse* where we sat for a while at the chipped table; strong local color was supplied by a little whore, a veritable midget, who uncrossed her legs and let loose an effluvium which could be smelled tables away, stables away, could almost be heard. . . . Then to that room where she had told me this and that, and her breasts and so on. Then Henniker, with her face flushed with rage, all red and bruised from the crying, protesting about Graphos and the whip. "He taught her to enjoy it, but he couldn't make her love him. No, if she loved anyone

[123]

sexually it was me. ME. I seduced her, I calmed her, I loved her and was faithful right to the end." What pitiful wounded stuff we carry around inside us; wounds that gush blood at the slightest touch of memory's lancet. He sat in a chair looking dazed, like some very old tame monkey, gazing round him and yawning; but when I told him about the breasts he put his face in his hands and went very still for a moment. Then he cleared his throat softly and said: "About death there is something curious—a sort of shrinking; if you copy the exact dimensions, the effect of your statue or dummy always looks smaller than the remembered original. In the waxworks, for example, everyone seems to have become reduced in size. Just over lifesize is the best recipe for copies. Let us go, I have heard enough."

He did not appear for dinner that night and I amused myself by reading Koepgen, ringing up Benedicta and leafing through *Figaro*. Much literary prize-giving and distribution of honorary titles; why don't we? The Epicurus of Letchworth, the great Aubergine of Clermont-Ferrand. Hum!

Next morning Julian decided that he must go to Holland, and, as I was impatient to see this new-old wife of mine, I took a plane, full of a vertiginous excitement and shyness. My impatience led to indiscreet arguments with everyone, officials, porters and lastly with an insolent cabby who had clearly never seen a man in love before, and made no allowances for this desperate illness. (One should be put in an ambulance with a bull; or someone should walk in front of one with a red flag crying: *"Enceinte. Enceinte."* But at last I arrived to find Benedicta in bed with a cold, so pretty and so woeful that I was tempted to ring up the whole of Harley Street. "You see what happens now when you leave me? I get ill."

"O thank you, thank you."

But nevertheless, in spite of the infantile euphoria, I had the most dreadful dreams. "Dreams are but the prose of quotidian life with the poetic quantum added." All right. All right. Cut it out now. They were horrible, and of course they made me wonder if perhaps I had been seduced once more upon the bitter path of . . . I interrogated her silent form, sleeping so calmly beside me, one hand on her breast: the rise and fall so reassuring, like the spring swell of a marvelous free sea—a Greek sea. And I felt suddenly terribly old and went into the bathroom to examine my old carcass with attention all over again. Bits were falling out—a tooth would have to go: O not another! The hair was coming back quite strong. But an extra magnification of the bloody glasses.

It was amazing that my balls hadn't dropped off after all I'd been through—like Vibart's champion novelist. It seemed to me that I had a very false cringing sort of smile, so I decided to change it all along and because of . . . But smiling from left to right instead of right to left set the wrong groups of muscles moving. Also the old knowing friendly *kindly* expression in the eyes looked just bleary to me. What despair! I knew exactly how I should look in order to rivet her attention forever. But suppose it got stuck, that smile, from being artificial? Suppose nobody could move it? I would have to go every morning to Harley Street and accept facial massage from some torpid Japanese. Perhaps acupuncture in the dorsal region, huge colored pins being driven into my inventor's dogged bum? O hell, please not that.

Marchant rang me the following day and at last I began to think that things were moving along as planned. He asked me to meet him at Poggio's which I duly did, enchanted to see my old stablemate again. But he had changed a good deal; his hair had gone very fine and quite silver and you could see pink scalp through it. He sported a set of new false teeth of fantastic brilliance. His clothes were much the same—the stage uniform of the absent-minded professor: baggy gray trousers and a torn tweed coat (acid-stained here and there) with leather patches on the elbows. And a huge college scarf of garish design, bearing his college colors I don't doubt. But he was full of energy and excitement, gesticulating and twitching his face as he spoke like a lively earwig. And yet somehow tired and highly strung; and I noticed that he was drinking rather heavily for such an abstemious man. Anyway, "How," he said, giving me the benefit of a Red Indian salute. "How," I replied gravely.

"I had all your news from Julian. Imagine my delight. To hear you were coming to work at Toybrook with me. I have been bored stiff among all those corpses."

"Wait a minute," I said. "First Toybrook. Isn't that a hush-hush plant of some sort?" Marchant nodded and said: "It's where we work on anything which might be on a secret list for the forces; it's a security A factory. I brought you a pass, all neatly made out for you. When will you begin? It's only a very few miles from the country house, if you have your car. You could drive over every day. Why the grimace, Felix?" I sighed. "Bad memories, painful memories. I wonder. I'll ask Benedicta."

"Do. It would be convenient."

"Now what about corpses?"

"A literal fact; working on these models which I must say are beginning to look quite frighteningly like the real

[126]

thing, we found we knew next to nothing about anatomy. We could have called in great surgeons and all that, but they work on living bodies; we were only imitating and where possible simplifying in glass, wool, nylon, jute and so on. In other words the inside of the Iron Maide did not have to be copied, provided we mocked out a musculature and a nervous system and allowed her to imitate human behavior, speech, gesture, mnemonic response. Of course Abel has been invaluable with his memory bank which we have now reduced spectroscopically to the size of a pea virtually—talk about writing the Lord's Prayer on the point of a pin! It's only a matter of detail. She'll have twice the vocabulary of Shakespeare, and all the *souplesse* of a mummy trained for a ballet. Gosh, it is really amazing. Julian is incredible. Do you know when they moved a model of her into Madame Tussaud's, he used to go there day after day to watch the crowds filing by her. One day I saw in the paper that this wax model had been damaged and I wondered if he had . . . well, I don't know . . . started kissing it or doing something even more drastic. He hasn't dared as yet to see what they've got. He says he will only come when you authorize him to. You know he is scared, Felix, very scared by this nylon Iolanthe; and she is coming along so well that I'm rather scared too. Suppose we get within three decimal places of a perfect copy? What are we going to do with her? Could she live an independent life as a free dummy, in a three-dimensional world? Eh?"

"What about the sexual stuff—is she designed to poke the other one? Will they be monogamous?"

"All that is feasible; but they will never be able to produce—the whole pelvic oracle is sketched in I'm afraid. But the vagina will please you. And incidentally, another chance remark of yours has borne fruit in a marvelous way. You've probably forgotten. Ejax!"

"Ejax?" I said vaguely. It meant nothing to me. Marchant chuckled and said: "One day when you were drunk you said that for real sexual pleasure the quantity of sperm was important. The heavier the discharge the greater the excitement of the female."

"I said that?"

"Yes, you did."

"Good god! Is it true?"

"Our new sperm-thickening pill called Ejax is having a wild success—surely you've seen the advertising in all the tube stations? No? 'Have you taken your Ejax today? If not, what will the wifey say?' It's swept the board. And it was so easy chemically to work it out. A very slight provocation of the prostate with an irritant does the trick. So far no side effects, but by the time these come along we'll have a counterblast to them."

"Marchant," I said, "are you happy?" I don't suppose it was the question to put at this time and place. He stared at me angrily for a long moment and then said indignantly: "Yes."

We went on looking at each other, critically and carefully. "Yes," he said, and again, "Yes, Felix." But it was stagy; he didn't want to be probed on this topic and I realized with a pang of regret the full measure of my tactlessness. Whose happiness is whose business after all? It was also a bit alarming to find that so much of my own was intimately bound up with Benedicta—surely this was a fearful weakness?

"Go on," I said, "go on, Marchant boy, and stop me from thinking. I have never heard of such a beautiful project with all the problems it raises. Why it's like having a baby!"

"Exactly," he said, resuming the flush of enthusiasm which I had cut short by my ill-judged intervention. "While society is happily creating a slave class of analphabetics, *'les visuels,'* who have forgotten how to read and who depend on a set of Pavlovian signals for their daily bread and other psychic needs—surely we have the right to build a model which will be at least as 'human' as these so-called human beings? Eh? Whether her limitations of freedom in action will have to be circumscribed for her I cannot get Julian to discuss. He turns a blind eye to the whole matter.

"But if we get what we might—why, we could turn Iolanthe loose one day, kiss her warmly, and say, now you are free—just as if she were being released from Holloway. There is no reason that I can see why she shouldn't hold her own in the world as it is today. Just release her, as a soap bubble is flicked off a child's soap pipe. 'Go, my child.' It's not an unfair analogy—babies are born this way; but they arrive helpless and have to be passed through the cultural mincer. Suppose ours arrived at the age of thirty—mentally mature; with all her experience digested? What is to prevent her taking her place with all the other dummies and pushing a lever for her living, her Pavlovian living? A trapdoor opens and the soup comes in." He was very drunk indeed in a cold and rational sort of way. His cheeks had a hectic flush. But he wasn't slurring and when he got up to go to the lavatory his walk was quite steady. "Will she have opinions?" I asked and he replied, "That is up to us; we are building the library of her conditioned responses upon the old graph you drew for Abel. Yes, she will feel certain things. But it's for us to decide to a certain extent." He absented himself and I reflected upon this weird assignment with a certain lustful satisfaction. Iolanthe!

"Faustus!"

Marchant, reappearing, said: "On the one hand it might seem complicated, but in fact it's only terribly detailed and intricate. Our responses are not infinite, from a muscular point of view, though of course they are various and numerous. Speech and so on—again it's not infinite; your sound analysis was most useful and adapts perfectly in the new materials. The voice is particularly successful in my view; here, I will play you a test strip." He crossed to where his coat hung and eased out a small tape recorder with a set of fine earphones. Through them, and clear above the breathing silence of the machine, I heard the real voice of Iolanthe saying softly, dreamily: "Worlds of memory, worlds of desire, echo will set them both on fire. Three two four, three two four. Answer me. Is there anyone in the room who has seen my, has anyone seen my, seen my . . . ? Darling, it could only have happened to us." It was a little unnerving—no, I'll go further. The reproduction was so beautiful that I was a bit blood-curdled by it. On the one hand it was all so remote, Athens, the Nube and all that. But I suddenly felt the wild pang of the Acropolis at dawn with that warm scented little body lying tangled in mine in a sort of holy ship-wreck; tasted those pious kisses. "Iolanthe!"

"Isn't it her to the life?"

"It's a funny way to put it, but it's true. I suppose you built up the vocal thing direct from Abel—I had quite a lot to work on."

"Yes, and her films, for example."

"The damnedest thing," I said, and for no known reason felt a disposition to laugh out loud. "Muscles powered by tiny photoelectric mnemonic cells."

"That's it, my boy." Marchant produced sheaves of boring-looking paper and drew out the circuits in very rough specification. "She has five zones of response; her power storage is a new kind of dry cell with a longish life, and is replaceable. We are weaving her from a selection of guts and nylons finer than any fisherman dreamed of, or any violinist for that matter. The hands are extraordinary—utterly beautiful; probably more so than the originals. She travels by the power of light, boyo, light-sensitized cells; becomes a trifle languid at twilight; and fades into sleep at any time you care to name. But of course she isn't done. It'll be weeks before it's all sewed into place and ready to walk down Regent Street."

"Soliciting, I suppose?"

"That is for you to decide."

"Why me?"

"Julian seems to think your word is law in these matters. Myself, I think he is playing a dangerous game—with your so-called sense of humor. But it's not my affair. I'm playing my part as best I can. But I realize now that I'm a mere interpreter of other men's ideas; you are the real scientist." It sounded pretty strange to me, put that way. I had always believed the direct opposite to be true. "But, Julian," I said, "is the real brains. None of us would be doing what we are doing had it not been for him." Marchant agreed, wiped his teeth in a napkin and replaced them tenderly. "We've photocopied the daily life of about twenty women to work out the range of situation responses for Iolanthe. It's really amazing how monotonous the ordinary range of movements, conversations, stock responses, can be. Even with the total range of thought we can conceivably stock her up with, it's perfectly adequate for most things that happen to most people. Response-provoking through sound and light. She will move about like some huge abstract dolly playing a perfect part in the world of our time."

"I'm getting to love her already," I said.

"Beware of Julian," said Marchant jokingly. "We've built her a set of sexual organs which . . . but I haven't done the detailed planning yet. Waiting for you to come in with new ideas. But the site of the temple is all there and the foundations of the thing are all sound."

"What temple?"

"Temple of pleasure. I'm too much of a puritan, I avert my face a bit from all that; and Julian supplies no sort of guidance as yet. But if we are to get her as perfect as a real person, we can't deprive her entirely of her sexual response, even if it's battery-driven."

It was all very well to joke, but inside I felt rather solemn and indeed a little uneasy. Marchant added an afterthought. "You'll find several old friends down at Toybrook—among them Said, the little one-eyed Christian Arab of your salad days who has been doing the most imaginative and intricate work on the light sensitization and the sound. The man who built your ear trumpet, remember?" Of course I did. An absolutely marvelous artisan in little; the firm was lucky to have such a master craftsman on hand.

"And the corpses will intrigue you, the real ones; it's funny how things tend to call up other things. Involuntarily, so to speak. Just when we were having the first troubles over anatomy and invoking the aid of the Royal College of Surgeons and so on, Julian was faced with another opening for the firm in Turkey: embalming! I know it sounds strange, and of course at first we laughed very much in an exasperated sort of way, because really we should have thought of it. It is the most ancient of all cultus ploys and we could have launched it years ago. Now, with the help of the two holy churches, East and West, we got everyone into a huddle and, basing ourselves on a profit-sharing scheme, with Rome and Byzantium we launched the whole thing with éclat. It was of course preceded with a bombardment of clerical propaganda from the pulpit, specially prepared sermons, telling you that it was wicked for you to leave your nearest and dearest to rot when you could embalm them and stick them on the hall hatstand as we used to stick wild boar or stags or whatnot. Also a very nice decoration to very old-fashioned pubs might be Mine Host resurrected in this fashion (if ever so slightly glazed) .

"Combined with this we got the avant-garde in Paris interested in it as a sort of beatnik curio with fascinating responses from all. They don't really want to live, the young. They want to be embalmed so that they can impress their friends. Moreover they are prepared to pay for automatic posthumous embalming as one pays for life insurance. The cult went off with a bang; we couldn't meet the demand. It seems to them, I suppose, the only future guarantee that they had actually been alive. And there's always the chance of lending out your mummy for that perfect party where everyone was so 'stoned.' In short we were in business. But . . . on the technological side we ran into trouble with the quality of the embalming.

"In Turkey they were using methods unchanged for hundreds of years. The result was a very friable effort which, if removed from the dry astringent desert air and moved into a more humid climate, deteriorated dreadfully. In fact rotted. Of course we moved 'Chemicals A' over on the job and we are still in the process of wrestling with the formulae for preservatives—it's more difficult than you can imagine. But while the embalmers were using our brains we were using their dead bodies, which can be played about with at will, in order to learn what we needed to know for Iolanthe. So you will find a rather strange Embalming Studio (so called) *chez nous*. It's very useful to us for checking; but they are training to conquer the whole Middle and Far East. Nature, beautiful are thy ways!"

"Do you mean to tell me you have been poking about in corpses with a notebook in one hand, Marchant?" By this time he was extremely drunk but not at all shaky; I mean one would have had to know him quite well to divine that he wasn't sober. Also he gave me a funny feeling of being a bit scared. Anyway he gave a great earwig chirp of laughter and said: "My dear chap, all that I know of the human anatomy is based on the dead. I could not play around with the living, and I'm no surgeon, as you know. But the dead have been of enormous help, specially while they are still fresh, while the motor responses are still working. The *rigor mortis* buggers them up from my point of view—at least on the suppleness and response factor. But it is most instructive and delightful to see them taken apart as clockwork is, bit by bit, and then pieced together into the sort of doll we are contemplating.

"In fact, one has to stop and ask oneself from time to time, 'Who is doing what, exactly?' I'm damned if I know. But anyway right next to us we have this vast Embalming Studio run by the Americans which provides us with models galore. Of course the American market was already very advanced when all this happened; Europe is terribly backward in some ways." We both cackled with the old-fashioned laughter which nowadays would merit a pistol fired through the skull. "But the Middle East," he said, "is going in for this with a vengeance, and Julian has already financed a couple of films based on the subject to orient public opinion toward the notion." He paused. "Always Julian," I said.

"I must go," he said, but he still sat on for a while, cupping his brandy in a warming hand and staring at me. Then he continued with remorse: "My God, I've done nothing but talk; I haven't asked you a thing, how you feel, how you are, whether you are keen to take this business on or not. . . .Forgive."

"I'm glad. I would have been incapable of answering any of your questions. I'm newly convalescent and very newly wed, if I dare to believe it, to a reupholstered ghost called Benedicta. I am just feeling my feet, as they say, but very uncertainly. But whatever the state of things, I'll come to Toybrook and look over the setup with you. Would you like Monday? I'll be there betimes if you think that it would suit?"

Marchant drank off his glass and rose. "Yes," he said. "Monday. I must let you hear a lecture by the top embalmer. You will hardly credit your senses. All good sense mind you. Ahem!"

I took the tube back, crushed in among my fellow countrymen who looked on the whole rather nice, after such a long absence from them. But it was like traveling in a parrot's cage; I was all but deafened when I finally crawled up the steps of Claridge's. I walked into the room and said: "Mark, Benedicta, Mark!" She jumped up, radiant. "Thank goodness you said that; I was thinking it. It's the sorest place of our many. So many thorns to be taken out of each other's paws, but Mark . . ." I sat down: "What brought it on was the discovery that the place where I am working is very near . . ."

"Yes. I see."

She lit a cigarette and marched up and down for a moment. "We must try and incorporate him, relive him a little bit inside ourselves. It's very selfish in a way, but I fear that if he goes on inside us like a suppurating thing, the memory of a bad act, then things will not grow right between us as they might. Mark still stands at the crossroads between you and me." She sat down thump in a chair and, still smoking furiously, gave a gulp which was as much rage and frustration as just tears of regret. I, too, could have beaten my head against a wall and yelled, but not being of that sort of minting I did damn all. I tried as hard as I could to yawn, look natural, that sort of thing. Tried to light a cigarette, burned my finger, got a fit of coughing. Went off to the lavatory to do a pee and swear quietly at the way things are arranged.

When I came back she was standing in the center of the room, very composed and with a fine haughty kind of determination in her eye. "We must go back to every place where we have been hurt, or where we have inflicted hurt on each other, and systematically exorcise the memory—what do you think of that?" I jumped at it. "But now," I said. "This very night." And she nodded. "Otherwise it will be no good."

It did not take long to raise a car and alert the housekeeper—nor truth to tell to drive down through the roads which were horribly empuddled and the countryside looking devilish sad. We didn't exchange a single word. I had organized a Thermos of coffee and some repellent ham sandwiches. The night was cold. It blew. I suppose the same sort of thing was going on in her—I mean for my part I was rehearsing the whole past of this period in that horrid garish mansion; it was less like a bad dream than an old abandoned tunnel into which one had fallen and been rescued. But now one had to go back and clear it of fallen debris. I thought too with a pang of Iolanthe's island cottage. Ghosts, they need meat too!

Benedicta drove while I fed her with cigarettes; drove in her brilliant fast vein as if anxious to reach the end of the journey as soon as possible. Long white headlight ribbons winding away over the hills, melting down long avenues littered with a detritus of autumn. Beauty and melancholy of the night country softening away toward winter and the white transforming snow. At last we came slowly, cracking down the long winding drive up to the house with its steely lake and horrid toffee-rose towers. O Coleridge where wert thou? A little bit slowed down perhaps by a temporary misgiving; everything hereabouts spelled Mark, spelled sickness, hag-drawn nights of sleeplessness, Nash, Julian, Abel, Bang. . . . I put my hand inside her velvet coat and touched her breast. "So," she said, "here we are, gentlemen of the jury, here we are."

I hammered on the door and rang the interminable bloody bell rope, while she turned the car and backed it up for shelter under an eave. For a long time nobody. Then the little old gnomish housekeeper came tottering down and tuttering about unaired beds and blown fuses. There was no electric light in the place, and despite all her telephoning she had not been able to get a man in to do the repair. Candles, then, a couple of big silver branches on the great marble table; perhaps more suitable in a way for visiting this great mausoleum of wasted hopes—in the sense of atrophy, I mean. Attrition. I saw her face rosy in the rosy light, so very grave and precious. (Julian had said: "Open your legs, I am going to kiss you," but instead he had shaken the candlesticks and the burning wax sprayed her unmercifully.)

The long desolate galleries grew awake and attentive as they watched us come walk, walking in this warm bubble of candleshine; watched us pass and then slipped back into the anonymity of darkness behind us. We went solemnly and without speaking, spending a moment at each of the stations of the cross in meditation. Like visiting the picture gallery of a lost life. Here we had married, here lain down in each other's arms in helpless silence, here quarreled, here shouted deafly at each other, here smoked and mused. Mark had slept here, wakened there, played further on. This death newly felt and revived vibrated on the heart like the concussion of some fearful drum.

Abel had gone—there was just a gaping hole in the musician's gallery; my toy of a pet of a monster of a brainstorm of a Thing. I was glad; it had integrated itself elsewhere, been melted down. Here for some reason she kissed me and wept a small tear. And so on through the tower bedrooms and thence down the great staircase to the larger of the two ballrooms. The mirrors had not been replaced, though the gunshot-splashed glass had been picked out to leave just the far gilded frames like so many reproaching frowns. Here the silence was immensely real silence, the air stagnant; there was no other resonance except ours in this place. Nobody had ever had a ball here, for a wedding or a birthday. Just she and I and a shotgun and the Lord's Prayer written on the mirrors with number three shot. The gun room too was now empty except for a few twelves such as cottagers might need to chase rooks out of a tree. But in the little fridge in the buttery, the thoughtful gnome had placed a bottle of champagne and two goblets as green as Venice. This too was appropriate.

We took it, tray and all, into the fake library with its tapestry of empty book covers; there was a fire laid in the grate which took no time at all to burst into bristling flame. I scouted out cushions from everywhere I could and built a huge Oriental divan reminiscent of Turkey in front of it. Here we sat, thinking each other's thoughts and sipping the green champagne, while the logs carved out their strange figures and stranger faces. Then of a sudden the telephone rang, which gave us both a tremendous start. We looked at each other in curiosity, touched with a certain consternation. Who knew we were there? Julian was in Divonne, gambling. It rang, and rang, beseeching and beseeching. I rose swearing, but she took my arm and said: "No. Just for once let it ring. Don't answer it, Felix, I implore you." I said: "Don't be superstitious, B." But she was adamant. "I just know we must not answer it." On it rang and on; I sat down again. We couldn't talk or think anymore for the noise of the damned instrument. Then it choked off. "Now we shall never know what it was, or who it was," I said with regret. But she sighed a great sigh of relief and said: "Thank goodness, no. Yet that one conversation might have made us change direction all over again —have put us back on a fatal course."

So we lay down at last and fell asleep by the warm fire, like hibernating squirrels, too drowsy to make love even. It must have been nearly dawn when I woke in the chill to revamp the fire and to scout out our coffee and sandwiches. Benedicta was yawning and combing her hair, quite refreshed. I went to test the water in a nearby bathroom but found no hot; boilers unstoked for ages, I suppose. Benedicta was saying: "There's that old cottage in the grounds which was revamped, do you recall? Why couldn't we live there for a while and acclimatize? I would like to live more alone with you. We could have a little boat on the lake. Felix, answer." But I was struck dumb by the brilliance of the idea. It was a very pleasant little wooden chalet, not too small; I had once started to build a studio in it. It had originally been built to keep a housekeeper in, but proved too far from the house. So there it was, yet another place lying empty. "If I remember right the sanitation and kitchen were done over."

"Brilliant. Let's go and see it."

This we did, cutting swathes of dew across the meadows. A tiny brook, a meadow, an abandoned mill. A small jetty for a boat. . . . How the devil had I never thought of it before? "Darling, you are speaking directly to the romantic bourgeois in my soul. The secret of a happy life is to reduce the scale of things, circumscribe them; a girl doesn't need to fill up more than the circumference of one's arms. I have never liked big women anyway." Yes, it was there, the cottage, but I had to force a kitchen window to get in. It was quite dry and warm because of all the timber, I suppose, and spotlessly clean. A pleasant studio looking out through a weeping willow onto the misty waters of the lake. "It's ideal." Was it too much to hope for a few happy years here without the nagging frontal brain intervening to muck everything up with its bloody hysterias? One hardly dared to formulate the sort of hopes it offered, this queer scroggy chalet, looking in a vague sort of way as if it had been influenced by Caradoc's Parthenon of Celebes.

"Don't you feel we should at least try here?" she said. "It hasn't the terrible gloom of the big house with all its memories—the horrid backlash of the past. But it's only across the meadow—we could go there from time to time like one goes to visit a friend in the cemetery." I said, "Yes."

With a certain amount of awe, though. What had poor Felix done to deserve all this? Invent Ejax by mistake?

"Yes. Agreed!"

You say you've never been to Toybrook," said Marchant with a certain happy condescension. "I can hardly believe it." No, I was sure I hadn't. "They were working on an obscure nerve gas and documented me once when I was doing Abel, but that is all I know. Central nervous system." He chuckled in a specious professorial way, like a don who is delighted to take you to lunch at the Athenaeum because you aren't a member. He settled the car rug round him and fiddled with the heating—I detected indications of old age and badly lagged pipes. The afternoon was mild and clammy. "As a matter of fact," he said, "I opened this morning's paper and got quite a start. I thought I was looking at Toybrook, but in fact what I was looking at . . ." He fumbled among his cases and bundles and produced a paper which he opened and spread before me, stabbing with a lean nicotined finger. The caption was one word, a familiar one: Belsen! We laughed very heartily about this—a long terrain of old-fashioned potting sheds with the two funnels, like a liner or a soap factory. All indistinct and furry.

"Come," I said, "didn't Caradoc build it? It can't be less than a Parthenon of some sort in that case."

"It's very beautiful," he admitted, sitting back and settling the rug around him, "really very beautiful. And also marvelous from our own point of view. There are no labs like it in Europe, nowhere. The nearest comparison is Germany, but even then I think we have the edge on them. No, Toybrook is quite something. Sounds like an invention of Enid Blyton, doesn't it? Do you know those children's books of her?"

"Of course. I read them in the tube."

"Then?"

"Well, I'm curious to see what you've got and to find out where you want to go." Marchant looked at me curiously, humorously. He said: "We want to get as real as we can." Silence. "You mean fundamentally you want to give yourself the illusion of actually controlling reality? How real can one conceive, I mean?" Marchant gave a chuckle. "Felix, Felix," he said reprovingly, putting his hand on my knee. "The old weakness is peeping out. You want to intrude metaphysical considerations into empirical science. It's no go. You are tapping on a door which does not exist. The wall is solid."

"It's quite a consideration if the things you make get up off the operating table and start being MORE real than you? You will surely be forced to reassess your . . . dirty word . . . culture?" Marchant shook his head vigorously. "We must move step by step, not in your quanta-like jumps—you can do nothing scientifically if you get the typical clusters; it's like seizing up your engine by over-heating, hence the Paulhaus." I watched the wonderful Socialist country rolling by with all its marvelous advertising. "Ejax makes a man of you." Why not a woman, I wondered? It damn soon would. Hair down to the waist and a costume from Napoleon's Grande Armée. Perhaps there was a future for poor Felix in all this?

"*Bon,*" he said, with a growing sense of familiarity. It was not simply the firm—it was the particular smell of self-satisfaction it unleashed. "And Julian?" I said. Once more Marchant gave a small earwig chuckle. "Gambling," he said, "all the time. But now he has started losing and this is not in nature—at least not in his. I love Julian, you know, now that I have really got to know him. He is humility itself—humble as the Pope. Self-effacing. Tender. Felix, what a man!"

"What a man," I echoed piously, and indeed the funny thing was that I felt it; I felt a strange sort of reverence for this . . . mummy. I don't know if that is the right word. But to have so much understanding of humanity as Julian had and to manage to live apart, to play no direct part in its strange or deformed operations—why really it was something to doff the hat to. "All that Planck stuff is fruitful from a theoretically viable point of view; but from our point of view it is a matter of scale, in our empirical test-tube business the three dimensions are all one can cope with." He was pursuing the argument like a sort of granny. He cleared his throat while I lit a cigarette. "Our only problem down in Toybrook is a simple one; namely does it work ninety-nine times out of a hundred? If it does it is real." I coughed slightly and scanned off the scenery a bit. We were traveling mighty fast with a chauffeur who, for all I knew, might have been a dummy invented by Marchant. Then I said: "And the hundredth? Is there no room in your system for the miracle? That trifling shift of temperature or wrong mixture of chemical salts . . . it's so easy to go wrong. What exactly would be the miracle for you, Marchant?" Chuckle. "Well," he said, "something like Iolanthe. She can for the moment be exactly controlled. Or so we hope. So we hope."

But reassuringly enough Toybrook was not in the least like Belsen—quite the contrary, despite the two stout brick towers exuding a lick of white smoke from the ovens in the experimental section. Toybrook was laid out with great dignity in two long complexes enfilading a piece of wild woodland, so that there was no laboratory or theater without its fine green view. Moreover in the woodland there were several families of wild stags which appeared and disappeared dramatically among the trees, mating and battling in full view of the scientists; sometimes even coming shyly down to put a wet muzzle on the plate glass of the aquarium-like laboratories. It was both elegant and very peaceful—the chemists' studios with their long rows of microscopes glinting, their scales and pulleys and grapnels. A long pendulum hung slowly swinging in the hall. They had everything, these boys, even a wind tunnel and a cyclotron. Marchant was in high good humor as he showed me round, stopping here or there to present me to a colleague. Thence to the elegant theater where the progress reports were read and recorded audio-visually for whatever posterity a scientist might believe in or hope for.

In the darkness Marchant flicked a couple of switches and a bald man appeared on close-circuit image. "That is old Hariot," he said, while the celebrated man read haltingly against a blackboard upon which someone had written in violet chalk: "Does perhaps the rate of blood sedimentation dictate the oxygen intake?" A vexing question, I should have thought. Anyway Hariot went on: "As you know, oxygen pushes carbon dioxide out of the blood and vice versa; as far as the circulation is concerned, about five liters of blood a minute are pumped by the heart of an ordinary resting adult. The distribution is not uniform; I mean that brain and kidneys get disproportionately large amounts compared to their relative size. As far as the brain is concerned, a decrease of ten percent oxygen will give the first signs of confusion; decrease it by twenty percent and you get the equivalent of four or five strong cocktails, say; around forty percent you would expect to get coma. If the total supply is cut you get unconsciousness in a few seconds; and after four to five minutes the damage to the brain may be irreversible."

I said: "I suppose you had to mug all this stuff up for your dollies?" And Marchant nodded as he faded down on Hariot and came up with an image of rubber hands occupying the whole screen, poking about in the entrails of something or someone. However it was Hariot's flat voice again which continued the exposition with: "From the umbilical cord of twenty-five newborn children an appropriate test length was clamped before first cry; blood samples were drawn anaerobically with special all-glass syringes from the umbilical vein and umbilical arteries. Coagulation and glycolysis were inhibited by heparin and potassium oxalate and sodium fluoride. . . ." Marchant chuckled approvingly. "You can call for any damn thing under the sun," he said, consulting a panel of data. Other images wallowed up, once more of rubber fingers moving about in a uterus as if performing some obscure rite of divination. "This particular demonstration monkey was merely anesthetized, its abdomen opened and copious amounts of Bouin's fixative solution poured into it, over and around the uterus *in situ*. At the end of three to seven minutes all uterine ligaments with their contained blood vessels were clamped and the specimen removed. . . ."

"Ugh," I said. "I think I must be getting home to the wife and kids if this goes on." He laughed and tried another lucky dip on the dial to produce this time a strange surrealist picture of three men in white coats gathered round a seal which had been lashed firmly to a board and suspended above a water tank. The poor animal was terrified and struggled with all its might, rolling bloodshot eyes and moaning through its long silky moustaches. One of the men was holding a stethoscope to its body and saying something grave about lactic acid levels. Then the pulley swung and down the whole contraption fell out of sight. Crank!

"Enough," said Marchant. "It was only to give you an idea of the data-processing side of the thing."

In the mathematical section there were a hundred small hanging mobiles gyrating slowly in the sluggish air of the studios; a tiny planetarium, mock earth, and God only knows what else. To Marchant's annoyance however the experimental embalmers had taken the day off and locked up the studio. "It's most vexatious," he said. "They have probably gone up to town for more dead. It isn't all that easy to get them, and one cannot run a Burke and Hare body-snatching organization from such a respectable address as this." Why not, I wondered, surely old Julian could provide? (Cut out the flippancy, Charlock.) At any rate there was nothing for it now but to proceed to business and visit his own section, which would later become mine as well. It had no name as yet, just Experimental Studio B.

He had doubtless been keeping this special treat for the last, deeming it the most exciting, which of course it was. He unlocked two sets of doors and locked them again behind us with a stealthy gesture that reminded me of the Rackstraw ward in the Paulhaus. A high, bright, airy studio almost as tall as a hangar for cub aircraft came to light; white silk curtains moved softly in the breeze. Silence!

The bed she lay in was a long white surgeon's operating table with gleaming leverage members in tubular steel. She lay so still, like the experimental aircraft she was, so to speak (still on the secret list) : covered completely in a sheet of soft parachute silk, which stretched down to the floor on both sides. But her silhouette gave the illusion of completeness—a whole, undismembered body of a corpse, woman, doll or whatever. "You said she was still in bits," I said and Marchant tittered with pleasure. "They are not completely joined up as yet for action, but I want to give you the illusion of how she's going to be by showing her to you bit by bit, so you don't see the joins. The power isn't in yet, but I get some traction off another unit which enables us to check the whole flexion patterns of our fine plastic musculature. I plug her into a g-circuit." He performed some obscure evolutions in the corner, switched on powerful theater lights above the body, and beckoned me over with a shy grin, lifting as he did so the corner of the silk to reveal the face. It was extraordinary to find myself gazing down upon the dead face of Iolanthe—so truthful a copy of the reality that I started with surprise even though I had been expecting something like this. But what really took me away was the perfection of that fresh and dewy skin. "Feel it," said Marchant. I put my finger to her cheek; "She's warm." Marchant laughed; "Of course she is, she's breathing, look now." The lips parted softly and a tiny furrow of preoccupation appeared on the serene brow. In her dream some small perplexity had surfaced here. It was skin, though, it was human flesh. Here she was, simply lying anesthetized upon an operating table. "Iolanthe!" I whispered and the lips parted as if to answer me, but she said nothing. Marchant watched my confused excitement with a happy air of complacence. "Whisper again and she will wake," he said, and in an incoherent, uncomprehending sort of way I said: "Darling, wake up, it's Felix." For a

[145]

moment nothing, and then the whole face seemed to draw a waking breath. The lids fluttered and very slowly opened. "Damn," said Marchant. "Said has taken out the eyes again for restitching. I forgot, sorry." But I was staring entranced through the eye sockets of the model into her skull with its intricate nest of coils and wires in different-colored threads, finer than the finest cotton. Marchant passed his palm over the eyelids to close them, as one does with the dead; I felt rather sick in an elated sort of way. "The eyes are over there," he said, indicating a small white glass bowl in which the eyes of the goddess floated in some sort of mucus—gum arabic? They lay there like oysters—unrecognizable now as the most famous eyes in the world, simply because they were detached from context.

Ah, Osiris, we must gather up the loaves and fishes; O Humpty-Dumpty, we must put you together again. But Marchant was irritated by this trifling misadventure and drew the sheet back over the face. He went on to a demonstration of the thigh and ankle flexion—a perfect beautiful leg was revealed, of positively Botticellian elegance, and again warm, palpably real, a breathing leg so to speak. "Of course most of the fun has been in playing with the surfaces, the decoration, since we were ordered to reproduce from a known model. But her skin, boy, is just as beautiful as the real stuff and rather longer lasting. I must say that nylon pencil you invented has been a godsend." So I had invented a nylon pencil—what the devil can that have been? "Once again you've forgotten," he said. "It was just a hint you threw out once which we took up. My dear boy, look." He took a fine scalpel and cut a long incision in the thigh, spreading the wound with a clamp. No blood, of course, nor sawdust as in an old-fashioned golliwog but a beautifully coiled nest of vivid plastic cones and wires, packed tight as caviar. "Now look," he says and takes a thick metal pencil which he draws along the lips of the wound. It closes instantly, leaving no trace of the gash in the warm thigh. "For running repairs—what would we have done without it? So swift, so easy. You can open it, her, up anywhere in an instant and reseal the wound. Good old Felix," he added with an incandescent admiration.

"Good old Felix," I echoed. We know not what we do, Bolsover, we know not what we do. I sank into an armchair and began to smoke like Vesuvius. "Mother of God, Marchant, what a treat she is. Will you give me the specifications, please?"

"Of course," he said, rubbing his hands. "I don't think there will be much you don't understand; most of the data comes from your old scrying board—only of course very much reduced and in finer-web materials." I shook my head doubtfully. I had never worked on this scale before—through a jeweler's eyepiece or a microscope, so to speak. I stared into the mental sky of science and muttered, *"E pur si muove."* That was the damnedest thing of all. Marchant stared at me with schoolboy glee and said: "Yes, you can't put your telescope to your blind eye on this lot; we are getting as near as dammit to the target objective."

He was acclimatized, I could see; but despite all he had told me about the project I found this experience to be quite a shock. Nor was it all. "Come and look," he said, "at the vagina, the real treasure." He made some artful disposition of the shroud and revealed the downy sex of Iolanthe. "Stick your finger in there and feel—a self-lubricating mucous surface imitated to the life." I felt an awful cringe of misgiving as I did so, albeit reluctantly. He cackled happily and slapped my back. "You don't like it, do you? It seems an intolerable affront to her privacy and her beauty? I know, I know. I couldn't do it for weeks, she had become so real to me. But I had to. I had to take myself in hand and remind myself that I was a scientist after all—a man rather than a mouse." I felt shaken by a sort of remorse; it was silly to feel like this about the private parts of a dummy. Yet, so deeply buried are these motor complexes derived from the education of the tribe, that they come to the surface in quite involuntary fashion. Poor Iolanthe, lying there asleep and in pieces, to be fingered over by mousemen! I felt as if I had insulted her dignity. Marchant knew perfectly well the feeling. He had already felt that way himself, and steeled himself against it. I mopped my brow and thanked him. "But why does Julian want this sort of thing copied?" I asked in an outraged and aggrieved fashion. "Does he expect them to reproduce?" Marchant shrugged. "I don't know; they won't ever be anything but simulacra of fertility. Not only that, they can neither eat nor excrete. But he won't say what he has in mind. What will she do for an *état civil*, my lad? No good asking me." He burst into a small cackle of helpless laughter and sat down in a chair to wipe his spectacles. "Phew!" I said.

The dossier on the figure was almost as thick as the Bible, though rather more intelligible for someone of my outlook. I riffled it and put it in my briefcase abruptly. I had a sudden feeling that I wanted to go away and be alone with myself, with my brief, with my dossier—and singularly enough with Benedicta. Marchant seemed a little disappointed that I had nothing much more to say at this stage. He eyed me keenly and said, "You are in on this thing, Felix, aren't you?" I smiled and nodded. "You aren't," he went on, "going to let theoretical considerations intrude on the work, are you?" It was as if he were pleading for Iolanthe's life—the life of that marvelous mummy lying so silently under her silken shroud of gray. "No," I said. "I'm in it all right."

He heaved a sigh of relief, as we went out to the car. I was to be driven home and dropped—the great *déménagement* to the cottage from Claridge's was only a day or so old. But I was glad when the chauffeur produced an afternoon paper for Marchant as it kept him busy, inveterate punter that he was. A headline said MOBS SOB AS DALI LAYS EGG. Good. Good. "I want to watch when you replace the eyes, remember." But I was thinking to myself about memory—is everything recorded in it from the first birth cry to the death rattle? Why not? Or does it simply wear out like an old disc? In Abel's system the sound unit, the πòγον, gave you a clue to the basic predispositions of character which was then modified by experiences, environment, etc. . . . Yes, that side of the thing was all right. "My God, it's begun to snow," said Marchant, and so it had; the sky fell out of its frame, turned into a great flocculent pane of melting confetti and came down over us, locking up visibility; we nosed down the country roads between spectral hedges and sculptured gateposts—griffins in wigs on the front gates of Drue Manor. Plastic elves in white cauls on the lawns of suburban houses. Ah, to be a quiet man, living sagely with a little plastic wife, following out the serpentine meanderings of my inner self . . . why hasn't God made me a quietist? *Nigaud, va.*

I made them keep the headlights on to enable me to grope my way across the meadow and skirt the disappeared lake; it was all crackly underfoot. When I looked round, the snow had swallowed them up. Like a blind man I clutched my way up the steps of the chalet and at last found the latch. Ah, the warmth inside, the blazing fire of thorn and oak, the smells, and Benedicta pajama-clad, asleep before the fire with Osmosis the cat on her stomach. "One side of your face is all burning, bottom as well," I said. "Better turn over." But she preferred to wake. "Caradoc has been ringing you this afternoon. He seemed to be rather drunk. I told him to record himself and go to hell, which he duly did." But either he had been more than just drunk or else his sound track had got itself mixed with other stuff for it was a mighty incoherent display of temperament beginning with a poem of which I could only make out the lines:

> *Fornication's pedaled jam*
> *Which has brought me where I am*

[149]

and ending with a request for a Christmas box of fifty pounds. "I am at the Metrofat Hotel in Brighton with a young lady who is all warm breast of Christmas Turkey; greetings of the season to one and all. Did you see my little thing in *The Times*? '*Grand génie, légèrement bombé mais valide, cherche organiste.*' Had no replies yet."

"Well," I said, "he sounds all right." I poured a drink and resumed my inward brooding on Iolanthe. I told Benedicta a bit about the marvels of the dummy—it, her?—and how it had given me quite a turn to see the faithfulness of the copy. She looked at me curiously, seriously, and said nothing. "I wonder if I could raise Julian!" I said. "I would like to have a talk with him about her. He hasn't seen her as yet himself. I wonder if he knows what's in store if she really works down to the last rivet."

"Try the Casino in Divonne. Anyway he always leaves his number wherever he goes."

The night switchboard at Merlin's took not much more than half an hour to trace him. That characteristic voice, full of the illustrious melancholy of a dispossessed potentate. . . . "What is it, Julian—you sound so sad?" He sighed ruefully. "Yes. I am losing so heavily. It gets more and more mysterious. I wonder what I have done to shift the axis, so to speak, of my luck? It was always in perfect working order. I lost at Divonne and am continuing to lose down here in Nice, where it is snowing if you please." He paused and in the background I could hear the yelping of croupiers. "Consult Nash," I said and he sighed again. "It would be useless. He could tell me why I played, but not why after always winning I have started losing—why the bunghole has dropped out my luck. I have done every-thing, changed my game more than once. Damn it all."

There was another long pause; of course Julian had always been of a melancholy and introspective cast of mind, but he had never given himself, his views, so freely to anyone. "It's your fault for taking Abel apart," I said. "He might have suggested an answer." You can't hear a smile on the telephone but I did—a world-weary sad smile. "It was another gamble. I had to try to suck you dry in case you never came back, to ensure the perpetuity of the firm!" A fine light irony played about the phrase. "Like Rackstraw," I said and he nodded invisibly. "The vulture always waits," said Julian. I heard the puff puff of his cigar. I stayed silent, feeling that perhaps there was something he wanted to get off his chest before listening to whatever I myself wanted to say to him. But he said nothing, and an operator asked if we were still talking: actually we were. All his loneliness and despondency were leaking down the wire like a low-tension current: also a certain anxiety. I felt he was glad to have even this mechanical contact with someone.

"Felix," he said hesitantly, as if he were feeling slowly, blindly along the Hippolyta-thread of an idea he wanted to express. "How lucky you are not to be a gambler. We constitute a different tribe, you now, belong to a different totem. I realized tonight that I am only really at home in a casino; I really have no *foyer,* no hearth of my own, except here. When I go from here I don't go anywhere in particular. A hotel isn't a home; and my so-called home is only a hotel. Now be a good boy, don't quote Freud. The matter is much more fundamental than that."

Pause for breath. "When you see all these pale, exhausted faces in the light of dawn, after their fruitless love affair with the wheel or the dice or the pack: this sterile love affair, because even the winners express a haggard lost feeling—why, you realize that masturbation isn't the real clue. The gambler is really dicing with death, as the popular saying goes. Just as all dancers are simply persuaders to the act, so gambling is a sort of questioning, an act of divination. How weary of it we all are, yet it is the only situation which enables us to feel vicariously alive, this side of death."

I said nothing; the sorrow in his voice was absolutely overwhelming. He went on very slowly, like an exhausted climber reaching for handholds, languid for lack of oxygen. "But then what is the question that the gambler put to himself by the act of gambling? What does he hope that the dice will tell him? Well, think of the strange symbolic pilgrimage he is forced to make to the casino when he can find one—as characteristic as that made by other men to a brothel. He enters, reveals his identity by producing a passport or other document; he fills in a *carte d'admission*. Then he passes in front of the *'physionomiste,'* a 'scanner' who subjects his face, hands and body to a close scrutiny. This is as intensive as a police check, though he does not touch you. My various faces must be on record somewhere in somebody's mind. A scar, a tattoo mark, a blemish—that is what they look for, this race of 'scanners.'

"Once past this barrier he is admitted to the temple of the supreme Game which he craves; and here everything speaks to him of the past, of a vanished epoch. An old-fashioned anachronistic décor, whole surfaces of dusty unspringing carpets, such as one would find only in abandoned Edwardian hotels or in late spa hotels at Vichy, Pau, Baden. The fuzzy chandeliers, broken-down *salons de luxe* festering away in their desuetude. Even the costumes of the croupiers and often the gambler's own partake of this strange out-of-dateness. It is as if everything had become stuck fast like an atrophied limb—death in aspic. The formulae too are all part of this strange marvelous stereotype, as superannuated as a half-forgotten liturgy. It smells like a page or two of Huysmans. Yes, but all this is deliberate; this atmosphere is anxiously preserved, conserved, watched over. And the premises themselves should if possible smell airless and ever so slightly dusty. You do not want fresh air in a casino. The ritual forbids it. The air must rest, tideless, scentless, and only just breathable. The gambler feels at home then like a fish in water of the right temperature. His nostrils breathe this warm welcoming balsam. He knows what he *must* do, he simply *must*."

In this slow near-soliloquy I felt once more all the

rancor and despair of his inner loneliness welling up in him—though why for the first time he should choose to allow me to be a party to it I could not tell. Somewhere a bell rang and voices buzzed to the tune of the big wheel. Julian appeared to be listening to it all with half an ear even as he was talking to me. So much of it I remembered myself, too, from my one brief flirtation with the law of probability—is there such a thing? Poking the cat with my foot I shared Julian's curious muse in silence for a moment.

Yes, he was right: the weight of the ritual, the entering, the form-filling. . . . Then the decision between *les Salles Privées* and the *cuisine.* . . . On which front to attack the demon of hazard, he whom Poincaré called "the real mathematician of genius"? Ah, those long interior debates on the thirty-seven slots in the wheel (alchemy?) , eighteen red and eighteen black with the somehow inevitable white zero. A sort of Tarot of probability instead of a calculus . . . (perhaps Abel?) . But behind the silence of Julian I heard a voice calling, as if from a cloud, *"Vingt-et-un rouge, impair et passe."* And I saw the lean face of the arbiter, the *chef de partie,* sitting up there on his throne, his baby chair, overlooking the celestial game, impervious to human feelings of gain or loss, a sort of God. And then I thought, too, of all the gambler's fevers and follies. In that expensive and beautifully cut suit of his, in the breast pocket, he carried a typical talisman, a rabbit's paw.

"Change your talisman," I said. "Why not get a fox's paw, or the dried paw of a great lizard, or a human hand?"

"Fatal," he replied dryly. "You know it."

Julian was a heavy staker in the *Salles Privées* and richly merited the French slang word for the breed, *flambeur,* inflamer: the flame of pure desire, the mathematical desire to *know.* Not to *be,* but to *know.* And of course he had always won. The croupiers had always passed him his mound of golden ordure which for him symbolized so much more than a unit of value. Negligently but voluptuously he must have fingered it always, before throwing it back into the melting pot—for only with gold can one make gold, whatever the wizards may tell you. I remembered too that when numbers run in a series they are said in gambler's slang to be *en chaleur*, on heat.

"None of this can have anything to do with what you wanted to talk to me about," he said, "and I apologize. I was in rather a reflective mood this evening. What did you want to tell me about, Felix?"

"Iolanthe. I went to see her with Marchant today, and I'm still a little groggy with surprise. It is the most astonishingly lifelike thing I've ever seen. And if everything he tells me is true it will be rather unique. But I haven't read the specifications in detail yet. I'll do that this week. But there were one or two things which struck me about her, it."

"I'm delighted that you are excited," he said, and sounded almost moved himself. "But," I went on, "I felt that I wanted to go over some of the points with you in case we hadn't fully understood your idea—I suppose, for example, the male will be much the same?"

"Same what?"

"Fair without, false within. I mean I found myself wondering why we were copying the outside with such fidelity when the inside is an artificially arranged thing with simply a stress, strain, flexion index."

"It's not entirely true—what about the brain box?"

"But they will never eat, excrete or fornicate. . . ."

"We are perhaps asking for too much at this stage. Let's go step by step. I wasn't hoping for reality so much as for the perfect illusion which is probably more real than reality itself is for most people; hence my choice of the screen-star symbol. As for fornicating, I suppose they can go through the motions, though it will be without result, sterile; but they *will* try to illustrate an aesthetic of Beauty, which is always in the eye of the beholder as 'The Duchess' tells us. Eh?"

"Eunuchs!"

"If you wish; but did Aphrodite eat and excrete? I am not enough of a classical scholar to quibble about it. After all these are only serious toys, Felix, *serious toys*."

"But Marchant insists they are so perfectly adapted from the point of view of responses that they could, according to him, be turned loose in the real world without danger of being discovered for what they are."

"Why not, Felix? They will probably be more real than most of the people we know. But of course I have no intention of setting them free; first of all, Iolanthe's face is world-famous. We mustn't run the risk of their getting damaged. No, I thought of them living in seclusion quietly somewhere where we could work-study them; they are far the most advanced things of their kind, after all?"

"Hum. And who will the male doll be based on; we only have legs and the outline of a pelvis as yet. Eh?"

He yawned briefly and then went on in the same even tone. "You can guess how much I would have liked to aspire to the role myself—but it would be too Pharaonic, a sort of embalmer's picnic. So I have stepped down in favor of Rackstraw."

"Rackstraw?"

"We will confer a vicarious immortality on him; he will end as a museum piece in some colony of waxworks. But of course I mean Rackstraw as he was once, not as he is now. Once again, we have all the information we need about him. Any objections?"

"No. But the whole thing seems bizarre."

"In one sense I suppose it is; but then Felix, it's only a gambler's idea. I remember you once insisting that habit grooves the sensibility, that even movements repeated endlessly generate comprehension, just as an engine generates traction, or sticks rubbed together, fire. What I wonder is this: will perhaps this creature of human habits one day, simply by acting as a human being, REALIZE she is a dummy?" The capital word was practically hissed into the telephone. "As much, I mean, as the original realized she was Iolanthe? It's a gamble, and like all prototypes our models may prove too clumsy for us to practise divination on or by them. But then if one does not live on hopes in this life what else is there to live on?"

"I see."

"Good night, Felix," he said. "Wish me a run of luck will you? I am in mortal need of it."

The line went dead. I sat for a long moment before hanging up from my end. Benedicta was laying out our dinner before the fire, ladling out soup into the bright earthenware pots which looked Italian. I was in a state of unusual and rather violent excitement—though I honestly don't know why. Of course in part it was all the implications of this extraordinary project; but I had seen others, far more theoretical, where the issues were much more in doubt. And of course, with one half of my mind, I could not help thinking of it as a bit infantile. Was it though? At any rate, whatever the cause, I ate in very perfunctory fashion while I dipped here and there into my brief—the dossier. . . . It was all as beautifully and methodically laid out as the specifications for a new aircraft. The only question was: would it fly, how would it handle, etc. etc.?

"Benedicta," I said, "I must go out for a walk. I simply must." She looked at me with surprise. "In this weather? It would be foolhardy, Felix." But I was already groping for a heavy sweater and the stout ski gear I had acquired in Switzerland. Seeing I was serious she sprang up at once and joined me. "I'm coming with you; I am not going to risk letting you fall into the lake or break your head against a tree. It's all too new this, Felix, to be risked." I felt a bit of a swine, but was really extremely glad to have her beside me as a sort of thinking generator. It had stopped snowing, everything was hushed back into whiteness—apocalyptic flocks of solid cumulus which had filled out the world and blotted out the edges of things. No moon, but an infinity of white radiance which turned the sky into an upturned inkwell. We found a stout storm lantern in the kitchen for want of a torch, and let ourselves off the dry balcony as gingerly as swimmers entering the sea splashlessly. The forest had still some edges left which were a help in judging our general direction—as if someone had spilled India ink over a lace shawl. Within a few yards we divined rather than felt that we were upon the ice of the frozen lake. The snow was so dry it screeched underfoot. Somewhere in the sky wild geese cranked out to one another.

We made our way slowly across the lake to the little island in the center, now piled up like a wedding cake of whiteness. At the far end of the lake itself a solitary figure, a gamekeeper, moved about in the grayness, absorbed in a task which could only be gradually identified as we approached him. With a crowbar and hammer he was knocking holes in the ice and pushing something down them—to feed fish perhaps? We called out a greeting but he was completely absorbed and did not hear us. We skirted the little islet—and gained the further shore, lengthening our stride at the feel of terra firma. "Science is only half the apple," I told myself aloud, "just as Eve is only half Adam." Blundering along thus the mechanized philosopher could hardly help falling over the odd tree trunk, or banging his head on a branch or two. But gradually we became accustomed to the light and were able to move about with as much certainty as one might have done by day.

A distinct violet shimmer in the light where it caressed the shoulders of the little hills. On a branch one old and perished-with-cold-looking owl, fluffed out in his mink like some run-down actor. (The margin of error in the case of such a talking mummy was, of course, enormous.) "There is little that I can guarantee about her once she is buttoned up and launched. I can't even say for certain that she will be good, for example, or bad; only that she is more likely to be clever than stupid." So we struggled on down the avenues of shrouded elms, along the firebrakes which once we used to ride down, and over the frozen gudgeon. Gradually the warmth came to our bodies despite wet boots and wetter trouser bottoms. Sometimes she looked at me for a moment without speaking. So we passed the little crooked pub called The Faun which was locked and barred at this hour; a bedroom window glowed like a jewel. Our boots rang musically on the frozen tarmac of the road as we traversed the hamlet. Then from one of the dark barnlike houses we were surprised to see a deep red flame spring up, and spit out a great gush of brilliant sparks; it spurted and subsided, spurted and subsided, and we heard the massy ring of the blacksmith's hammer on the anvil, and the wheeze of his bellows. In the shadow of his smithy, bobbing his shadow about on the roof, moved the huge creature, stripped to the waist and sweating profusely. We stood to watch him for a moment but he worked on methodically without giving us a glance. Perhaps he did not even know we were there.

On we went, up into the white night, and it was only when we reached the old crown of Chorley with the famous "view" from its summit that Benedicta said: "By the way, I meant to tell you before. I have completely surrendered, made away, all my share in the firm. I now own nothing but what I stand up in, so to speak. I am a public charge. All that stands between me and starvation is your salary. Do you mind?"

We stood up there gazing at each other, smiling—like a couple of explorers on an ice floe, oblivious of everything but the extraordinary pleasure we were deriving from the new sensation of harmony, of comprehension and trust. "How marvelous," I said. "Is that what Julian meant about you having betrayed him?" Benedicta nodded: "Only partly, though. He was also thinking of the young German baron; I was supposed to make him sign on the firm's strength, but I did the opposite and the firm didn't get him. It was the first time I had deliberately set my face against Julian—he didn't like it; but so long as he needs you he can do nothing."

"O! O! O!" Marchant was humming under his breath as he worked on Iolanthe. "You great big beautiful doll! I'm so very glad I found you. Let me get my arms around you." A low current was discharging itself through her throat and she stirred slightly in her sleep, turning her head from side to side, then yawning and smiling. Marchant still adhered to his superstitious convention of keeping her covered while she was in pieces; so that we were working on different sections at the same time. We would see her whole, so to speak, only when she came to be launched; by that decisive stage it would be hard to make rectifications without totally dismantling the power box with all its hair-fine infratopes—it would be as if we were forced to begin again at the beginning. God knows how long she had cost already, probably years of amazingly detailed work. I had a great reunion with Said, who was very smart in hefty British tweeds and who had assumed the habits and the dignity of the uniform with his usual equanimity. It was good to feel that all that infinite patience and delicacy were really making their mark on a world which could reward him as I had never been able to when I began work with him in the Greek capital.

"Now," said Marchant, "try her for kisses, Felix, just in case she ever needs one, or feels that way. Eh?" He gave her a scientific kiss on the lips and pronounced himself satisfied by their marvelous springiness, better than the real thing. "And the mucus imitation is wonderful—like fresh dew. And look!" Iolanthe sighed and pouted like a child in her sleep, seeking another kiss. Adorable! "Your turn," he said, so I tried her out. "I say, this is wildly exciting," I said. "It's so damned . . . well!" Marchant burst out laughing. "Art imitating nature," he said. "But what about this?—come over here. I just geared up Adam's penis yesterday for a simulated orgasm. Man, it's perfect.

Shades of my prep school!" On another table he uncovered, with a proprietorial air, the thigh and pelvis
arrangement of the male dummy. "Now watch," he said
and began to rub the penis, which rose strongly, darkening
as it became tumescent, to discharge its mock semen.
"Talk about Ejax," said Marchant in high delight, wiping
his hands on a towel. "Once again, it's a much heavier
orgasm than Dad was ever able to manage. We could
perhaps rent him out, Felix, and make a little dough. Why
shouldn't somebody love him a little, bring a little light
into his male life, eh? He should have as much chance as
you or I?" Gutta-percha, plastic, rubber, nylon . . .

"And to have done away with those two time-wasting
and boring activities, eating and excreting, surely they will
be grateful to us for having done it." I scratched my head.
"Suppose she becomes too inhibited by half—I mean what
does she do at mealtimes?" Marchant replied tartly: "Exactly what any other actress does—takes out a cigarette and
says, 'Darling, I think I'll just have a glass of water.' She
will go through all the motions without actually eating.
She is not forbidden tobacco, by the way. My dear chap,
she is fully fashioned, this girl. Easy to be with, easy to
love. . . ." He was humming again, in high good humor.
What a strange thing the human body is—I was feeling
that warm hand with its lazy fingers moving slightly under
mine. Strange foliage of toes and fingers, elaborate patterning of muscle, striped and streaky.

So the great work moved slowly forward toward launching day; it was arranged that Iolanthe should imagine
herself to be waking in hospital after an operation, recovering from the anesthetic. Once dressed she would be
moved into a small villa which had been furnished for her
with her own possessions—Julian had acquired them all,
furs, and ball gowns, and shoes and wigs. In other words, to
give her reaction index and memory a chance to function
normally, we would provide ideal test-conditions in ideal
surroundings. All around her would be the familiar furni-

ture of her "real" life—her books and folios of film photos, her cherished watercolors by famous artists (careful investment: all film stars buy Braque) . . . . There would, then, on the purely superficial plane, be very little to distinguish between Iolanthe dead and Iolanthe living. Except of course . . . The dummy would be living the "real" life of the screen goddess.

But if we were working, so was Julian in his tortuous way; he had returned from his gambling bender both poorer and richer—for the fever had left him abruptly as it so often did for months at a time. It was like an underground river this illness, appearing and disappearing, now aboveground now below—never constant. But he spent long evenings now in the little projection theater he had built for himself, playing through the films of Iolanthe in a quiet deliberate muse; beside him sat Rackstraw mumbling and nodding with flickering attention, and on the other side the strange graven image which was Mrs. Henniker. There they sat, the three of them, fixed by the silver dazzle into silhouettes of hungry attention. Mrs. Henniker was going to take up her old post as companion-secretary to Iolanthe as soon as she "awoke." As for Rackstraw, there was little enough to be squeezed out of him. At times he seemed to have glimmers of recognition, but then his attention would slip, and he would mumble incoherently before subsiding into sleep, the softly nodding drowse of old age. Yet in some way, and for some particular purpose, Julian held this group together for a whole winter—though really I could not understand for what reason. At least, Henniker had a role to play, but what about Rackstraw? Julian must clearly have had something fairly clear in mind which prompted these sudden periods of self-dedication to what might have seemed a futile activity. There was also in the case of Julian a curious intermittent play, an alternating current, so to say, between intellectual boldness and cowardice. Perhaps the word is too strong—but when you think that the Iolanthe we were building was his particular obsession: why did he never come and see her? He used on the contrary to ring up Marchant and myself and discuss the various stages of our work with a kind of voluptuary's nostalgia. But when I said: "Why not come and see tomorrow what you think of her?" he replied at once. "No, Felix. Not until she is word-perfect, until she is complete." I sensed a tremor of something like fear in the words; but of course it was always accompanied by that wonderful self-deprecating charm. "You see I have never met her, I shall have to be introduced."

As for Io, she was getting so real as almost to be a pet. Machinery has this peculiar tug on the crude affections of the human race; why else do men christen their cars and sailing boats? I must confess that the first time we hooked up the memory-reproduction complex I had the most extraordinary thrill, almost sexual, in hearing that marvelous, rather husky voice saying (as if she had a hangover): "And I told Henniker it wouldn't do, it simply wouldn't do; Felix, love is all in compartments, otherwise it wouldn't be a universal disease. It's silly that we only have one word for it. And the ones we have are very inadequate to deal with its variety—like esteem, affection, tenderness, sympathy. It isn't classified as yet in any language." I sat down with a bump on my chair and Marchant thrust a glistening, sweaty face up against mine, exulting: "Do you think one could improve on her? Now tell me honestly." I could only shake my head wonderingly. It really was quite devastating the extent of the dummy's habituation to the ordinary terms of what we might call the human condition—if you can just simply imagine an object called "self" operating with a frame of memory, habit, impulse, inhibition and so on. It looked as if in another month or so she might be safely placed in the orbit of an ordinary life—held in harness as all of us are, purely by the routines of the daily round. Feeding on the rarefied air of inner space, correcting by willpower the gravitational pull of the passions—which to so many modern scientists seem little better than a bundle of assorted death wishes. But of course inevitably the unlegislated-for quality made its appearance—for an example, we hadn't really thought of "charm" as an ingredient when we specified her; but her charm was devastating—and surely it is the one thing you would expect her *makers* to remember from the original actress? So that, on the one hand, while we really knew all about her, she continued to surprise us during the long period which passed between her being in pieces, and being united. The day I mean when she woke up completely, yawned, knuckled her eyes and said: "Where am I? What time is it?" And then as she gradually took in her surroundings and the men in white coats around her, added: "Is it all right—that old appendix?"

At the moment she was still a set of intermittent responses; her eyes were in, but had to be left a week or more to "set" properly so that she might use them. So that she still slept all day, and still kept her eyes closed when she spoke, the sound welling sleepily out of that beautifully formed humorous mouth. We had even forgotten (how is this possible: please tell me?), we had forgotten that she would know all about us, even our names. Or let me put it this way: we knew with one part of our minds, but not with such conviction that it didn't give us a tremendous start to hear her use them. It was even stranger when, fetching back a memory from the very beginning of our Athens days, she spoke to me in Greek. "They say I shall never have a child, but I am glad. Would you like to have a child, Felix?" And it was here that *my* memory was faulty while her artificial one worked perfectly; I had forgotten what my answer was on that particular occasion. She was full of small surprises like these. But we still had to select a date for an awakening.

FOUR

Perhaps the most cogent reason for our habit of walking down the corridor into the embalming studio was that we wished to compare what we were building with what they were preserving with such care. There was not much trade in their business—somehow embalming had not really caught on, even among publishers. Nevertheless that mere trickle of corpses provided Cyrus P. Goytz with a theater of operations in which he could train staff. He was an endearing man with a face like a spade and a swarthy skin which occasionally flushed in a dull way when a pupil made a mistake. He was clad in black to lecture, which he did with his hands clasped in front of his stomach. A big smooth minatory-looking man, dressed in such heavy materials that he looked not unlike one of his own products—drained of all blood, like a kosher dish, and not as if he had just been warmly sacrificed on the altars of gluttony. He wore a very obviously short-cut wig which gave his face a curious expression of transience—again like his subjects, who apparently began to melt after about a month. But he was a pet Goytz, the soul of patience, and (so they said) the best embalmer in the universe. On New Year's Eve, at staff parties, he had been known to take out a glass eye and

[167]

show it to everyone on the palm of his hand. In the evenings he played the violin to timid little Mrs. Goytz (who looked like a taxidermic waterfowl) in a semidetached at Sidcup. He was spearheading the firm's embalming attack on the Middle East.

But this was not all; it was really his homely philosophy which gave us so much pleasure; he was so full of a benign desire to spread light and goodwill, dispel the clouds of gloom—or whatever misgivings his students might have about an avocation so, well . . . unusual. "Contrary to what many might assume," he might say, taking up his penguin-like stance with hands joined in front, "a corpse can prove a friendly, even a companionable thing—while it is relatively fresh, I mean." This sort of thing Marchant used to treasure, and whisper it into Iolanthe's ear as we knelt beside her, working on the eyes. The embalmers, by the way, worked to music—mostly the strains of *In a Monastery Garden* played in a reverent sort of way by a Palm Court Orchestra. Goytz kept it low so that the sound of his voice was not drowned as he instructed the students in the use of the trocar or the siphon pump which drained the bodies on the slabs. He was such a kindly man that he could even pretend to take a mild teasing from Marchant— as when the latter suggested that the appropriate motto for his little parlor should be "The More the Messier or the Nausea the Better."

His specimens, though, had rather a different feeling about them; they were vulnerable, you see; the decay could be contained but only for a while. They had not that noble abstract quality of Iolanthe, lying there asleep under her silk sheet. You could smash her, but she wouldn't rot away, or melt under the coating of resin poured over her in her coffin—I am thinking of Egyptian kings and queens. All this of course Goytz knew and perhaps at times he smelled a little condescension in our tones, in our way of questioning him about his work. At any rate he once or twice uttered a phrase about our work which might have seemed barbed—as when he said: "And when she wakes up and asks you imploringly: 'Is there any hope for a little happiness for me?' what will you reply?" Marchant chuckled. "Nothing, of course; for she knows the answer, just like every human being knows the answer to the questions he or she poses. The question contains the answer in capsule form."

Mr Goytz smiled briefly and said: "You see I have no such problem with my children; they have entered into the Great Silence, borne on the wings of their nearest and dearest. For them there are no problems. But for us, of course, they are numerous; we must dress them as if for a fancy-dress ball. And darned quick. Come in by the way, we have a few most unusual specimens this week." He turned on his heel and led us through a curtain into the main studio where three or four corpses were laid out on trestles—the "cooling boards" where they are trimmed and coiffed before the makeup goes on. All but one were covered, or half covered, in sheets so that there was a superficial resemblance to the other studio across the way where we ourselves worked. But the resemblance was a very superficial one, and ended when we saw the venuous system being pumped out into a bucket. The pump hissed, the pink blood tinkled. (Rather like having the oil changed on your car, I suppose.) A young man devoutly pumped and pumped. The body was much mutilated by a street accident, and a second youth kept the wounds free with a sponge. Goytz touched the cheeks with a quick white hand, as if to judge their springiness, and seemed satisfied with the rate of progress. He consulted a watch. "You got an hour I guess," he told his acolytes who did not so much as look up from their work. They had expressionless faces and square Jewish heads. Goytz inspected with some care the bucket which was half full of the pumped blood of the subject and said, in his lecture-room voice: "One of the characteristic features of carbon monoxide poisoning is the bright cherry-red color of the blood, and a greatly delayed coagulation time. One must not, of course, confuse it with the similar blood coloration in drowned subjects."

So we moved from slab to slab while Goytz talked pleasantly and discursively about corpses and their habits, of the different ways of enbalming them through the ages, of the methods used to secure anatomical subjects for study—and a hundred other fascinating sidelights on his art, which showed us plainly that we were in the presence of a master of the trade; but more, an enthusiast. He knew all the names and dates of embalming history by heart. And he spoke of his own particular hero, William Hunter, the Scot, with a reverence that was almost tearful. "It was this great man," he said, "who not only gave the world a method of embalming which advanced the whole technique a hundredfold, but also listed the chemicals he used in so doing. He was the first to use the femoral artery as his point of penetration for his mixture of oil of turpentine, oil of lavender, rosemary and vermilion; this he allowed to diffuse through the body tissues for several hours before he started to open the cavities and remove the viscera for cleaning and soaking in essential oils and wines. These were then of course replaced and covered with preservative powders like camphor and resin and magnesium sulfate as well as potassium compounds. The powder was also packed tight in the cavities like mouth, nose, ears, anus; and finally the whole body was placed on a bed of plaster of Paris and allowed to remain there for about four years. In this way he dehydrated the subject and prevented the decomposition which comes about with bacterial growth." All this seemed to move Goytz very much.

"And here," he said, "is an Eastern potentate who died of an embolism on his arrival in this country as an Ambassador to your Queen. He is quite fresh and will come up very nicely indeed, yes very nicely indeed. He will give them all a thrill by his naturalness back there in Abyssinia."

The sheet turned back revealed a dark hairy man with enormous clenched hands which Goytz soothed out flat at once, tenderly elongating the crude fingers. He was anxious that no trace of an apparent arthritis deformans should remain when he had completed what he was pleased to call his final "composition" of the subject. I thought, as I saw him, how the fingers of our Io did not need to be kneaded into softness; her hand lay in yours like a snowflake of softness. Goytz was forced to knead and rub his subjects, to massage them, rub them down with rollers—all to squeeze the blood out of them before he could start work on the outside. In this case the corpse was a huge dark simian brute of a man, part Negro, but whose face strongly suggested that of Jocas Pehlevi, the half-brother or whatever of Julian. Something about the swarthiness contrasting with the bright blushing warmth of the skin in which the beard grew, black as the bristles of a warthog. The same tips of gold in the teeth which were very slightly revealed by a retracted lip. But of course no earring. The abundant hair and nails would outlast the great part of the final decay of this "potentate." He was clad only in a blue underpant. His toenails were huge, broken, and very dirty, as if he had always shoveled coal with them. Goytz again gave the flesh of the corpse a quick almost affectionate runover, patting it here and there with some of the complacence of a woman rubbing cold cream into her face. In a sense I could see that his subjects had become a sort of extension of himself; it was his own flesh that he patted, smoothed, stroked, like some great painter his canvas. "He'll be no trouble," he asserted. "We shall compose him something lovely. Eosin," he added somewhat cryptically.

I remembered. Of course: one of the interesting properties of eosin is its capacity to fluoresce when exposed to ultraviolet light; to some extent even in bright sunlight it can do the same. But the best is when a shaded ultraviolet bulb is used—the so-called "black light." It was the use of eosin which enabled Goytz to obtain what he called his "internal cosmetic effect"; his subjects looked lit from within, they glowed with an illusion of warmth and life. We were also taking advantage of it, but our skins were finer, more supple, and at least a thousand times more durable than his. But I could see his weakness for swarthy subjects because of this luminous dye which removed the residual grayness caused by the kosher treatment of the body, the draining out of its blood. At points then our preoccupations chimed; at others they diverged. For example he had been always far more preoccupied by the question of odor than we had been, though in an opposite sense: we had to invent smells which were indistinguishable from the real animal smells of the human body. But he had had to disguise, first of all the smell of decay, and then the smells of all the powerful agents he was using in order to preserve the illusion of life, or the quasi-life of his subject; an abbreviated life in time? No, but heavens! Surely both were dead in the technical sense? Well, Iolanthe was a little less dead because of a perfect memory which *she could use:* it was her radar. So that dying . . . was a case of loss of memory, both mental and physical? "The first thing," said Goytz with the air of a hunter giving a colleague a tip, "is to select your drainage points with the full knowledge that here and there you may discover a clot or other blockage to free movement which will have to be sucked out by the trocar syringe. But it's not very hard.

"The intercapillary pressure of the blood during life is very low, and movement of the blood itself can be accomplished only by the squeeze action of the muscles against the veins. This squeeze we imitate when it comes to voiding the body of blood. But the first really important thing is to select your drainage points and then raise and open the veins you have chosen. In them you place the largest possible drainage tube to facilitate the movement of the blood." He illustrated this for us with the unerring skill of a seasoned darts player scoring an "outer." The harmless simian arms of the "potentate" lay there; Goytz drew on rubber gloves ("always guard against infection," he said under his breath) and made a couple of magisterial incisions on the inside of the forearm, some way below the elbow; then, with an experience obviously born of long practice, he took an elevator and raised a dark vein, passing the instrument through it, so that it was indeed raised above the surface and ready to be tapped. This he repeated with a kindly absorption on the other arm, saying to Marchant in abstracted tones, "You see, all we know is thanks to the great anatomists; you may laugh, but Leonardo prepared specimens this way." But something went wrong, the wounds began to bleed. "It's nothing," he said. "You will see." He called over some students and with them proceeded to tug the arms of his subject above his head, pulling them as far as they would go, and in such a fashion as to squeeze the maximum amount of blood out of them; meanwhile the arms were being sponged from fingertip to shoulder by the students. It was in a sense a kind of Japanese massage that the "potentate" was receiving. "Poor drainage," said Goytz, "has been universally recognized as the cause of embalming failure. We use surface manipulation, vibration, even a roller stretcher—anything to get the blood moving. After all, in terms of quantity, you can calculate that there is about seven pounds of liquid blood per hundred of body weight; now with the best will in the world and the most up-to-date equipment (taking one gallon of blood per one single 150-pound body) we should expect to remove perhaps one-half of the total quantity, certainly not more: that is to say, two quarts of blood from this 150-pound fellow here." He tapped the potentate lightly on the forehead, demonstrating with kindliness; now he was like some champion fisherman, standing beside a huge white shark almost taller than himself, and talking modestly about the means he had employed to take it.

"But," he went on in cautionary vein, "continuous and

uncontrolled drainage is one of the common causes, for the situation in which the body is firm and clear and, on the face of it, well preserved when embalmed . . . yet," he raised a finger to the ceiling and paused dramatically, "becomes soft and begins to decompose a few hours later. That is the tragedy! In other words, the embalmer's work is really an art based on a calculated judgment of a given situation. Both underembalming and overembalming result from inaccurately judged drainage control. With overembalming you get wrinkling, leatherizing and dehydration in low-resistance areas; with underembalming you risk premature decomposition areas of high resistance. Scylla and Charybdis, my friends, that is what you might call it! Ah!" He sighed again.

When he was in this vein—which Marchant called his "Sermon on the Mount" vein—he was irresistible, and we did everything we could to encourage him to continue. Indeed the subject was so dear to him that his features took on a rosy tinge, almost eosin-tinted with the enthusiasm he felt for "composing" his subjects. But he was also a modest man and feared to bore a nonprofessional audience, and so from time to time he paused, smiled vaguely and self-deprecatingly round, and gave a little sigh of apology. "Don't stop, man," said Marchant. "This is fascinating; we are learning from you, Goytz. Don't stop now!" The Compleat Embalmer simpered and said: "Very well. Let me then just run over the main points in regard to this Eastern potentate. I think we will have to consider some of the main factors of cavity embalming with him—attacking the main points of putrefaction with a trocar."

He snapped a finger and one of his acolytes held up for our inspection a heavy metal syringe with a sharp nozzle, looking for all the world like some article of gardening equipment; Goytz smiled. "I know," he said. "It has been often said. Yet it is the most invaluable piece of embalming equipment there is." (The sort of thing one sees old ladies using to spray soapy water on their roses.) Goytz took it in a cherishing fashion and presented it at his subject in a manner obviously perfected by long practice. "I will just outline what must be done!" he said. "First we must penetrate at the intersection of the fifth intercostal space and the midaxillary line; press down until with a slight puff you enter the stomach. Next we must tackle the cecum which is slightly more complicated. Direct the point one-fourth of the distance from the right anterior-superior iliac spine to the pubic symphysis; a tiny bit tricky here; you must keep the point well up near the abdominal wall until within about four inches of the right anterior-superior iliac spine, then dip the point two inches and press softly forward and . . . with a puff you are in the colon." His smile was beatific, his audience rapt. He paused to blow his nose in a tissue.

"Now," he said, "there remains the urinary bladder and, most difficult of all, the right atrium of the heart." He issued his instruction for these two delicate operations with burning enthusiasm, though his voice was modulated and serene. He took a pencil from one of his students and, as he spoke, marked the places on the skin of his subject. The "potentate" said nothing, though he also appeared to be listening attentively to Goytz. "Onward until it touches the pubic bone; you will feel the slight jolt. Withdraw about half an inch and dip the point slightly and you will find yourself in the bladder. Now as for the atrium, the target is a small one; you must imagine a line drawn from the left anterior-superior iliac spine to the lobe of the right ear; keep your point firmly up against the anterior wall of the cavity until you pierce the diaphragm. Then dip down and you are in the heart." He sighed again and looked around him benignly, apologetically.

"You see, Marchant," he went on. "And you also have had to take such simple matters into consideration: the combined weight of the viscera in the average adult is around fifteen or twenty pounds, and since this material is so highly putrefactive a considerable amount of fluid is required to disinfect and preserve it. We generally reckon upon between twenty-four and thirty-two ounces of concentrated cavity fluid as a mean dose. But of course cases vary. Sometimes you get blowback from intestinal gases, specially if the subject is not too fresh, or if it has succumbed to a disease which has filled a member with some putrefactive fluid. But one can judge usually after a bit of experience." At this moment the "potentate" gave out a noise, a strange rumbling of the stomach, for all the world as if he were hungry. Goytz smiled and raised a finger, saying: "Hark at that! The formation of gases. You must learn how to interpret the sound." There was a slight hiss from the anus of the "potentate," like the noise made by a torn balloon at an Xmas party. "That is normal," said Goytz. "But if things have gone too far we are frequently obliged to make an incision and snip the gut here and there with scissors in order to avoid it. It is a messy system and is better avoided if possible. But in this craft one is always up against unknown factors like freshness or serious illness; and sometimes we have to take emergency steps and use aspiration to void the chief cavities. A six-inch incision, for example, through the ventral wall, along the median lines of the abdomen between the umbilicus and the xiphoid process of the sternum. . . . Then clip-clip and void by aspiration; then the viscera are quickly covered with fluid, embalming powder or hardening compound. But of course the trouble with the holes you make is that they have to be sealed. Yet here we may take courage; to stitch up an embalming subject is less delicate than the stitching up of somebody alive who has been operated on. A simple sailmaker's stitch will draw the lips together; and then you may coat it with a wax sealer as a final operation." He paused in order to give emphasis to what must have been a staple lecture-room joke. Then he said benignly, "Your body is as good as new." There was a slight ripple of sycophantic laughter from his little group. One of them made an involuntary gesture of the hands as if he were about to applaud, as one does at the end of a concert. Goytz nodded his thanks at the youth and went on to demonstrate the various types of suture he would use according to nature and size of the incisions made. It was of course fascinating for Marchant, who had been laying lifelines so to speak, made of almost invisible thread, through the photoelectric body of Iolanthe. How crude, compared with our work, it all seemed. Nevertheless there was an affinity of attitude. It lay in our attitude toward Beauty!

There was a long pause for breath, during which Goytz paused, as if hovering on the edge of a final peroration: but in fact he was drawing strength to deal with the trickiest part of his art, gazing down with quiet attention at the face of the "potentate." He placed a finger reflectively on the mouth of the personage and gently eased the lip back to reveal a white wolf's tooth before replacing it with care. Then he turned back to us and continued.

"Now the great painter Sargent once said that the hardest thing to get right in portraiture was the mouth of his sitters. One would have thought that it was the eyes, which are so mobile and so full of variety and expression. But in fact he was right. The position of the mouth is absolutely the thing which must be right or else the whole expression goes wrong. The eyes may smile, the eyes may blaze, but if the mouth is wrong, everything is wrong, and your subject will instantly be criticized by his beloved ones as unnatural. Now if this was true for one of the greatest portraitists the world has ever known it is much truer still for the embalmer.

"The mouth position is the most delicate of all, and is also the weakest part of the physical structure—for in death the jaw often falls, the musculature tenses or yields, the lips shrink. Here some swift action has to be taken. We must rub in our embalming cream and massage well before proceeding to the 'set' of the mouth. But in very many cases one has to do what we have called an 'invisible mend'; technically speaking there are two sutures of great importance, that of the musculature and that of the mandible itself. The first is really a septum suture. A full curved needle is passed through the muscle tissue at the base of the lower gum, at the septum. The needle is kept as close to the jawbone as possible and the stitch should be quite wide. The needle is then directed upward between the upper lip and gum and brought out through the left nostril. It is then pushed through the septum of the nose into the right nostril and back down between the upper lip and gum. The loose ends are then softly pulled together to coax the jaw into position. When the operator stands at the head of the table, he can hold the mandible in position with the little finger and tie the knot with the remaining fingers. But a bow knot is advisable here, as it leaves a little play for any future adjustments one might be called upon to make.

"Of course in this domain, too, the rule of chance obtains, and very small factors play a large role; dentures, for example, or heavily retracted gums which death will shrink out of shape all too quickly; decomposition, ulceration . . . many imponderables with which only the skilled embalmer can cope and still remain true to his vision of reality—if I may make so bold as to call it that, for he tries to get as near to life as possible. He is an artist trying to re-form the effects of death in a subject, particularly those of the *rigor mortis* and associated conditions. But sometimes too, in subjects which have suffered a long illness, his kind of beauty treatment is up against many of the problems faced by beauticians who have to compensate for a lifetime of sadness or selfishness or stupidity showing on the faces of their patients.

"I'm thinking, for example, of the *facies hippocratica,* so called because first described by the greatest little doctor of All Time, Hippocrates. All literatures both before and after have drawn attention to the fact that the faces of those about to pass on tend to have a sort of stamp of death about them. Of course it is almost infinitely variable according to the causes of the death, but sufficiently consistent to have been noted down. It is not just folklore, my friends, though each embalmer may cite you different characteristics of the condition. I myself would cite a sharp pinched quality of the nostrils, and a general semblance of skin shrinkage around the temples. But of course each case is modified by circumstances; those who die in peace will not show the same signs as those who die in high emotion, shrieking, or suicides who have blown their brains out. It takes all kinds to make a world."

He smiled round at us in kindly and abstracted fashion, and then turned back to reflect upon the problems which his "potentate" would pose to the class. "In his case," he said, "we can congratulate ourselves on his freshness but on little else—for there is a problem or two connected with his mouth. I have asked for some photographs of him in life. His lower jaw must have protruded a good deal and I think we will have to consider a mandible suture—inserting the needle straight down between the lower lip and gum and bringing it out at the point of the chin; then reinserting the needle into the same hole but pushing it upward behind the mandible, in order to bring it out through the floor of the mouth just beneath the tip of the tongue. The actual decision of course depends on our documentation.

"By that," he went on, "I mean that if he has no friends and relations to mourn him here and to complain about the likeness; if he simply has to be casketed and package-shipped to Abyssinia: why then I might in the interest of pure speed resort to a more primitive method known as 'tack-and-thread.' This is much swifter. You take a long slim carpet tack and a tack hammer such as picture framers use; you drive the tack into the mandible, between the roots of the teeth. Then you drive a second into the maxilla. Then a strong piece of cord attached to the two tacks will draw the mandible into position and hold it. But the method is not foolproof, and often not professionally attractive. On the other hand I have to take into consideration other factors. For example, his own folks back home may want him gilded from head to foot, not just painted like a photographic likeness hand-tinted by however expert a hand. We must first secure the cavities while we are waiting for a word from his Embassy." He smiled, pulling off his gloves, and prepared the air for yet another lecture-room jest. "You see," he said, "often the dead are just as choosy as the living." This too was acknowledged with rapturous respect.

"And now it's past my work time," said Goytz. "So I will invite you into my study for a cup of tea." He led us as he always did into his smart white office, the walls of which were covered with charts and graphs showing the progress of the embalming campaign. There were advertising leaflets everywhere. A trolley with freshly made tea on it stood by the desk, and this he dispensed with care. "At the moment it may seem very slack," he said, "but the buildup is impressive. I reckon within ten years everyone in this country will have taken to the idea of embalming; already the advance sales to the young with our special bonus have soared into millions. It's become a bit of a fad, if you like, specially since that pop group launched that song 'My mummy is a mummy,' but nevertheless the advances have been *paid for* on these policies, and they will have to be honored. There is no time to be lost. We shall soon need hundreds of embalmers working through the length and breadth of the land. I have warned Julian that a special effort will be needed. Of course in my case I am concentrating on Turkey and the Middle East where totally different methods both publicitywise and sciencewise will be necessary; we can do a cheaper job, use cheaper fluids and cruder methods. More bright colors and less representational art if you follow.

"But that too is virtually presold, thanks to the brilliant campaign that the firm organized with the clergy. We offered free embalming to the Byzantine church, and after our second Greek Archbishop there was a stampede. The lying-in-state of the Archbishop of Belgrade was for the first time prolonged for weeks thanks to our up-to-date methods. Normally in those lands of the Noonday Sun the decomposition sets in all too swiftly and after three days or less even . . . why you can't get near enough to show your reverence. Then came the Catholics; they don't like to be left behind, and they smelled the political power behind the drive. At once they issued a special bull authorizing the embalming of everyone. It averted dangerous riots. But the last and most positive victory of all was over the Communists when we pointed out that Lenin had used our own patented cavity fluid! Fancy! After the first suspicious hesitation Toto, the dictator of Bulgaria, signed a full policy, and he is next on our list.

"So you see by the time I send out four or five fully trained embalmers to the Middle East we shall have captured the whole market to a point where it only remains to sweep up Mecca and we're home. Then . . . gazing even further away to the Lands of the Lotus we might envisage Persia and India playing their little part. . . ." Goytz was in a sort of dream as he sipped his tea and waved vaguely at these vast horizons. Marchant rubbed his hands in high delight. "Yes," he said, "you are right. Nothing will stop the march of science." And he gave forth a characteristic titter; Goytz, still in his creative muse, smiled upon us from behind his desk. "How long," he said, "before the reign of Real Beauty begins?" This was rather a harpoon for Marchant who put on a somewhat schoolmistress' expression and said with a touch of tartness, "Our own Iolanthe won't be long now, Goytz. Another month or two at the most." The embalmer raised a hand in kindly benediction, and then a faint cloud passed over his serene countenance. "For me," he said, "the only trouble is that Julian's brother is not pulling his weight; something is wrong. He is ill perhaps. But at any rate he has disappointed us rather, because he won't play any part in our scheme, or so it appears. And Julian is vexed with him. That's all I know of the matter." Suddenly I recalled with a start Julian saying something about Caradoc building Jocas a tomb . . . when was it? But the tea party went on with decorum until the duty cars arrived and we all went home for the night. Goytz shook hands with both of us and charitably invited us to come back whenever we wished.

That evening I was sitting by the fire, reading a book when the telephone rang and the quiet voice of Julian sounded—a voice which was perhaps just a shade less languid than usual, yet nevertheless controlled and modulated. He was phoning from Paris, he said, and added: "And particularly to thank you, my dear Felix, for thinking up so charming a gesture; you will have guessed how much it meant to me to hear her voice. . . ."

"Whose voice?"

"Why Iolanthe's," he said in puzzled tones. "It was only a few words, of course. But what a thrill for me after so long. Thank you."

"But wait," I said. "She couldn't possibly have talked to you Julian; the magazines aren't dated and placed yet. She is still asleep, my dear. Yes, she can say a few words all right, but she couldn't get up or lift the phone as yet. Has Marchant been playing you some recorded stuff to try it out? I wonder."

"I assure you," he said, amost pleading, "there was no mistake. She said: 'We have never met, have we, Julian? It is as if I had missed a vital part of my real life.'" His voice shook a little. "Then she went on: 'Now the doctors will remedy that together with a lot of other things, and when I am well I will ask you to come to me.' It was terrifying in a way, but so very real. . . ."

I was on my feet by now, full of a very real perplexity. "I'll check back," I said, "and let you know."

The thing was how, and in which order? I rang Marchant and cleared him from suspicion. He was as mystified as I was. Then, on a sudden impulse, I phoned to the studio itself—though on the face of it this was an absurd thing to do; for I myself had locked up that evening after drawing the covers carefully over Iolanthe. And here was a funny thing. The phone returned an engaged signal, which clearly showed that the receiver was at least off. I listened to the monotonous bleating tone and my thoughts began to race. And then, even as I listened, there came the decisive click and silence which could come only from the replacing of the receiver. Click, followed by the engaged tone again.

"Now what the devil?" I said. Benedicta looked up to see me rushing myself into an overcoat and scarf. "I must just go to the studio and check," I said. "Come with me; only hurry, darling; you can drive me if you wish."

Light powdery snow drifted across our headlights, a shadowy distracted moon wandered in the sky; B. drove at full tilt, a cigarette burning between her lips. The car had been well christened when the makers chose the name "Spear" for it. I chewed the inside of my lips, chewed my ragged thoughts. I felt an extraordinary despondency arise in me. It was too early for things to start going wrong, before we had even got our model onto its feet. It was partly fear, I think, of finding some mechanical defect in our dolly which might cost us months' more intricate work—but also: fear of an unknown factor which hinted crudely at a sort of physical autonomy for which we had not yet made room *in our minds.* How *free* was the final Iolanthe to be? Freer than a chimp, one supposes . . . yes, infinitely; but free enough to pick up a phone and charm Julian? "You are looking scared," said Benedicta quietly.

"Is it my driving? I'll slow down." I shook my head. "No. No. I was debating a little matter of free will, of conditioned reflexes. . . . Drive faster, in fact. Much faster. One is only scared when something happens which one can't explain to oneself. She could not, for example, have done what Julian says she did, namely, lift the telephone and talk to him. At this stage, at any rate."

"I'm dying to see this dummy."

"You have been very patient, Benedicta; why you have never even asked me, darling? Of course you shall. Now."

"I knew my voice would shake with jealous rage and you would suddenly look at me in astonished fashion. To be deprived of the female right to be jealous by the logic of things—that is the unkindest thing that could happen to a woman." She laughed.

"Are we jealous of Iolanthe, then?" I said.

Some hefty branches torn from a tree by the wind lay astride the main road and we swerved to a halt, nonplussed for a moment, for there seemed no alternative way forward. Fortunately the wood was not quite so heavy as it looked, and I was able to shift it enough to clear a fairway for the car. Panting, I sank back at last beside her, reveling in the warm gushes of air from the heater as we raced on again toward our destination. "Who could have done it then?" she asked. "Could he have imagined it in his sleep?" There was nothing to be said as yet, until I had seen Iolanthe with my own eyes. Of course when she woke such an act would be part of her enormous repertoire of "autonomous" acts. Ring anyone up and say anything, in fact. "Did you say she could not eat or excrete?" I placed another lighted cigarette between her teeth and explained. "She won't know it. We built her the reflex movement and the functional pattern which go with them; only she doesn't have to trundle a disagreeable bundle of fecal matter around with her. She will feel the same punctual need as you do, and like you will sit down on the bidet and run the taps. But unlike you she only imagines the act of defecation, though she has all the same enjoyment—why she even gives the little shudder that we men find so endearing. But she is full of laborsaving devices like that. O God, Benedicta, she is marvelous; you will have quite a surprise, truthfully you will. Maybe feel a little scared as well—I confess that at first blush I was quite taken aback, awed."

We swerved at long last into the driveway, to find the whole complex of buildings in darkness, which of course was what we would have expected. There was a bright green light in the lodge which housed the two security guards whose duty it was to make two late night patrols through the studios and labs. The tagged keys to our studio hung on a nail behind the grizzled head of Naysmith who lumbered to his flat marine's feet to welcome me. "Is there anything wrong?" he asked, catching, I suppose, a touch of urgency from the expression on my face. "Not exactly. It may be me. But I thought I'd come back and check over my section. There's a little matter of a phone call I have not cleared up as yet. By the way, Naysmith, come with me and bring some fingerprint snuff would you? I'd like to see if our inside phone has any prints on it. The last lot should be mine or Marchant's."

Benedicta was waiting for us in her lamb furred overcoat and boots; and together we cut across the main pathways and walked the hundred yards or so toward the studios. We entered, turning up the white lights of the theater of operations as we advanced; I was relieved to find everything as I had left it. Though why I should have imagined or looked for a hypothetical disorder I know not. "That phone over there, Naysmith. Give it the gold dust treatment, will you, and see what you find?" Obediently the security man dusted his goldish powder over the instrument, puffing it softly from an atomizer. Then he took out a large magnifying glass from his professional kit and ran it over the suspect instrument, grunting as he did so. "There's nothing *at all* on the damn thing," he said at last, stretching his back straight with relief and turning to me in a mild perplexity. "It's been wiped clear by someone." For a moment this too seemed strange, but then I was determined not to invent mysteries where none existed. The air was kept at a specially moist heat to be kind to Iolanthe's skin, which had been woven from pure Mel, a derivative of nylon. I explained briefly to Naysmith and he seemed satisfied enough with this explanation as indeed I was myself. I could think of no other; an invisible skin of moisture particles formed upon the Bakelite receiver and washed out any fingerprints. And Iolanthe? Well, she had not moved at all under her sheet; poor dear, she was still in pieces, though nearing the final joining together. There was quite a lot of juice roaming about inside her because we had plugged her in to a low-power induction current to keep her body at a satisfactory temperature. And it was this factor which suddenly presented me with a solution—or the sketch of one. Benedicta stood at the door, looking very pale and extraordinarily youthful all of a sudden. She was afraid of what lay beneath the sheet! I didn't want to unveil the head until Naysmith had taken himself off—a twinge of proprietorial jealousy, I suppose? But this the good man did in a few moments and now was my chance to show off my beauty to Benedicta. I took her cold hand in mine and together we crossed the room to the operating table.

"I mustn't forget to show you the weaver team that made the skin for her; you'd think you were in a Japanese watercolor in their studio—finer than the petals of any flower you might conceive." I turned back the sheet and we gazed down upon the still serene features of the screen goddess. I could feel that she was terrified, Benedicta. And when, at this juncture, the telephone suddenly shrilled, we both nearly jumped out of our skins and into each other's arms. I picked it up with trembling fingers and was relieved to find that it was only Marchant. "I've thought of an explanation," said he. "She's still on the feeder, isn't she? Well there's a fairly big buildup of juice, enough to enable her to pass a thought or a phrase along a wire without using the phone. It doesn't sound very plausible, but I think that must be it."

"It will have to be," I said. "There's isn't any other solution." Marchant sucked his teeth cheerfully and went on. "If you switch on and pin her onto feedback she might even answer the question herself." But I wasn't keen to start fooling round at this time of night. "It'll keep," I said, "until she walks in beauty like the night." There was a gasp and stirring sound; I turned to see Benedicta gazing fixedly at the face which had suddenly altered its expression. And then, even as we looked, the two sapphire bright eyes opened and gazed fixedly, unwinkingly at Benedicta. B. moved back a few paces with obvious fear. "It wants to speak," she whispered. "Poor thing. Poor thing." She was about to faint but I caught her. In the little lavatory next door she was violently sick.

"Leave me a moment," she said, between spasms of nausea. "She wants to tell you something. Please go back." But I waited until she could accompany me back; I wanted her to get over her shock and come to accept Iolanthe for what she was—a modest enough copy of reality, not a creation. I hung about obstinately, not saying a word, until she shook herself at last and said: "There! It's done with." She washed her face and dried it on the little white napkin behind the door, then slipped her arm through mine. "What an experience!"

Iolanthe's head had hardly moved, but her features tenderly sketched in a shoal of transient feelings, impulses bathed in memory or desire, which flowed through the magazine of the coded mind on the wings of electricity. For such low-voltage feeding it was remarkable to find her "live" at all. Yet she was. Her blue eyes gazed into the white glare of the theater lamps with a sort of abstract curiosity; then, attracted perhaps by the glimpse of our shadows moving upon the general whiteness, lowered their gaze and came to rest at last, in troubled and loving confusion, upon my own face. You could have sworn she recognized it—the little mischievous pucker of the mouth came, as if she were about to utter her sardonic greeting in Greek, *"Xäire Felix mou."* And yet also timid, abashed, a *gamine* who fears she may be reproached. But of course with a current so far below optimum, the threads had got jumbled as they do in an ordinary delirium—in high fever for example—and what she said she uttered in the back of her throat and not too clearly at that. The tone of course was low contralto, not very like her ordinary one because of the fallen levels. "The deep inside wish to be level with the grave, Julian; you are worn out with the sin of wishing you had died in childbirth—how well we understand! Now that I have come back from this great illness I shall bring you some comfort, you will see."

"Christ!" Benedicta vibrated with a mixture of fascination and horror. "She's jumbling," I said; and I ran my hand softly and tenderly through the hair of Iolanthe in a gesture which I knew would elicit the response she must have so often made in life. She arched her head slowly, flexing it on the lovely stem of her neck, and breathed in deeply, voluptuously; then she expelled her breath slowly, uxoriously through her mouth and gave me a sleepy smile. "Kiss. Kiss," she said. "Felix." And pursed her red smiling mouth for a kiss which I gave her while Benedicta looked on in a kind of scandalized amusement mixed with loathing.

We kissed and she brushed my ear with her lips murmuring: "Precious. But life could have been full of so much hope, only we're cripples, cripples. I spoke to Julian." Well, if there was enough juice for all this there might be enough for her to get back on to the mnemonic register without an additional charge, and actually answer a "real" question. "How did you do it?" I asked. She closed her eyes, appearing not to have heard, not to have understood; then she opened them again and the tiny dimple appeared in her cheek. "The Arab doctor is kind; he got me Julian. Just for a minute. It's so tiring." So that was the answer! Said had obtained the call and placed the receiver to her ear and mouth. Switched on the power. Ah, my schizoid goddess, you are falling asleep again. She couldn't help it; her long lashes declined softly and she subsided quietly once more into nescience pillowed on the sea rhythms of the current. Receding, receding into the tide-less sleep of scientific time; her bloodstream was a wave-length only in her tissues, its force measured now upon a small dial with a face no larger than a lady's wristwatch. A little nodding blue bulb of pilot flame winked on all through the night. Such silence and such beauty!

"Well, we've solved the mystery," I said. "Let's go home. I am beginning to feel tired."

"Kiss me just once," said Benedicta. "I want to feel how it must have felt to her . . . to it. No, you don't kiss very well. Inattentive. Your mind's always elsewhere, you are woolgathering. You should plunge it in like a spear." But I was tucking back the white sheets round my dolly, drawing the transparent curtains once more. It was very late, and for some reason I felt very excited and nervous—a relief reaction, I suppose, to find everything as it should be. Naysmith had left an evening paper and in this mood of slight disorientation, anxiety-powered, I suppose, the most banal headlines took on a tinge of almost sinister am-biguity. "Attendants steal fittings," "Birds lodge in soil," "Work-providers for landless," Amen. Amen. I locked up with method, whistling under my breath. Then with a sigh I clicked the studio door behind me. "Now," I said, "when I tell you I am working late at the office, you'll know who I am kissing. Would it be possible to become jealous of a model? I suppose so; one can about a child or a dog, and in cases of great mental cruelty brought before the Cali-fornian courts you even find inanimate objects playing a perfectly satisfactory role. A man who went to bed with his golf clubs for example. Extreme mental cruelty. Benedicta, when you read cases like that and then think of me, don't use bad language, will you promise?" But Benedicta would not rise to my nervous banter; she remained pale and abstracted, her hand clasped hard in mine as we found our way across the grass to the asphalt car park. She sensed that it was mere diversionary babble, that all of a sudden this trifling incident had upset me, had made me feel hesitant, unsure of myself. Yet I could not formulate any special reason why. There was nothing really wrong, nothing at all.

She drove slowly on the way back, and indeed took a longer way round, through Croley, Addhead and Byre, which must have added some forty miles on the clock. I wondered why for a while. Of course. Then I remembered the road all but blocked with fallen branches. I was glad anyway of the long detour; I always think better out of doors than in, and best of all when I am traveling as a passenger in a fast car. But it was mighty late when at last we came back to the cottage, sharing the last puffs of the last cigarette. It had stopped snowing. A large limousine lay at the stile across the fields, with its headlights blazing. It was the office Rolls that Julian always used. Indeed his chauffeur sat inside at the wheel. We pulled in alongside him and he saluted when he recognized us. "He is waiting up for you, sir. Mr. Baynes let him in and made him a snack to eat. I am to pick him up within the next hour or so, so I'm keeping the car warmed up to run him down to Southampton."

We docked the little Spear and cut a glittering path across the field to where the cottage stood, with its one warmly lit window. The latch was off the door and it opened with a slight touch to reveal a blazing fire and the figure of Julian sitting in a high-backed chair, holding a dossier on his knee; the little silver pencil raised in his small neat hand was poised over some abstruse calculation. He looked completely different once more—perhaps it was the clothes, for this time he was dressed in morning dress with a high stock, for all the world as if he had just come from a wedding or Ascot. A gray topper and gloves lay on the windowsill, together with a copy of the *Finance World*. The man appeared to be eternally surprising, unpredictable.

He had chosen, too, a highly dramatic point of vantage in the room—over against the old fireplace and directly under a brilliant lamp with a dull, blood-colored vellum shade. The result was bright light upon the crown of his head and on his knee, but a subdued swarthy reflection on the skin of his face, making it seem deeply sunburned. With this great contrast of tone, one could not but find his hair very white, or at least much whiter than usual. Yet the warm tone shed by the vellum'd light gave him all the benefit of a whole skiwinter of snowburn. "Ah," he said, and recrossed his legs in their polished shoes, "I took the liberty of calling in on my way to Jamaica. I hope it is all right? Baynes has looked after me like a child." He indicated with his chin a tray with sandwiches and some champagne in a pail. But he did not stand up. Benedicta slipped across the room to embrace him in perfunctory fashion while I busied myself in pulling off my storm coat and slipping my feet back into my lined slippers.

Baynes must long since have gone to bed; so while foraging for a cigarette I implored Benedicta to put some coffee on the hob. "You were right, Julian," I said, and all of a sudden I recognized my own relief by the tone in which I uttered the words. "But you gave me the devil of a start. What you suggested was impossible at this stage without outside aid, and when I rang Marchant he swore that he hadn't taken a hand in it. All kinds of gross scientific short circuits flashed into my mind. But of course we had both forgotten Said—he provided the number and arranged the call. Phew!" I sank down in front of the fire, and a silence fell—the deep rich silence of the countryside; I could feel him drinking it in with nostalgia, his head cocked like a gundog's. "How still it is here," he said, in a wondering sort of way. "Somehow much stiller than the big house—there were always noises there. It's the small rooms, I expect." Benedicta came with coffee on a tray; she had already changed into her pajamas and combed out her hair. We sat down before the fire, stirring it into flame, and pouring ourselves mugs of the steaming stuff.

Julian stared hard into the fire over our shoulders. He seemed very calm, very much at peace—and yet with the sort of peace which suggested the resignation of old age rather than the inner resolution of, say, conflicting anxieties. "You said she would be ready next month, didn't you? We must start of course insinuating her into our lives a little, no? She is, after all, from her own point of view, taking up a long life from the point at which she left it off. One wouldn't want her to have the cold comfort of being some scientific orphan." I was very touched by a curious sort of plangency in his tone, rising and falling like the rosined note of a viol; it had an accent of rather naïve sympathy. Even his face looked somehow juvenile and unlined in the firelight as he spoke. "Wouldn't you say, I mean?" he ended a trifle lamely, but with the same unemphatic wistfulness which I found somehow touching. "I only hope," I said, "that you don't identify too closely with the model we've made, and mistake it for the actual subject! It wouldn't be too difficult, as a matter of fact—she's so damn true to life, if I may use such an expression. Indeed Marchant and I have both found ourselves thinking of her as if she were real and not merely a man-made doll, however word-perfect." He nodded once or twice as I spoke. "I know," he said softly, "I know." And his lips moved as if he were whispering some *sotto voce* admonitions to his inner self. I suddenly said impulsively: "Julian, how did it come to you to . . . think of having her copied, made?" He looked at me now with such a reproachful sadness, such a concentration of unanswering pain, that the superfluousness of my question became all too clear. Damn! "One does the obvious thing in given circumstances," he said at last. "It never occurred to me that anything else was possible." He was right. What question was there to be answered which could not be so within the terms of the experience we had both undergone with Merlin's? The apprenticeship I myself had served, for example. No, the fantastic was also the real. It was all as clear as daylight, as the saying goes.

He lowered his head for a moment and hooded his dark eyes like some bird of prey, and watching him there in the reflection of the vellum shade I could not help reflecting that the whole power behind his mental drive, and indeed that for the firm itself (they had become coequal) rested really upon impotence; the slowly spreading stain of a self-conscious ignominy, a shame, and all the spleen which flowed from it. Nothing much more than that—as if that wasn't enough! But it was something at least to be able to formulate it, to indicate the region in which it lay. It threw into relief so much that I had wondered about, so much that I had been quite unable to explain to myself before. Indeed the article of value about which we were all fighting, brandishing each his sterile and desexualized penis, was the eternal anal one—the big tepid Biblical turd of our culture which lay under the vine shoots of modern history, waiting to be. . . . ("The Moldavian penis all back and no sides," writes Tinbergen, while Umlaut adds the rider, "And not seldom glazed like the common egg-plant." Where would we be without the studies of these northern savants?) The enormous cupidity of impotence!

"You have been lucky in a way," said Julian slowly while my attention had been wandering, "in that you came to us fresh from the outside. What you had to fight— or felt you had to fight—was something quite apart from yourself. But if, as in my case, your adversary is more than half yourself . . . ? What then? I found myself trying to do two different things at the same time which were mutually contradictory—trying to harness and direct the firm's drive, and at the same time to enlarge the limits of my own personal freedom within it. I *belonged* to Merlin, you see; you never did. And yet I feel a greater need for freedom than you ever could. And then, other things which nail me down—family, race, environment . . . all these things held me spellbound and still do. Benedicta, don't cry." Unaccountably Benedicta had given a brief sob before bowing her head upon her knees; but it was only the noise of a child troubled in sleep by some fugitive day memory of a quarrel over a toy.

"Her death *halted* Me," said Julian with a meek softness of tone which carried a sort of weird hidden intonation in it—the provisional hint perhaps of a madness which one had come increasingly to feel was not so far away? No, this is too strong. "This week," he went on wearily, "has been a week of great misgivings, all due to Nash, who has suddenly appeared on the scene with all kinds of new questions to ask about her. None of which I am able to answer, though I am quite as much up in the lingo, and anal-oral theology, as you are. Nash, incidentally, wants to have her destroyed."

"Destroyed!"

" 'She will do us no good,' he says. 'Indeed she carries buried fatally in her construction the thumbprints—the Freudian thumbprints of her makers.' So he says. In other words, she can't, as I suggested, stand for an aesthetic object related to our culture because you have deprived her of the very organs upon which it is based. I am repeating only what he said. Where is the *merde* that sank a thousand ships? That is what he asks. In fact he has been trying in his clumsy way to analyze why I should have decided to have her created, and specially in the image of the only person . . ." He broke off and stared into the fire, following with restless intentness the shifting flames as they patterned themselves upon the wall. "They are satisfied with so little," he went on, "these psychologists, and the most trifling analogy offers them an apparent explanation to something. As when Nash analyzes why I should choose her, above all women, as my prime symbol—the money goddess, the goddess of the many. It smells too easy, doesn't it? And analysis is often along a very shallow trench; it isn't very far down to the Paleolithic levels either. But on Nash plods, with his free association. The screen itself is a sterile thing in essence—bed sheet or winding-sheet, or both; but lightly dusted over with alchemical silver the better to capture the projected image so dear to the collective unconscious—the youthful mother-image with its incestuous emphasis. . . . On the one hand one would have the right to burst out laughing, no? Yet on the other . . . ah! Felix.

"Yes, this week of misgiving has been chock-full of questions about Iolanthe; it would have been better if you yourself had been there to answer them, however provisionally. I tried my best to get Nash to see her as simply a small observation post upon the field of automation—nothing much more. But that does not quite satisfy him. It was a mistake in the beginning to talk to him about culture or aesthetics—unconsciously we were all trying to disguise the base metal of our search in a number of pretty ways. Yes. To the psychoanalyst it is dirt. By the way, have you ever seen a gold brick? I happen to have one with me; I am taking it off to Jamaica. Let me show you."

It couldn't well have been more incongruous, the juxtaposition of tailcoat, top hat, and the small brown paper parcel which lay under them, tied up with string. A middle-class-enough-looking parcel which he undid with an air of dogged, modest triumph and then set the little greenish loaf with its deeply indented seal squarely upon the carpet between us. It sat there glinting saturninely in the firelight.

Julian said: "Freud says that all happiness is the deferred fulfillment of a prehistoric wish, and then he adds: 'That is why wealth brings so little happiness; money is not an infantile wish.'" He sat down, musing deeply for a moment; then he got down softly upon one knee and began to do up the little green loaf in its brown paper, tying the string carefully round it. Having secured it he replaced it once more upon the windowsill, in the folds of his overcoat, under the topper. "I have been studying the demonic of our capitalistic system through the eyes of Luther—a chastening experience in some ways. He saw the final coming to power in this world of Satan as a capitalistic emblem. For him the entire structure of the Kingdom of Satan is essentially capitalistic—we are the devil's own real property, he says: and his deepest condemnation of our system is in his phrase 'Money is the word of the Devil, through which he creates all things in exactly the way God once created the True Word.' In his devastating theology, capitalism manifests itself as the ape of God, the *simia dei*. It is hard to look objectively at oneself in the shaving mirror once one has adventured with this maniac through the 'Madensack' of the real shared world—this extended worm bag of a place out of which squirm all our cultural and gnomic patterns, the stinking end gut of a world whose convulsions are simply due to the putrefying explosions of fecal gas in the intestines of time." He paused, musing and shaking his head. "And then gold itself, as Spengler points out, is not really a color, for colors are natural things. No, that metallic greenish gleam is of a satanic unearthliness; yet it has an explicit mystical value in the iconography of our churches." He relit his cigar with a silver lighter.

"And then from gold to money is only a very short jump, but a jump which spans the shallow trench of our whole culture and offers us some sort of rationale for the megalopolitan men we are and our ways; *our ways!* For money is the beating heart of the New Word, and the power of money to bear *interest,* its basic *raison d'être,* has created the big city around it. Money is the dynamo, throwing out its waves of impulse in the interest principle. And without this volatility principle of Satan's gold, there would have been no cities. The archaeologists will tell you

that they have noted the completest rupture of the life-
style of man once he had founded his first cities. The
intrusion of *interest-bearing* capital is the key to this
almost total reorganization of man, the transvaluation of
all his rural values. From the threshing floor to the square
of a cathedral city is but a small jump, but without interest-
bearing capital it could never have been made. The economy of the city is based wholly upon economic surplus—it
is a settlement of men who for their sustenance depend on
the production of agricultural labor which is not their
own; it is the *surplus* produce of the country which consti-
tutes the subsistence of the town. But Nash will hasten to
tell you that for the unconscious the sector of the surplus is
also the sector of the sacred—hence the towering cathedral
city with its incrustation of precious gems and sculptures
and rites; its whole economy becomes devoted to sacred
ends. It becomes the 'divine household,' the house of
God."

He put back his head and gave a sudden short bark of a
laugh, full of a sardonic sadness. He looked so strange,
Julian, bowed under the weight of these speculations; he
looked at once ageless and very old. "I've had difficulty in
convincing Nash that our science is still so very backward
that for comfort's sake we still feel the need to build
ourselves working models of things—whether trains, tur-
bines, or angels! In aesthetics as against technics, of course,
a whole new flock of ideas comes chattering in like starlings.
We are at the very beginning of a phase—one can feel that;
but one wishes that the bedrock were newer, fresher,
contained fewer archaic features. No? The old death figure
is there, side by side with creative Eros, longing to pull us
back into the mire, to bury us in the stinking morasses of
history where so many, innocent and guilty, have already
foundered. As far as Iolanthe is concerned, I freely confess
that I am at a disadvantage as compared with you; you
knew her, you knew the original, you have something real
to compare her with. But I have only a set of data, like

outworn microscope slides, with which to compare her; her films, her life—I have assembled the whole dossier. But when I meet her it will be a momentously new experience—I feel so sure of that. Yes."

Suddenly he seemed to be almost pleading, like a schoolboy, his hands pressed between his knees, his eyes searching mine for a trace of reassurance. I felt it was in some way unhealthy to become so intense about a dummy—the whole thing filled me with unease, though it would have been hard to explain to myself why. Nothing could have been saner than his glance, nothing more unflinching than his grasp on language when it came to trying to disentangle all these interlocking concepts. Julian sat for a long moment, staring into the fire and then continued. "I am probably ready for her in this new form. I have always behaved as much like an immortal as I could—the negative capability, you might say, of deprivation. Like a Jap prince or a Dalai Lama, I have been forced to develop in captivity, all by myself. But if I haven't been evil I have been a keen student of evil—in alchemical terms, if you like; I was prone to the white path by nature; but I trod the black in order to divine its secrets. Some few I managed to appropriate for myself—but pitifully few. I wanted like everyone else to assuage the aches and pains of humanity. What an ambition."

"I wonder, Julian," I said, gently caressing the nape of Benedicta's neck. "I see you rather as enjoying it as pure experience, for its own pure sake." He gave a soundless little chuckle and half admitted the truth of the charge. "Perhaps. But then that *is* the black path. It admits of no compromise, one has to become it, to tread it; but there is no obligation to remain fixed there, like a joker in a pack. One can extricate oneself—albeit after a long struggle against the prince of darkness, or whatever you might call the Luciferian principle. The struggle of course makes one unbelievably rich; if you keep your reason, you emerge from the encounter with a formidable body of psychic equipment at your disposal. Not that that does much good to anyone in the long run. . . ." He yawned deftly, compactly, like a cat, before resuming. "I must be on the high seas tomorrow. Look, Felix, you do understand why I have been having these long sessions with Nash? I wanted to plumb as far as possible the unconscious intentions behind my desire to make a neo-Aphrodite—one who cannot eat, excrete, or make love. In terms of her own values—and I use the phrase because I know that you have endowed her with a built-in contemporary memory which can give an account of any contingency. Total memory, seen of course from our own vantage point in time. But suppose her to be free—suppose the world were in charge of a dozen models as perfect as she is—various other factors would obviously come into play. What, for example, would be their attitude toward money? What sort of city could such creatures come to found and finally to symbolize? Eh? It's worth a thought. Then, what would happiness represent for her, since she is free from the whole Freudian weight of everything that makes us 'un'; could you arrange for her, ideally, to have the free play of a natural lubricity, an eroticized function which ideally need never rest? No, because she isn't fertile—that's the answer, isn't it? And yet she is word-perfect, she walks in beauty like the night. Felix . . . could such a thing . . . could Iolanthe in her dummy form *love?* And what form would such an aberration take? I suppose when we have Adam we will be able to see a little more clearly into this abyss. I am so looking forward to seeing her, knowing her in natural surroundings—pardon the phrase. This free woman, free from the suppurating weight of our human mother fixation. She can neither love nor hate. What a marvelous consort she might make for someone. Does she know good from evil? There is no such question; does anyone? We are impelled to act before we think. No, let me finish. . . .

"Action, whatever they tell you, in almost every case precedes reflection; what we recognize as right and wrong action is almost always the fruit of a retrospective judgment. God, what a host of ontological problems she could raise . . . could she, for example, realize she is a dummy as much as, say, you realize that you are Felix? We don't really know, do we, until we ask her? And even then, one slip on the keyboard might give one totally unknown factors to consider. At what point could she invent, could she be original, supposing she slipped among the mnemonic signatures?"

He had begun to walk slowly up and down the room with a kind of burning, I could say "incandescent" concentration upon this conversation to which I myself did not wish to add a word. I was an artificer, I was simply there to wait and see at which angle the thing went off; and then to correct its trajectory whenever possible like a good mathematical papa. No, this isn't quite true; it would be truer to say that when one is dealing with inventions it is safer to go step by step, and not lose oneself among theoretical considerations before the actual model can start ticking over.

"Julian," I said, "give yourself time; you will soon be able to call on her in her own snug villa, take tea with her, converse on any subject under the sun; listen to her as she plays jazz to you, cherish her in every way. We can promise you a degree of the real which you will find quite fascinating, quite disturbing. I wouldn't myself have believed that our craftsmen at Merlin's could have been capable of such fine workmanship. Indeed she's so damn near perfect that Marchant suggested that we build a small fleet of them—our 'love machines' he called them; we could turn them out on the streets and live on their immoral earnings. From the customer's point of view they would be virtually indistinguishable from the real article—better dressed and better bred, perhaps, that is all. And from a legal point of view our position would be quite unassailable. They would, after all, be dummies: nothing more."

He smiled and shook his head: "I wish you wouldn't use

that word," he said softly. "It always suggests something old and primitive and creaking, studded with levers and buttons. Not something sophisticated, something of our decade. By the way, when she is launched will there be any way of controlling her?" It was my turn to stretch my aching legs, and prop B.'s head with a pillow. "That's the whole point, Julian. Once launched there is no stop-go button or rewind or playback; she is as irrevocably launched as a baby when you hit it on the bottom and force it to utter the birth cry. I had to confer full human autonomy on Iolanthe, don't you see? Otherwise our whole experiment would have been diminished; I could not have given her the mnemonic range if we had had to allow for cutting out the current every ten days, rewiring, recharging—as if she were a model train or yacht, run by remote control. We simply leaped over all these considerations; and when she rises from her bed of sickness and roams abroad in the world, there will be no calling her back! We'll have to take her as she is, for better or for worse, in sickness or in health, in fair weather or foul. But that is how you wanted her, isn't it?"

"God, of course!" he cried softly but passionately. "I wanted her absolute in every way." I heard the words with a pang, so charged were they with love, with desolation, with hunger. "She's breakable, of course, and ultimately wear-outable, I suppose, but probably less than you or I. She will outlive us all, I dare swear, if she isn't smashed or run over by a car. The organization is pretty delicate but the substitutes we've used for bone and cartilage and vein paths is a hundred times more durable and dependable than what God gave us poor folk. And of course she won't age, relatively speaking; her hair and skin will keep their gloss longer than yours or mine."

Benedicta said suddenly, without opening her eyes, "Julian, I'm afraid of this thing."

"Of course. You must be," said Julian, his voice full of a vague reassurance. "Nothing like it has ever been done."

"What good can come of it?" said Benedicta. "What will you do with her—she cannot breed, she's just a set of responses floating about like a box kite, answering to every magnetic wind. Will you just sit and watch her?"

"In holy wonder," said Julian greedily, "and with scientific care."

"Benedicta, there hasn't ever been one," I said mildly.

She lay there still, my wife, her head supported by the cushion, her eyes closed, but with an expression of intense concentration on her face—as if she were fighting off a painful migraine.

"No," she said at last, almost below her breath, with a tone of firm decision. "It won't do. Something will certainly go wrong."

Julian looked at his watch and whistled softly. "My goodness, it's getting late and I haven't yet come to the real subject of my visit to you two; of course I was worried about that phone call but really there was something else on my mind. It concerns my brother Jocas in Polis."

"Jocas."

The wind rose suddenly and skirled round the house. I had not thought of Jocas for ages now; and the memory of him, and of Turkey, had faded like an old photograph. Or perhaps it was simply that in this rain- and snow-swept countryside it was hard to evoke the bronze-stubbled headlands where the sturdy little countryman rode to his falcons, calling out in that high ululating muezzin's voice of his as he urged his favorite bird in to the stoop. Jocas existed now like a sort of colored illustration, an illuminated capital, say, in some yellow old Arabic text; yet he was after all in Merlin terms all of Africa, all of the Mediterranean. "First of all Jocas believes he is dying, and perhaps he isn't wrong, although the information comes to him from his Armenian astrologer—a very acute man, I must admit, who has seldom been at fault. Well, anyway, there he is, for what it's worth. He has several months ahead of him, he believes, in which to prepare himself, and is apparently doing it in customary Merlin style, in the high style, that is to say. In my own case, this new turn of events has sort of blunted the edge of the lifetime of enmity I have borne him—I can confess it freely only now. It had ebbed away now, the hate, leaving only respect and regret for the man."

"Julian!" cried Benedicta sharply, opening her eyes and staring angrily at him. "I don't like you in the mock-humble mood. It is false. You cannot stop being a demon now just because Jocas is dying, just because you will get your way at last. You have been at each other's throats ever since you were born."

Julian paled, his dark eyes flashed briefly like precious stones before hooding themselves once more under their heavy lids, to give his whole face an expression of massive and contemptuous repose—like an Inca mask, I thought. He paused for a long moment and then went on in a quiet voice, ignoring her and addressing himself to me, as if he were seeking a sympathy or comprehension which I was more likely to accord him than she. "I shall leave myself out of the picture, then, and simply sketch in the details of the matter for you, supposing that the business of his death is a fact, and actually takes place a few months from now. It will raise of course the question of his replacement in the Eastern field; and I have no doubt, Felix, that the senior boardroom will be extremely keen to have you take over the responsibility from him. It doesn't surprise you, does it? Of course the decision is yours and hers, Benedicta's. That is the first point."

"My God," I said with a mixture of wonder and distaste, never having visualized myself as occupying any position of administrative power in this octopus of a firm. "As I say," went on Julian, a trifle sardonically, "all that is contingent upon the movement of a few planets across the natal chart of Jocas. When and if it does happen you will have to think about it. But for the moment all Jocas wants is to see you again; he wants you to visit him briefly. I leave the question of timing to you. Obviously you won't want to abandon our experiment before it is complete; I mean Iolanthe. But once she breathes, once she walks, you might feel like taking Benedicta for a short visit to Turkey. Or perhaps before. It's how you feel."

The thought itself was full of the meretricious dapple of unfamiliar sunlight—seen through the long gray corridors of an eternal English winter; one forgot the damp, one forgot the scorching winds on the uplands, the miasmic stenches of the great capital at evening. . . . No, all that remained was this travel-poster sunlight with its enticing glint. Benedicta looked once more sunk in thought. "The timing is up to you," said Julian again softly, "but I shouldn't leave it too long. As a matter of fact we are sending out a small party of people at the end of the month—we've chartered a plane. You know some if not all of them: Caradoc, Vibart and Goytz, for example."

"Caradoc! Why?"

"He's coming back to us again on the circular staircase. Jocas has been on for some time about building himself, indeed all of us, a mausoleum—if that's the word. He wants to unite the remains of my mother and . . . father." A funny little contortion traveled over his features as he uttered the word. It was as if the word itself cost him something to bring out. He repeated it in a whisper: "My *father*," as if to secure a firmer purchase on it; to possess it more thoroughly. "I think perhaps Caradoc is the man to talk to him about it; I have no views one way or the other. As far as parents are concerned, I am hardly aware of having had any; my father was something quite different— he was simply Merlin. I owe him everything good and bad that has happened to me in my life. I am not a sentimentalist like Jocas—more particularly now he is growing old, and feeling, I suppose, his childlessness. Anyway, that is roughly the picture as he has sketched it for me. O and by the way, according to the soothsayer I myself don't outlive him by very long. As if I cared . . ." His weariness, his sadness rang out clearly in the silence of the little room, and the phrase hung fire, remained unfinished. "When I was young, and could not sleep at night, Benedicta was sent to read or recite to me to calm my spirits. I can still remember one of the poems you recited—perhaps you have forgotten?" In his soft negligent tones, so fluent and at the same time so full of charm, he repeated the lines:

> "Merlin, they say, an English prophet born,
>   When he was young and govern'd by his mother,
>   Took great delight to laugh such fools to scorn,
>   As thought, by nature we might know a brother.
>
>   His mother chid him oft, till on a day,
>   They stood, and saw a corse to burial carried,
>   The father tears his beard, doth weep and pray;
>   The mother was the woman he had married.
>
>   Merlin laughs out aloud instead of crying;
>   His mother chides him for that childish fashion;
>   Says, Men must mourn the dead, themselves are dying,
>   Good manners doth make answer unto passion. . . ."

He hesitated for a moment, hunting in his memory for the next line; but Benedicta took up the strain and finished the poem in a voice which seemed charged with a queer mixture of pride and sorrow.

> "This man no part hath in the child he sorrows,
>   His father was the monk that sings before him:
>   See then how nature of adoption borrows,
>   Truth covets in me, that I should restore him.
>   True fathers singing, supposed fathers crying,
>   I think make women laugh, that lie a-dying."*

Julian smiled and said: "Thank you. That's it. And it's a fitting note on which to wish you an apologetic good night. Felix, make your own decisions about Jocas. I shall be

---

* Fulke Greville.

away anyway if you decide to go now. And another thing, could you give Rackstraw a glimpse of your handiwork—I fear he is really completely useless for my purposes; he's too far gone? I would really like him out of the way before the others come into the picture. And so good night to you. My God, it's nearly morning."

He had slipped into his coat and muffled himself up in his white scarf; the brown paper parcel with its trophy was tucked under his arm. He hesitated at the door for a moment, as if he were hunting among all his available expressions for one which might seem perfectly suitable to this leave-taking. "Don't worry," he said at last, lamely, to Benedicta, and to me, "until very soon."

Thus he outlined himself for a second on the spectral snowscape and then was gone, softly closing the door behind him. An effortless disappearance as always.

There was a long silence; Benedicta stood drooping with fatigue and staring into the fire. "He is no Greek," she said at last, grimly. "Our Julian does not know the word *hubris;* he thinks you can give life as easily as you can take it—and you are following him blindly, perhaps into a trap, my poor foolish Felix."

"Come," I said. "He is transformed since we gave him back the hope of an Iolanthe. He's a new person!"

"You don't know him," she said. "His form of ambition is so absolute that he could crush anyone in his path without a thought. I have been his victim once. I could tell you a strange enough tale of his alchemical experiments on me, his powers over matter—a long sad tale of false pregnancies, mock miscarriages, even the birth of a changeling with the head of a . . . thing! Murder, too, if you wish. But it was all sanctified by the fact that these were scientific experiments conducted not from evil motives but purely in the name of alchemical curiosity; rather like your scientific self-justifications for the torture and vivisection of animals and so on. He has abandoned all that now— or so he says."

"I don't know what you are getting at."

"I am only saying that whatever his final intentions are he is masking them from us; he is using you as usual."

"Of course. What is wrong about it? I am doing a job for him—but a job after my own heart as well."

Suddenly she turned round and put her arms round me. There were tears in her eyes as she said: "Well, I am so happy to have escaped him, to have freed myself. I can't tell you the relief. I should be the one to put red roses on Iolanthe's tomb every day as a thank offering. Free!"

Nevertheless that night, for the first time for ages, I surprised her sleepwalking; rather, I woke to find her standing at the window, having drawn back the curtains. I thought she was watching the wonderful snowfall of the early morning, but when I moved to her side and put my arm round her slender shoulders, I saw with surprise that her eyes were shut. And yet, not entirely, for she felt my touch and turned her sleeping face to mine in order to say: "I think we must really go and see Jocas. I think Julian is right. We should go and see Jocas as soon as possible."

"Wake," I said, shaking her. She came to abruptly and shook herself. "What have I been saying?" I kissed her and said, "That we should go and visit Jocas. It was exactly what I was thinking. But you were sleepwalking, an ominous sign."

"Fatigue," she said, "nothing more. Kiss me."

FIVE

Some ten days later, having made my arrangements with Marchant and Said to keep Iolanthe "feeding": that is to say "charging": and to fill in the time by working on the male dummy Adam until my return . . . having done all this, I drove a patient Benedicta down to Southampton, our point of embarkation for the journey to Turkey. A freezing rain fell upon a muted landscape of rime-stiffened hills and clay pits—the winter at its beastliest. Perhaps it was a trifle wicked to allow the heart to lift with every thought of a spring-pierced Mediterranean, with its oranges glowing on faraway islands and its lofty March seas . . . but lift it did. Only she was thoughtful while I whistled to myself cheerfully to drown the skirling of the tires on the black wet roads. Moreover it was impossible not to feel that this would turn out to be some sort of holiday—despite, I mean, the sobering news of Jocas and his death-oriented preoccupations. A holiday feeling was in the air, and it was accentuated when we at last ran Caradoc to earth in a dockside pub on Pier 3 to which, for some mysterious reason, we had been directed. We were not going by sea, were we? I would have preferred the old Orient Express with its long romantic rumble across the heart of Europe. But we were in the hands of the firm's travel people. Everything had been arranged, as usual.

As for Caradoc, he looked both flushed and incoherent, as much with pleasure as with alcohol; but it was quite appalling the physical state he was in—his clothes dirty and torn, his new shaggy beard ungroomed. "I know," he said, taking in our consternation. "Don't look now; I've been camping in Woodhenge and Stonehenge—damn disagreeable month I can tell you, living like an ape under a bush. But the firm is sending me down a couple of suitcases of decent clothes and shaving kit. I'll soon be worthy of your respect." He made a hermetic gesture which the barman instantly translated into three double whiskies. "I'm back in the firm," he said suddenly, jubilantly, laughing a harsh ho-ho. "Once more into the breach, dear souls. For the moment I'm being forced to work in the graveyard section it seems, laying out cemeteries, designing mausolea and all that; but Julian says if I'm a good boy I can work my way back through public conveniences and council houses toward some real architecture. For the moment it's a sun-oriented mausoleum—once more Jocas has called for a funeral monument! It may be my last really free job—but who am I to worry? Two more mnemons in today's paper, have you seen?" He was beside himself with self-congratulation.

"And now to cap it all," he added, jerking a thumb, "look what the firm has hired. Just look." The mystery of our presence in the dock area was at last explained by the old gray flying boat which lay at anchor in the swell, snubbing the light craft surrounding it, and presumably waiting for its passengers and crew. My misgivings were only to be allayed when we finally did go aboard by tender and found out just how spacious and comfortable it was with its two decks, its bars and conference room where we were to dine and pass most of our time. It was a good choice, really, but as a craft she was slow, slow as the devil; moreover I gathered we would have to touch down almost everywhere to refuel—Marseilles, Naples, Bari, Athens. . . . Ah, but that was something else in its favor, for we could stop overnight anywhere. Perhaps in Athens we could look in on the Countess Hippolyta? I conferred with Caradoc and dispatched a telegram warning her of our threatened descent upon Naos, her country house.

What was not easy was the takeoff, however; we leeched up and down the sound, trying to get up sufficient speed to free ourselves, to get airborne, but in vain. We were stuck to the water as if to flypaper; the great engines groaned and screamed, the spars shuddered, the hull vibrated under the thwacking of waves. But at long last, after a run which seemed to last an eternity, she suddenly broke free, tore herself loose from the shackles of the water and swayed up into the free air, turning in a long slow curve over the land with its toy houses and gardens and infantile piers and railway stations—turning her prow toward the tall blue spring sky which waited for us somewhere off Corsica. And all at once the noise diminished and speech became possible; from everywhere stewards appeared with drinks and sandwiches. A few light pantomime clouds puffed around us in glorious Cinerama, giving us the illusion of speed and mastery. Our spirits rose.

There was so much room that each of us had a choice of different corners if we wanted to read or work or doze. Vibart, for example; he had gone off to the far end of the saloon to sit alone, briefcase on knee, gazing out of the window. We had hardly had a chance to exchange a nod. He had arrived at the last minute in an office car, and had been forced to gallop down to the tender and crawl aboard with scarcely enough time to exchange a wave with his friends and colleagues. But he looked sad and somehow withdrawn in his dark city clothes and broad-brimmed Homburg. Goytz, on the contrary, looked splendrous but completely relaxed. One might imagine him to be perhaps a great violinist on his way to fulfill an engagement abroad. He had a mysterious leather box which, though somewhat like a gun case in shape, could easily have housed a master's Stradivarius. Spectacles on nose he benignly if sleepily leafed his way through what looked like a large seed catalog—though the illustrations were of corpses in various states of prize-winning splendor. But if Vibart looked unhappy and withdrawn how much more so did Baum, the firm's overseas sales representative? He looked as if he were listening intently to his own inner economy and trying to ascertain whether he was going to be sick or not. I went to pass the time of day with him, for he was very sensitive, very Jewish, and quick to imagine that neglect by a senior might be a slight. I found though that his preoccupations, though unusual, had nothing to do with airsickness. "I am worried about England," he said broodingly, gazing down at as much of it as swam into visibility through the low cloud. "I am worried about the young, Mr. Felix. They are all studying economics. They are all taking degrees in it—you can get them anywhere now. Now you know and I know that economics isn't really a subject at all. But the mental evolutions necessary to study it can easily fix one at the anal stage for the rest of one's life. And people fixed at the anal stage are a danger to humanity, Mr. Felix. Is it not so?" It was. It was.

I agreed seriously with him; his brooding concern for the national fate was so well grounded and so sincere. I wondered if Goytz was fixed at the anal stage . . . and Nash? Or Julian, trotting about with that golden turd in the brown paper parcel? I patted Baum's shoulder in silent sympathy and signaled the steward for another reviver. Benedicta slept, so innocently, so discreetly. If I had to be murdered, I thought, by somebody I would like it to be by somebody like her. Caradoc's voice poured in upon me, raised half a tone against the massive thrum of the great engines as they pushed us across the skies of France. "I haven't wasted my exile one bit," he said exultantly. "Although this trip to Stonehenge nearly killed me with cold. I went down with Pulley and a sextant to take some readings and do some drawings. You know my old interest in deducing a common set of principles for all our architectural constructions? It still stands up, and wherever I touch the matter I get verifications, whether the Parthenon or the Celebes—whether ancient or modern, whether Canberra or Woodhenge. It's as if city-builders had a built-in gyrocompass which pushed them to build in respect to certain cosmic factors like sun, moon and pole."

He sipped his drink and adopted a pleased and somewhat glassy expression as he divagated about megaliths aligned to the sun as early as 1800 B.C.; about early Pole Stars like Vega and Betelgeuse and their influence upon the orientation of cities and temples. "Why," he said regally, "Pulley and I even discovered a magnetic field at Stonehenge—a certain place near the center which gave off enough juice to demagnetize a watch, or make a compass squeal with pain. It's reminiscent of the spot at Epidaurus where the acoustic wave is at its highest and clearest. I hadn't got anything to leave as a marker but my drawings have it. I don't know yet what such a thing might prove. And by the way the same goes for St. Paul's Cathedral— there's a magnetic spot in the main aisle, about where they've sunk that black hexagonal stone. Again I'm not surprised as perhaps I should be. St. Paul's is of course more an engineering feat than any of the other cathedrals and naturally much less aesthetically beautiful. It was built by a great artificer in conscious pursuit of mathematical principles; it was not a dream of godhead full of poetry of frozen music or what not. No, it belonged to its age; it was a fitting symbol for a mercantile country in an age dedicated to reason, hovering on the edge of the Encyclopaedia and the Industrial Revolution. It is no accident that the business part of the city, the moneyed part, grouped itself round this great symbol of the stock and share. Nor is it an accident that it should in some ways feel strongly reminiscent of a railway station—say Euston or Waterloo. It stands as a symbol for the succeeding ages which produced both. But after St. Paul's where do we go? The dome's rise is like the South Sea Bubble. The Mercantile dream has been shattered. And now that the mob has too much pocket money we can expect nothing so much as a long age of bloodshed expressed by the concrete block. It is hard nowadays to distinguish a barracks from a prison or a block of dwellings—indeed I'd go so far as to say it was impossible. They belong to the same strain of thought—Mobego I call it after our old friend Sipple. I wonder if we'll see him in Turkey? It is quite impossible to predict what might come out of it, though one can almost be sure that some sort of universal death by boredom and conformity is being hinted at. And I won't live to see what happens after the bloodbath. . . ." He mooned on, slowly drumming himself into innocent slumber with his tongue rocked by the soft drubbing and jolting of the huge plane in the air currents of the French mountain ranges.

I wondered what Julian might make of these considerations. Obviously he would have seen the results of Caradoc's work.

As Benedicta still slept with the new *Vogue* on her knee, I started to make my way across to Vibart in order to exchange a word with him, but I was waylaid once more by the pensive Baum who motioned me to sit down with the obvious intention of opening his heart to me. I hoped we would not have to dwell any longer on the English nation and its habits, as I had long since given up worrying about it; fortunately not, it was now the turn of the Jews. "I am wondering," said Baum *sotto voce,* looking around to see if we might be overheard, "if there isn't a touch of anti-Semitism entering the firm from somewhere. Lately I have been troubled." When Baum was troubled he had a very troubled look indeed. "From where?" I said, longing to break free from what threatened to be a curtain lecture.

"From Count Banubula," he said surprisingly enough, suddenly staring me in the eye in a challenging manner.

"Banubula?" I said with genuine puzzlement. Baum nodded with compressed lips and went on slowly, with emphasis. "Yesterday I overheard something in the senior boardroom which made me pause, Mr. Felix. He was there addressing a very large group of salesmen. I don't know what the meeting was about or where they were selling, but what he was saying was this: I made a note." Always meticulous, Baum produced a pocket diary with a note in shorthand. He cleared his throat and read in a vague imitation of Banubula's aristocratic drawl the following: "Now the foreskin, as everybody knows, is part of the poetic patrimony of man; whether firmly but gracefully retracted or in utter repose it has been the subject for the greatest painters and sculptors the world has known. Reflect on Michelangelo, his enormous range . . .'" Baum put the book away with pursed lips and said, "That was all I heard because they closed the door, but I was very struck. I wonder if all those salesmen were Jews and whether he was . . ." I drained my drink and took the dear fellow by the forearm. "Listen," I said, "for God's sake listen, Baum. Michelangelo was a Jew. Everybody was a Jew: Gilles de Rais, Petrarch, Lloyd George, Marx and Spender, Baldwin, and Faber and Faber. This much we know for certain. BUT THEY HAVE ALL KEPT THEIR FORESKINS. What you don't know is that Banubula himself is a Jew. So am I."

"He is not. He is Lettish" said Baum obstinately.

"I assure you he is. Ask anyone." Baum looked mollified but in some deeper way unconvinced. He said: "Now that this work of his is so delicate that it is on the Top Secret list, one doesn't quite know what he is doing. I hesitate to accuse the firm of course; but with a Lett one never knows where he is." He looked overwrought. I took my leave of him in lingering loving fashion, smoothing out his sleeve and assuring him that everything would be all right. "Above all resist the impulse to become anti-Lettish," I said, and he nodded his acquiescence. though his face still wore a twisted and gloomy expression. He buried himself in his papers with a sigh.

Nor did Vibart seem the less gloomy as he sat looking sideways and down across the clouds to where somewhere slabs of blue sky were beginning to fabricate themselves. "Ah, Felix" he said moodily. "Come and sit down; you never answered my letter." I admitted the fact. "It was hard to know what to say; I was sorry. One couldn't just be awkwardly flippant—and flippancy has been our small change up until I ran away, got banged on the head, and wound up in the Paulhaus munching sedatives."

"I had to tell someone," he said. "And I was hoping that you would stay mad and locked up with the information. But it didn't work."

"Heard about Jocas?"

"Of course."

"Are you coming to see him? Or are you on some other mission and just using the firm's transport?" Vibart peered sideways at me and shot me a quizzical twisted look. He said nothing for a long time; then he replied with conciderable hesitation: "I deliberately made an excuse to come, a publisher's excuse. But I wanted really to see him once more in the flesh."

"But you know him, have met him."

Vibart sighed. "I knew him without really recognizing him as the man who had completely altered my life. I suppose it is a common enough experience—and always a surprising one. But what puzzles me is that in getting me my job with the firm he knew full well that I would be transferring myself to London and taking her with me. Why did he, then, feeling as he did and she did? Why not let me molder away for another four-year spell in the Consular, rising by slow degrees to a Chancery and some trite Councillorship in Ankara or Polis? When I suddenly heard the truth, I closed my eyes and tried to remember this benign little man's face. 'So *that* was *him*,' I said to myself 'all the time *that* was *him.*' All right, it's not good grammar; but the surprise hit me between the eyes. And death was the result. It's so very astonishing that I don't believe it yet. But I want just to look at him for once—my only link with Pia now on earth, Felix. My goodness, what a sublime trickster life is, what a double-dealer."

His eyes had filled with tears, but he conjured them away manfully by blowing his nose in a handkerchief and shaking his head. He stamped on the floor and cursed, and then all of a sudden turned quite gay. I recognized this feeling: after one has talked out a problem there is no longer the weight of it upon the heart; one can get almost gay, though the situation remains as desperate or as disagreeable as ever. "Now," he said, putting away his handkerchief with an air of decision and clearing his lungs. "Now then. That's enough of that." Poor Vibart and his lovely wife; I felt rather ashamed to have the figure of the reclaimed Benedicta lying asleep in one of the seats back there. But then death . . . ? We were all crawling about like ants on the Great Bed of Ware, choked with our so-called problems; and with this extraordinary unknown staring us in the face. "To hell with death," said Vibart robustly, as if he had read my mind. "It is merely a provisional solution for people who won't take the full psychic charge."

"What on earth's that?"

"To live forever, of course. Immortality is built-in, my dear boy; it's like a button nobody dares to touch because the label has come off it and nobody knows what might happen if one dared to press it. The button of the unknown."

"You are romancing, Vibart."

"Yes: but then no. I am serious." He shot another look at me, pensive and thoughtful, and settled himself deeper in his seat. "The thing is," he said, "that things turn into their opposite. For example, this man wounded me to the heart, and naturally I hated him—hated him long and with concentrated fury. But after some time the hate began to turn into a perverse kind of affection. I hated him for what he had done, yes; but in the end I was also feeling affectionate, almost grateful for the fact that he had made me suffer so much. Do you see? It was something that was missing from my repertoire, a most valuable experience which I might never have had without him. So now I am ambivalent—love-hate. But I am also consumed with curiosity just to see this chap—this demigod who could hold the future and the happiness of a fellow human being in the palm of his hand. Could administer such advanced lessons in suffering and self-abnegation to others—for I presume that in sending me to the firm in England he knew that I would take her away from him. Did he think more of the firm than of *her?* And was the inner knowledge of this what decided her fate, made her commit suicide, eh?"

What could one add or subtract? These long and furiously debated questions had obviously gnawed him almost away; they were responsible for the new gray-blond hair, thick and dusty, which had given his features a rare glow of refinement. They were equally responsible for his present slimness—for people who don't sleep well usually get thin. He had never, in fact, looked handsomer or in better physical trim; the weary, well-cut features had lost the last suspicion of chubbiness, had become mature, had settled into the final shape which the death mask alone could now perpetuate. Vibart was complete. (I found myself thinking rather along the lines of a dummy builder, occupied with the stresses and strains of false bone and ligament, nylon skin.)

"You know," he said, "that *we* had a child very late in the day? No? Well we did, or rather perhaps *they* did. At any rate it was too late in the day for Pia, for the result was a Mongol—a horrible little thing with flippers. Thank God, it died after a very short time—but there again I am not sure: did it fall or was it pushed? I think Pia did away

[220]

with it in pure disgust, and I am glad that she did, if she did. And so on. And so on in endless *mélopée*. Ouf! my dear Felix, here I am chewing your ear down to a stub when you yourself have really been through it. I came to share your distrust and terror of the firm after I had been in it awhile, after I had watched your antics, your long battle in and around the idea of a personal freedom which must not be qualified by this Merlin octopus. I too wanted to react against all this moral breast-feeding and might well have run away like you did, in order to hide myself away and start something uncontaminated, something really my own. But I decided that we were looking at it from the wrong point of view. I mean that in thinking of the firm as a sort of Kafka-like construct exercising pressure on us from without we were wrong; the real pressure was interior, it was in ourselves, this pressure of the unconscious lying within our consciousness like a smashed harp. It is this which we should try and master and turn to some use in the fabrication of . . . well, beauty."

"Lumme!" I said. "Beauty? Define please."

"In the deepest sense Beauty is what is or seems fully congruent with the designs and desires of Nature." We both burst out laughing, like people discovering each other for the nth time in the same maze—instead of finding each other outside the exit, I mean.

"Enough of this," I said and he bowed an apology, his eyes full of laughing exasperation. "Anyway, now it's too late," he went on. "So we must put a firm face on it; here, have a look at this outline will you? Some spy in the industry has unmasked all the activities of the firm in the drug business. Fortunately for us the manuscript was sent to me; they—he must have been unaware that my house was a Merlin subsidiary. So it gave me a chance to look at it and to muse; how much of this do we want out, and what can be done about it if we don't? That is why I am here; the Polis end of the drug business is shrouded in mystery, simply because business methods are so different;

abacus-propelled, old man. So I want Jocas to see and judge. That's my excuse anyway."

He absented himself for a while and I took a look through his drug dossier which was written in rather a jaunty journalistic vein which reminded me vaguely of Marchant's minutes—though the paper could hardly have been by him. . . . "Resin of cannabis is collected in various ways including, in Turkey, running through the fields naked to catch it on the bare skin. . . . Cigarettes are dosed with the dried tops, the shoots, or the flower pistils powdered. . . . As for qat, you must chew leaves or branches of the plant, but smoke while you chew and drink water copiously. In Ethiopia it is mixed in a paste with honey or else dried into a curry powder for use with food. In Arabia the leaf is rolled and smoked. But these are only some of the humbler drugs in which Merlin's has come to deal. The firm has also a virtual corner in Mexican morning glory seed—*ololiuqui*. But if the Oriental end of the firm handles products which give it rather an old-fashioned air, the London end is fully aware of contemporary standards and demands. The pharmaceutical subsidiaries of Merlin have gone further than any other such organizations. Befotenin, for example, is a drug first found in the skin glands of toads (the Bufo vulgaris) and also in the leaves of the mimosaceae of the Orinoco. This is already finding new medical uses as a hallucinatory snuff, though it is still on the secret list of the firm. Merlin subsidiaries are also working on a protein fraction obtained from the blood serum of schizophrenes which has been named taraxein; injections of this substance induce apparent schizophrenia in monkeys. But most disturbing of all the new secret drugs is Ditran—which is calculated to be very much more powerful than LSD or mescaline. . . ."

Here at last I came upon some marginalia in the characteristic handwriting of Marchant. "Ref Ditran. A single dose of 15 mg. rocks the world, old man; for extreme cases in the Paulhaus they supply multiple doses of 30 mg.

intramuscularly. God, you should hear them scream! It is so painful and so terrifying that the cures are often instantaneous as Lourdes and often much more general. The author is also slightly out about LSD. When the syndrome gets out of hand chlorpromazine can save the day with 20 to 50 mg. intramuscular doses repeated every thirty minutes—unless the heart gives out."

Vibart was back from his wash and brushup. "Well I see nothing wrong about all this." He lit a cigar and said: "I don't know. It's a question of degree. For example we have launched (under the counter, so to speak) a new cocktail with immense adolescent appeal—equal parts of vodka and *Amanita muscaria* juice—the hallucinogenic mushroom, no less. It's called a Catherine Wheel, after Catherine the Great, I suppose, who used to mushroom herself insensible in between love affairs. For my part I just don't know how much of all this should go out or not. We shall see what Jocas thinks, and then what Julian says." He read in a sententious voice a phrase which went: " 'Since earliest times a change of consciousness has been accredited with great healing power; this was recognized since the Eleusinian Mysteries and long before them.' " Then he snapped the ms. shut and thrust it back into his glossy briefcase. "We shall see," he said.

Night was falling over the dark sea, the clouds were straining away westward. We had lost altitude and gained the last frail blueness of the evening; softly we came down with an occasional rubbery bump, as if an air bladder had been as often smacked with the flat of the hand, until we were moving along almost in the water. Under us a fresh spring sea tilted and coiled back on itself, its simply lazy gesturing suggesting all the promise of sunshine which could not long be deferred. The lights went on and turned the outer world to lavender and then to dark purple. We were running along a heavily indented coastline with an occasional mountain pushing its snout into the empty sky. Somewhere a moon was rising. In another hour or so we should be skating and strumming across the Bay of Naples, where the captain had elected to stay the night and refuel. But it was not worth going ashore, as his plan was to start on the next leg of the flight a good hour before dawn, to gain as much light as possible for the Greek touchdown which he seemed to regard as rather more chancy than the Naples halt. None of this was our affair; we dined early and slept in our comfortable bunks.

Athens, when at last it came, was something quite other —at least for me, poised in its violet hollows like some bluish fruit upon the bare branches of night. The day had been brilliantly calm with here and there a mountain in the deep distance showing its profiles of snow, and a sea calmly pedaling away to a ruled horizon. But of course it was not only the old and often-relished beauty of the site, it was really the thronging associations. I suppose that Athens will always be for me what Polis must be for Benedicta—a place as much cherished for the sufferings it inflicted on one as for the joys. I had spent part of my youth here, after all, that confused and rapturous period when everything seems possible and nothing attainable. Here I had lived for a while with Iolanthe—not the semi-mythical star whom we were trying to re-create out of the pulp of rubbers and resins; but a typical prostitute of a small capital, resolute, gay, and beautiful. (I repeated her name to myself in the Greek way, reclaiming the original image of her, while I pressed Benedicta's arm with all the recollected tenderness I felt for this other shadow woman whom I had not recognized as a goddess when I actually owned her. Was I later to start almost to love her retrospectively, so to speak? And perhaps this is always the way? The amputated limb which aches in winter? I don't know.)

We moved now in a great fat bubble of violet and green sunlight, sinking softly down into the darkening bowl to where the city lay atremble. The night was darkling up over Salamis way. The outlines were turning to blue chalk, or the sheeny blue of carbon paper. But always the little white abstract dice of the Acropolis held, like a spread sail, the last of the white light as the whole of the rest of the world foundered into darkness. Hymettus turned on its slow turntable, showing us its shaven nape. We were just in time. We circled the city and its central symbol in time to see what was to be seen. Ants waved to us from under the plinth of the Parthenon and Caradoc waved back in a frenzy of amiability—to what purpose I could not discover, since nothing could be seen of us save smudges of white. Nevertheless. Meanwhile my eye had taken a swift reading, basing itself upon the plinth, and was racing through the streets to find the little hotel where, in Number Seven, so much of my life had passed. But I was not quick enough; by the time I got my bearing right, the street had slid into another and the buildings formed fours, obscuring the site I was hunting for. By now of course we had come down low for our landing, but must perforce carry out a long loop which would take us several miles out to sea, thus enabling us to run landward into Phaleron and touch down upon its placid waters. Everything went calmly, smoothly; a naval tender full of chattering Greek customs officials carried us joyfully toward the shore, making us feel that we had been anxiously awaited and that our arrival had thrown everyone into ecstasy. It was simply the national sense of hospitality manifesting itself; later on land we started to have trouble with an elderly official, but all at once Hippolyta's chauffeur appeared. "Grigori," we all cried and there was much embracing and dashing away of happy tears. Overcome by our bad Greek and obvious affection for the venerable Grigori, the customs people passed us through with bows and smiles. We were in. There were two cars, and after a short confabulation we decided on our various objectives. Caradoc, Benedicta and myself were to go to Naos and stay with the countess, while Vibart elected to spend the night in Athens with the other members of the party.

Caradoc was strangely subdued as we set off; Benedicta peeled a mandarin which a child had handed her; I thought, for no known reason, of the sunken rose garden with its nodding yellow tea roses, and of the draughts of music which flowed out into it on those still summer nights when we would sit so late by the cool air which hovered around the hushing lily pond. It would be too cold to dine out as yet. It was an age since I had seen Hippolyta. I asked Grigori how the countess had been keeping and he shot me a glance in the mirror. "Since Mr. Graphos died," he said, "she hardly goes out anymore. She is gardening very much and has built a little church for St. Barbara on the property." He paused, racking his brains for something else to tell me, but obviously there was not much. Or perhaps he did not wish to speak too freely before the others. Grigori was a northerner and had rather a fanatical sense of rank and the general proprieties. Chauffeurs should be reluctant to discuss their mistresses, even with old friends. So!

It was dark now, but the house was ablaze with light as we crossed the garden, leaving such luggage as we had to Grigori. She came to the door, she must have heard the engines of the car—Hippolyta, I mean. She stood rather shyly, holding it open and gazing shortsightedly into the darkness from which, one by one, her friends—her lifelong friends—would emerge. The greetings were long and tender. Back in the firelight in the huge room with its medieval vaulting, one could see how thin she had become.

"Welcome to Naos," she said softly. "O strangers to the Greeks." A quotation doubtless, and perhaps a soft reproof for so long a neglect. "But still out of season," she added, leading us in to divest ourselves of our coats. Yes, the rose gardens, the green citrons, the oleanders would have to wait until the spring became more generous with its sunlight. But the big awkward country house was gay with light. Fires blazed hospitably in the long vaulted rooms with their oil paintings of three generations of Hippolytas echoing each other. Degenerate trophies of the past—she had once called them that. The vaulted monastic rooms echoed with our voices. We had a chance really to look at each other. Hippolyta, though very much the countess still, and though transformed by age and experience—as we all had been—registered no really critical change for the worse. She had become thinner, yes, but this only emphasized the new frail boyishness of her figure, the slenderness of her arms. But nothing could submerge the dark mischievous Athenian eyes, with their swift sympathies and swifter touches of mirthfulness. The naïveté, the candor, these were there still; and from time to time touched by a kind of lofty sadness. Watching her smiling, and thinking about her love for Graphos, the politician, and what it had done to her life: and then of his death—I searched in my mind for a word which might do justice to this new maturity. She had the fruitful, sad yet happy look one sees on the faces of young widows. "Undamaged," I cried aloud, at last; and she gave a tiny shrug.

"I mean you are still living a life," I went on.

Now she laughed out loud and said: "Get thee to a nunnery, Felix, and see how it feels. The boredom! Ouf!"

The servants brought in trays of drinks and olives now, and we pledged each other in the firelight. Once Hippolyta had hated Benedicta, but now this feeling appeared to have given place to a warmer one. At any rate she held B.'s hands and shook them until the bracelet of ancient coins on her wrist clicked. Then she said in her frank way: "Once I remember hating you; it was because I was jealous of Felix and sorry for him and you were hurting him. But it didn't go really deep with me. Do you think we could be friends now? Shall we try?" Benedicta, with a word, put an arm round her waist, and together the two slender women walked the long length of the room in sisterly comradeship, saying nothing. I was delighted.

The companionable silence was broken only by a vast and somewhat typical hiccough from Caradoc. "Alcohol provokes the fruitful detonations from which ideas flow. But my digestion is not what it was, I must beware." Hippolyta smiled down upon him benignly. "An echo from the past," she said. "For when did whiskey never detonate you?"

"I am old, my locks are white," he replied gravely.

But she clapped her hands softly together, saying, "No; it is just that we have all changed places, haven't we? The pack has been shuffled. Everyone will be going round counterclockwise now. I expect the good to get badder and bad to get gooder; except in the exceptional cases—where one or other have got up enough momentum to stop the pendulum. Then if bad, they will achieve greatness by becoming horrible, unspeakable. If good they will become angels. What do you say to that?" In the calm of the great country house such propositions did not sound what they perhaps were—a trifle sententious.

"All change for the worse," said Caradoc testily. "Why since last we met I have been dead in Polynesia. I have been a bigamist, a trigamist, and heaven knows what else. I have been unrepentantly happy, Hippolyta, and still am. I am just in the right mood to build Jocas the mausoleum he wants."

"Good Lord," she said. "Has he started all over again, poor darling Jocas? There's an echo for you. Do you remember the last time?" She laughed and replenished Caradoc's drink. He too gave his histrionic lion's roar and slapped a knee. "Damn him, yes," he said. "He wanted nothing less than the Parthenon. At least he wanted the Niki temple—I just had to add a few rooms to that for members of the Merlin triple and he would have been quite happy. The ass!"

I remembered in a vague and indeterminate fashion the movement and bustle—and not less the mystery—of this long ago period. I had first met Caradoc here, in this house, and had subsequently spent a night in a brothel called the Blue Danube with him—a brothel run by Mrs.

Henniker, of all people, and where Iolanthe herself had worked for a while before being swept away on the wings of good fortune into the world of the film.

"I simply never got to the bottom of that business," I said. "Nobody would explain anything."

"Nobody could; or rather everybody thought something quite different. We were misled by Julian and also by Graphos. I only pieced it together slowly over the years. I don't think even Benedicta knew what was going on; all she knew was that you were in some sort of danger in Polis—you were then regarded as quite expendable, since the firm had complete possession of your notebooks. Yes, but here in Athens something else was going on; first of all a tug-of-war between Julian and Jocas, all over this blasted temple. Julian, as you know, had set his heart on getting control of the Parthenon for the firm. Now of course it's a *fait accompli*, everyone is used to it, but then . . . where would he find a politician daring enough or crooked enough to sign a secret protocol vesting the Parthenon and the hill it stands on in Merlin's? Of course Graphos was the obvious choice, but he demanded a very heavy price, partly out of patriotism and partly out of personal greed. On the one hand Merlin's must wipe out the National Debt, on the other rig an election to get him in as Prime Minister and keep him in until he had invested a personal fortune in Switzerland. They all told me lies: Graphos said he was saving the Parthenon from Julian, not selling it behind my back. Jocas, getting wind of this, wanted to walk off with the temple of Niki. That would have given the show away, so he had to be stopped. Julian did it somehow. But then came another complication. You remember a small, rather despicable figure called Sipple, the ex-clown? Caradoc does. He admired him extravagantly I remember. Well Sipple got wind of the protocol from some indiscretion of Caradoc and rang me up, hinting at blackmail. Silly fool . . . one word would of course have ruined Graphos. So Sipple had to be neutralized and sent away. We did that, and we were lucky to be aided by a personal scandal which made the little spy anxious to leave Athens and hide away somewhere. There, that is my story, at any rate. How right and how wrong I don't know. I still don't know."

"It was all my fault," said Caradoc.

I thought vividly of the boy with his throat cut lying on his side in Sipple's bed; of the birds beginning to chirp and preen as the dawn came up over the Salamis sea line; I saw Sipple standing there in his braces with traces of clown's makeup still on his face, round the eyes. I thought of Iolanthe who had committed the murder. It was unbelievable really. Unbelievable.

"It's all like a dream," I said.

"So much is. Time plays such strange tricks. Do you remember the old brothel, the Blue Danube, Caradoc?"

"Of course," he said robustly. "How could I ever forget what it taught me from the great book of life?"

"Well," said Hippolyta, "the other day I was driving along the corniche and I suddenly thought of you; I was passing the place in the car and I decided to stop and look at it. But my dear, *it had gone*. There was nothing but an empty sand dune where this quite considerable villa had once stood. I could hardly believe my eyes. I stopped the car and started to search like a lunatic. I knew the spot like the back of my hand. No good. There was nothing there. Yes, by dint of poking about in the sand I uncovered a few pieces of plaster and the tracing of what might have been a bit of foundation . . . yes, but an archaeologist would not have dated it as different from the old pieces of the Themistoclean wall one sees down toward Phaleron. *Gone!* The windows, the doors, the cupboards, the beds . . . all vanished. Even the *house* had vanished. What do you make of that? I wondered if there weren't gaps like that in the middle of our memory, vanished people and events. I felt so awful that I had to lean against a wall. I was very nearly sick when I thought of you and Felix moving from room to room there. I suddenly thought of

you as if you were dead. So long ago, all of it." She repeated the phrase in Greek in her low musical voice, and
then added under her breath, "And death behaves in such
an arbitrary fashion, striking when you are not looking,
not expecting."

"I refuse to be sad," said Caradoc. "May my dying
breath be a giddy oath, that's all I can say." Benedicta
patted his hand reassuringly as if to comfort him.

Hippolyta turned to me and in a lower register said: "I
saw a good deal of Julian, of all people; he was in Switzerland when I was. To my surprise he decided to manifest
and was most attentive in his strange way. You are building him some sort of echo of her—Iolanthe—aren't you? He
told me and I felt suddenly alarmed. Not for the fact but
from his way of speaking about it. What has come over
Julian? He seems to have lost his devil, to have become
somehow subdued. For example he said in a sweet resigned
sort of way: 'Obviously Felix will betray me when he can,'
and I wondered whether he was serious or not. As for what
you are building, any Greek would warn you against
hubris—tempting the wrath of the gods. . . ."

"The gods are all dead, or gone on holiday," I said
gloomily. "They've left their looms and spindles behind
for us to use as we see fit. Has Julian really changed so
much?"

"Yes. A sort of resignation. 'The firm has given and the
firm has taken away; blessed be the name of the firm,' " she
intoned softly but mockingly with her arms crossed on her
breast. "No, Felix. Some new element has entered the
picture. Julian has become so *human!*" I don't know why,
but the remark seemed to me to be one of the most sinister
I had ever heard. It was ridiculous, of course, but a sort of
shiver ran down my neck. I looked over at Benedicta and
saw, or thought I saw, that she herself had turned quite
white; but it may only have been her hair, the candlelight.
"Human," I said, turning the word over like a playing
card and gazing at its face, so to speak. Spades or hearts,

which? There was a silence broken only by Caradoc's champing of celery. He was not paying the least attention to what was said.

Hippolyta went on. "He told me a great deal of his last long wait by her bed all that night when she was dying—the last night. How he felt so crazy with grief and surprise, so unhinged that he found himself doing strange things, like making up his lips in the mirror with her lipstick. It terrified him but he felt compelled to do it. And then the lines of Heine kept going through his mind; his lips moved, he kept repeating them to himself in a whisper, over and over again, quite involuntarily. Do you know them, remember them? The Faustus ones?

> *"Du hast mich beschworen aus dem Grab*
> *Durch deinen Zauberwillen*
> *Belebtest mich mit Wollustglut—*
> *Jetzt kannst du die Glut nicht stillen.*
>
> *Press deinen Mund an meinen Mund;*
> *Der Menschen Odem ist göttlich!*
> *Ich trinke deine Seele aus,*
> *Die Toten sind unersättlich.*
>
> *You conjured me from my grave*
> *By your bewitching will,*
> *Revived me for this passionate love,*
> *A passion that you'll never still.*
>
> *Press your cold mouth on my cold mouth;*
> *Man's breath's by the Gods created.*
> *I drink your essence, I drink up your soul,*
> *For the dead can never be sated."*

A silence fell once more, in which the tenebrous and perverted verses of the returned Helen talking to her Faust echoed on impressively in the mind, vibrated on the heart, lighting up with their fitful shadow play the figure of Julian crouched there batlike in a clinic chair, watching a fly moving upon a dead eyeball. A picture to inspire both pity and despair. Hippolyta went on in a low voice: "It was clear that only some sort of vampire would do for him—nothing less."

Benedicta pressed her hands to her cheeks and said: "I know, Hippolyta. I know only too well. But he has had reason enough to become what he is; I tell myself always that it should still be possible to love him despite it all. But I don't know whether I can myself anymore. I don't know whether I can. And who else will? It's all so unlucky, so meaningless."

A draft blew in from a window and the candles wagged and danced on the long refectory table; we were quite startled, as if in some intangible way it was the breath of Julian which had entered the room; attracted perhaps by the verses or by the mention of his name. "An unquiet ghost," she said in Greek; and shivering drew her shawl about her shoulders. The impression of some such silent visitation was slightly heightened when, in a little while, the telephone began to peal in the depths of the house, insistent as a child calling. Hippolyta went out into the hall to answer it while we took our cigars and coffee back to the warm firelight in the outer room. We sat down, each absorbed in the thoughts set in motion by the verses of Heine and the mood they evoked. Presently Hippolyta came back and said: "The firm is calling you from London; they've traced you here. Shall I say you are out or in bed?"

"Why?" said I. "I'll see what they want."

I went out into the hall where the little phone booth stood; it had been converted from a satin-lined sedan chair. Inevitably the line was poor and the voices were crisscrossed with whirrs and clicks—it was like talking across the reverberations of some giant seashell. But yes, it was Nathan, waiting patiently for me. "It's Mr. Marchant, sir. He has been asking for you rather urgently. Hold on while I put you through to him."

Marchant sounded testy, as if he had been called out of

bed in the middle of the night, and yet relieved. "I wouldn't have bothered you," he said, "only Julian told me I should try and make contact and tell you that we've had rather a nasty accident on our hands here."

"Iolanthe!" I cried, my heart beating faster from sheer anxiety. "What has happened to her?"

"No. No," said Marchant. "It's the man, Adam. He's a total wreck, a write-off, I fear; but he's gone and killed poor old Rackstraw, of all people. Completely unexpected."

It could not well have sounded more astonishing, more improbable. "But how? Where?"

Marchant sighed with exasperation and said: "You know we had orders to let old Rackstraw into the lab to acclimatize himself to Iolanthe, and to test any reactions he might have. It was Julian's idea; I wasn't keen on it, but he said he'd discussed it with you and that you had seen no reason why not. Well, anyway, we drew a blank from the point of view of reactions. The old boy simply stared at our girl friend for ages without moving a muscle; I think he would have gone on forever had he not been led away by Henniker. Incidentally the effect on her was terrific; I have never seen anyone cry so hard and so long and so passionately. She kept saying, 'My God, she's so real,' over and over again and going into paroxysms, leaning against the wall. She is hardly calm as yet and they've been visiting us in the lab every day for a few hours. The old boy just hissed and croaked and wagged his eyebrows; but really they'd drawn a blank with him. He kept asking about the whereabouts of a chap called Johnson, that was all. Then yesterday we got so used to him standing there motionless that when I went to lunch Said forgot to lock up; or rather he just went out of the lab for a second, overlooking the fact that Rackstraw was still there. The next thing is he heard a crash and smelled a roasting smell. He rushed back to find Rackstraw rolling all over the floor like a centipede with this Adam creature wrapped round his neck; it was what you'd call a muscular reflex with a vengeance. I don't know what he could have been trying to do but he was badly burned and concussed and covered with Ejax into the bargain. Well, Said gave the alarm, and of course we had some difficulty over the current; the dummy had become live. But anyway they finally turned everything off and disentangled Rackstraw who was led away to hospital. The next thing we heard in the middle of the night was that he had died of heart failure. It's being hushed up, the whole episode, and presented as a normal death—heaven knows it was about time; he'd long overstayed his welcome, the old man. But Julian said that you ought to be told. There is a bit of electrical damage to the big feeder but that can be repaired. Otherwise we are moving along; you will have to make a much stronger temperature control stat, or else she will overheat, and then she's likely to write free verse: I suppose as any normal person might do in a delirium. It all happened yesterday. She lost optimum temperature control and committed a poem. Felix, are you there still?"

"Yes. I was thinking of Rackstraw. Poor old thing. Is the dummy completely smashed, irrecoverable?" Marchant thought for a moment. "Yes," he said, but doubtfully. "But the funny thing is that Julian has told us to stop work on it and get on with Io. I had a funny sort of feeling that in a way he was almost jealous of the mate. He said, 'We don't really *need* a male dummy, do we?" He said it in a funny sort of voice, too, kind of complacent and rather pleased—unless of course I am romancing, which I don't think. Indeed when I spoke of trying to recover the outline drawings of Adam with a view to rebuilding, he looked extremely peeved and told me sharply to lay off and consign the plans to the wastepaper basket. So there. The funeral was yesterday afternoon. I don't believe anybody went except Julian. I didn't, though I am sorry for the old sod. Anyway, I have told you all and done my duty. There is nothing else to report unless you would like to hear the fever verses that Iolanthe produced yesterday. First verses from beyond the grave, my boy, and not half bad. I thought of sending them to a paper."

"Have you got them on you?"

"Just a sec. Yes, I, have."

"Read them, then."

It was a strange feeling to hear these dissociated ramblings which had been produced by a simple temperature rise; was it an illusion or did they make a strange kind of sense, perhaps "poetic" sense—since poetry isn't a stock report on experience, or written for a seed catalog. (So I have been told.)

> *Just supposing because*
> *death is never too fervent*
> *though water suffer little damage*
> *and women have a descriptive function*
> *simple conjectures about loving*
> *in adolescence sweet and turbid*
> *brief caption on the love box merely,*
> *will announce her engagement to spring*
> *or winter or one of its forms, yes,*
> *its memory kicks back and throbs*
> *if bivouacked on Windermere*
> *made one with the ferny forms.*
> *All and none of these functions*
> *would be valid, a cause for surprise*
> *when reality is so taut and gnomic,*
> *digestible and without unction,*
> *all and none, I say, all and none.*
> *just supposing because, now*
> *surely every allowance should be made for such things?*

"Bravo," I said, but in a confused, puzzled sort of way. The line went dead. The roaring in the seashell stopped.

Somewhat to my surprise they had all taken themselves off to bed save Hippolyta, who was waiting up for me; she sat, lost in thought, and gazing into the fire. I poured myself another drink and joined her—extremely depressed by the story of poor Rackstraw. I had got quite fond of him, of using him as a sort of touchstone for my own sanity in the Paulhaus where, at a certain time, I even placed Benedicta among the disorderly figments of my own waking dreams. Fancy to find when I woke that she was really there, in my arms! Not just a daymare. "Thinking?" I said and she: "Yes. A lot of muddled and inconsequent thoughts—what a jumble. Thinking about you all with an affectionate concern—it's allowable in a friend, no?"

"Concern, Hippolyta?"

"Yes. For example this new Benedicta—she's suddenly normal, sensible, in full possession of herself; won't you find her diminished, less interesting than the other?"

I groaned. "My God, you aren't wishing me another long spell of misery with her, are you?"

"But the whole mystery must have gone."

"Thank God it has, if its only manifestation is in hysteria. Besides, she's exactly how I wanted her, always imagined her. I almost invented her. It was written on the package so to speak; if the contents were different there was many a good reason. We now know the reason. But when I fell for her I saw the possible person embedded in the witch. I fell for the blueprint of what she might be. It was a terrific gamble, but I've won, don't you see? Hippolyta, you've always thought of me as one of nature's mother-fixated cuckolds who reveled in his suffering; but it doesn't go very deep, my masochism. You must have misjudged the issue."

She looked at me with smiling relief tinged with doubt. "And you don't hate Julian anymore?"

"How can I now I can see him in close-up? His life has been such a calamity, and the type of genius he was given was a catastrophic gift for someone condemned to impotence."

She put her hand on my cheek and I kissed it. "You are an ass," I said. "I'm sorry," she replied, and then went on. "Strange how we ascribe fixed qualities to ourselves—and really we are only what others think of us: a collection of others' impressions merely."

We sat a long time in silence now, smoking and pondering. Vague thoughts passed through my mind like shoals of fish. I thought of the effect that her love for Graphos had had on her life. Then of a sudden a fragment of my intuition stirred and an original thought made its appearance which was disturbing and upsetting. It was: "Hippolyta has outlived the death of Graphos now, it has melted, with all the luxurious pain and emptiness it conferred. She is now in mortal danger of relinquishing her hold on life, of dying from pure ennui." I took her hand as if to hold her back, as if to prevent her slipping downstream. And as if to confirm and echo this dispiriting thought she said: "We can't believe it, can we? That we are all condemned; that it's only a matter of time? Death is something we accept as part and parcel of others. Why do we never get used to it in regard to ourselves? O the boredom of waiting! One has the impulse to race toward it, get it over." There! I had no consolations to offer; neither love nor opium ever really meet the case. For a pure scientist and an impure man—how to steer a safe course between the inconsequent and the outrageous?

We said good night; Hippolyta spent all her mornings in bed, reading, and would not be awake when the cars came for us at nine. She opened a window to purge the room of its cigarette smoke. The smell of lemons came in out of the darkness like a friendly animal. We did not know when we would meet again—if ever.

We had been put in the room with the icons and the heavy old-fashioned beds; the sheets were of coarse island linen. Prison bars on the windows. By the light of a single guttering candle Benedicta slept, her pale blonde head on her arm; so utterly motionless was she that she might have been dead. I climbed in beside her. She was naked and deliciously warm. She turned in her drowsing and asked me about the telephone call, and I told her of the death of

Rackstraw and the destruction of the model. This awakened her. She stared at the ceiling for a long moment, and then at me. Then she said: "There! You see?" as if the mishap proved something, as if she had foreseen it. "But I wish to God it had been the dummy of Iolanthe. That would have solved something."

I was outraged. "Darling," I said, "take pity on me. You aren't developing a jealousy of my poor dummy, are you?"

"In a perverse way, yes. I expect you will want to sleep with it out of curiosity one day—to see how real it is, to compare it with me, perhaps." My breath was taken away by this scandalous statement. "With Iolanthe?" I said in tones of mortal injury. "And why not?" she went on, talking to herself almost. "It must stir up all the most perverse instincts. Wait, vampirism. I know exactly what Nash would say."

Ah! so did I, so did I. And not merely the matter but the manner as well—oblique regard of the cuttlefish, fussy voice and so on. And the ideas all neatly laundered and folded by courtesy of Freud. (Now *him* I love for his modesty, his hesitancy, his lack of a dogmatic theology; it is what poor Nash has done to him that I condemn, avaunt, conspue.) Anyway I had a long dream colloquy with him in which I manfully defended my dear dolly against the penetrating criticism of this marvelous but as yet incomplete science. Ah, the infantile theory with its congeries of undigested impulses jumping about in the mud like fish leaping from the subconscious water. Who was I, poor Felix, to deny the double fantasy—both of birth and of coprophilia: the fecal matter which the infant will one day knead into cakes, and then from cakes, into sugar dollies and statues of bronze and stone? Yes, but dead dollies these. Ah, there we were—poor Iolanthe forever dead, forever part of the *merde*, that cosmic element which makes up the *Weltanschauung* of the groping analyst; element in which the poor fellow struggles waist high, holding his nose, and yet convinced on the basis of the evidence that what he is slithering about in is really gold. GOLD, remark you—the cement of a basic material value which binds together the shabby cultural brickwork of the times. The citizen's toy and talisman, the giver's gift and the receiver's wafer. . . . Gold, bread, excitement and increment pouring from the limited company of the dreaming big intestine. And then, via the same nexus of associated ideas direct from the chamber pot to Aphrodite, the austere and terrible and mindless, her sex tolling like a bell. What a vision of judgment for a simpleton like Felix . . . I heard Marchant singing at his work!

> *O, O, O,*
> *You great big beautiful doll.*

Benedicta stirred in her sleep, dreaming no doubt of the scarlet Turkish slippers she had promised herself, of the slices of holy muslin out of which she would make a ball gown. Softly breathing as she circumnavigated those vast and shadowy fields of sleep—the other reality which is a mirror image of our own. A living corpse like myself suffering only from the beta decay of the world within us. (The wish to die together is the image of the wish to lie together.)

And then all the shaggier motives which wake and howl like ravening mastiffs after dark. Through them I could align my fecal image of the ideal Aphrodite with everything that woke and stirred in the bestiaries of necrophilia, in the huge syllabaries of vampirism. Sliding, sliding the good ship Venus through the conundrum of the *anus mundi*, plop into the ocean where time has run wild: to circle the huge constipated Sargasso of the reason and melt at last into the *symbolon tes gennesiois*, the symbol of rebirth which Plato knew was the sea, cloaca of the archetypal heart. ("The grave so longed for is really the mother's bed." "All right, Nash, I take your point.")

And then of course a natural and completely ineradicable sadism is always inflamed by the thought of communion with a dead body—partly because of the helplessness of the latter: it cannot defend itself: "lie down, dead dolly, and come across": and also partly, but much more important is the idea (so firmly implanted) that the dead mistress cannot be wearied by excessive caresses. In death there is no satiety. Yet beyond the fetal pose and the fecal death, the mystery of decomposition offers the promise of renewal, of a new life for dolly. Grave Aphrodite, formed from the manure out of which we are all constructed, has coaxed the gift of fertility—for manure also nourishes; death is defied by a change of code, of form. The smoking midden is also of this world, of this culture, of our time—indeed of all time. The compost generates another life, another echo, to defy with its heat the fateful laws of decomposition, of dissolution.

"You groaned, my darling, in your sleep."

"A nightmare; I dreamed we were at the World's Fair and I bought you a pretty sugar doll. And you ate it, crunch, and the paint ran all over your tongue, turning it scarlet. And when we kissed my lips grew bloody too."

Somewhere a dog barked, and the wind lightly shuffled the sleeping trees; listening hard I thought I could perhaps discern the sound of the sea. I rose mechanically and lit a candle under one of the little icons in the niche; other eyes in other corners woke and winked. Then I got back into bed and took her in my arms. The pretty seizures of the love act brought us once more to comfort, to wholeness and at last to sleep—a sleep so innocent that it seemed we had invented it for ourselves, as the only fitting form of self-expression.

Tomorrow would be Turkey. Tomorrow would be Turkey.

So we embarked on the next long leg of our journey, skimming over the taut and toothy ranges of the northern chain of mountains—much higher now, and a good deal snowier; although we in our heated cabin were blissfully warm and were made welcome by innocent morning clouds, soft cirrus. No boundaries to this airy world save the very last peaks stretching out their necks like upward flying geese. Then at long last, clearing them, we moved down once more to a lower octave over an evening sea which played quietly, half asleep. Water and sky here divided the lavender dusk, parted and shared its clouds, and presaged a spring nightfall.

Here somewhereabouts scouts came out of the sky to salute us—grim visages staring out of the fighter planes like Mongolian dummies; faces like medieval armoured knights of the Japanese Middle Ages. Yes, but they were all smiling and beckoning, and they wished us softly down until we landed in a dense whacking of waves and great spools of white foam, almost under the heroic bridge itself. Through this thick water we taxied like mad, hunting for a windless lea which might let us moor safely.

We had taken it all in, however: there had been time and light enough: the huge thickets of spars moving in soft unison, the beetle grooves carved by the tankers and small brigantines upon the blue skin of the gulf. It was sunset, too, and blowing fresh and keen from Marmara. And my goodness, how sinister it all felt to me as I sat smoking and gazing down upon the long walls once more—the long irregular buckler of hide or mud-daubed osier such as savages might run up about a stockade. From a great height they looked absurdly flimsy, but, as we scaled down out of the sky, the whole mass began to take up a denser stance, obdurate and threatening: and softly the tulips rose like the horns of shy snails, to take the colors of the sinking sun upon their pale skins. Benedicta, leaning at my side, stared down with me; her nostrils dilated a little, and with an expression of mingled horror and anticipation, of nostalgia and regret, upon her pale face. We were swimming together once more into the great tapestry of Polis—and at a certain moment, quite precisely, everything spun round as if on a jeweler's turntable, to present its profile: fused into the single dimension of an old shadow play manipulated by the fingers of some great invisible shadow master.

The journey had been tiring; everyone had been grumpy, out of sorts, in some way or another. Vibart buried himself in his papers, was offhand with me and noncommittal. I had the feeling that he was angry with himself for confessing as much as he had to me on the day before—I know not why. Caradoc too was in a scolding mood, and only the promise of a glass of authentic raki or mastika seemed to give him a hope. I think in a way all our thoughts had begun to turn one way, to quest out toward that long bare headland where, among the jumble of forts and kiosks and shattered palaces—the fabled Avalon of old Merlin's dream—somewhere out there Jocas, the brother, was waiting for us. I suppose that Benedicta must have read my thoughts, for she said softly, echoing in a strange way the recent thoughts of Hippolyta: "We tend to forget it, but people do have this awful tendency to die."

"Come. Come," said Caradoc peevishly. "You will never console me in this way. Cut out all this nonsense."

It was natural that in this developing gloom, this heavy preoccupation with what waited for us, I should take refuge in Baum: for he had business of his own, he was not heading for Avalon as the rest of us were. The town itself was his objective. Yet even he was depressed in a smaller way, though of course his behavior was exemplary. I was soon to learn the reason. It was our good friend Banubula who was causing him anguish. "You see," he said, "I am disquieted because the count has begun to hunger for the power to initiate. So long as he was quietly working for the firm his role was a fulfilling and useful one. But now . . . you see Mr. Marchant has played this dirty trick on him and he has taken it seriously. And the awful thing is that it has *become* serious. The thing is launched. You must never joke the hearing of the firm, Mr. Felix, because the firm takes everything deadly seriously."

"What dirty joke, Baum?"

"Fresh sperm," said Baum moodily, poking his ear with a long spatulate fingernail, as if to clear it. "Fresh sperm!"

"What is that all about?" I asked, perplexed.

"Mr. Marchant was very drunk and he said that the latest findings of the chemical section showed quite clearly that the only really nourishing skin tonic for women was fresh male sperm. This is all very well, Mr. Felix, but he went on to add that there was really nothing to stop the firm marketing the stuff if only it could be collected on a large enough scale; and of course if one paid for it well enough one would be able to get as much as one wanted from private producers—just like any other commodity in our modern civlization. From donor to factory, at controlled temperatures, presented (according to Mr. Marchant) hardly more complicated a problem than picking lavender and taking it to the perfumery. This was very wicked of him; he should have known how gullible the count is. But he should also have known that the firm takes everything very seriously indeed. Just what Mr. Marchant envisaged I have no idea—I suspect he had none himself when he made the joke; it was simply to tease his friend. On the face of it the idea is mad—thousands upon thousands of people making this sort of contribution to a factory which fills up phials with it and markets the product. On the other hand, as Marchant said, conserved sperm was already used in artificial insemination, why not in skin food? I was of course horrified when Count Banubula told me this; but what is worse the whole thing was set out as a memorandum and discussed by the chemistry board, and *passed*. I could hardly believe my ears when I heard. Not only that, a subsidiary called Lovecraft Products had been set up, and a subscription list for willing donors has been opened. Moreover it shows every sign of sweeping the continent. Can you imagine it, hundreds of thousands of males all over the world selling their ... product? And yet the chemical group say that they can sort and grade it, keep it in a temperature emulsion form, and distribute it to all who seek beauty through skin tonics. I must admit I was sharp with the count when I saw what had happened. But he produced a number of disingenuous arguments in which is immediately recognized the drunken hand of Mr. Marchant. Why, he said, was it any worse than the sale of Chinese or Malayan hair by the women of underprivileged nations? Why should the over-privileged nations be denied the right to part with their surplus—assuming it was a surplus? At any rate, whatever my own reservations, the scheme has gone ahead so fast that I fear it will get out of hand; so many donors have joined that new factories have been opened and the whole project has had to be twice refinanced by the Germans and Americans. Meanwhile, too, all the letterpress and the advertising devised by the count and Lord Lambitus I find distasteful to a degree. Look."

He whipped out his briefcase and groped about in it, to extract at last a thick batch of letterpress which bore the unmistakable imprint of Banubula's innocent genius. I was surprised that Marchant was the author of the jest which the firm had so swiftly turned to profit. It was the sort of thing Caradoc might have done, but not Marchant. Yet here it was.

Nor was it hard to see and to sympathize with poor Baum's misgivings, for he was in the advertising and promotion department, charged to dish out all these pamphlets and advertisements to a weary world. They were designed both to attract new donors ("Why not give your all for Lovecraft and be in the swim? You can make a fortune if you work at it. Study our bonus scheme. Moreover it's work you can do at home in your own time. Why not have fun with the firm? Take life in hand and double your income," etc., etc.) ; and also to appeal to a gullible beautician's market ("The safest natural skin food, so kind to the thirsty pores") . . . but why go on? I could see that Banubula's literary side had been quite carried away by the whole scheme.

Baum had been scanning my face as I read in order to gloat sympathetically on my expressions of horror. "You see?" he said, as I handed back all the gaudy letterpress. I did. "Moreover," he went on, "I have been sent out here to try to sound out the Turks, to get them interested in the scheme as possible donors. Of course everything has its market value, Mr. Felix—I would be the first to admit that. But there are dangers here; we might make a mistake. The Turks are Moslems and deeply religious—suppose we started a holy war without meaning to, eh? I prefer simpler, more material ideas; I like to know where I stand. Now when Lord Lambitus proposed marketing whips in gold lamé I saw the possibilities instantly. But this could prove to be . . . well, grotesque! I am supposed to meet the religious leaders tomorrow to outline the scheme. I am much afraid of what might happen. How, for example, will all this stuff translate into Turkish, eh? One doesn't know. I don't want to die with a spear through me just for encouraging Turks to . . . well, market their product through Merlin's. Yet on the other hand it's my duty to obey orders." He sighed heavily. I wondered whether he was wearing a bulletproof waistcoat.

There was no time, however, for long-drawn-out commiserations, for by now the officials had come aboard, clucking like hens, and stamped our passports. Long strings of colored lights had demarcated the outlines of the bay; the nether sky was still molten but cooling fast, like the steel lid of a furnace. Out of the nearby darkness a large white pinnace whiffled once, and then, at a signal from a man in uniform, began to sidle toward us sideways—like a smart cat.

Our belongings sorted and our various destinations decided upon, we crawled aboard her—Benedicta, Caradoc and I. The others had other duties and would spend the damp Turkish night in the magnolia-scented gloom of the Pera. But Vibart? "I thought you were coming with us?" But he had made one of those inexplicable *volte-face.* "So did I," he said. "And now suddenly I'm not. I'm not even sure I shall come and see Jocas—I don't seem to need to anymore. It came over me just as we hit the water." He looked suddenly elated, his smile had grown younger, more self-confident. "I shall walk about Polis tonight and think myself over," he said, and with a brief nod joined the others in the pilot's launch. I was curious enough to want to question him further, but Benedicta pulled softly at my sleeve and I desisted.

The wind was fresh as we came out of the sea, but the sturdy little pinnace rode sharp at fifteen knots. In the comfortable little cabin with its smart leather-upholstered seats we found a small insect-like man dressed in white who turned out to be the doctor who was looking after Jocas. He spoke only French, and he smoked very slowly and thoughtfully as he spoke. He held the white bone cigarette holder in a tiny clawlike hand which suggested that of a mantis. But what he had to say to us disabused us immediately of any notions we might have had about astrology and destiny and suchlike. Unless of course the progress chart could accurately trace the course of a long-drawn-out metastasis. It was our old friend, the contemporary scourge. On the other hand he said: "He is weak, but in very good courage, in spite of knowing the truth. But the place is in an awful mess and needs clearing out. He has got rid of many of the servants and has more or less moved in with his birds. *C'est gênant* from the medical point of view—washing him and so on." We were silent now for the rest of the journey. B. looked at her fingers.

Caradoc contented himself with a heavy sigh from time to time. The little doctor sat watching us and smoking and reflecting. The journey seemed to last an age. But finally our nose sank into still water, we throttled down and softly ebbed along a dark landing stage where a figure from the past—the old eunuch of my first visit—stood holding a lantern high above his head and giving the Islamic greeting to the darkness. Mouth, forehead and shoulder, mouth, forehead and shoulder. But even when we stepped ashore he gave no intimate signs of recognition—perhaps because Benedicta had her head done up in a scarf. He did not at any rate recognize me. We huddled ashore in the humid darkness to the slapping and slobbering of water along the wooden piers. A sense of desolation invaded me, I do not know exactly why. One felt that everything here had run down, gone to seed—but how one could feel such a thing when one was surrounded by darkness I really cannot imagine. Perhaps the little doctor's few brief words had prepared us for such a thing. At any rate, leaving our baggage we followed the majordomo with his hissing white light, the doctor leading us. The paths had been marked out with little kerosene lamps which faltered here and there in the wind; but they gave hardly any light, and were simply markers upon which to orient ourselves. Uprooted trees and creepers and bushes lay about beside the path, and once a couple of starved-looking mongrels emerged from the dark to sniff at us and retire. I thought of the fine pack of hunting dogs with their lustrous fur which had been Jocas' pride in the old days; they would have simply wolfed mongrels like these, or driven them into the sea.

The air of desuetude must have been largely imagined, then, for we could take in few details until we reached the cypress glades with their kiosks. The eunuch was talking now to the doctor, with a soft high clucking voice; it appeared that a once elaborate electrical lighting scheme which illuminated everything had recently foundered owing to a faulty generator, and that nobody had bothered to have it repaired. He wagged his huge bald head in resigned disapproval. "You will see," said the doctor.

There was more light in the two villas with their cracked windows and starred mirrors—but the smell of kerosene was everywhere. The flagged floors were full of chicken bones and unswept feathers. We were asked if we would eat first—indeed in the old salon a table had been clumsily laid with a dirty tablecloth (of the finest Irish linen), several branches of dribbling candles and a solitary bunch of dusty artificial grapes in a cracked plate of alabaster. Here the stink of the birds warred with the kerosene. The walls showed cracks. The doorjambs heaved and creaked—the sea salt had been at them. There was a swallow's nest in one corner of the room.

But it was to Jocas that we were going, and he had apparently moved out lock, stock and barrel into the old shot tower—on the eastern ramparts of what had once been a fort with a high keep overlooking the gulf. Here in the old days he had spent his time delecting in a huge marine telescope pitched on a low tripod. Sitting in a deck chair, pausing only to eat an olive from time to time, Jocas could follow the whole movement of the shipping in the gulf below. But to gain access to this martello one had to walk along a crazy broken parapet built along the sea face of the headland; a ruined staircase which Benedicta as a girl had come to know as "The Battlements of Elsinore."

On this stone ramp we embarked in single file. I could hear the squinch of my rubber soles on the stone. Hereabouts too an occasional lemon-yellow lizard darted for cover—they are always first to emerge with the spring sunlight. But the climb was steep. Smell of thyme. So at last we crossed a walled courtyard skirting an uncoped well disguised by tall thistles, and then climbed onto a balcony and opened a huge door.

It couldn't have been much smaller than a good-sized parish church, the room in which Jocas had taken up residence; but the height of it was such that the upper shadows pressed upon the lighted areas like a whole sky of darkness. One expected to see stars upon that black-damascened darkness. For the rest it was a robbers' cave from some old fairy tale. A huge fire of thorns blazed in one corner. Branches of candles and small oil lamps picked out and punctuated the foreground where the figures of men and boys worked and moved. Wait. We stood upon the threshold and gazed into this cave with its dark flapping shadows, expectantly, hesitantly. We had come at an inconvenient moment. An enormous Victorian hip bath was being filled with steaming water by a small boy, while two other shapes were carrying a shrunken form from the bed toward it—the figure you'd say of a large white frog, legs spread apart. The bed itself was enormous and was hung about with a dark red velvet baldaquin whose ropes bore the unmistakable signs, even in that erratic light, of greasy hands. The curtains were drawn back. Jocas therefore advanced toward us, carried by four arms, helpless as a child, but cheerfully smiling, the smiling languor of the small infant longing for the surcease of hot water. It had a powerful resonance this sudden glimpse—like some somber oil painting of the Spanish school. Moreover there was enough light here on the ground to take in the dirty deal tables, the flagged floor covered in droppings of bats and birds, the smashed windows.

Our natural instinct at this unwitting intrusion was to draw back in some confusion, but the white figure waved at us with cheerful languor and cried: "At last you come. Very good." His tone, his mien, transformed the tableau suddenly into something different, say a friendly rag in a boys' dormitory, something which might end in a pillow fight. But he was shrunken and much withered, had lost the sturdiness of his buttocks and thighs. Yet his face was still agleam with intelligence and the little gold caps on his canines glittered as he smiled upon us. "Don't go," he said. "I will soon be washed." The two expressionless figures carrying this pale frog deposed their burden with slow carefulness in the tub. Jocas sighed to feel the water rise up round his waist. He leaned his head back against the high rim of the bath and then extended a pale hand for us to touch. There was a kind of lucid and rather moving simplicity about the gesture; his helplessness was as disarming as his smile.

His magnificent head of hair, now plentifully touched with white, was combed loosely back; it fell in a straight shock almost to his shoulders. Benedicta knelt down to kiss his cheek and then turned aside to order the rumpled bed while Caradoc and I stood looking down at him. His servants sponged him softly and rhythmically. "Well this is a fine business," said Caradoc harshly, disguising his affection and concern in a habitual gruffness. The doctor made some professional movements among the bottles and pans which were laid out on one of the long white tables in the corner. What a jumble of spoons and forks, of half-eaten dishes, and broken fragments of meat for the birds. The birds! They would account for that heavy rotting fragrance in the vaulted air of the room. They were ranged like trophies along the end wall, the darkest corner of the room, all but invisible, but one could hear the tinkle of their bells as they stirred and sighed. His belongings stood about in isolation, as if they had lost context. It was a trifle surrealist, the old horn phonograph with its records (Jocas loved military marches and had quite a collection). There was a tall cupboard whose doors hung open. A few articles of attire were hanging up in it; but for the most part his belongings occupied the other wall, and were hung on nails. A fez, a deerstalker, binoculars. An old-fashioned typewriter lay on the floor beside a flowered chamber pot. Thigh boots. Two gaunt armchairs, of the style called Voltaire, stood beside the bed with a strip of tattered carpeting between them. Everything looked quite haphazard, the result of a series of hasty afterthoughts.

But now they were finished with him and carefully lifted him from the bath. He let them with the same air of wary innocence, smiling, but delightfully unashamed of his nakedness. They laid him out upon one of the white deal tables to dry him—and I was reminded at once of the white "cooling tables" of the embalmers. He hissed in with pleasure at the harsh touch of the towels and in a whisper urged the men to curry him harder and yet harder, like a horse; until at last his pale flesh took on the faintest warmth of tone. Then they produced an old-fashioned nightshirt and slipped it over his head. Now it was the doctor's turn; first an enema and then various injections. The little man whistled softly, abstractedly as he worked on his patient. Jocas had a whole lot of new and very beautiful expressions on his face—a whole new repertoire it seemed, born of the illness, no doubt, and all the considerations which it raised. Had he thought very much about death, I wondered?

But once in bed, lying back like an emperor under a Byzantine covering, pressed into puffed pillows, he became suddenly completely himself. I mean one would not have thought him ill at all. He held Benedicta's hand in his own confiding childlike grip and spoke in a new calm voice, smiling. "I wanted just to take leave," he said, and I realized that he was planning to die in the time-honored, traditional Eastern fashion. Here death itself had a ceremonial value and form; in the East there always seemed to be time to gather all one's relations together and take a formal leave of them. To distribute alms to the poor and order the family estate. We used to die like that once in England, a hundred or so years ago. Now somehow people are rushed into the ground unceremoniously, like criminals thrown into quicklime. Jocas was doing it in the old style. I caught sight of his scarlet slippers (les babouches) ; there was an ink-spot on one. Under the bed, as if hastily thrust aside, there was a bit of railway line and a model train lying on its side. In the far corner under the window stood a huge and beautifully colored box kite with a long tail. Of course! One could lie in bed and fly a kite through the window.

He said suddenly: "But they must be hungry. They must eat."

It took some time to penetrate the heavy Turkish skulls of the servants, but at least the message got through and several heavy silvery trays made their appearance with two huge loaves of village bread, some olives, tinned meat, and a rank black wine. Caradoc carved all this into the semblance of helpings and we all fell to, suddenly ravenous.

The fire was built up with wood shavings until it bellowed and bristled, throwing our shadows about the room. The small dark eyes of Jocas watched us with a benign affection—the expression on the face of a mother watching her children eat. I took my doorstep-sandwich and sat on the edge of the bed to share a friendly smile with him; he sighed with deep satisfaction as he watched us dispose ourselves around his bed. Like a child arranging his toys upon the counterpane. And I saw also that this whole visit of ours was part of a design, a deeply considered design. His architect was there to consult about a funerary monument; the embalming team were already on the spot. Jocas was good at mind reading and followed my thoughts clearly, like somebody reading print. "Yes," he said. "It is like that. I had at first difficulty in my ideas because Julian could not understand; but now he's united with me. He has agreed with me. The need to have all our unhappy family—Merlins—under one roof, in one ground." He spread his hands in the direction of Caradoc who was munching. Then from under his pillow he produced a piece of parchment and handed it to me. It was in Greek. "Permission of the Orthodox Church to remove the body of the old man; Koepgen will bring it. He is still alive there in Spinalonga working, happy. I saw him last week." He chuckled softly. "Then what else? Yes, I wish myself to be golded, or do you say gilded? All gold. I have a firman for the whole headland, Caradoc." But this sort of talk made Caradoc extremely uneasy and shy; it seemed to him rather ill-mannered to talk so openly about death. "It's bad form," he said severely and munched his bread. Moreover he was very superstitious, had no intention of dying himself, and didn't want to hear about such matters. I watched the new vivid imperial face of Jocas and racked my brains to think of the prototype; at last click, up came the Ravenna mosaics, together with a whole lot of half-forgotten debris about Justinian and Theodora, that brave soul. I felt the long heavy night of the Turkish soul exemplified in its old half-dead capital—the Venice of the East. "And Julian will give me a service in St. Paul's." It is impossible to describe the smiling childish joy with which he uttered the words. His eyes sparkled with cupidity. "St. Paul's!" He crooned the words almost. He had begun to make everything sound extremely attractive—death should be like that. It was the ancient Greeks who couldn't take the idea.

He took a long drink from a glass at his bedside and subsided again into sighing happiness. "Though I have never seen it," he said, "Julian once had a photograph faked to appear as if I was there at a memorial service. It was politically necessary, Amin Pasha. Here everyone thought I was in London specially for him; but it was a fake, I was here. Julian did it. Ah Julian! Only now I have come to understand him a little bit. He will never love me, but now he doesn't care. And he fears death very much. O yes."

The little doctor coughed. It was time for him to take his leave. He shook us each by the hand and said good night, placing a hand briefly upon Jocas' forehead and nodding, as if to say that he was satisfied with his patient. The bald old eunuch recovered his lamp from the outer darkness and led him slowly away. They had put some knobs of frankincense on the fire and the air had become rich and fragrant. The servants had retired, though one remained on call. He sat on an uncomfortable-looking kitchen chair in the shadows by the birds; appeared to sleep, head on breast. But Jocas was not done with us; he still radiated energy, and it reminded me of the Jocas I had first encountered, the tough and tireless countryman, hunter, swimmer. We sat around him on the bed—the stiff brocaded counterpane of some Byzance weave, the candles, the frail oil lamps . . . all that. And the past sat heavily on us, too.

"Felix," he said, still holding the white hand of Benedicta in his, "I followed with so much interest all your attempts to destroy us, to sabotage the firm, to escape from us. It was all in my heart, and it was so very interesting, so very passionately interesting to me. You see, I could understand you, but Julian not really. For Julian the firm perfectly expresses something, perhaps his impotence? Eh? I am not clever like him, and because I am not clever I was always in danger from him. O but I love him so." An air of rapturous infantility took possession of him. He licked his red lips and went on slowly, picking and choosing his words from his limited knowledge of English as one might pick flowers at random in a field. But he could express himself well, and here and there tumbled upon a mistake which itself was a felicity. "But you I sympathized," he said, "and for why? Because I myself had the great search for the freeing of my soul, Felix. I too made a great calculation. But I had no courage to do it because I was afraid of Julian. He was so clever, he could simply kill me." He thrust out a hand to arrest my interpretation of the remark. "I was not afraid of the death. But I did not wish to join everything else in Julian's conscience; you see he pretends he has none. You must not have with the firm. But he has. Julian has seen much weeping." He swallowed and looked sad for a moment. One saw that he really did love this enigmatic figure, it was not simply Oriental exuberance. One detected too the kind of pity that the simple, uncomplicated and healthy man can have for the cripple. Julian had never shot, flown a bird or a kite; yes, but he had made love, I suppose. I caught a glimpse of Benedicta's white serene face. She sat to me in profile, still holding Jocas' hand and gazing at him with an air of admiring confidence. He had sunk back among the pillows and closed his eyes—not out of weariness but in order to recover the thread of his argument.

"In the old days," he said, "at the very beginning when the firm was a small thing, a [he inserted the Greek word for a newly born infant] . . . in those days every one of our transactions had to be done on trust, on an exchange of salt mostly. Arabia and so on. People could *not write,* Felix. All was human memory. Even quite late our whole accounting was with the old-fashioned abacus which you still see in Greek grocery shops today. The only factor that made for our security was mutual trust. When I thought about freedom and remembered the old days I thought very heavily—elephant-heavily—round this quite small but precise condition. All our money was deployed around the sea of the East, and while here and there were some little scraps of paper signed with thumbs, the most was in risk of trust. We had to *believe* in such a thing as an exchange of salt with a sheik. It was the only strong thing, the only plank. Now then all this paper came, all this contract business came. The whole firm became so big, so complicated. The sale had lost its savor, doesn't it say somewhere in the Bible? I thought. I thought. When Julian told me that the whole of the contracts of the firm had been photographed on film and that one little house held them all, I had an extraordinary idea . . . I thought one night very late, while I was talking to myself. I thought: suppose we destroyed all contracts—the whole of the written thing. What would happen?"

He looked terribly excited, swallowed twice heavily, and then joined his hands on his breast. I suddenly felt myself face to face with one of those tremendously simple, but at the same time critical, veins of thought which belonged to what Marchant and I (in the case of Iolanthe) had labeled the contingency vector; it was the "supposing scale" and I imagine it represented in rough mechanical terms that sector of the human consciousness where the full horror of the idea of free will comes to be understood or felt. It is this terrifying idea which causes people to throw themselves off cliffs (just to see what will happen) : or to play Russian roulette with a pistol they just happened to find on a shelf. . . . If is the key of If. And then I thought of the little library which housed the total contractual commitments of the firm on microfilm. There had been a good deal of newspaper ballyhoo when Merlin's went onto microfilm; its contract department had by then grown to the size of the Bodleian. Now all the paper had gone. A special little funerary monument—not by Caradoc this time—had been erected to house the film in a London suburb. An ungainly little building, something between a Roman villa and the old Euston station. I recalled Caradoc's fury at this awkward neo-Egyptian monster of a creation with its four stout elephant columns. Above it was a small flat where the egregious Shadbolt lived (the same old chap who had drawn up Benedicta's marriage contract with me). He was now Registrar of Contracts. Well, it was not unlike a small and hideous crematorium. But I interrupted this train of thought to concentrate rather more deeply on what Jocas was trying to tell me. "What would happen?" he repeated again, dramatically, but in a lower register. "Either the whole thing, the whole construction would dissolve." He threw his eyes back into his skull, showing the whites, which is the Turkish way of illustrating total catastrophe. "Or else . . . *nothing* at all. Without the bonds of the paper and the signatures *trust* might come back, the idea of obligation to one's word, one's spoken bond, one's salt." I realized that I was in the presence of a great, but completely insane idealist. Trust indeed! But he went on headlong.

"Now I am so happy to know that you will try this freedom yourself—you will do this thing when once you are the head of the firm. Zeno has seen it all very clearly. He sees you give a last supper with twelve people in the big house. That same night you will completely burn every contract and announce it to the world. Very exciting. It will be a big fire. One old man will be burned in it. But it will be the crown of your career. Only what happens after, if the firm continues or if it dissolves, Zeno cannot see clearly and he is too honest to pretend all this."

He gave a little chuckle, and added, "Of course Julian doesn't believe in these nonsenses; perhaps you don't either. But she does, Benedicta does. She has lived long enough in Turkey to know how sometimes strange things are real."

"Who is Zeno?" I asked purely to avoid taking up a definitive position vis-à-vis all these shadowy postulates. It seemed that he was an old Greek clerk who worked in the counting house in the city; subject to visions. Genus epileptoid, I had no doubt. It was as if the great aborted dream of Byzance lived on in the weaker psychic specimens of Polis, troubling their sleep with its tenebrous floating visions of a future which chance had aborted. I suddenly seemed to hear the disagreeable yelping of the barking dervishes ringing in my ears; how they flopped about the floor of the mosque, yelping and foaming just like the schizos in the Paulhaus. Or else fell about like toads, beating up the dust and screaming. It was all part and parcel of the same type of phenomenon I have no doubt.

Beside the bed lay a stout old-fashioned family Bible encrusted with colored wax from the candles. From between its leaves Jocas produced a small piece of paper written over in a very fine Greek hand; there was a drawing of a table plan. From the red thumbprint (the attested signature with date), I recognized it as a witnessed prophecy—the sort of thing that idiots and hysterical soothsayers produce on saints' days. But the writing was skillful and very beautiful, the hand of an educated man. I took it and put it away to study at leisure—cursing the infernal rustiness of my Greek. "He does not know the people," said Jocas, "but he described them and I put the name in with a pencil. You shall see. Anyway." He made a vague gesture and sank back, drooping a little from fatigue at last. I wondered whether we should leave him.

Benedicta seemed disposed to stay awhile as yet, and he for his part seemed to derive comfort from the touch of her hand on his. But Caradoc provided a slight diversion by picking up a lantern and saying that he must attend to the calls of nature; and I took the chance of joining him to get a breath of air. We climbed out upon the unwalled shelf, the balcony above the sea, and made our slow way along the paths which led to the headland of which Jocas had spoken. A cloudy sky obscured the nascent moonlight; far below us the ocean gulped. Somewhere in the obscurity below us ships moved, their lights glimmering frail as fireflies. But clouds were rolling in slowly toward the shore and a heavy dew had fallen. At last we came out upon the site of this proposed building—perhaps it was an old threshing floor, built up belvedere-like over the sea. Despite the general darkness one could feel the dominance of the position, could divine the splendor of the surrounding views in fine weather. But Caradoc was morose; he set down the lantern to attend to his business, and then came and sat beside me on a boulder, shaking his head and growling a bit. "What is it?" I said. "Don't you think you can do it?" I said this to annoy him, and the remark was quite successful. "Do it?" he snarled. "Of course I can do it. That's not what's worrying me. The problem is Jocas. He has got ancient Greece on the brain, and has been pining for the bloody Parthenon for half a lifetime now— he will never pass my drawings; not of the sort of thing I have in mind. Not in a month of Sundays. He does not realize the first thing about building; his idea would be something between a cassata ice cream and a Georgian rotunda. He doesn't realize that a real piece of building must be responsive to the emanations of the ground upon which it stands. To a certain extent the available materials create limitations and point out clues. In the Celebes, for example, bamboo, fern, leaves, lianas, they all dictate the weight and form of the construction—but they also echo the soul form of the man who inhabits them. For those islanders the notion of life and death is dreamlike, unsubstantial, poetical; their culture is born in a butterfly's soul. Just as Tokyo is all mouse culture, a mouse capital. We must build with this sense of congruence to place. The Parthenon would be a joke propped up here on this Turkish headland. Why? Because the soul-form of the Greeks was different, their metaphysical attitude to things was sensual, relatively indifferent to death and time. And their sense of plastic was really related to plane surfaces decorated on the flat, not to volume. All their stuff is radiantly human because the scale is small, nothing larger than lifesize. Their sunny philosophy domesticated not only life, but also death; one has the feeling that even the huge gods were homemade, perhaps formed by the hands of children in a cookery class. No morality either to shock and frighten. Innocence, a gemlike trance. All the ominous or minatory elements in their history were imported from death-saturated lands like Egypt, like this here bloody Turkey?" He flashed me a glance of righteous indignation from under his shaggy prophetic brows. "Just sit here and listen to Turkey, listen to what it says," he went on. "It's a heavy death-propelled wavelength, the daze of some old alligator slumbering in the mud. It has all the solemnity, the heavy somnolence of Egypt, the one country above all which specialized in death; if Turkey ever showed flower in a cultural way, it will echo Egypt, not Greece. That is why all this embalming business of Goytz is a stroke of genius. Some cultures are so death-weighted that they store up their dead, they are ancestor-obsessed like the Chinese. *That* is the call sign of this gloomy old land. Consequently if one tunes in and tries to set it to an architecture, one is almost driven to echo the grave ponderous style of an Egypt; the bright blue and white of Greece would never work. But how to tell Jocas that?"

I changed the conversation abruptly. "That well over there," I said gravely. (I was surprised to find myself a trifle drunk.) "That well already houses the genius of your mausoleum. Jocas has imported a snow-white python from the island of Crete; and he has planted an almond tree for it to climb. Prophecies will spring from this tomb, Caradoc." I invented all this of course in order to scare him. I knew he was particularly frightened of snakes. It had the desired effect. He secured his lantern and said irritably, "Why didn't you say so before? We might have sat on the damn thing."

When we got back to the house it was to find most of the lights turned low and Jocas asleep with a smile on his face; Benedicta had disappeared. The attendant drowsed on his upright chair. We made our uneven way back to the villa where we had been allocated rooms. Caradoc, holding his lantern high, examined the cracked plaster cherubs, the broken marble fireplaces, the litter on the dirty flags, with a sustained curiosity. I found a candlestick and lit it. Benedicta had been given a room to herself on the balcony side of the house. I had been allocated a sort of uncomfortable box room. Though I was weary I found it difficult to sleep, I suppose because of the atrocious but heady black wine we had been sluicing. So I wrote a little letter to Benedicta—something to read when she woke up alone in bed. "Dear Benedicta, the whole point—why will you never grasp it? The whole point is that time gives birth to space, but space gives death to time. (The ancient liver mantic was an attempt to read forward into time—and it might have worked for them.) That is the only reason for my loving you—because you simply cannot grasp the meaning of causality in the new terms. I would add an equation or two but I am rather drunk and the light is bad. So I will content myself by warning you gravely about the perils of such homely ignorance. It saps the will and rots the cortex.

Squinch. Felix." I suppose it lacked warmth; and it certainly wasn't what I intended to say when I took out my pencil. I pondered, and at last traced the missing component. My postscript read: "I would be quite willing to dismantle and abolish Iolanthe if you asked me to do so."

An uneasy night of shallow dreams, bird noises, howling of dogs; but then I dozed off and slept quite a way into the morning. It was a dark and gloomy day with huge shaggy clouds hanging motionless over everything; the gulf was the color of gunmetal. Beside my bed I found the response to my letter of the night before. "It's my job now to see that you do what you feel you must. Anything else would be fatal to both of us. I must say you are an awful fool, which is consoling in a hopeless sort of way. Meet me at Eyub at four."

I was startled to find that it was already ten o'clock; she had taken the launch into Polis, in order to spend the day wandering about its streets and mosques. Meanwhile the returning boat brought the little doctor with it. Jocas was wide awake and alert in his birdlike way. "She wants you to meet her in Polis," he said. I said I knew. From the only bathroom came the sound of prodigious swishing—as if a herd of elephants were hosing each other down. "It is Caradoc taking a bath" said Jocas solemnly, and then added (for all the world as if he had mind-read the whole of our conversation of last night) : "I have told him that I do not wish to see any plans. He is free to design what he pleases. He has the money and the site. I will trust him to make a most characteristic thing for the family." I whistled with surprise and pleasure. Presently Caradoc, hale and ruddy after his ablutions, emerged from the depths. He was looking happy for a change, indeed radiant. "Did you hear?" he boomed. "Jocas is going to trust me all the way." This seemed to call for a celebration and, despite the earliness of the hour and the slight trace of hangover, I coyly accepted a glass of fiery raki.

I left the company gathered about the huge bed and

(grateful for an old umbrella I had brought) found my
way down through the gardens to where the white launch
lay at the landing stage, waiting with steam up to take me
into town. The sea was black and calm, luminous and
bituminous all at once; we rustled across it at full speed. I
studied with interest (perhaps amusement, so foolish am
I) the prophecy of Zeno and the elaborate table plan he
had drawn for this classical last supper of mine. What the
devil was it all about? It reminded me a little of the
Banubula Tunc talisman—twelve places of which three
were empty. But the penciled names were those of my
friends—Vibart, Pulley, Marchant, Banubula, Nash, etc.,
etc. There were empty places, too, at this table and I
wondered a little about them. It seemed that neither
Julian nor Jocas was to be of the party; and perhaps one of
the missing places might belong to Iolanthe? I don't know.
It was all pretty vague as these things so often are; and of
course there was no precise date for the thing—there never
is! However I felt charitably disposed toward occultism on
Tuesdays, and I pocketed it with a sigh, and turned to
regale myself with the black water and the livid marks we
were making in it. And the somber city came up like a
long succession of "states": I am groping for the image of
an etching evolving through a number of different stages,
slowly as the elaborations of detail are multiplied. I wondered what Benedicta might be doing; I closed my eyes
and tried to imagine where she was—perhaps sitting on a
block of masonry by her mother's grave in Eyub or else
(more likely) sitting in the little garden by the mosque
where Sacrapant fell, drinking a Benedictine and smoking
a gold-tipped cigarette. There was time to kill. In this
gloomy sodden-looking weather I found my way across the
arcades of the grand bazaar to the little restaurant where
once (how many centuries ago?) I had dined with Vibart
and his wife, and listened to his histrionic dissertations on
good books and bad. Pia, I had almost forgotten how she
looked; I had a recollection of brilliant eyes, watchful,

amused. For the life of me I could not associate her with Jocas—but there it was. And following out this train of thought I bumped into Vibart himself just as he was about to seat himself at a table. "Join me," he said, and all of a sudden it was a new version of my old friend which presented itself to my vision; no more was he morose and cast down. He radiated rather a recovered composure, a temperamental calm. He saw me looking at him and smiled. "It's come out, the equation," he said at last, turning his handsome smiling head sideways to examine himself in the mirror. "I spent all last night walking about until I found the missing collar stud. I've solved it, man. It's the smallest thing imaginable but it has been teasing my reason for so long now that it was a great relief to catch it by the tail. I was right to do it for myself and not ask poor Jocas foolish questions. It has to do with the quality of my loving, the subtle thing that didn't click between Pia and me. It came from the fact that I loved her not as a man loves a woman, but as a woman loves a man. In a subtle sort of way my attitude qualified my masculinity in the exchange. I wonder if you see? It is so clear to me. I'd turned the flow of affect or whatever upside down; and she was too much a woman to love except as a woman. It's such a relief, I feel like singing."

"I can see Nash," I said, "bicycling like mad toward you and muttering things about the 'homosexual component.' "

"Yes, it would seem from my diagnosis that I am a common or garden bugger at heart. What do you know?"

He burst out laughing. Thunder crackled and a brief skirl of rain fell. "Just like last time we were here, isn't it?"

"What a weird light; the whole damn city so subaqueous and *sfumato*. How is Jocas?"

I gave him an account of the patient to which he listened thoughtfully, patiently, nodding from time to time as if what I had to say confirmed his inner convictions. (The strictest style in classical painting limited its palette to yellow, red, black and white. Why? This singular fact has never been satisfactorily explained. Must ask Caradoc what he thinks about it.)

"I bet you," he said, falling to work with knife and fork, "that Benedicta hasn't gone up to Eyub with all this uncertain weather; bet you she's hiding in Gatti's, eating ice cream or something. Anyway it's on the way so we shall see. And by the way there's a telegram for you from Marchant which they gave me down in town. Take."

It was a simple and brief message to tell me that our model was "critical"—a word we used to denote the final stages before she woke up. That meant in about a fortnight's time. I felt my pulse quicken at the thought that we were so near launching day. Perhaps mingled with the feeling was a small touch of misgiving; this parody of a much loved person, how would it stand the test of scrutiny by those who had known her?

There was time before my rendezvous with Benedicta, and we elected to dawdle away an hour or so in the Grand Bazaar where I surrendered completely to the long stride of Vibart and the longer memory he had for everything in it. It was delightful to hear him talk now, with nostalgia and affection for the past—no longer hatred and shock. As for the bazaar—despite its size he knew every flagstone, every stall; and despite gaps and changes brought by the times, there was enough for him even to evoke what was absent as we rambled about it. The circumference of the place cannot be less than a mile, while about five covered arcades radiate from its hub, the so-called Bezistan. It is really a walled and gated city within the city, and it claims to contain 7,777 shops. Mystic numbers? Vibart walked about it all with a sense of ownership, like a man showing one round his private picture gallery. He had, I think, come to realize how intensely happy those long years in Turkey had been for him, and indeed how formative; yet he had spent the whole time grumbling about books he could not write. The little square Bezistan, so clearly

Byzantine in feel, is less than fifty yards long; square and squat, it spiders this stone cobweb. The one-headed Byzantine eagle over the Bookseller Gate places the building as tenth century, after which time the eagle became two-headed. The gates are called after the quarters which they serve, each characterized by a product—Goldsmiths, Embroidered Belt Makers, Shoemakers, Metal Chasers. . . .

I could see now that Vibart was living in the romantic schoolboy glow of the mysterious East. These empty rainy stalls once held damascened armor, silver-hilted pistols, inlaid rifles, musical instruments, gems of every water, seals and terra-cottas and coins. Even what wasn't there he was able to describe with complete fidelity in this new youthful voice. I think too that in a way he was talking to Pia in his mind, remembering for her, so to speak. I fell silent and let him go, as one lets a hound off the lead.

"And to think," he said, "that in a few days we'll be back in bonny Blighty facing up once more to all the contingencies which face the creative man—buggery, gin, and menopause Catholicism. Well, I shall take it all calmly from now on. To each his well-deserved slice of sincere dog. To each his cinema picture—the best way of trivializing reality."

But despite the characteristic grumbling tone and matter of his discourse, one felt his calm elation. Nor was he wrong about Benedicta, for she was indeed at Gatti's, sitting at the end of the terrace in a brown study with a cassata before her. In her absentmindedness—or was it due to old memories, old hauntings?—she had adopted a style of sitting with one gloved hand in her lap. One glove off always—that seemed once so characteristic of her; the glove hid a ring Julian had given her, a ring which came from the tomb of a dead Pharaoh. But with the new dispensation she had thrown it away, thus symbolically marking the new freedom which she claimed to have won.

Catching a glimpse of her sitting this way, her blonde head turned away to scan the nebulous city with its turrets and minarets, I suddenly thought of what Vibart had been saying about Pia and realized not only how much I loved her but also why; and by the same token why she must love me, why she would never break free again. It was one of those cursed paradoxes of love which hit one like an iron bar. I sat down with a bump in the chair next to her and said to myself: "Of course, we are most united in the death of Mark, our son. The child we unwittingly murdered. At bottom what brings this hallowed sadness to our loving is a sort of criminal complicity in an evil deed." I longed at that moment to embrace her, to comfort her, to protect her. But this train of thought would not do. Instead we listened to Vibart in full exposition while she let me hold her ungloved hand in mine. (Bookstores near the Mosque of Bayezid in the old Chartopratis or paper market; here in an old Byzantine portico resided a turbaned and gowned old gentleman who sat at a table with reed pen and color box, with gold leaf and burnisher, filling page after page of parchment with exquisite illuminated script. Left over from a forgotten age in which his art was as necessary as it was graceful. Now all he got in the way of commissions were a few petitions from government clerks or illiterate farmers. For the jewelery and the silks you must try Mahmoud Pasha Kapou. . . .)

"Astonishing how much you've remembered and how much I've forgotten," said Benedicta; to which Vibart replied with a certain smugness, "Isn't it, though?"

Clouds furled back to admit a streak of sunlight; we were joined by a relaxed and almost gay Baum. "So they didn't put essence of powdered rat in your soup?" He shook his relieved head and sighed. "To my intense astonishment I found them most receptive to this new idea; the religious leaders heard my exposition in complete silence. Am I to assume that there are passages in the Koran which sanction solitary practices—unless I misunderstood the interpreter, I think that is the case? What impressed them was the insistence on the modern world with its change of viewpoint. After all Turkey abolished the fez out of a desire to make itself a modern state, and then the Latin alphabet replacing the Arabic . . . I rubbed it all in. And when I had finished they practically gave me a standing ovation, if I may use the phrase without indelicacy, and rushed to fill in membership forms at once. Moreover from every minaret and pulpit in the city the news will go out and true believers will flock to the standard. I am so relieved." He smiled all over his face.

Our rendezvous with the pinnace was for dusk, so we idled away the afternoon in the shelter of Gatti's awnings while Baum and Vibart completed several small purchases in the immediate environs. Once again we were favored by a calm sea. It was dusk by the time we landed once more at the jetty and straggled our way up to the house, to the bed, the lamps and candlesticks; to Jocas who was completing his toilet, but in a very good mood. "Everything has gone well," he said. "All our plans agree. Even Caradoc is happy and when has he ever been happy?"

Caradoc was enthroned in a Voltaire and was playing with colored bricks, absorbed as a child; it was indeed a child's toy—this architectural kit. And I could see that having sat for an hour or two on the site by daylight had fired his fancy and given him the itch to begin his task. The evening passed very pleasantly indeed; we almost forgot the plight of Jocas he was in such a good humor, and so lively. But at last when dinner was brought in he said: "So you will go tomorrow, will you? Yes, I think it is best. Now that I have seen you all I am quite content to say good-bye."

It was the end of an epoch I suppose, but it did not feel very momentous so natural were the talk and banter in the firelight.

It is retrospectively that one marks up and weighs the value of experiences. Looking back—as a matter of fact looking down—over Polis as the huge lumbering airplane swam in widening gyres, gaining height over the capital, I was touched by a nostalgia which I had not felt on terra firma. Benedicta too I suppose felt it, and perhaps more sharply than I. Yet she said nothing. Dawn was breaking over the forest of tilting masts and spars, the long walls turned briefly poppy-colored before the lengthening rays of sunlight made them revert to bronze, then to umber. I had a feeling that I should not come back for a very long time, if ever; and I was also glad in a perverse sort of way that the pilot had decided to overfly Greece on the return flight. The melancholy and solitude of Hippolyta had saddened me; it was so absolute that one could think of no consolations worth the offering—you cannot console anyone against reality.

"Thinking?"

"Yes. Thinking and cross-thinking, all the map references are crisscrossed. I was thinking of Jocas, of you as a child, of Hippolyta in Athens. And I was thinking of that absurd prophecy of Zeno's." I took it out of my pocket to study once more. The idea of destroying the firm's entire contract system had begun to tease the edges of my mind; of course it was preposterous, but then everything was. What was more preposterous than returning to England to set Pygmalion's image walking?

"I saw Sipple," said Vibart. "He's blind now and pale and ghostly as a mouse. He is head of the embalming section which Goytz has started up. He does everything by touch, like a mouse nibbling at cheese. He was at work on a small corpse, a boy, silently, happily. It terrified me. I buzzed off hastily."

He looked round carefully to see that Goytz was sleeping tranquilly, and had not heard the remark. Goytz was so easily offended when his craft was mentioned in flippant tones. "He's become like one of those pink transparent eyeless lizards which live in caves in total darkness. Opaque, completely opaque. You can see the sunlight shining right through him, Sipple."

I had forgotten until now that the clown was still with

us, in the land of the living, the land of the dying. A steward brought drinks. Benedicta had fallen into a doze now with her head on my shoulder. Soon we would be booming across the high spurs of Albania, bound for England, home and Iolanthe.

SIX

I have the impression that if anyone had seen us that evening as we wheeled our trophy of love across the crisp green lawns, down the winding gravel paths, through the woods, until we could settle her into the little villa—if anyone had, he would have been tempted to smile at the solemnity and concern written upon our visages. As for her—why she was breathing softly but regularly under her parachute-silk shroud; you could see that faint rise and fall of her breast as she lay stretched out on the long steel trolley. She was gradually coming out of the anesthetic, so to speak. The last threads had been snipped which attached her to the machines that had been feeding slumbering life into her all these long months; the life which, in due course, she would be free to turn to her own uses, to the exploitation of good or evil. "Today she wakes, today she walks," Marchant had chanted with schoolboy enthusiasm which masked, I think, a concern nearly bordering upon hysteria. He had worked harder than any of us on the model. When first her breasts began to rise and fall, her lips to move into the soundless shapes of words, his surprising reaction had been to burst into peal upon peal of laughter, high girlish laughter. And he was still poised on the edge of a triumphant giggle whenever she gave the smallest sign of responding to the demands made upon her by the life currents into which she was entering. His pink scalp shone through his thin silvery hair; his silver-rimmed spectacles, which gave him a slightly White Rabbit look, steamed over all too easily with emotion. He had to wipe them in his apron. It alarmed me, this laughter, I must say.

I confess that I too felt a nudge of concern and perhaps even horror as she began to take her cues—sorry, *it*. She was moving like a planet in to camera range, telescope range. . . .

She licked her lips slowly, tentatively, and her small red tongue flickered over them like that of some marvelous copperhead. Then she sighed once, twice, but it was a very small boredom as yet. We had allowed ourselves a quarter of an hour to dress her and conduct her to the little villa where she might wake in surroundings appropriately familiar to her intricate memory codes. After all, we wanted her to feel at home, to be happy, just like everybody else. So here we were, wheeling her away across country, with Marchant dressed in the elaborate white intern's coat and Mrs. Henniker tricked out as a nurse. Myself, I was still a civilian, so to speak. Marchant was going to play the doctor who by a brilliant operation had saved her life. As for Mrs. Henniker, she was ashen pale, her hair was glued to her scalp with perspiration. But she was behaving very nobly. I had given her a long talking-to about this excessive emotion. There was no need for it, after all, and there was a risk that the experiment, so delicate in its various contingencies, might be spoiled unless she kept a straight face, so to speak. "Above all nothing must be said in the presence of the dummy to suggest to her that she *is* one, that she is not real. She must not be made to doubt her own reality—because that might lead to some sort of memory collapse; whatever doubts she may eventually have must come out of her own memory fund and its natural reaction increment." Easy to say, of course, but the thing was that she was so damn real that it was difficult not to think of her as a "person" . . . already! And she not walking and talking as yet—the acid test of her mock humanity! Yes, she could even read, and by her bed lay the familiar bundles of film papers and weeklies which she would nose through like a dog, quizzing the fashions as she picked her front teeth with a slow fingernail. Yes, she was typical, as contemporary as a mere man could make her.

Julian was there at this briefing, if I can call it that, sitting very still with his hands in his lap, listening intently, looking somehow diminished, somehow like a schoolboy. He too had been showing signs of strain from all this cruel anticipation—symptoms more suited to a young bridegroom than to a grown man playing games with a dummy. Yet there it was: changing his clothes several times a day, studying himself with somber attention in mirrors, fussing over the freshness of the carnation in his buttonhole. I could see that he was going to choose his clothes for the first meeting with the Ur-Iolanthe with great care, for all the world as if it mattered. Yet perhaps after all it did to him. (She would hold out long phthisic fingers toward his, smiling, saying nothing.)

We had chosen the evening as the best time for her to start; it enabled us to see if our settings were right, by her reaction to nightfall and bedtime and so on. Iolanthe used to wake punctually at six every morning, and was usually in bed by eleven at the lastest every night. Henniker had promised to reenact her usual role of nurse-secretary and friend with all the fidelity she could command, and I presumed that she would soon get over her initial worry and take everything naturally; she would familiarize herself with the new Iolanthe in the long run. It was just a question of the initial awakening. If the dummy was as "real" as we expected, its memory-reaction code would instantly throw up the whole of Henniker's history together with "her own" past—every damned thing. Yes, from the simple point of view of memory, she would simply be coming back to life after a critical illness—the gap created by the real Iolanthe's death would be filled in the memory of the false one by vague intimations of an illness, an operation, an absence. Her life henceforth (though we had not made out any elaborate schema to cover the range and scope of her activities: how could we?) —but her life henceforth would be a sort of long convalescence. At least so we thought. She was not "coded" or "programmed" forward. She was, so to speak, free.

The little villa in the woods was unobtrusively surrounded by a tall wire fence and entered through a gate. It was very pretty, set upon a deeply wooded knoll. The garden was a riot of wild and tame flowers; behind ran a brook and beside it lay an apple orchard. It was if anything prettier and more comfortable than the house in the woods which I myself occupied with Benedicta. Inside this elegant little place Henniker had arranged all the possessions (they were astonishingly few for such a rich woman) of Iolanthe, senior; laid them all out in familiar dispositions to reengage memory, yet also haphazardly to suggest perhaps that she (who had lived out of suitcases for half her life) was simply on location for some film or other. But it was beautiful, it was peaceful, the little house. A fire sparkled in the dining room with its new novels and *bibelots;* the Renoir hung upon the wall. On the small upright piano stood the sheet music of a film score and a volume of Chopin's Études. *Eh bien,* the sheets had been aired. On the bedside table were two novels she had been reading when she, the real one, had suddenly lapsed into death. (Some underlinings in one.) Everything in fact conspired to produce a normal setting and atmosphere for this softly breathing Other, lying under her airplane silk. I touched her fingers. They separated easily, flexibly. They were warm.

Marchant had timed it all very accurately. We unpacked her body softly and slipped on the blue silk nightgown while Henniker brushed out her hair with long strokes (she sighing luxuriously the while). Then we lifted her to bed. She smelled the newly ironed freshness of the sheets with appreciation, wrinkling up a newly minted nose. There were also the faint wisps of odor from the lighted joss sticks which burned in a small Chinese vase. It was time; there was nothing to do but wait. Marchant hung over his watch like a demented crystal gazer, his lips counting silently, a smile upon his face. "A minute," he whispered. And then *"Ahhh"* with a long delicious inspiration the lady woke; the two eyes, bluer than any stone, inspected first the clean white ceiling, and then traveled slowly down to take in our own surrounding faces; recognition dawned, together with that famous mischievous smile which was so warm that it had always suggested a marvelous intimate complicity, even when projected on a screen. The slightly husky and melodious voice said: "Is it over? Have I come back, then?" While she addressed the question to Marchant, her long slender arm came out and touched me, grasped my fingers, giving them a tender squeeze of recognition as she whispered in Greek, "Hullo, Felix." Marchant was bobbing and ducking his affirmative and vaguely going through a repertoire of Chinese gestures, shaking hands with myself, as if to congratulate himself for this feat—this living and breathing feat of science, with her china-blue eye and scarlet, rather ravenous mouth. "It's all over," he said. "A great success; but you must rest for a while, quite a long while." She yawned as naturally as a cat and whispered, "I feel wonderful. Felix Doctor, may I go to the loo?" She had not as yet recognized the blenching Henniker, but now as she turned back the sheet in order to stand up, she did, and gave a sharp delighted cry like a bird. "But it's you—I didn't see!" In some curious way the very naturalness of this embrace seemed to allay the emotion and anxiety of the older woman. Perhaps a sense of verisimilitude, of the reality of the flesh and blood, the gesture, released her from a very natural fear—I don't know. But all at once she looked unafraid again. "I'll come with you," she said, and accompanied Iolanthe to the bathroom, smoothing her hair with her hand as she sat on the lavatory and gave her little mechanical shiver of pleasure. "Is it really all over?" she asked Henniker. "Are you sure?"

Henniker reassured her gravely and then escorted her back to bed, puffing up the pillows behind her head and smoothing the sheets with her hard scaly hand. Yes, she had ceased to tremble now. Marchant played the doctor damned awkwardly, swinging a stethoscope in his hand. "Well," he said. "It has all been a great success." She turned her smile on him and expressed her gratitude by taking his hand in hers. "I am so grateful," she said gravely. "I had given myself up for lost, in a way." We studied her gravely, amazed at what we had done, and wondering a little if she would keep up this extraordinary performance of an understudy who had so thoroughly mastered an intricate part. I could well understand Marchant's unease, his desire to get away. It was like the first impact of falling in love—one paradoxically wants to get away, to be alone, in order to ruminate upon the feeling. His love was scientific, that was all. Dolly worked! Iolanthe was saying dreamily: "When you come out of the anesthetic, it's with a soft bump that you land in the middle of consciousness—like those lovely flying dreams one has when one is a child." Marchant stood on one leg and then the other. Finally he took his leave, promising to call on her in the morning. "Henny," said Io, yawning profoundly, "O, Henny dear, can I eat something? Something small, a boiled egg?"

"Of course, darling."

Henniker retired to the kitchen and left us staring at each other with amusement, yes, affectionate amusement. It was a very unreal feeling indeed. "I must just see," she said at last, "what they have managed to do about my breasts—that was what really worried me and brought on the other, I think," She got out of bed with a swift lithe gesture and turned her back to me to enable me to help her divest herself of her blue nightgown. Naked she walked toward the full-length mirror at the other end of the room. She gave a little crooning cry of relief as she caught sight of the beautiful new breasts the doctors had given her, cupping them in her palms, head on one side like a parrot. Then she leaned forward and stared intently into her own eyes as if to make some critical assessment of her own looks; then, sighing, turned to me as naked as sunrise and put her arms round me to kiss me lingeringly on the lips. It was the old affectionate, concerned kiss of Io, quite unbearably real yet utterly without any new sexual connotation. It was as sister to brother, not as lover to lover; but I was thrilled to have a chance to put my arms about her, to test the smooth flexion of her muscles, to stroke the pearly haunches of my darling, proud as any sculptor to have confided such a thing to nature. She giggled as she got back first into her nightgown and then into her bed. "You look so serious," she said. "Still the same old Felix, thank goodness. How is Benedicta?" she added with a faint frown of concentration as if she were trying to summon up an image of her face. "Happy at last," I said. "And me too, Everything has changed." She shot me a cool and rather quizzical look, as if she were in doubt as to whether I was being ironical, or pulling her leg. Then she said, "If it's true, then I'm glad. It was about time, I must say, that you had a decent break."

Henniker came back with the long-legged bed tray on which lay her boiled egg, some nursery bread and butter, and a glass of milk. I watched with anxiety, for all this she would eat only in her imagination; the plate, the glass, would seem to her quite empty, though all she had done was to cut the food up and mess it about a bit. But ideally the reflex hand-to-mouth action would satisfy her sense of participation in a natural ritual; one could hardly have denied her that. (I was reminded of the slow imaginary meals of Rackstraw in the Paulhaus.) She did her act and leaned back, pushing the tray away and wiping her lips. "Gosh, I'm full," she said, and then, "Felix, is there an evening paper? I want to see what plays are on." I found one and she consulted the theater pages with attention, her lips moving. "I don't know a single one of them," she said, and then looked at the date. "How long have I been here, Felix?" I parried this with talk about long sedation and memory lapses and so on. She wrinkled her brow and wandered through the headlines of the paper before abruptly putting it aside.

"By the way," I said, "Old Rackstraw is dead." She looked at me with wide-eyed regret for a moment and then turned away to fold up her napkin. "It's probably for the best," she said in a low voice. "He was so ill it was to be expected, I suppose. And yet everyone who dies takes a whole epoch with them. Racky was a saint to me, an absolute saint. Sometimes quite recently when I thought how contemptuously I had let him sleep with my body— not my me, my *you*, so to speak—I felt shocked and disgusted with myself. In a way I owe him everything; he made my name with his scripts. Felix, do you ever think of, do you ever remember, Athens?" The words came over with a kind of wild pang, saturated with a sort of forlorn reserve. "Ah yes, Iolanthe, of course I do." She smiled and shaking out her hair said: "I tried to reconstruct us in a film at one time, you and me. It didn't work. Racky was doing the writing and couldn't get it."

"I'm not surprised," I said. "But then, why?"

"Because. I do things backward. Experiences don't register with me while they are happening. But afterward, suddenly in a flash I see their meaning, I relive them and experience them properly. That is what happened to me with you. One day by a Hollywood swimming pool the heavens opened and I suddenly realized that it had been a valid and fruitful experience—us two. We might even have christened the thing love. Ah, that word!"

"I took it as it came, with perfect male egoism."

"I know; I suppose you thought we were just . . . what was your pet expression? Yes, 'just rubbing narcissims together and making use of each other's bodies as mirrors.' Cruel Felix, it wasn't like that; why you got quite ill when I left. Well then, I got quite ill too, but retrospectively, by that Hollywood pool, and within the space of a second; people wondered why I suddenly burst out crying. Really it is absurd. Then later I tried to build a film about us in Athens in order to cauterize the memory a bit; but that didn't work. So I just had to let it dwindle away with the years. How absurd. Yes, the film got made, but it was rotten."

She had spilled egg on her nightgown. It was so natural, so babyish. I wiped her with my handkerchief, clicking my tongue reprovingly the while like a nanny. "Now, Iolanthe, please be a good girl, won't you, and obey Dr. Marchant to the letter? No originality, no tricks, no bright ideas. You have got to take it easily for some weeks at least."

"But of course, my dear. But will you come and see me often, just to talk? Bring Benedicta if you wish." She hesitated. "No, don't bring Benedicta. I haven't got rid of my dislike for her as yet. It would make me shy."

"Come. Come."

"I know. Sorry! But still . . ."

I stood up and removed the tray from the bed. "I'll tell you more about Racky," she said, settling herself more comfortably in the bed. "I'll tell you anything, everything. Now I feel at ease. Now my career is finished, the company bought out. I feel a new sort of relief. I have a little time in hand to do the things I want. See Bali properly, read Proust, learn to play the tarot. . . ."

I didn't want to ask her but I had to. "Tell me, do you feel the capacity for happiness inside you? Happiness!"

She considered. "Yes," she whispered as I stooped to kiss her forehead. "Yes, I do. But, Felix, everything will feel indeterminate until I meet Julian, the author of all my professional misfortunes."

"How so?"

"I'm exaggerating of course, but he hangs over me like a cloud, always invisible. Have you ever seen him up close?"

"Yes, but only recently."

"How is he? Describe."

"He is coming to see you tomorrow."

She sat bolt upright in bed, clasping her knees, and said, "Good. At last." Then she clapped her hands and laughed. Henniker came in to draw the curtains and remake the bed and I took the opportunity to take my leave. I was glad to. This first encounter made me feel weak; my knees felt as if they would buckle under me. I stumbled out into the garden with a feeling of suffocation and relief. On the way to the car I had a moment of faintness and was forced to lean against a tree for a moment and unloosen my collar.

On the way back home, at a deserted part of the road over the moors, I came upon the black Rolls laid almost endways across the road in a fashion that suggested an ambush or a holdup. As I hooted I recognized Julian's car; his chauffeur replied with a warning ripple of horn like a wild goose sounding. What the hell? Julian was in the back of the car. I got out and opened his door; he was dressed as if he had come from some official reception. A black Homburg lay behind him on the rack, and in his hands he held a pair of gloves. The funny thing was that he was sitting with his head turned away from me, stiffly, hieratically. I had the impression that he may have been trying to avoid showing the tears in his eyes. Probably false—it was just a fleeting thought. But he swallowed and said: "Felix—for goodness' sake—*how is she?*" The intensity of the question was such as to bring on my shakes. I climbed in beside him and told him—I fear with growing incoherence—all about her awakening, her naturalness. "We've done the impossible, Julian. They talk of portraits taken from the life;

[282]

but this is liver than any portrait. Liver than life. It's bloody well *her*." I was shivering and my teeth began to chatter. "Have you any whiskey, Julian? I'm shaken to the backbone. I feel as if I am getting flu." He pressed a button and the little bar slid out of the wall with its bottles and bowl of ice cubes. The telephone rang but he switched it off with an impatient gesture. I drank deeply, deeply. It was nectar. He watched me narrowly, curiously, as if I *myself* were a dummy, astonishing him by my lifelikeness. "Julian, you wanted this creature and we've produced her, it, for you. I wish you the *densest* happiness in the words of Benjamin Franklin. Her sex is more in the breach than the observance, though technically she could make love, Julian." It was extremely tactless. He struck me across the mouth with his gloves. I didn't react, feeling I had deserved it.

"You are babbling," he said contemptuously.

"I know. It's pure hysteria. But I tell you, Julian, that on the present showing the damned thing is as real as you or I."

"That is what I'd hoped." Now his little white fingers were drumming, drumming upon the leather armrest. "How much does she recall?" he said. "Did she mention me at all?" I laughed. "You still don't realize, Julian; she remembers all that Iolanthe did and more perhaps; we won't know for a while until she has a chance to develop her thoughts. So far though . . ." His eyes looked queer, vitreous; he hooded them with his heavy lids as he turned them on me, sitting there with his brooding vulpine air. He sighed. "When shall we meet, then?" he asked in a low resigned voice, as if he might be asking the date of an execution. I finished my drink. "Tomorrow, at teatime. I told her you would be there." I got out and banged the door on him. He put down the window to say: "Felix, please be there; remember we have never met. This is the first time."

My nerves reformed by the whiskey, I got back into the

car, and felt a sudden wave of elation mingle with my exhaustion. I don't know when I have driven quite so fast or taken so many risks. I was in a hurry to get back to Benedicta, for better or for worse, in slickness or in stealth. . . .

It was so natural—Benedicta before the fire reading, with a sleeping kitten beside her, it was so familiar and so *reliably real* that I was suddenly afflicted by almost the same sense of unreality I had had in talking to Iolanthe. The comparison of two juxtaposed realities like these gave me the queer feeling that might overwhelm a man who looks in the mirror and sees that he has two heads, two reflections. But she didn't ask, she didn't question; I simply slumped down beside her, put my head on my arms and went straight to sleep. It was dinnertime when she woke me. Baynes had unobtrusively set out a tray in the corner of the room on a table which we moved into the firelight. By now of course I was as ravenous as a pregnant horse and bursting with euphoria. She looked at me quizzically from time to time. "I can see it's gone well," she said at last.

"It's not quite believable yet." That was all I could say. We embraced. I exploded the champagne, laughing softly to myself like a privileged madman. " 'Eternity is in love with the productions of Time,' says Will Blake. You have nothing to fear Benedicta; drink my dear, let us toast reality awhile."

It could have had its funny side, too, the meeting between Julian and Io—I suppose—to an objective observer. I mean that he for his part had dressed most carefully, his hair was neat, his nails newly manicured; moreover he had developed a new and stealthy walk for the occasion, a sort of soliloquy glide out of *Hamlet*. He was at pains perhaps to disguise his fear? Whereas now I had more or less got on top of my own anxiety—the primitive terror that all human beings feel when faced by dummies of whatever kind, representations of hallowed reality: an Aurignacian complex, as Nash might have called it. I was indeed swaggering a little in my newfound relief. Like a young man introducing a particularly pretty fiancée. I smiled upon my *patron* indulgently as I led him across the green lawns and down the long gravel paths, Julian snaking slowly behind me, rippling along. He had brought a small bunch of Parma violets with him as an offering. But suddenly he threw them away and swore. I think he was saying to himself, "My God! Here I am thinking of her as if she were *real*, instead of just an expensive contemporary construct." I chuckled. "You will get used to her, to it, very quickly, Julian. You'll see."

Henniker was in the room when we arrived. She pointed; apparently Iolanthe was in the lavatory. Julian seated himself with the air of someone taking up a strategic position, choosing a chair in the far corner of the room. At that moment Iolanthe entered and, catching sight of him, stood stock-still, smiling her soft hesitant smile with all its shyness welling up through the superficial assurance. "Julian, at last," she said. "Well!" And walking across to him, took both his hands in hers and stood staring down into his eyes with a candor and puzzlement which made him turn quite white. "At last we meet," she said. "At last, Julian!" He cleared his throat as if to make some response, but no words came. She turned triumphantly aside and got back into bed with the help of Henniker. "Henny, let us have tea, shall we?" she said in rather grandiose tones, and the older woman nodded and moved toward the door. Then Julian from the depths of a recovered composure said: "I don't know where to begin, Iolanthe; or even if there is a place to begin, for I think you know everything

by now. At any rate every bit as much as I know. Isn't it
so?" She frowned and licked her lips. "Not entirely," she
said, "though I have made some provisional guesses. But
now you own me, don't you? I wonder what you plan to do
with me? I am quite defenseless, Julian. I am just one of
your properties now." His nostrils dilated.

His upper lip had gone bluish—like someone in danger
of a heart attack. Iolanthe continued in a dreamy voice,
almost as if she were talking to herself, recapitulating a
private history to fix it more clearly in her own mind.
"Yes, you were always there behind us, sapping us, sniping
at us from behind the high walls of the company. How
cleverly you disposed of Graphos too when you found he
was my lover; I mean of course his career. He was very ill
of course; that wasn't your fault. And I kept expecting you
to appear so that I could perhaps make a deal with you,
plead with you, trade my body, even to save my little
company, save my career. Nothing. You never did. Sometimes I thought I knew why really; I worked out reasons
from what people told me about you—feminine reasons.
Were they wrong I wonder, Julian?"

The artless blue eyes, inquisitive and chiding, rested
fixed on his face. He stirred uncomfortably and said:

"No. You know all the reasons. I don't need to explain
at this stage, Iolanthe, do I? You haunted me just as
much."

He spoke gently enough, but at the same time I felt a
sort of fury rising in him; after all, here he was being
ticked off by a *dummy* for defections of behavior toward
an all too real (though now dead) Iolanthe! It was very
confusing this double image. Moreover he could not lean
forward and, tapping her wrist, say: "That's enough now;
do you realize that you are just a clever and valuable little
dummy, fabricated by the experts of the firm? You are
simply steel and gutta-percha and plastic and nylon, that's
all. So kindly hold your tongue." He couldn't do that, so
he just sat still, looking stubborn, while she went on in the

voice of reminiscence. "Yes, when the production company failed, when Graphos died and when my career collapsed and I got ill, I expected some word from you—after all so much of this had been your deliberate design against me. I was puzzled, thought I might find some sympathy, some understanding of my plight. But no, you were out to smash me and take me prisoner. And now you have, Julian. But for a long time I dreamed about you: about how you would appear one day, all of a sudden, without warning. Yes, sitting just where you are now, dressed as you are, and a little tongue-tied for the first time in your life by a woman's *love*. You see, part of my fantasy was to imagine that you loved me. Now I know I was right. You do. Poor Julian! I do understand, but when Graphos went out, the mechanism rusted, broke, and now I have an empty space where the thing used to live." She gave a short and sad little laugh. "I grew tongue-tied."

"Tongue-tied," he repeated ruefully, seeming somehow put out of countenance. They looked at each other steadily, but with an extraordinary air of mutual understanding. Then she said: "But not any more somehow," and a renewed cheerfulness flowed into her. "I have half recovered from that period and perhaps so have you. Now there seems to be something else before us—I don't know how to put it, perhaps a friendship? At any rate something unlike anything I have ever known before; Julian, do you feel it too?"

He nodded coldly, critically. His face betrayed no emotion whatsoever at this somewhat extraordinary speech. Then she added calmly, with an air of simplicity, a QED air, which was completely disarming, "I don't think I can do without you anymore, Julian. It's more than flesh and blood can stand." It was terribly moving, the way she said this.

"Of course," he said softly, greedily. "It's the loneliness. No, you won't have any more of that, I promise you."

She extended her long languid waxen hands and he got

up to take them and carry them to his lips with swift precision, yet without any trace of deep feeling. I could see however that the strain of his first interview with Iolanthe was beginning to tell on him as it had on me; he was being slowly flooded by the same unreasonable sensation of gradual suffocation. Just like me. We of course were both conscious that we were talking to an experimental dummy; but she, unconscious as yet of her own unreality, was at ease and as perfectly sincere (if I can use the word) as . . . well, as only a dummy could be. What am I saying? It was an extraordinary paradox, for we were literally worn out by having to act a part while she was fresh as a daisy. One wanted to laugh and cry at the same time—how well I understood Julian's desire to be gone! "Now there will be time," said Iolanthe coolly, "all the time in the world, to take a leisurely look at everything I have missed in my rush through life. Later maybe you may help me to rebuild my career once more; unless you think I am too old to act anymore?"

He shook his head decidedly and said, "First things first; when you are quite well we shall see."

"But I feel so well already," she said.

"Nevertheless."

At this point Henniker produced the tea and I could see the proconsular eye of Julian fixed upon Iolanthe to admire the excellence of her teatime deportment. His alarm had subsided somewhat, the temperature of his anxiety had dropped a little. Then she added: "In a way we were well-matched enemies . . . parricide against infanticide . . . no, that is not the way to say it."

"What a memory you have got," he said bitterly, and she nodded, taking an imaginary sip of China tea. "Mine is as long as my life," she said, "but yours is as long as the firm's, Julian."

I was in bliss. A dummy that could forge repartee like this . . . . better, cleverer than a real woman; because less arbitrary, less *real*, less feminine. And yet, on the other hand, the little note of bitterness in her voice was very human, very feminine. If she were absolutely identical with Iolanthe, surely she *was* Iolanthe? Obviously we must spend a bit of time to work out the differences between the real and the invented; but if there were none? Julian was talking again, softly, indifferently it seemed: "Well, you would not join the firm so how could I reach you—for I am more the firm than I am myself in a manner of speaking; what could I bring to you or offer to you that did not bear the fingerprints of Merlin's? But you refused all my offers, you evaded me." He paused to take out a cigar and crackle it in his fingers; but then he replaced it in his cigar case with an air of irresolution. Her lips curled as she said with a tinge of contempt, "But now? I am broken and bridled, am I not? The firm has swallowed my little company. I am your captive at last, Julian, amn't I?"

At this a sudden little flash lit up both pairs of eyes, a sudden spark of fury, of antagonism, of sexual fury. I had not seen this look on Julian's face before. Then she drawled with her most mischievous air, "I could come to you tonight, Julian, if you wished. Just tell me where and when!" He went deathly white at the insult but he eyed her contemptuously, his eyes glittering like those of a basilisk. He said nothing, and it was obvious that he was not going to say anything. "Just tell me," she repeated, and I thought she took a sort of savage delight in provoking his male pride thus; surely she knew the sad story of Julian— the fate of Abelard? Nevertheless she stayed there, staring at him with the same expression of provocation on her face, outfacing his silence, trying to discountenance him. He was absolutely still. But now I saved the day by putting in a word or two. "Now. Now. You are under Dr. Marchant's orders, Iolanthe. Don't forget it please." It broke the spiteful spell. She pouted adorably and said, "I was only teasing, Felix; just to see how far one could go with Julian." But she began to pick at the tassels of the bedcover with long painted nails. I did not particularly care for the note of insolence in her voice: I thought it might be a good moment to make our exit. I announced that I must leave as I had an appointment and Julian immediately elected to come with me; yet he seemed without visible emotion, visible relief. I kissed the warm cheek of my angel, and gave her fine fingers a squeeze. "Until tomorrow," I said, confiding her to the faithful ministrations of Henniker who stood at the foot of the bed, smiling tenderly at her; the older woman was by now quite cured of her original fright and dismay. But she had overcome it in the simple fact of *believing* in the new Iolanthe—of *believing her to be real!* By some simple *déclic* of the mind she had abolished the knowledge of Iolanthe's dummyhood and replaced it with a fully conscious belief and acceptance of her as a real woman.

We walked slowly along the gravel paths toward the car park; Julian was sunk deep in thought, gazing down at his feet. "I suppose you have a set of experiments to subject her to?" he said at last quietly. "Yes. For the time being we are recording her night and day to study the general patterning of the memory-increment apparatus. I propose later to set her back into the Iolanthe picture by letting her meet a few of the people Io knew in real life—people like Dombey, her agent—just to see how capably she works."

"I abolished the mate, you know," said Julian quietly. "I wonder whether it was right of wrong. You say she could make love this creature?" I said I saw no reason why not, she had the organs. "Of course when she speaks about love and so on, you have to make a sort of mental correction in realizing that the words are simply coded into a machine by an echo master, and in the final analysis simply come out of a metal box."

"I know," he said, "it's weird. But she is so word-perfect that one wonders if she couldn't live happily with a member of the human species, as a wife, I mean." The chauffeur opened the door of the car for him, but he still stood, shaken to the bottom of his soul by this interview and the possibilities it promised. "We must be careful not to feel too much affection for it," I said. It was easily said, I know. "But *you* are half in love with her already," said Julian, smiling up at me suddenly, and of course he was speaking the truth—I was mad about my own invention, like every inventor is. O yes I was. He went on slowly, thoughtfully. "And what sort of future do you envisage for her, for it? Will she ever be allowed out into the world?"

"Nothing very definite was worked out for her—we didn't know how real she might turn out to seem; she might have been vastly more limited both physically and mentally than she is. The whole operation was done on spec, Julian, you know that. Now I think we must really submit her to extensive testing before letting her increase the range of her activities; we must think about her a bit as one does about a handicapped person, which of course she is, because she is only a machine, a love machine." I don't know why I used that stupid phrase, it simply popped out. "I see," he said, frowning at the ground. "We can begin by bringing the world to her for a while; then if she satisfies every requirement, if she is foolproof, we can gradually insinuate her into quotidian reality, so to speak; in the end we might accord her an autonomous life of her own, like any other taxpayer, lover, wife or dog."

He hoisted himself slowly into the car, still sleepy with thought. "I will see her every day with you until I get over that extraordinary feeling of panic," he said; and then very suddenly: "Felix, if we wanted to abolish her it would be an easy matter, wouldn't it?" I jumped as if he had stuck a pin in me. "Abolish her?" I cried sharply, and he smiled. "I'm sorry; but one must think of every possible contingency, mustn't one?"

"Not that one," I said. "Never that Julian."

"Well, I am in your hands."

Slowly the car wound its way down the leafy roads. I betook myself to the studio to study the schemata that

Marchant had worked out for the daily life of Iolanthe in these initial stages. A masseur who did not know she was not real had turned in a most interesting report on her body which made me swell with pride. That at least showed no particular anomalies in the disposition of the muscle schemes; he had found her musculature if anything too firm. He wondered if some predisposition to sclerosis might not be envisaged! No, in every way so far she seemed to be of a mechanical perfection that eluded all criticism. Every word she uttered was also being monitored, and playing through this library of speeches one could find nothing disoriented, nothing out of key. She had a fully grown organ of memory to fall back on as she lived her real life. Marchant had scribbled a note or two about his visits to the patient. She had proved very docile and cooperative. "*Too* damn real for my liking," he added sardonically. "I keep almost forgetting she is an It."

So we embarked thoughtfully and I hope skillfully upon this experiment; but it was hard to shed the feeling of unreality which crept over us as we watched the perfected mimicry of her gestures. heard this highly articulate woman talking, arguing, even singing. It was a good ten days before we let her out of bed, but finally there seemed little reason to deny her the right to walk about her house and garden. Julian was away for part of this time, and I had to visit Geneva for a week. We took it in shifts to attend her levees. Nor did Benedicta react in any particular manner to my absorption in the life of this model—I had not really expected her to; yet her little speech in Athens had filled me with a certain misgiving. I felt that, like the rest of us, she would get used to Iolanthe, conquer an initial repulsion and panic, and come to accept her for what she was—an experiment. But I told her quite candidly what Iolanthe had said about disliking her, and asked her if she would mind waiting awhile before risking a meeting with her. In the meantime the daily life of Iolanthe herself was being gradually filled in at the edges by designedly quotidian events. For example, we got hold of her agent and invited him down to see her; now, *despite* the fact that he was fully briefed about the doll, the impact of Iolanthe was so marked and so faithful to the original which he had loved that he passed out cold upon the carpet and had to be revived. He *was* revived, of course, but he was badly shaken. Naturally we explained this away as relief to find her recovered from her illness. We tried as far as possible never to let her doubt the reality of herself—to make her self-conscious in the true sense of the word.

But gradually, inevitably, she began to feel a sense of constraint; after all, she was being pretty closely watched and monitored, and up to now had not been allowed to go beyond the garden fence. The excuse we gave was of course medical. But the minute a patient begins to feel better he or she is tempted to throw good advice to the winds. This aspect of things was a trifle preoccupying; but Henniker was always unobtrusively there to follow her movements. She reported the fact that Iolanthe had asked if she might go down to the village, and had shown some pique when told that Marchant had forbidden it. Later she tackled Marchant himself about it, and I must say I thought the reasons he gave sounded somewhat shallow if not downright shifty. "We are fighting a losing battle," I said. "She has got through all her tests so quickly, I don't see how we can keep her locked up much longer without arousing her suspicions. Indeed it might be a good idea to start letting her out a bit, though of course someone will always have to be with her; she's too valuable to lose, or to let get damaged."

Julian asked to see her alone during this time, and spent many long hours in the house talking to her; I could hear him pacing up and down slowly in her room. Once I heard his normally low voice raised as if in anger; another time I had the illusion that she was shedding tears. But there was nothing much to be done. When I was in Geneva I opened a weekly paper and found a picture of the gambling rooms at Gunters—baccarat in progress; and there to my surprise stood Julian in his dinner jacket, shoulder to shoulder with a bewigged Iolanthe who was watching the play with great interest. As soon as I got back I rang up Julian and he confirmed that he had taken her out for an evening, with Marchant's consent. "I can tell you something new," he said. "She has the devil's own *luck*, computer luck you could call it. We made a packet. Felix, I want to thank you; I feel extremely happy. When do you think she can be declared absolutely autonomous, absolutely free?" I could not really think up an answer to this question. "It raises one of those bogies, Julian, and I think you've heard enough choplogic about freedom, specially from me. How free will she be? How will her freedom compare with our own imaginary freedom? Goodness, I can't answer you; the whole thing is still in the realms of pure experiment. But why should you ask? Are you in danger of falling in love with my little toy, are you going to ask for her hand in marriage?" Once again I had slipped tactlessly; I felt rather than heard him grinding his teeth, and in a low voice, almost a whisper, he uttered an obscenity. "I'm sorry," I added vaguely, "but the question just set me off on a long train of thought. Her precarious freedom against ours . . . but we mustn't start taking her too seriously, Julian." I had the impression that he gave a little groan. The line went dead. And that was all.

But after that gambling outing she seemed to show an increased impatience with constraint, and I began to fear that she might take the law into her own hands. She said to Marchant, "In the long run you can't deny me my freedom forever. I have the right to start to rethink my career, to rebuild it if I decide I would like to." Then she discovered that one of her teeth had been given a small filling which she could not remember having had placed by her dentist. It was just a passing cloud, so to speak, and she was easily persuaded that her memory had slipped. But she was right; when we had another look at the dentist's jaw diagram we discovered our mistake. "How could I have forgotten," she said, "I who live in such terror of dentists? Ah, well, my memory must be failing—it's old age, darling Felix, that is what it is."

Ten days later I braked the car violently in the middle of the village; there was Iolanthe walking nonchalantly out of the door of the Gold Swan, lighting up a cigarette. She burst out laughing as she saw my alarmed face. "I couldn't resist," she said. "I gave Henny the slip and trotted down for a whiskey." Like the real Iolanthe, who had had so much trouble from her public, she had taken to a brown wig which completely transformed her face. In this way no fans would pester her. I didn't know what to say; it seemed ridiculous to chide her. After all there was nothing intrinsically dangerous or harmful in what she had done—it was just an agreeable escapade for her. But it made me think. I had a long confabulation with Marchant. We wondered perhaps whether it might be time to move her into a large hotel, say, where there would be plenty of movement, plenty of life around her. Or whether we should buy her a dog—no, but like the real Iolanthe she wasn't keen on dogs because of the infernal quarantine restrictions in Britain. Well then, what?

"Felix," she said, "I've had a strange feeling growing up inside me that I must change everything—make a break for liberty." This is what I had been fearing; but she went on in a low, infinitely touching tone: "The awful thing is that the inevitable has happened—I always knew it would." She paused, and her beautiful eyes filled with tears. She put her hand on my arm and said, "My dear friend, the worst that could happen—I have fallen in love with Julian. That is what frightens me so much. I was always ferociously independent, as you know. I feel now that I mustn't sink any deeper into this adoration. I must, so to speak, negotiate from a position of strength. But he won't help to set me free; he wants me bound and gagged, and at his mercy."

She walked slowly up and down the room with her

hands in her armpits, thinking. On the table lay a fat bundle of five-pound notes and a specimen signature-card form such as bank managers present when one opens an account. She caught my gaze upon it and smiled. "I was going to open an account but I've changed my mind. It's better to have the cash in hand. Funny thing is that when I'm with Julian, when he bets for me, I turn tremendously lucky. Did he tell you? We won a fortune." She groped for her slippers and sat down in a chair, frowning and pre-occupied. "You see," she said at last, "I must envisage some way of remaining myself, of not being engulfed; I've played snakes and ladders with the firm long enough—and at the moment I am snaked out, so to speak, sent to the very bottom of the board. But I can't stay there; so long as I have health enough and will enough I must try and climb. Unfortunately this is not what Julian wants. It makes him angry. Do you know he even insulted me? He called me 'the parody of a woman,' said I wasn't real, that I had a heart of steel wool. . . . That sort of thing has never been in Julian's repertoire, has it? Well, it just goes to show that we are both under some strain. Felix, something's got to change to make it all right between us." O! God!

Naturally all this talk made me feel ineffectual and dis-tracted, for I could not image any practical changes in her "life" which might meet with these inherited feelings—feelings which belonged to the dead woman whose mind and body he had had foisted upon her in so Faustian a fashion. "But what?" I said vaguely, noting with another part of my mind that her signature was perfect—I mean that it was unmistakably Iolanthe's handwriting. No pro-fessional forger could have produced such a perfect copy. "Let's not do *anything* impetuous," I said in the feebly admonishing tone which would be bound, I knew, to irritate her, to fill her with impatience, "until you are quite clear of Dr. Marchant. Then we'll really go over the whole position. By that time perhaps Julian will have thought of something; he may invite you away on the yacht, he may take you to the villa in Ischia or Baalbek. Don't be too impatient and hasty, that is all I beg."

It was all too easily said, and secretly I rather echoed in my heart the impatient sign that she gave now as she sat, looking into my eyes like some distraught jungle cat—a cheetah, perhaps. Nor did I see really why she should not be allowed to travel about a bit, provided she always came back. Of course it would mean that she was out of the range of our monitors, and it was Marchant's expressed intention to do some depth findings in the memory code of the doll's "mind"—laborious and perhaps as unfruitful (for the most part) as Nash's depth analysis which kept people nailed to the horsehair sofa for years on end. She was talking again. "I have been very shaken these last weeks by the fact that Julian is so exactly what I knew, dreamed, felt, he would be. It gives me a strange feeling of unreality—as if he were an artificial man, constructed by my own mind, by my dreams or something. . . . When he speaks I feel I am listening to someone who is word-perfect reciting a part. It is very queer. But, Felix, what a strange mind he has; what extraordinary passions—yet all locked up in steel strongboxes inside his mind. He attracts and scares me at the same time." Naturally this did not surprise me; I knew enough about him at first- and secondhand to gauge the impact of a character like his upon her. The real Iolanthe would not have been any different, of this I was sure. Were they not as alike as two signatures, the dummy and the dead memory?

"He has offered to let me see all my old film successes again—there's a projection room apparently in the labs. But that also scares me a little bit; at the moment the mirror seems to console me on the score of beauty—perhaps I should say still flatter? But I don't really know if I am past it all, films, or whether there might be just a glimmer of chance about recovering my position. Have you any ideas on the subject?" I had none, naturally enough. If she were sufficiently lifelike to live in Claridge's, surely she could act in front of the camera? What I *couldn't* say was: "That would raise a capital problem for us—you see, you were once a world-famous screen star, your face was known to the whole world. But you *died!* It would take some explaining if you reappeared and competed for the crown all over again. You see, darling, it would put us in the jam of having to find an excuse for your being here. If we told the world you were a dummy, you would find out the truth yourself and it would destroy your confidence in yourself, and in the esteem of the world. In fact, you might very well commit suicide or take to drugs—or adopt any other conventional form of self-abasement. In some ways, Io, you are all too human, despite the fine firm construction of you; you are still as affectively mentally fragile as any human counterpart." All this I said in my own mind. "What are you mumbling about?" said Iolanthe peevishly. "Reciting the creed?" I blinked bashfully and stood up. It wasn't far off the mark.

As a matter of fact a muddled series of quotations had been bubbling about in my mind, among which was "I am the resurrection and the life, saith the Lord God." Where that came from I have no idea, I am not well up in Holy Writ. And then again a line—"freedom, freedom, prison of the free"—from the best of our modern poets* But none of this provided a coherent frame of reference upon which we could base a discussion of her preoccupations. I had a feeling that everything was beginning to slip a bit; the feeling of ineffectuality grew and grew. I finished my drink and said that perhaps I ought to be going. "So you can't think of anything?" she said with a touch of grimness. "If of course I am seriously ill and likely to die soon, and if you are simply keeping the truth from me . . . ." It might have offered a way out but in my naïve way I omitted to take the chance. "Far from it," I said, "you are healthier than you have ever been."

I took my leave, kissing her softly upon her impatient

* Lawrence Durrell.

forehead; and I was glad to do so, in order to think things over a bit in the quietness of the cottage.

In view of this steady development toward some attempt to claim a margin of freedom of herself, I was not unduly surprised to find her sitting in the garden one morning in a bathing costume, half asleep in a deck chair, and radiating a high good humor. She chuckled with pleasure as she said: "Henniker is not on speaking terms with me. She is *furious*, Felix, and swears she will report me to you and Dr. Marchant. I ask you, *report;* I was astonished by the choice of a word, it belongs to prisons or girls' schools. And all just because I spent half the day in London without telling her. I knew she wouldn't let me go—why should I tell her? And whose permission should I have sought? Yours?" As a matter of fact, yes; she should have told somebody. But I said nothing. She looked at me quizzically, uncertain whether to scold me or to remain aggrieved, defensive. "I had to see this new film of Escroz'. He is one of my oldest friends. So I went. The bus service is very convenient. And I was back by seven. I've sent him a telegram to tell him I am well again. I'd like to see him if he could get down here." I made a mental note of this; Escroz had been at the funeral of the real Iolanthe, and may not have realized that she was once more in the land of the living so to speak. "How was it?" I said, more to conceal my sense of misgiving than anything else. "Not too strong," she said, "but some lovely camera work as usual. He's marvelous on atmosphere."

I coughed. "I've had a word with Dr. Marchant," I said, "and we were wondering whether you would not be happier in a hotel like Claridge's or the Dorchester, with a bit of life and movement around you; you could finish all your tests there for a while and at least get about, shop, and so on." She was suddenly contrite. She put a hand on my arm. "I'm not trying to be a trouble, Felix," she said. "It's just that everything is going so slowly and my health seems wonderful; and I have been made a bit impatient by

[299]

these meetings with Julian. He is coming back from New York on Saturday. That's all. A very nominal freedom would satisfy me and cure my boredom for the present; later of course I shall decide what I will and won't do, naturally." I did not quite know whether to like or dislike the tone of this last sentence. "You were always an impatient soul," I said, and she nodded humbly. Then she produced something which, considering the terms of reference, sounded out of character. "Last night I hardly slept a wink, and had to take a sleeping tablet or two. I hope it isn't a return of the old migraine I had in Athens long ago. What a *supplice*." Of course it *was* part of the old memory code coming back, and from that point of view unexceptionable; nevertheless it hinted at strain of some kind. She had taken a very strong dose of M.I.S.T.[2] I presumed the taking was an imaginary act, for the tablet could not by any conceivable manner of means have had any effect on her body as it was then constituted. "Did you sleep at last?" She nodded. "But I had palpitations and nausea and so on."

Beside her on the lawn lay a long gunnysack full of her fan mail. (I had a whole department busy writing nothing else; they were part of our verisimilitude team, as we called them, filling in and reviving the quotidian life of the Ur-Iolanthe.) The letters were of course all fabrications; any answers that she wrote back to these imaginary fans came straight back to us for analysis. Henniker spent a part of every evening taking letters destined for fans and sending out signed photographs and so on. All this part of her life worked impeccably so far, it seemed. A mountain of glossy screen stills lay neatly stacked on the rack above her writing desk with its many pictures of leading men in silver frames. There was one empty photograph frame among them which I knew was going to be destined for a picture of Julian (she had asked for one and he had promised to have one sent to her). But which Julian—that was rather the point? Yes, which?

You will appreciate that I am simply recording all this matter of fact as I can for the record—both personal and scientific, I suppose. I don't remember being particularly surprised by the denouement when it started to work out— I mean the sudden fugue and disappearance of Iolanthe; but just about the same time other events started to impact themselves so that when I think back upon this period I see a succession of juxtaposed images rather than a straight chronology of events. But the whole thing led up in a steady series of small surprises to St. Paul's. Benedicta is sitting beside me following the recording; from time to time I switch off to debate a date or an event with her. It's taken a hell of a while, and in this summary I am of course dealing with quite a long extent of serial time. Since Iolanthe disappeared, of course, all our monitoring pre-occupations were so much wasted machine food. Marchant and I, Julian and Benedicta, we seemed to spend all our time on the phone; and every time it rang it was something to do with her, some polite hint, or a tip-off from a friend.

But her disappearance was very quietly and confidently planned; Henniker woke up at early light to find herself pinioned to the bed with a length of stout cord. Skillfully, too, for she could not free herself and had to wait for Marchant's regular morning visit. Iolanthe was walking about the room, chuckling in a rather sinister, disoriented way, and packing two of her pigskin suitcases with the most indispensable articles of wear. Clothes, wigs, personal notepaper, etc., etc. She was deaf to the protestations of Henniker who by now was almost beside herself with fury and anxiety. She tried to get her to say where she was going, but the busy figure would not even turn its head, let alone answer. She packed with miraculous speed and dispatch, still making this queer crepitation. Henniker gritted her teeth and renewed her appeals. She wondered whether to scream for help—but who would have heard her at such an hour and in such a place? Useless! Once the task was complete Iolanthe drew the curtains and looked out, as if expecting someone, and the thought did cross Henniker's mind that perhaps Julian might be abducting her. The clock struck. Quickly, like a master cracksman after a night's work on a safe, Iolanthe made herself a cup of tea and drank it in imaginary fashion. She came and stood before the pinioned figure of her profoundest human friend, slowly sipping and staring down into her eyes, saying nothing, sunk apparently in the profoundest reflection. Then there came the sound of a car. Iolanthe was shaken by little sobs, tiny youthful little sobs, so separate, so painful. Nor could Henniker now restrain her own tears. "Iolanthe, don't leave me." But the mechanical maenad was already humping the two large suitcases to the door, and thence down the garden path to the car. Later we found that she had simply ordered the village taxi to come for her and take her into the town where she caught the morning train to London. That was that. It may well be imagined that this event threw us all into a frightful disarray. Marchant first flew into the most terrible rage and threw equipment about, and then sat down on a stool and cried. It was curious what we had come to feel for this creation; one felt a little as if one's own heart were broken.

Julian appeared looking as if he were fresh from hell. An urgent conference was held; it was first necessary to try and work out the places she might visit, the people she might call on. But this was a task of the greatest complexity; Iolanthe was a citizen of the world. Besides, nothing could have prevented her from taking a plane to Paris or Rio—she even had Iolanthe's old passport. It was necessary to invoke the aid of the police, but on what terms? Could we ask them to watch the ports and air terminals by saying that she was wanted for some crime—larceny, perhaps? An excuse must be found so that the law could weigh in and help us trace her. "She must be brought back alive and undamaged," Marchant kept repeating, somewhat absurdly I thought. Alive! The police when we finally alerted them were kindly, understanding and very efficient; and we did have a collection of pictures of Io in her various wigs. But it took a long time to try and formulate a story which might not seem too preposterous; somehow one didn't dare to talk about a dummy which was at large. Yet there was hope; between the firm itself and the police force, we managed to throw out a fairly effective net into which, with any luck, she might stray.

Somewhere in the real world, freed from the dead sanctions of science, strayed the new Iolanthe, perfectly equipped to mix into the background of people and events without raising the smallest suspicion that she was not as others were. But it was a blow, and there was no disguising it; moreover until we were sure of her whereabouts, or indeed of her fate, we had no stomach for anything else; we had concentrated so deeply upon her that all other work of the firm seemed suddenly stale, profitless.

She went to see her agent who reported the fact at once to Julian; but though we tried we could not trace her. However it proved that she had been in the London area and was still traveling about incognito in a wig—apparently fully aware that if her fans recognized her she risked being compromised with us. She was clever and agile. We could not watch all the cinemas and all the theaters, but we managed to keep an eye on some of them, and in particular those where likely films or plays were being put on. She was signaled as coming out of the Duchess one night; but if it were she, she slipped through the net once more. Other sightings were reported from various parts of the country now, as if she were moving about fairly quickly. Harrogate was a likely one—she had always liked Harrogate. But again we were too late. One day she even walked into the firm, though nobody saw her, and left a note on Julian's desk.

He seemed disinclined to let anyone see it, and we did not press him; but it contained no news of her whereabouts. It was simply about their relationship—so much he vouchsafed in a low voice. I must say that since her disappearance Julian seemed to have aged very much; he walked with a stoop, his hair seemed whiter, and his suave swarthy features appeared more deeply lined; this touched something profound in Benedicta, and her sympathy for his . . . well, his plight . . . made her demonstrate a new warmth and affection for which he seemed deeply grateful.

Ipswich, Harrow, Pinewood: these visitations were all characterized by the same deftness, the same unerring choice of time; the same cool disappearance. There seemed nothing to be done. Perhaps we would never find her again; she had so perfectly integrated with reality, one supposed, that there was hardly any need. Was there nothing to be done, was there nothing which might lure her back? Julian! He had been told to write to her, but she gave no address, so he was constrained to imagine that she meant him to put a notice in *The Times* which he dutifully did, imploring her to come back to him. But she contented herself with ringing him up once from Dover to say that she was going to Paris. That she was very happy. That she missed him, and all of us. That she would come and see us all after she had experienced a number of unspecified events which were of great importance to her. She visited a producer in Paris for a moment, and telephoned to Nury, the film star, who thought she was a madwoman impersonating the other Iolanthe. By the time we heard of this she had vanished again.

Then one evening, one dark and rainy evening, I found myself in Chatham, in a dockside street, walking back from some appointment or other in the harbor master's office. A sordid drizzly evening with the bluish streetlamps casting a greasy glow in the darkness like disembodied heads. I was picking my way through the slime and wet of the broken pavements when the swing doors of a pub flew open and a woman walked out on the arm of a young sailor; in the bar of light thrown by the open door I saw them turn, and I was at once struck by some small singularity of pose in the way the woman turned her head. "Iolanthe!" I gasped with delight, with ecstasy I might say; for when she turned her head I saw that it was indeed she. But she screwed up her face into a vile simian expression and pretended not to recognize me. I advanced toward her in my usual naïve and ineffectual way—feeling tolerably sure that when she recognized me she would at least greet me. What to do? Somehow I must try and capture her, make her see reason; perhaps if we had a talk . . . I took off my dark hat so that she might recognize me the more easily. But still she wore this common expression, and then in broad Cockney she said: "What the 'ell do you want, sonny? I don't know you." The impersonation was so good that for a moment I almost doubted; she had blacked out a front tooth which gave her whole face a gap-toothed, lopsided look. I hesitated and made as if to put my hand on her arm; whereupon she cried again in this baroque Cockney accent, "Lemme go, will yer?" And the young sailor turned all gallant and stepped in between us to deliver a blow which hit me between the eyes and knocked me flying. They walked on unhurriedly, arm in arm; at the end of the street she paused under a streetlamp to look back and give a coarse little laugh. Then they turned the corner and disappeared from view. I scrambled together all the papers which had flown out of my briefcase onto the pavement, and nursing my jaw followed them. But by the time I reached the corner they had vanished. I did not tell Julian about this unsuccessful encounter, I don't know why; but yes I do. In the afternoon paper of the following day, I came across an item which reported the discovery of the body of a young sailor in Chatham; there was nothing very unusual about it except that it was standing up in a doorway. But these things happen almost everywhere, and all the time.

Then late at night Julian suddenly appeared at the cottage, holding in his hand the buff telegraph form which announced the death of Jocas. We sat for a long time in complete silence, staring into the fire. I don't know what hopeless regrets, what formless memories, stirred in the mind of Julian, but for me it was as it we were looking down the long curving vistas of the Turkish capital toward the origins of Merlin's—toward the blue waters of the gulf, the masts, the walls, the colored kites floating and tugging against the sky. I was reminded of someone saying something about each death marking a whole epoch in one's life. Was it Benedicta or Hippolyta? So Jocas had gone! The thought had a heavy resonance; even when one had forgotten his existence or had passed months without consciously thinking about him, he had always somehow been there, a swarthy presence that represented the weird complex of colors and sounds which made up the patchwork quilt of the Eastern Mediterranean. An old benign spider, sitting at the center of the Merlin web. How pale Julian looked, and suddenly how vulnerable! "Zeno was out in his prediction, but only by a couple of months," he said with a kind of melancholy zealous calm. "Things are changing round us," he added. "And all this business about Iolanthe—that has been a blow, I don't deny."

"Has she written again?"

He shook his head slowly and said softly, "Neither has she phoned me. Goodness knows what has become of her." Benedicta said suddenly, surprisingly, "She has been here, you know. I was away yesterday, and Baynes says that she came in and said she would wait for me to come home. He went up to the house to try and tell someone, to try and phone to Felix; but when he came back she had vanished. She may have got into a sudden panic at the sound of a car, as it seems that Nash drove up to the house about that time."

"But how can you be sure it was she?" Benedicta crossed the room to the cocktail cabinet and extracted from it a woman's handbag—a rather chic new handbag; she turned it out before us on the carpet, and among the visiting cards and other trivia which identified the visitant was something which gave us all a start. It was a small pearl-handled revolver. I thought at first it was a stage prop, but no. It was a real weapon and was fully loaded. We looked at each other with surprise, perhaps with consternation. "What on earth could that mean?" said Julian at last. "Who could she be afraid of?" But I had another idea. "Who could she hate enough to . . . ?" For the first time we felt that Iolanthe was starting to behave right out of character. It was late when we went to bed that night, all of us very preoccupied by these mysteries.

SEVEN

Boom-treacle . . . *Boom-treacle* . . . The big bell was punctuating the ruminations of the organ which succeeded in weaving an almost tangible curtain of sound across the great doors of the western face. *Om mane padme boom.* The spendthrift monotony of the Gothic soul trying to realize itself, to anchor itself in the infinity of darkness created by the ample dome. Clock of ages cleft for me, let me in thy tick reside. The cars and buses had disgorged their freight of workers—practically the whole of Merlin's London staff had turned up. In my own case I had had a drink or two—I must admit it—which gave me, according to Benedicta, an air of melancholy sincerity. It was not perhaps the time or place to feel gay, with the thoughts of Jocas on the edges of the mind. So few of us had seen him. But I could now, and very clearly. I wondered what thoughts hovered like dragonflies above the now placid surface of Benedicta's mind. This was what he had wanted, and here we all were full of the fragile self-deluding hope that somewhere he might be listening to us, perhaps smiling under the mask of gold. Here in this old petrifact which crowned London town. The organ growled and prowled about among the shadows, about the narrow fallopia of the naves, dull and repetitive as the Saturnalia of Macrobius. Long long ago, somewhere in Polis, Benedicta recited to me some children's verses about the sound of bells—a touching onomatopoeia which came back now to me under the hammer strokes of the heavy clapper. The small bells in Turkey exclaim *Evlen dirralim* over and over again, while the big ones intone on a slower note *Soordan, Boordan, Boolaloum.*

What was he dreaming about, old Jocas? Surely not about this rainswept London where the fat blue pigeons ruffled and crooned about the statue of Queen Anne? No, but of the islands of Polis, of Marmara threaded through by its fishy migrations, of Smyrna, of the famous wharves stacked high with merchandise. Of the slow plains with their black herds of goats and horses and fat-tailed sheep. In fields and arbors where the jackals come out by moonlight to scavenge the muscat grapes; or in glass-penned coffeehouses suspended over flowing water where the hubble-bubbles clear their throats in rose water. . . . Something like that I suppose. Well, here I was at last in St. Paul's, reflecting on the vehemence of great art and regretting that Caradoc had missed his plane and stayed behind in Turkey.

I had bought a shilling guide to the monument and put it inside a prayer book, fearing a long sermon. Thus in the intervals of standing up and sitting down, I was able to inform myself (I imitated Caradoc's voice in my mind) that the nave is narrow (forty-one feet), while the exterior length of the church (without the steps) is five hundred and fifteen feet, and the height of the church to the top of the dome approaches three hundred feet. Doubtless all this was of the utmost esoteric significance, if only I could grasp it. A hundred feet above our heads was the Whispering Gallery, and above it again the gamboge cartoons of Paul basking in the white light of twenty-four windows of clear untinted glass. Characteristically in this house of Paul, this Paulhaus of ours, there was no Lady Chapel. Well, Felix whispered an irreverent prayer, touching elbows with his pale girl in black: "O Lord, deliver us from the primacy of the Mobego whose genetic silhouette is the Firm, and its closed system. Suffer us to wander like rational men in the fair psyche-haunted fields of Epicurus, inhabiting our own fair bodies. If you can't do this, Lord, you should say so clearly and resign."

Somewhere about now the terrible thing began to happen. Julian was quite a way up front, flanked by numb-looking members of the senior boardroom. Though the service was in progress, the broad side aisles of the church were still full of Dutch and German tourists, buying postcards and making the sort of noise that people only manage to make when they are trying to be respectfully quiet. How everything echoed, every scrape of shoe or thwack of hassock! I was in my usual bemused dream when Benedicta prodded me with her elbow and said in a shocked whisper, "Look over there. Isn't that her?" At the far end of the aisle a tall girl was just turning away from the postcard stall, having purchased some sort of souvenir; she was hemmed in by the press of tourists which clogged all movement, and for a moment she disappeared from view so that I could not get a clear look at her. Then, as the shuffling crowd moved forward, she reappeared once more and I saw that it was indeed she, my one and only Iolanthe; yet somehow subtly transformed. She looked flushed, as if she had been drinking, or had had some strange inner revelation. Her wig wasn't quite snug, and looked badly in need of cleaning, as indeed did her whole person. The heels of her shoes were worn down to stumps. A torn raincoat. There was a small gash in her left calf which had been mended with a piece of surgical tape. She limped.

For a long moment I stood frozen into a statue of surprise, and then I started out in her direction; and as I did so I saw another figure detach itself from the front pews and start to glide toward her, as cautiously as a child trying to catch a rare butterfly. Julian had seen her! We were still quite a way off when all of a sudden she turned her eyes (they seemed to blaze with a fierce and somewhat distraught glare) upon the congregation. It was her turn to feel surprised—for the whole of Merlin's was there! How common she looked now, like some down-at-heel whore; her features had gone drawn and ugly. But recognition was swift. She started so sharply that she dropped her handbag. In a flash she retrieved it and tried to struggle back into the crowd, to regain the west door; it was pure panic, for we were moving with relative freedom while she was clogged in the mass of visitors. Baffled in her attempt to penetrate the solid mass and thus gain the street, she suddenly changed her tack, and tried to lose herself in the crowd ahead of her—the crowd which was trickling forward into the church. Here there was less resistance and she was able to get herself pushed and shoved forward. But we were now close behind her, and her desperation was obvious from the way she looked this way and that, hunting for an escape route. "Iolanthe," I hissed in a blood-curdling stage whisper, but she did not turn round; she simply burrowed more deeply into the sheltering crowd. Julian was ahead of me, crouching like a wrestler as he pushed and shoved his way toward her. We were both expelled at the end of the aisle, like cartridges from a gun, by the sheer press of human bodies. And here to our dismay we lost her to view. A moment of despair held us motionless and then Julian gave a little cry and said: "Up there, Felix." She had darted up the spiral stairway in the south side. We could hear her panting as we started after her. Everything began to get blurred in my mind now; what, after all, were we going to do, pinion her? I don't believe Julian had really thought about it; he just wanted to grab hold of her and never let her go. . . . We heard the footsteps running across the gallery of the south triforium. We galloped after her, panting, disheveled, incoherent—and so up into the famous Whispering Gallery which my guide had just told me was a hundred feet from the floor of the church; if you stand where we now stood, glaring hungrily at her, panting, pale as hunters, you can hear with perfect clarity the whisper of someone opposite you 107 feet away. . . . But she had come here to hide, not to whisper; nevertheless she was whispering now, talking to herself under her breath in the most affecting way. I heard: "O please God don't let them get me. Don't let them take me back. I'll do anything, anything." It was bloodcurdling this little whisper. She did not address a word to us as we stood there trying to catch our breath. It was to herself she was whispering; and in the midst of the whispered appeals came little clicks like sobs out of focus, and little clucks like a tiny chick. There was no need for us to concert our plan—the design of the gallery made it automatic. Julian went one way round, while I took the other; there was, at last, no escape for poor Iolanthe. But now her rage and despair had once more transformed her features into those of some sick demon let loose from the lower floors of the Inferno. Now at last she began to gabble and click and whistle at us, to deride us, to defy us. Never have I heard on the lips of a woman such obscenities as she uttered now. Julian was faster than I, and she spat and spat again into his white face as he approached her with the expression of a sleepwalker. Indeed, we both felt caught up in some waking nightmare so unreal did it seem. Below the leather-bound booming and crooning made an almost solid sea of sound, washing back and forth; above the bright white light illuminated the cartoons in grisaille which pointed up the main events in the life of Paul. And here we were on this echoing catwalk, holding on to the low golden balustrade in order to grapple with a raging steel maenad. "Iolanthe!" I cried in despair as I approached.

Julian had reached her now and they began to reel and struggle like drunkards. And now, just as I came up, the horrible thing happened. She gave a sudden leap, like a high-tined stag, over the balustrade; in a flash Julian had caught at her frock and held it, himself hanging over the rail. For what seemed a hundred years they hung thus like some human snail, and then the cloth began to tear. Julian made a desperate grab to increase his purchase, but in vain. They fell together into the echoing nave; in a wild and shattering moment of vision I saw them flatten out like arrows as they fell. But the scream I uttered deafened me to the noise of the crash as they hit the marble floor with its black brooding hexagonal stone. Hardly knowing what I was doing, I lurched back across the gallery and down the spiral stairway. Like the rings made by a stone in water, the impact of their fall had deflected the crowd. From the corner of my eye I thought I had seen something small and white fly from Julian's body as it hit the floor; strange how in moments of utter panic some small observation gets registered with the utmost fidelity. I could not see the body of Julian, there was a crowd round it; but I crossed to the pew and verified that the white object had indeed skimmed there. I picked it up. It was the little white rabbit's paw he always carried on him—the gambler's mascot.

But if I could not get to Julian, Iolanthe presented no such problem; she had, so to speak, cleared her own space. At this moment, this very moment, she was slowly turning on her axis and making a low humming sound. Sometimes when a motorbike falls on its side with its engine still running, it turns in an arc in just this manner. I felt the tears rise in my eyes. Everyone was there, the confusion was raging like a cataract: Baum, Marchant, Benedicta, Banubula—all shaken out of their wits, white with surprise and horror. But it was really Iolanthe who had broken my heart, as I had hers. And the danger now was that she was "live," could electrocute someone. I suppose I should have used a thermal lance, but all we could raise was a boy scout's sheath knife. "Felix, for God's sake, *careful!*" shouted Marchant above the din of voices, but somehow I didn't care. I crawled into the magic circle she was tracing with that lovely body of hers, and plunged my knife into her throat. I knew just where, in order to stop the whole works. And that is the story of the Fall, and how I slew my darling more in sorrow than in anger, more in sickness than in health. Iolanthe! Benedicta cried, "Felix. Don't cry like that," in a voice of anguish; but what's a poor inventor to do?

The days pass.

"I, Felix Charlock, bound in mind and body!" You will see now why I had to bring all this up-to-date, in order to straighten the record—for now the whole responsibility of the firm has fallen on my shoulders. These last weeks have been full of boardroom conferences, votes of confidence, resolutions, and so on. I have not hesitated to shoulder the burden for the vanished Julian and Jocas. Outwardly nothing much has changed—or else I went through everything in a sort of dream. Baum fed the press some story of an advertising firm with a dummy, and successfully accounted for the accident, which satisfied the law. When Julian's will was proved we found that he had agreed to let his body be taken to Polis to share the family mausoleum—probably the only concession to Jocas he had ever made in his life.

For the rest, we have come to a great decision, Benedicta and I; it will not be hard to guess that the prophecy of Zeno has been occupying me, preoccupying me very much. Indeed I now feel it less as a prophecy than as a sort of command, from myself to myself, so to speak. I have hardly had to mention it to my wife; she knows full well what I am planning. The microfilm archives which house all our contracts—I have had a careful look at the small building. Fortunately all the stock is in nitrocellulose film, so highly inflammable that a single time-pencil should be enough to set it off. This is a relief—I feared that we had transferred it to some new acetate which might be hard to dispose of. Marchant is in full agreement with me. The job is an easy one. It should burn fine in the archive vaults with their 118 degrees controlled temperature. I feel tremendously calm and composed, very much master of myself.

We are already in the big house and preparing for Christmas; I have chosen Xmas Eve for the send-up. I have explained carefully to our guests that the fire will be lit while they are at dinner. The first reactions should come in within a day or so. The only one who has shown alarm is Baum who said, "Either everything will disintegrate, the firm will begin to dissolve; or else nothing, Mr. Felix, absolutely nothing. People will be afraid to take advantage of the fact that they have no contractual written obligations. They might stay put from funk or . . ." So it will be either/or once again; it will be now or never.

I have been working all day and am enormously weary. Benedicta has had fires lit in the big ballroom where once she shattered all the mirrors. It has been transformed now into rather an elegant room. It is full of flowers. There is some fine black jazz playing and we have been dancing, dancing in complete happiness and accord. And we will keep on this way, dancing and dancing, even though Rome burn.

THE END

POSTFACE

Dear C.-M.V.,

Well, here it is, the second volume I promised you. As always I have tried to move from the preposterous to the sublime! It was you who said once that all my novels were inquests with open verdicts. This was true. But in this one I have tried to play about with the notion of culture—what is it? The provenance of the ideas will be familiar to you. It's a sort of novel-libretto based on the preface to *The Decline of the West*. Freud is there too, very much there. I remember too that you remarked once about Spengler, "He's not pessimistic at all. He is a realist, that is all." Well in its way this novel in two parts tries to take a culture reading merely. Of course the poetic game is to try and put a lid on a box with no sides. But when you go on deck, for example, to find that the ship is out of sight of land you are pleased to see a map in the chart room with a flag in it, stuck there by an invisible hand. It marks your position. By intention this is such a flag.

For the rest, the form presents no singularities. A two-part novel of an old-fashioned sort; perhaps you might say an Ur-novel. Nor do the epigraphs present any mystery. It's always now or never—since we are human and enjoy the fatality of choice. Indeed the moment of choice is always now. For the rest, the fabled two is the human couple, but it is also the basic brick out of which our culture is constructed—mathematics, measure, motion, poetry. And so cheers,

ever thine

LD

P.S. To Ur is human to forgive divine.